REDEMPTION

Also by Jon Grahame:

REAPER

ANGEL

REDEMPTION

Jon Grahame

MYRMIDON

Myrmidon
Rotterdam House
116 Quayside
Newcastle upon Tyne
NE1 3DY

www.myrmidonbooks.com

Published by Myrmidon 2014

A catalogue record for this book is available from the British
Library.

ISBN 978-1-905802-86-9

Set in 11.75/15.5 Sabon by Reality Premedia Services, Pvt. Ltd.

Printed and bound in the UK by
CPI Group (UK) Ltd, Croydon, CR0 4YY

1 3 5 7 9 10 8 6 4 2

This one is for Kevin Andrews,

a true Jedi.

Daily Telegraph, February 5, 2010

China's reckless use of antibiotics in the health system and agricultural production is unleashing an explosion of drug resistant superbugs that endanger global health, according to leading scientists.

Chinese doctors routinely hand out multiple doses of antibiotics for simple maladies, like sore throats, and the country's farmers' excessive dependence on the drugs has tainted the food chain.

Studies in China show a 'frightening' increase in antibiotic-resistant bacteria such as staphylococcus aureus bacteria, also know as MRSA. There are warnings that new strains of antibiotic-resistant bugs will spread quickly through international air travel and international food sourcing.

'We have a lot of data from Chinese hospitals and it shows a very frightening picture of high-level antibiotic resistance,' said Dr Andreas Heddini of the Swedish Institute for Infectious Disease Control. 'Doctors are daily finding there is nothing they can do; even third and fourth-line antibiotics are not working.

'There is a real risk that globally we will return to a pre-antibiotic era of medicine, where we face a situation where a number of medical treatment options would no longer be there. What happens in China matters for the rest of the world.'

Associated Press

An outbreak of SARS (Severe Acute Respiratory Syndrome) has been reported in Guangdong Province, China. It was discovered by Canada's Global Public Health Intelligence Network (GPHIN), an electronic warning system that monitors and analyses internet media traffic, and is part of the World Health Organisation's (WHO) Global Outbreak and Alert Response Network (GOARN). The disease comes on top of the problems caused by the violent earthquake that devastated the region two months ago. Members of worldwide aid agencies are still working in the area.

Guangdong Province previously suffered a SARS epidemic in 2002, although the Chinese Government did not inform WHO until four months later. It spread to 37 countries and there were 8,096 known infected cases and 774 fatalities. SARS is a viral disease that can initially be caught from palm civets, raccoon dogs, ferret badgers, domestic cats and bats. Initial symptoms are flu-like and may include lethargy, fever, coughs, sore throats and shortness of breath.

Les Knight, founder of the Voluntary Human Extinction Movement

(As quoted in *The World Without Us* by Alan Weisman, Virgin Books)

'No virus can ever get all six billion of us. A 99.99 per cent die-off would still leave 650,000 naturally immune survivors. Epidemics actually strengthen a species. In 50,000 years, we could easily be right back where we are now.'

The Rt Hon Geoffrey Smith, spokesperson for HM Government, UK

By now, you will all be aware of the terrible affects of the SARS pandemic. It is estimated that fifty percent of the population has already died of this dreadful virus and we fear that many more will succumb. Hospitals are full and medical staff have fallen victim at the same rate as the civilian population. All known medicines have failed to stop the devastating effects of what scientists have described as a virus aberration. No one could have foreseen this modern plague, and no one, it seems, can save us from it, not just here in Britain, but all around the world. We don't know when this pandemic will end. But we do know there are some who have a natural immunity. This small percentage is our only hope for the survival of the human race. All I can do is urge you all to make your peace with your god and remain in the safety of your homes as we truly face the apocalypse. God bless. And good luck.

July, Year One

HE LAY IN BLOOD, BRAINS EXPOSED UPON HIS HEAD. A nightmare had been unleashed and he should be dead. But he could still hear the voices of the living through the smoke; laughing, taunting, boasting. And he remembered. He was numb and in pain but he was alive even though it seemed he was in hell.

The bodies of the dead were around and upon him. Their souls called to him. Perhaps it would have been best if he had gone with them, to a place where the emotion couldn't reach. All he had to do was remain supine and inhale the smoke and he would follow. Except the souls of the departed were urging him to stay. Vengeance, they said. Live, they said.

Now the smoke was thicker; the heat growing. The voices were retreating.

He rolled onto his side and gently removed Joe's arm from across his chest. He moved slowly on hands and knees away from the fire that would reduce the crime to ashes. Except in his mind. In his mind, he knew it would remain white hot.

Vengeance, his friends whispered. Vengeance.

July, Year Two

Chapter 1

ALBERT WAS MENDING THE BARN. It was an old wooden structure and he was nailing new boards across a gap he had made by pulling out rotten ones. Not the best repair in the world but, in this world, it would be enough. He was seventy and his eyesight was not as good as it once was, but his hearing was sharp as ever. At least, that's what he told Billy, and that was why he kept the fully loaded pistol close to hand. He was crouching to nail the boards in place and the position was beginning to hurt his back. He sat down on the dirt floor for a rest.

The day was hot and the barn was hotter. An early heatwave. Weather forecasters might once have claimed this was the start of a barbecue summer. Albert snorted to himself. How many of those had they had? They hadn't enjoyed a proper summer since 1976 when the reservoirs ran dry and people had complained it was too hot. Never satisfied, some people. The next memorable spell of good weather had been 2002 or 2003 sometime, but he couldn't remember exactly when. Not that it mattered these days.

Nobody worried anymore about having a barbecue summer. Not since the virus had killed most of humanity and civilisation had collapsed. These days, they judged meteorological conditions only on whether they would be good for growing crops. Strange bloody world, these days, although he couldn't say so to Auntie Marjorie. She wouldn't disagree with the sentiment but she would object to the language. As if *bloody* was bad language. He'd used a lot worse in his time, which gave him pause to think again.

His time? It had been and gone and he cherished his memories. He'd been lucky to have had a happy marriage and lucky that his wife had died three years ago – before the virus. He'd been able to grieve properly and see that the proper funeral rites were followed. Lucky, too, he'd had no children, so that when the plague arrived, he had no close relatives to lose. Whole families had been taken, for Christ's sake – whole towns. He had heard it said that less than one per cent of the world's population had survived because of some built-in immunity, but who really knew? He laughed. He had also heard there were still pockets of survivors who were living on tins and waiting for the Americans to come and save them.

Albert now had more family than he'd known in years. Eight of them lived at Nab Farm. Auntie Marjorie was cook and ran the domestic arrangements and he odd-jobbed as best he could because a bad back stopped him working in the fields. He had become surrogate grandad to Billy, a lively six-year-old. In fact, most of the others treated him as a grandad figure and called him Pops, even though he claimed 70 was not old, these days. These days. Mind, if he was honest, he did look and feel older than he actually was, a consequence of a lifetime of hard manual work as a builder that had resulted in a damaged back and two buggered knees, and he didn't care if Auntie Marjorie didn't like bad language. Why had an old wreck like him been spared when all those young people, like Billy's parents, had died?

The barn was a pleasant place to be, even though it held the heat, and he could smell the fresh tang of sawdust from when he had cut the boards to size. Soft footsteps outside the open door alerted him. The little bugger won't get me again, Albert thought, with a smile, and picked up his weapon. He aimed it at the slab of sunshine.

His eyes weren't good but he could tell it was a man who stood in the doorway and not a six-year-old.

'Who's that?' he said.

'Death,' said a voice, and a flame and roar came from the man and a bullet ended Albert's doubts about being spared. It hit him in the chest, throwing him backwards onto the floor, his finger tightening on the trigger of the blue plastic pistol he held that shot a jet of water into the air that fell to mingle with the blood pumping from his wound.

Chapter 2

JAMES MARSHALL WAS STILL CONVALESCING but had insisted on getting back to duty as soon as possible. Although he hadn't told anybody, he felt guilty that he had survived. He had always kept his feelings under control, which was probably the result of a formal upbringing and seven years at public school. He had survived the virus when almost all his fellow pupils and the masters at his school had died. That was guilt enough, but then he had survived again, in the action that had become known as the Battle of York, and he was still only fifteen years old. Despite his age, he wore the blue t-shirt and combat pants of the special forces known as The Blues. He was one of the chosen few. A crack shot who could kill without compunction. One of the guardians of the community called Haven.

The first time he had taken life had been at a distance, through the barrel of a Heckler and Koch G36 carbine. He had been fourteen. They had been defending Haven itself from an attack by a private army. The action had been fast and furious with little time to think. Afterwards, the euphoria of victory had swiftly faded as they counted the cost of friends and comrades who had died. The anger at their loss had kept at bay any regrets about dealing death so efficiently. Much later, he had assessed his personal body count with detachment. There had been no doubts, no angst, no tortured moments. Those he had killed had deserved to die. Then had come the Battle of York where a handful of them had taken on and beaten a much larger force of invaders. More friends had died and he had been wounded. But he had survived.

Kev Andrews drove the Range Rover through the sunlit lanes. He was a big, bluff Yorkshireman of fifty, who had been an electrician in the world that had gone, with twenty-two years' service in the Royal Navy that had left him with a penchant for jackspeak – navy slang – and calling people 'me hearty'. In the victory celebrations after the Battle of York, and after a suitable intake of alcohol, he had been coerced into showing his tattoo to anyone unlucky enough to be in range in the bar of The Farmer's Boy. A pair of eyes had stared unblinking from his buttocks.

'Now I'm getting on a bit, my eyesight's going,' he said. 'So I'm thinking of having a pair of glasses tattooed on them.'

There were no volunteers to do the job.

Kev had an unfailing upbeat personality. But he, too, had been a victim of the plague. He had lost his wife and daughter. Everybody had lost someone.

James himself had lost mother, father and younger sister. Men he killed never bothered him; but his family did when they returned in the silence of the night. He still mourned them. Why was he alive when they were dead? His father had been a successful lawyer with a great sense of humour and a wonderful way of bending the truth. As a youngster, James had thought his father really had been a member of the Rolling Stones, so eloquently did he tell the tale of how he had eventually opted out for the greater good of justice and the people. Mind you, he had said, he still sent the odd song or two to Keith and Mick. *Satisfaction?* That had been one of his.

His mother had been a beautiful and elegant woman who, to James's embarrassment, had caused several of his school friends to become moonstruck with love. A hint of her perfume still came to him at times, unbidden. And his sister who, in the final year he had known her had left her gawkishness and childish tantrums behind, and had also been developing into a stunning beauty.

He felt guilt about surviving and guilt that he had not returned to the family home, just in case one of them might have still been alive, even though he knew the odds against it were astronomical. Maybe one day.

The plague, virus, judgement of God, whatever people called it, had arrived in the spring of the previous year. James had been found by Reaper and taken to Haven. He had volunteered for the embryonic commando unit that Reaper had formed to protect the community against marauding bands of violent men who preferred to take what they wanted – food, petrol, women – rather than work towards a future. He had been teamed up with Kev for nine months and they had become close. You had to be close when you covered each other's back.

In the first days of his recovery from his wounds, James had been aware that Kev had never left his bedside. The ex-matelot had encouraged him, given him strength, particularly when he learnt that two of their number – Tanya and Keira – had died in the battle that he had survived. Two wonderful young women. At that point, James hadn't been sure he wanted to live. *Why me?* He smiled. Greta Malone, their chief medical officer, had explained that anybody with a conscience who was still alive, had probably asked themselves the same question after the plague had done its worst.

And then Kev had chipped in with his own words of wisdom.

'You and me, James. We're good together. A nice balance. You're posh and I'm rough as a bear's arse. Who the hell would they team me with, if you're not there? Come on, me hearty. Get better for your Uncle Kev. I need you.'

And he had resolved to get better.

This was only their third day back on patrol as a team. They visited outlying farms, hamlets and groups on a regular basis. They were the police whose presence was reassuring to the loose confederation that looked to Haven for leadership and safety. They were guardians of a border that covered the plain of York, much of the Wolds and the North Yorkshire Moors. To those in the outlying hamlets, they were paramedics, security and friends combined. They brought news and essential items, as requested by the communities they served.

Kev said, 'This is the one you've been looking forward to isn't it?'

'What?'

'Nab Farm. Special attraction.'

'Shut up, Kev.'

The older man laughed.

'It's all right. You can tell me. I've noticed the way you look at that girl, Bren.'

'Gwen.'

He laughed again at catching him out.

'Gwen. Nice looking girl. You play your cards right ...'

'Don't be vulgar, Kev.'

Kev put his hands up in apology. 'Sorry. I didn't mean to be smutty. But if you need any advice on making an impression on the opposite sex ...'

'Forget it. I do not intend to have a tattoo on my arse.'

Kev let it go but continued chuckling. He chuckled all the way to Nab Farm. Until they realised something was seriously wrong.

There was nobody in the fields as they approached. They both sat up straighter. This was an anomaly on such a day made for work. James flicked the safety off the carbine.

Kev, driving one handed, took the Glock handgun from the holster strapped to his right hip and laid it in his lap. It already had a bullet in the chamber. Both wore Kevlar stab and bullet proof vests as standard, but they still felt vulnerable as they drove into the farmyard. A body lay sprawled on the cobbles. The amount of flies surrounding it, suggested it had been there some time.

They got out of the vehicle and Kev depressed the trigger of the Glock one click to remove the safety. The man and the boy warrior remained by the Range Rover for a long time, senses seeking danger, totally alert for any sudden noise that would intimate an ambush or a hidden assassin.

There was an extended market garden behind the farmhouse, part of it under the cover of heavy duty plastic. They had hens and a couple of cows for milk, but most of their livestock consisted of pigs. The body was that of one of the men who lived there. Had lived there.

'Hello!' shouted Kev. 'Anybody?'

Nothing but silence and the buzz of flies laying their eggs in the corpse.

'It's Kev and James from Haven. Anybody?'

The kick was muffled. A small kick. The cry so faint James wasn't sure whether he had heard it at all. 'The house,' he said.

Kev went first towards the open door, James backing after him, carbine at his shoulder, covering the yard and barn and any hiding place that might portend danger. He stopped at the door, maintaining his guard. Behind him, Kev said, 'Jesus.'

James risked a look. Auntie Marjorie lay on her back, dead, her face a mass of flies. He recognised her by her clothes and her shape. A dumpy lady who pretended to be older and dottier than she was, and who looked after everybody on Nab Farm like a mother hen. The kick came again from the cupboard against which Auntie Marjorie lay, her body acting as a dead weight that would not allow it to open.

Kev put the Glock back in its holster and pulled the woman's body clear by her arms. She was holding a saucepan in one hand. He pulled open the cupboard door and a small boy fell out sideways, his face pale, eyes glassy, mouth dry and cracked. In his hand he held a water pistol.

'Billy?' Kev said, picking up the lad and laying him on the kitchen table. 'Christ. How long have you been in there, Billy?'

The farm had its own spring and a pump in the yard. Kev grabbed a bucket from near the door and went outside. James continued to cover him but suspected whoever had done this was long gone. He pumped water until he got a flow, half filled the bucket, and returned. He lifted the boy upright on the table so that he cradled his shoulders and used a cup to pour water gently onto his face and, when his lips parted, dribbled the liquid into his mouth.

At the touch of the water, Billy's mouth opened and he gulped to try to take more.

'Not too much, too soon, me hearty,' Kev whispered. 'A bit at a time.'

The boy coughed and drank some more. His eyes opened. They still held fear and dread.

'You're all right, Billy. You're safe.'

Billy coughed some more and was content to be cuddled in Kev's protective arm. He still held the water pistol, his grip tight.

'There's no one here,' said James. 'They've gone.'

Kev gave Billy another sip of water, and another. The boy revived and his eyes moved around the room. Kev made sure he couldn't see the body of Auntie Marjorie on the floor.

'What happened, Billy? Can you tell us?'

'Men. I hid.' Another sip. 'Guns.' He shuddered and his eyes closed. 'I thought I was in the cupboard for ever.' His eyes opened again. 'Where's grandad?'

Kev gave him another sip of water and looked at James, helpless, as the boy took another drink and then appeared to slip into unconsciousness.

'Put him in the Rover,' James said. 'We need to search the place.'

He remained on guard while Kev laid Billy on the back seat of the Range Rover. He left windows partly open but activated the child locks on the rear doors. Hopefully he would sleep while his dehydrated body responded to the water.

James went straight to the open door of the barn and found the man everyone had called Pops. He lay on his back. More flies around face and chest wounds. A blue water pistol in his hand. Thank God for the water pistols. Without his, Billy might not have survived.

In the covered market garden, they found the bodies of a young man and a black and white collie. Near the pigs was the corpse of a middle-aged woman. They exchanged a look. Two women were missing. Two young and attractive women. Gwen and Nina. This had been a murderous and rapacious raid by a gang who were probably passing through. James had thought rogue bands were dying out, but he was wrong.

Would he lose sleep about killing those responsible? Not in the slightest. They deserved to die. They would die. And they would get the girls back.

*　　　*　　　*

Kev insisted that James take the boy back to Haven in the Range Rover and, once he was within range, radio an alert to Reaper and the Angel. He shook his head at falling into the nicknames others had bestowed. Jim Reaper, the former policeman who had become their leader, was hardly surprisingly known to the wider population as The Grim Reaper. Sandra was his nineteen-year-old second in command. They pretended to be father and daughter, although few believed it, because no other two family members had shared immunity and survived the plague.

But they were, to all intents and purposes, as close as blood relatives. They had teamed up in the early days when the world had gone mad and every town and city had its gangs of violent men, seeking booze and women and food. They had collected the first members of the group that had travelled north to the flat lands between York and the coast to a place called Haven, a manor house and farm in a walled valley, surrounded by purpose built holiday cottages. They had given this small part of the world the chance of a fresh start and had recruited and trained their small body of special forces to provide protection.

They had also provided its code of ethics. The old world was gone, where young thugs and feral gangs had been excused their behaviour with a slap on the wrist and a trip to swim with the dolphins; where murderers were sentenced to life only to be released for good behaviour a few years later. Where rapists and paedophiles never got their just desserts.

In this part of the new world, instant justice ruled. Murderers and rapists were shot. No trial, no mercy. The bad guys were put down so they could not offend again. The population was small enough without letting the bad guys roam and deplete it further.

Kev used a Hitachi mini digger that was parked at the side of the barn to excavate a grave. He chose a pleasant place behind the farmhouse, with a view across fields towards a distant treeline. Moving the bodies was more of a problem. He rolled each one in turn onto a tarpaulin, batted away the flies and covered them sufficiently so he could pick them up in his arms and carry them to their last resting place. The collie, that he remembered was called Bess, went with them. It was not pleasant work but someone had to do it and it was better him than James. Besides, he let it fuel his anger.

He replaced the earth, leaving an identifiable mound. He doubted anybody would want to take over the farm in the near future after the killings but, maybe sometime in the years ahead, others would carry on, because the land was good.

He washed at the pump, drank his fill of the cool, fresh water, and ate the sandwiches he had brought. By the time he had finished, two motorcyclists and two Range Rovers drove up the lane and into the farmyard. James was driving one of the Rovers and from the other stepped down Reaper and Sandra.

Reaper was in his middle forties, under six foot tall and of average build but he had a sense of purpose that marked him out as different. The only way to stop him would be to kill him. Many had tried and Reaper bore the wounds of their attempts. He wore Blues, Doc Martens and a Kevlar vest. He had a holstered Glock on each thigh and a 10 inch Bowie knife in a sheath on his lower right leg. On his left wrist was strapped a cache of three throwing knives.

Ammunition magazines were in the pockets of the vest and the belt at his waist.

Angel was blonde and petite, hair short. At first glance, an observer would notice how pretty she was, but then the prettiness would be forgotten, washed away by the calculation of eyes that were the blue of sharpened steel rather than a summer sky. She had survived plague, rape, bullet and knife and had left many dead in her wake. But only those who had deserved to die. She, too, wore Blues and Doc Martens, the Kevlar vest, a single Glock on her right thigh and a Bowie knife sheathed below it on her leg. Once this total impression had taken hold, the prettiness would return and an observer would realise it bordered on beauty. Deadly beauty.

They both carried carbines. They looked ready for retribution.

Kev showed them where he had buried the bodies of the former residents of Nab Farm. Reaper touched him on the shoulder. A sign of a job well done.

'Nick is following. He'll say the words.' Reaper licked his lips and stared out over what had promised to be a successful farm and home for a disparate group of people who had come together to embrace life once more, after so much despair and desolation. 'Gavin is bringing trucks to move the stock.'

Sandra crouched near the fresh turned earth, picked up a handful of dirt and crumbled it between her fingers.

'They were nice people,' Kev said.

'They were our people,' she replied. She looked angry enough to combust.

Reaper said, 'We'll find them.' He turned away and walked back to the farmyard. A moment later, the two motorcyclists left, travelling in opposite directions. The search had begun.

James joined Kev and told him the two other teams of Blues had been sent out to warn those of their community who lived on the fringes of the Outlands.

'Billy's recovering,' said James.

'Poor little sod must have been in there two days.'

'He'll be okay.' James gave a half smile. 'Children are resilient.'

Kev took it almost as a comment on the fifteen-year-old's own experience. He stretched his neck and looked out across the land, beyond the farm. 'We need to get the girls back,' he said.

'We will,' said James, with grim determination.

*　　　*　　　*

The Rev Nick Waite arrived in the first of three cattle wagons. They all gathered by the grave while he put the dead to rest. Nick was a small man in his late twenties with a neatly trimmed beard. He was the keeper of Haven's conscience, their voice of reason. He also had an ingrained courage that had seen him wounded in the community's fight to remain free.

He intoned sombre words and asked God to receive the souls of Auntie Marjorie, Albert (otherwise known as Pops), Marianne, Geordie and George. He also asked for divine intervention in helping to bring back to safety the two missing young women: Gwen and Nina.

The brief service was concluded with the saying of the Lord's Prayer. Only Reaper didn't recite the words. He still had a suspicious relationship with any god. He was agnostic with a born-again belief that he had been left alive for a purpose: to smite the wicked and allow the innocent the chance of a new beginning. There might or might not be a god but he didn't need divine intervention to direct his wrath.

Chapter 3

REAPER HAD NO ILLUSIONS. THE VIOLENT marauders who had visited Nab Farm could be at the other end of the country by now, but he suspected they were much closer at hand. They were probably strangers who had never heard of Haven. They had not behaved like a group on an exploratory excursion, or as the outriders or emissaries of a much larger force. They had behaved like vandals: they had taken only what they wanted for their immediate needs and continued on their way.

Cities were still dangerous places because of the urban gangs they housed. After a year of surviving amidst concrete, broken shop windows and apartment blocks filled with corpses, some city dwellers had discovered such places had a limited lifespan. Eventually, the tins and bottled water would run out. They began to realise the future was in the countryside where food could be grown, where rivers were cleansing themselves, where springs and wells of pure water could be found.

A few were beginning to leave the dereliction and make the transition. Haven had accepted many who wanted to learn how to work the land and raise crops and animals in this new agrarian society. But others were leaving who were unwilling to work. Who still thought they could take what they wanted with impunity. Some gangs still followed the same rules feral gangs had followed before the plague. Reaper guessed this was such a gang. They would leave a trail.

If, after leaving the farm, they had continued south into the Haven heartland, they would already have been discovered. They had most likely gone north towards Newcastle and Scotland, or could be heading west into where there was little but countryside until they neared the burnt-out city that had once been Leeds.

Pete Mack and Ronnie Ronaldo were searching for them on trail bikes. Such a group would leave signs of their passing and Reaper suspected they had not gone far. Why should they hurry when they might reason on easy pickings in the next village? There was no reason for them to hurry. They did not know they were being pursued. He was confident they would be found.

Pete had been with them since the beginning; stocky, muscular, shaven head, a bulldog tattoo on his arm. He could have been mistaken for what had once been the popular image of a white supremacist except that his best friend was Ash, an Afro Caribbean and a former sergeant in the Paras, who was now chief of homeland security. Pete was transport manager and the man you went to see to get things done. He was resourceful and tough as a pit bull.

Ronnie was their chief forager: mid-forties, wiry, unhealthy pallor as if raised on cheap cigarettes and cheaper booze. He came from the northern town of Castleford, where he seemed to have had a special relationship with the local constabulary, mainly over his fondness for articles that fell off the back of a lorry – any lorry, any article – and their desire to catch him in possession and lock him up. They had never succeeded.

He was, he had once said, misunderstood, but Reaper didn't think that was the real truth. He had been a misfit in the old world. He was a perfect fit in the new one. A brilliant scavenger who could smell out intact warehouses and anything the community might need. Like finding the bastards who had wiped Nab Farm off the map.

Reaper knew that waiting was always the hardest part. It gave time to brood over mistakes, regret the past and worry about the future. They had all lost so much, they should have all been suffering from a collective phobia about their right to life, love and happiness. Perhaps they were. Relationships had formed, sometimes out of desperation, other times with an ingrained fear that all could be lost again. Wives, husbands and children of the old world had not been forgotten, but the horror of their deaths made everyone highly aware of the fragility of the present; that life could be gone in an instant; be snuffed arbitrarily from their grasp.

Pete Mack and Ronnie both had new families; new wives and adopted children. How could you not care for children when they had no one else? The Rev Nick had conducted marriage services and, as a holy man, given interdenominational blessings to couples of other faiths. Their citizens were mainly white, from traditional Christian backgrounds, whether they believed in formal Christianity or not, but they had amongst them small numbers of different races and creeds. In their post-apocalyptic world, the boundaries of religion had blurred and, in Haven at least, colour or faith no longer mattered.

In the old life, Reaper had been a policeman. Content to be an ordinary copper, maintaining the social fabric of the community, safeguarding its citizens and upholding the law. He had been content with the job and thought he had been good at it, until his daughter Emily was raped. He had been unable to save her from becoming a victim of that most heinous of crimes and, after the rapist had been caught, justice had failed his family. The perpetrator had been given a derisory sentence, his daughter had been maligned in court when the judge suggested she was partly to blame for her own misfortune and, despite rules that were supposed to respect her anonymity, people knew. His daughter had become a victim for a second time and had taken her own life because of the shame.

Reaper's first failing. He still carried the blame of not being able to protect her, to help her, to save her. Rather than face the world with him, she had hanged herself from a hook in her bedroom. She had been fourteen years old.

Reaper's second failing had been his marriage. He and Margaret had stayed together because of their daughter. Once Emily had gone, they remained together, at first because Reaper needed the penance of a bad marriage, and later because of the cancer his wife contracted. How can you leave a woman with a terminal illness? They shared the same house, bonded by the despair of their daughter's death and the mutual loathing they felt for each other. In extremis, she turned to alcohol and religion and he bore her viciousness as a punishment for his own deficiencies.

His widowhood had left him in a state of semi-existence. He stopped being a policeman. His days passed by routine, he was a cog within a greater machine. He had no motive to live until the day he saw his daughter's rapist on the street, freed from jail, alive and well and chatting up a young girl who knew no better. From that day, Reaper regained a purpose. He trained, he planned, he plotted and he took the bastard's life, and found himself in a custody cell in the same police building where he had once worked.

He counted it his good fortune that he had committed his act of righteous revenge in the weeks before the virus took its final grip on the nation and the world. If he had delayed, the bastard would have died from the SARS virus. As it is, he died from a meat cleaver in the skull and a carving knife through the ribs. As the unrelenting plague took its final grip, the custody sergeant had unlocked all the cells. Reaper had survived as all around him died.

Reaper had surmised that if there was a God, She had a bloody funny sense of humour. He concluded his survival was a rebirth, a second chance. He had failed both his daughter and his wife in the world that had gone. He had to do better in the new world.

The first person he saved was Sandra. She was eighteen, the same age his daughter would have been if she had not taken her own life; if she had survived the virus. The significance was not lost on either of them, once Sandra learned his story. They had become de facto father and daughter and Sandra would never again be a victim. He had trained her in weaponry and she had learned the rest as they had fought side by side. Reaper was cold in battle, Sandra had an edge of fire that consumed those who stood in her way.

They had led the others to Haven, helped establish the community, and protected its people and boundaries. Since then, both of them had suffered yet again. Sandra had married Jamie and lost him weeks later when Haven was invaded by vandals. In the same action, Reaper had lost Kate, the woman who had taught him how to love again.

Almost a year later, they still nursed their pain and they fought with more determination than ever. Which is why they had become known as Reaper and the Angel, a duo whose reputation had spread to other parts of the country as travellers carried the tales of their exploits, often exaggerated, but not by much.

Their latest battle had been in York where they had suffered again, with the loss of two of their special forces comrades. Keira, the auburn haired girl from Ireland, had given her life to save that of her Blues partner Anna, the American everybody inevitably called Yank. Tanya had been shot in the head after manning a machinegun with her partner Jenny during the fiercest fighting. The losses had scarred them all, but Yank and Jenny had acquired a new edge to their characters. Reaper and Sandra had recruited two replacements to their ranks. They had no preference, either way, as to the sex or sexual orientation of those they chose to wear the uniform Blues. It just so happened that the best applicants were again women.

Kat, short for Katrina, was twenty-eight, pale skin and dark hair, a natural athlete who had competed at Yorkshire county level in pentathlon and marathon. She had worked for the BBC in Leeds. 'Nothing glamorous. I was a research assistant.' She had lost her husband Josh, who had competed in the marathon in the 2012 London Olympics, and one-year-old baby girl to the virus.

'We were competitive but it never got in the way of our marriage. He knew I could beat him hands down at one discipline. Having babies. He watched the birth and knew straight away that women are the tougher sex.'

Their baby, Karen, had died first, after the virus had already bitten deep into the population. Law and order was on the verge of breaking down, funeral directors were no longer able to operate, mortuaries were overstocked and the military were using industrial incinerators for mass cremations. They buried Karen themselves in the back garden of their suburban home and, when Josh became ill, he had smiled at her and said: 'I told you women were tougher.' As the world went to hell, she had dug a grave for her husband, exhumed their baby, and buried both of them together.

Kat had subsequently suffered hardships she preferred not to talk about before reaching Haven. Not many women wanted to remember rape, but for her, it didn't compare with the despair of burying her own family.

She was teamed with Jenny. The former public school teacher was still in her twenties and had been the epitome of a blonde English rose until the pandemic, sudden and violent death and gang rape had come along. She had grown into her role in the Blues and had developed a cold bloodedness that was chilling. It was no surprise. Tanya, who had died at York, had been both her partner and lover.

Dee was a slightly built mixed race girl of be twenty-four. Mother white, father Indian. She was unmarried, had two sisters and two brothers, all younger than her. She lost them all and found herself alone with their bodies in the flat above the family run store they owned in a suburb of Sheffield. Her mother had died early in the pandemic and the rest of them had thought they were immune, but a later wave had returned more virulent than ever, and taken them all. Her father had been away at one of his other stores when he fell ill and never came home.

The supermarket downstairs had become a target for the few who had survived. When the wilder male survivors realised she was alone, she also became a target. Her father had had the foresight to obtain a gun, totally illegal, but a solution of last resort. She had shot two of the men, one fatally, put supplies in the family Ford, poured oil over the bodies of her siblings, whom she had laid together in the back bedroom, placed gas canisters at their feet and lit a funeral pyre. They went to heaven in cleansing flame and an explosion that shook the car when she was half a mile away. She still carried the Smith and Wesson Ladysmith .38 revolver, a small and easily concealed five-shot gun, as a back-up to the 17-round Glock that was strapped to her thigh.

Dee was teamed with Yank. The American was thirty-four, with a punk haircut and a bitch of an attitude. She had arrived at Haven alone on a motorcycle with a shotgun strapped to her back. She had served three years in the US military, including one tour in Afghanistan, and was a martial arts expert. You messed with her at your peril. She had married an Englishman in Oregon and returned with him to become a personal trainer in a fitness centre he owned in Manchester.

The Blues were back to full strength but Reaper recognised the need to expand their ranks further. The

Community was growing and more specialists were needed.

He knew they were all impatient to get on the road and chase down the marauders who had visited Nab Farm, but all they could do for now was wait for intelligence, for a sighting. He was sure the killers had not known upon whose territory they had intruded. The reputation he and Sandra had acquired usually acted as a deterrent. They must be renegades from elsewhere who knew no better, possibly from an inner city, renegades who didn't want to face another winter confined by concrete and hungry rats.

If their future had been unsure when they arrived at Nab Farm, it had now gained an inevitability. It would be short and end in death.

*   *   *

Ronnie radioed in the next day in the middle of the afternoon. He had found them thirty miles away, camped at an empty farm off the main highway to the Lake District. Five men. They seemed in no hurry to leave.

The animals at Nab Farm had been transported to Haven and the Rev Nick had gone with the convoy. Reaper tried to make radio contact with Pete Mack but he was out of range. Instead, he left a note in the kitchen to tell him where they had gone. They met up with Ronnie twenty miles off and he led the two Land Rovers northwest along empty highways. He stopped as they approached a hill and motioned the cars to a halt behind him. Reaper drove alongside him.

'They're on the other side of the hill,' said Ronnie. 'There's a lane to the right. The farm is a half mile down the lane.'

The hill blocked the sound of their engines and the gang would be unaware of their presence. Ronnie pointed to a track on the left that disappeared into a copse of trees and Reaper nodded. They drove into the copse and out of sight.

Ronnie had drawn a rough map of the farm and outbuildings. It lay in a dip and was supplied with water by a stream that came down the hillside. The men had been travelling in two vehicles, a six wheel Transit and 4x4 Mitsubishi. The vehicles were parked on the far side of the buildings.

'Perhaps they thought they were being clever,' Ronnie said. 'Hiding the cars behind the farm. But then they went and lit a fire and sent out smoke signals. Silly sods.'

'Let's go take a look,' said Reaper.

They crossed the road and climbed a fence into an overgrown pasture where the grass was tall enough to hide in. The day was again warm and they sweated as they climbed the hill, taking a route so they would emerge above their target. A line of trees was on the crest and they slipped into their shade. The trees stood above a rocky outcrop and gorse bushes in bloom. They had a clear sight of the farm. Music came to them on the still afternoon air.

'What the hell is that?' Kev said, in a low voice.

'It's a Mozart string quartet,' said James.

'Stuff me,' responded Kev.

The music was incongruous but Reaper had learnt that not all villains were teenage thugs with a fondness for rap or heavy metal. The leader of this mob could be a chartered accountant making up for a lifetime of office boredom.

'I got here last night as the light was going,' said Ronnie. 'Saw their smoke, then the fire. I got quite close, to make sure, and saw the girls. Five men. Two young, late teens, early twenties. One in his thirties. Two middle aged, forty, fiftyish. The leader is one of the older blokes. He wears a safari suit.'

'A what?' said Sandra.

'You know. Khaki shorts and a khaki shirt that's like a jacket with lots of pockets. Khaki socks, too, and flipping chukka boots. Done up like a dog's dinner. But he's the bloke in charge. I stayed late this morning to make sure they weren't planning another move. Oh, and they have two dogs with them. Terriers.'

'Sensible,' said Reaper.

Terriers were good ratters and any building, abandoned or not, would have its fair share of vermin until they were cleared out by cats and dogs. That was why Haven had so many canine and feline pets.

They all carried binoculars and studied the scene below them. The farm was a two-storey brick building that had an open shed or lean-to on one side and a barn that was located across a cobbled yard. It looked as if it had been in need of repair even before the plague. There were no animals in sight and no corpses, either. Next to the barn was a caravan. The sort that during summers past had clogged the highways of England whilst being towed behind a family car. Judging by the weeds that grew around its wheels, this hadn't been touring for years.

The two vehicles were where Ronnie had described them. Out of sight to a casual visitor. With both vehicles in place, all five men would be present. The white van was covered in bright psychedelic designs.

A young man who was wearing just a pair of baggy shorts and flip flops and carrying a towel left the main building and began to walk towards the stream that tumbled down the hillside thirty yards away. His body was muscular and lightly tanned.

Another man came to the door and shouted and the young man stopped, shook his head and returned reluctantly. When he re-emerged, he was carrying a shotgun and had a handgun in a holster slung over his shoulder. They watched him walk to a part of the stream that pooled before the water continued its downward course. He dropped his weapons and towel, removed the shorts and stepped into the pool. He shuddered at the chill and then sank beneath the surface so that only his head was showing.

'They all slept in the house,' Ronnie said. 'One kept

watch. There was a changeover at two. The guard was sitting in the chair by the back door when the relief came out. The guard spent his time mainly outside. He would take a turn around the yard. Sometimes sit in the chair for a fag. Walk to the caravan for a piss.' He glanced at Sandra. 'To relieve himself, like.'

'A piss would do that,' said Sandra, and Ronnie grinned.

'When do we take them?' said Kev.

'Tonight,' said Reaper. 'At two.'

*　　　*　　　*

They made themselves comfortable. At least one of them, and quite often more, kept watching through binoculars. Sandra alerted them all when the girls were brought outside and taken to the pool. Gwen was seventeen, a small girl with a slim shape and a mass of wild auburn hair. Nina was thirty-six, curvaceous, tall with dark hair cut short, a style many women had chosen for expediency during the last year.

The girls were accompanied by a middle-aged man in khaki shirt and shorts and chukka boots. He was close to six feet tall and had a rangy build. No excess weight. He had two black and white terriers on extended leashes. They ran and sniffed and pissed like dogs do. With him was a squat man who looked strong enough to pull a plough. He wore a red vest, white trainers and blue jeans.

'Very patriotic,' said Sandra.

The girls were subdued. They had retreated inside themselves to hide from the abuse. Sandra chewed her lip. She knew the state they were in. She'd been there. For a moment, she wondered where she would be now if Reaper hadn't come along when he did? Quite possibly she would have taken her own life rather than face a future as a sex slave. Did anyone ever get used to such conditions? Did hope remain eternal? Or did hope finally become a sharp blade across the wrist or a noose on the back of a door? The hope of ultimate escape?

She glanced at Reaper. His face was set. There would be no mercy when they moved in tonight.

They watched the small group reach the pool. The man in khaki gave an order and the girls stripped off their dresses. They wore no underwear. Sandra noticed that James lowered his binoculars and looked away, his expression grim. The girls stepped into the pool and submersed themselves. The squat man threw a bottle that Nina caught. It was some kind of shampoo or body wash. The girls used it to cleanse themselves and wash their hair.

Sandra felt sick. They were getting themselves nice and clean for the evening's events.

She would have liked to have gone in, there and then, guns blazing, taking the bastards out and freeing the girls. But the dangers were too great. The girls might be hit in the cross-fire and the attackers might take casualties from the men still inside the farmhouse. Reaper was right. Tonight was the time to move in. Whatever the girls suffered between now and then, they had already suffered. The experience would not be new, just extended for a few more hours. And then would come a reckoning.

Chapter 4

WHEN DARKNESS FELL THEY WATCHED two and two about and let Ronnie catch up on the sleep he'd missed the night before. The guard at the farmhouse followed the pattern Ronnie had described. He stayed inside part of the time and, when he came out, sat in a chair by the back door and smoked. On one occasion, he strolled across the yard to the old caravan to urinate.

They applied dirt to their faces and hands and any exposed flesh that might be translucent in the dark and, at midnight, they set their watches and moved down the hill to take up agreed positions: Ronnie to keep watch over the men's vehicles, which were parked opposite a side door; James to cover the other two sides of the house from an oblique angle at the rear, in case of an escape bid through the windows.

James had been particularly quiet all day, as if locked in an inner turmoil. Kev had quietly mentioned to Sandra that his young friend had an unspoken affection for Gwen. 'They've done nothing more than exchange looks. But it's there,' he said. 'Young love.' He shook his head. 'And then this.'

Kev went with Sandra and Reaper, a position she knew Kev was happy with. He wanted to go in and kill someone, preferably with his bare hands. That was acceptable, as long as he did it to order and not on his own whim.

They were in position soon after one and found plenty of shadows in the farmyard, despite a bright moon and no clouds. They kept a radio silence. The guard had gone inside the house. They listened to the night sounds and the rustle of rats in the barn. One ran across the top of the caravan, outlined against the sky, and then dipped inside through a gap. Sandra shuddered.

The guard came outside twenty minutes later. It was the young man they had watched take a bath in the pool. Sandra was positioned alone, round the corner of the house, and would take him if he opted for the chair and a cigarette. She slid the Bowie knife from its sheath and waited.

Instead, he strolled across the yard, a shotgun hanging from a strap on his shoulder, enjoying the few more seconds of life that his choice had given him. The man unfastened his trousers and let forth a stream of piss with a soft sigh of satisfaction, and Sandra watched the shadow of Reaper leave the deeper shadows, silent as death, cover the man's mouth with one hand and push the ten-inch blade that he held in his other, into the unprotected throat.

Blood spurted now, along with the piss, and they mingled on the dirt and cobbled floor of the yard. Reaper lay down the corpse and wiped the steel on the man's shirt.

Kev ran across the yard and, together, they carried the body back to the farm and sat it in the chair, which they positioned three yards away from the door. Reaper broke the double-barrelled shotgun and removed the cartridges. He leant it against the man's legs. Kev joined Sandra. Reaper went back into the shadows by the caravan.

'Half an hour,' Sandra whispered to Kev, and they sank on their haunches to wait for the relief guard.

*   *   *

The door opened before two o'clock. Sandra used a mirror at ground level to look round the corner. The stocky man was standing in the moonlight, scratching. He was unarmed.

'Richie, ye idle sod!' he said, in a rough Scottish accent. 'Wake up! Merrick'll kill ye.'

He took a step towards the figure in the chair and Sandra came round the corner with a Glock in her hand that was levelled at the stocky man's head. Kev followed, the carbine at the ready, and moved past the man to take up a position on the other side. The man's eyes were wide. Then he noticed Reaper emerging from the shadows as he crossed the yard, lean, darkly clothed, two guns at his thighs and the 10 inch Bowie knife held casually in his right hand.

'Fuck,' he said.

'Exactly,' said Sandra, the barrel of her gun pressed against his head.

Reaper stopped in front of them. He didn't speak. He didn't have to. His stare was enough.

Sandra said, 'How many inside?'

'What?'

Reaper raised the knife and pricked the man's throat, very slightly.

'How many inside?' Sandra repeated.

'Three guys. Two girls.'

'Where are they?'

'Upstairs.' Reaper moved the knife in front of his face to encourage detail. 'Two bedrooms. Merrick's in one. The young girl's wi' him. Barney and Jonesy are in the other. The other girl is with them.'

'Upstairs…' Sandra said. 'Tell me about upstairs. We go upstairs and then what? Where are the bedrooms?'

The knife moved again. His eyes followed it.

'Top o' the stairs is the bathroom. Turn left, that's where Merrick is. Turn right, there are two rooms. The others are in the second room.'

Sandra was standing slightly behind the man and she glanced at Reaper. They had the information they needed. Reaper gave a slight tilt of his head and dropped his knife arm and the man exhaled, as if he'd been holding his breath. Then his eyes widened in shock and his mouth made a perfect O as the knife was pushed swiftly into his body at the apex of his rib cage and up into his heart. He made no other sound and was held for a moment longer on the tilt of the blade until Kev put down the carbine and took his weight and they lowered him to the ground.

Reaper spoke to Kev. 'Top of the stairs, you go left. We'll go right. We go into the rooms at the same time. No noise. We want the girls safe.'

Kev nodded and left the carbine where it lay and took the Glock from its holster. They entered the house silently. Moonlight provided sparse illumination through the uncurtained windows to show them a kitchen littered with cans and bottles. It was darker when they moved to the internal staircase, shadows dense at the top. Kev led the way, treading carefully, using the outside portions of the stairs to avoid worn areas that would squeak. Even so, the old boards made a noise. He paused halfway up. They could hear snores from above them.

He continued the climb and turned left. Reaper and Sandra went right; he was still holding the knife, she was holding the handgun. They exchanged a look across the darkened stairwell and Reaper raised and dropped his arm and they moved simultaneously. Reaper opened the door and Sandra stepped past him and into the room, the Glock levelled. The light was much better. Three people were in the bed, Nina in the middle. She was awake, her eyes wide and staring. Sandra raised a finger to her lips to urge silence. The men on either side of her were asleep. The one on the left was doing the snoring.

Reaper followed her inside and paused. Behind them, they heard Kev struggling with the other door. Dogs began to bark.

'Kick it in!' Reaper shouted, and moved swiftly round the bed to the silent sleeper and put the knife to his throat. At the same time, Sandra stepped to the snorer and put the barrel of the gun in his open mouth.

The two men in the bed awoke and, probably because sleep still clouded reality, attempted to fight. Sandra didn't hesitate. She put a bullet through her man's head. Reaper dragged the other man onto the floor, taking the covers with him. Nina lay unmoving, still terrified, totally naked. Sandra realised she might not know who they were; perhaps she thought they were yet more marauders come looking for spoils of war.

'Nina. It's okay. It's Sandra. From Haven. You're safe now.'

Realisation began to dawn and then Reaper stood up from the floor where he had finished with the final bedfellow. This time he hadn't been able to avoid the blood he had spilled and it glistened on his face. The girl fainted.

The sounds of splintering wood and dogs barking came from across the landing and Reaper went in that direction. Sandra rolled the other dead man out of bed, throwing with it the pillow that had been beneath his head and now contained brain, blood matter and fragments of skull, and began to look for clothes for Nina.

Kev had only just forced open the door as Reaper joined him. The dogs continued to make a noise.

'Bastard had it barricaded,' he said.

They pushed together and furniture, on the other side, scraped across the floor. Then Kev was in, gun raised. The window was open and the only occupants were two terriers who were now wagging their tails in delight at meeting someone new.

*   *   *

The window was above the lean-to shed that had a sloping tiled roof. James saw it open and lined up his shot. But it wasn't a man who climbed through, it was Gwen and she was naked. A man followed, also naked, but carrying a revolver. He stayed close to her as they crouched on the roof. James couldn't be sure of his target.

From inside the farmhouse came the sounds of someone kicking a door and a single gunshot. James ran down the slope. The man pushed Gwen so that she fell from the roof onto the ground, crying out. He dropped down after her and grabbed her roughly by one arm. James was closing fast when the man saw him and raised the gun he held. He fired once and the sound was loud but the shot wide. James dropped the carbine and, running full pelt, ran into him, taking him around the middle and knocking him backwards.

The three of them sprawled on the ground and James had a moment's advantage before the stronger man realised what was happening. James grabbed the wrist of the hand holding the gun before it could be pointed at him again and reacted with all the pent-up anger he had carried since the day before. He used elbow, head, knees and feet as he fought the man. The viciousness of the attack took his opponent by surprise, but then he began to react with his own desperation, and his own kicks and thumps pounded against James's still-healing wounds.

It was an uneven contest and James had to use both his hands to stop the man bringing the gun to bear, which meant he took even more blows to his body. He swung his elbow desperately and struck it into the man's throat, which provided a momentary respite, but he knew he couldn't last much longer, and then the fight went out of his naked opponent and James knelt up and began to swing a fist until his arm was held.

'It's over,' the voice said, and it took a moment to realise that it belonged to Kev.

He sat back on his haunches and the confused action of a few moments before began to slot into place. The first thump had been Kev dropping from the roof. The second thump was the kick Kev had applied to the side of the naked man's head. James moved backwards. He could feel blood from the re-opened wounds inside his shirt and Kevlar vest. Gwen? Where was Gwen?

The girl came to him and he wrapped his arms around her and they sat together and nursed their wounds and each other.

'We came,' he said, in a hoarse whisper, and meant to say more, but the words got lost and he felt tears in his eyes.

Gwen said nothing but hugged him tighter, hiding her nakedness against him, relief seeping out with the tears. The tightness of her grip hurt his wounds even more but he did not complain. Others moved around them but he was content to hold Gwen, content to let events now take their course.

Merrick was dragged to the front of the farmhouse. Nina came and stroked Gwen's hair but she would not relinquish her grasp of James. Nina went away again, to return some minutes later with a dress and shoes. Only when James urged her to clothe herself did she slip the dress over her head. He fitted the canvas shoes to her feet and they stood up but still they remained alone, behind the house. It seemed as if she needed time to gain strength from him before she faced the others.

*　　　*　　　*

The group stood around the naked figure of Merrick, who was sitting on the ground, his hands fixed behind his back with plastic cuffs. He glanced around the group, although most of his attention was directed at Reaper, whom he had identified as the leader.

Nina, arms folded tight across her chest, trembled as she looked at her former captor. Sandra stood by her side, one arm around her shoulders.

'Where are you from?' Reaper said.

The man didn't answer.

'Where were you going?'

He still didn't answer, but glanced around the group as if assessing his chances of survival.

'I could be useful,' he said. His accent was soft Scottish, educated, Edinburgh. 'I'm a professional. You're going to need professionals. Leaders. I'm a trained engineer. I was MD of a major conglomerate.'

'You're a murderer and rapist,' Reaper said, conversationally.

'You're a bastard,' Nina said, in a low voice that threatened to break with emotion. She looked around the group. 'Gwen was a virgin. The rape didn't happen until we got here. Gwen refused.' She stared back at the naked man with pure hatred. 'Merrick put her in the caravan.' She paused, taking a deep breath, her voice still on the edge. 'The caravan is infested. He put her in with the rats.'

The horror sparked through the group like a current. They stared at Merrick with a new intensity.

'It was only a few minutes,' the man said. 'Just a persuader. They didn't have time to bite her.'

Nina said, 'She was in there a while. Never stopped screaming. When she came out, she did whatever they said. She was a wreck. She hasn't spoken since.'

Kev began to take a step forward towards the cringing Merrick, who had sensed the mood change. James and Gwen came round the corner and joined them. The girl still clung to the youth; his arms remained protectively around her. Kev stepped back again slowly and put a hand on the boy's shoulder and James nodded, an acknowledgement for his timely arrival a few minutes before and thanks for his friendship and understanding.

Reaper said, 'Ronnie? Get the Mitsubishi.'

They all waited, uncertain about what was to happen, until Ronnie brought the Mitsubishi round to the front of the farmhouse. They collected all weapons and put them in the back.

'Everybody climb aboard,' Reaper said.

James said, 'What's going to happen to him?'

'I'll take care of it,' said Reaper. They exchanged a look and James nodded and led Gwen to the 4x4. 'Sandra, will you come back for me?'

She nodded and she and Nina climbed aboard.

Kev said, 'I'll stay, if you don't mind.'

'Don't trust me?' Reaper said.

'I trust you. I just want to be here.'

Reaper nodded and waved the car away. Kev saw James looking out of the window. They exchanged a nod. Justice would be done.

'What are we going to do with him?' Kev said.

'He's going in the caravan with the rats.'

'What?' Merrick looked from one to the other, utter panic in his gaze. 'You can't. For Christ's sake, you can't. Good god, man. What are you?'

'I'm a professional,' he said. 'I'm the Reaper.'

Merrick continued pleading. He tried to get to his feet and Reaper kicked him back to the ground.

'He'll scream,' Reaper said. 'The girls have suffered enough. I didn't want them to hear that.'

'After what he did, they might enjoy it,' Kev said.

'Only as a concept. Not as a reality.' He looked down at the sobbing man. 'Now, Mr Merrick. Why don't you tell us where you came from? Who knows … If I like your answers, I may just put a bullet in your brain instead.'

'We came from Scotland,' he said. 'Three of us came from Scotland. We met the others on the road. Teamed up.'

'How many others have you killed and raped on the way down here?' He asked the question as if enquiring about the weather conditions they had encountered.

'Nobody. We hurt nobody.'

'Except at Nab Farm.'

'Someone shot at us. The lads over-reacted.'

'And you took the two youngest women.'

'We couldn't leave them.'

'Of course not. How noble. On your feet.'

Kev helped pull him up. The man looked pathetic but Kev had no pity. He understood Reaper's rules. The crimes these men had committed were beyond the pale. There was no mitigation. Merrick had to suffer a penalty of death and he didn't deserve the mercy of a clean execution. They walked him towards the caravan, and when Merrick realised they intended to carry out Reaper's threat, he dropped to his knees and begged again.

'Please,' he said. 'I'll take a bullet. But not that. It's inhuman.'

'And totally appropriate,' said Reaper.

'It was a joke!' he cried. 'We didn't leave her there! It was a joke.'

Kev and Reaper took an arm each and dragged him the rest of the way. A rat emerged on top of the caravan and stared at them. The man fell to the ground and Reaper took out a second pair of plastic cuffs and applied them to Merrick's ankles. A third pair linked wrists to feet. He opened the door to the caravan and they all heard the scurrying inside. The man was sobbing, no words emerging any more, mucous running from his nose in his horror and despair.

They picked him up and threw him into the interior.

'Enjoy the joke,' Kev said.

They closed the door, and Merrick began screaming

and rolling about on the floor so that the caravan swayed. Kev found an old wooden pallet near the barn and jammed it against the door, just in case it came open. Reaper went into the farmhouse and returned carrying a spray can of red paint and Kev remembered the psychedelic van. One of the gang must have had artistic aspirations.

Reaper sprayed one word down the side of the caravan in big letters: RAPIST.

Five minutes later, Sandra returned in a Range Rover. She turned the car around in the yard and got out. She made no comment about the screams that were coming from the caravan and disturbing the night.

'Coffee?' she said, holding up a flask.

Reaper and Kev had coffee.

'How's Nina?' Kev asked Sandra, feeling guilty because most of his concern had been directed towards James and Gwen.

'Coping. She knows there's no alternative.' Her face was grim and she glanced away into the night for a moment. 'It wasn't the first time for Nina. It happened to her before.' She shrugged. 'I don't know if that makes it easier or worse.'

'Jesus Christ,' Kev said. He looked skywards, making the words a prayer.

'Get the dogs,' Reaper said. 'It's time to go.'

Kev collected the dogs from upstairs where they were once more sleeping after the excitement of the break-in.

They came with him happily, climbed aboard and waited with him in the back of the vehicle. Sandra exchanged a look with Reaper and Reaper nodded.

He walked back to the caravan where Merrick still thrashed and screamed, kicked away the wooden pallet and pushed open the door. The screams stopped and sobs could be heard coming from the man inside. His eyes gleamed white in the gloom and held Reaper's gaze with panic and hope. Scurrying sounds filled the edges of the darkness. Reaper drew a Glock, pointed and fired and the sobs stopped. He pulled the door closed on the sight and smell of the blood that would invite the rats to a feast.

Chapter 5

THEY WENT BACK TO NAB FARM, Ronnie leading on his trail bike, Kev driving a Rover with Nina in the passenger seat, and James and Gwen in back, still entwined. Reaper and Sandra brought up the rear. The farm had regained its night sounds and, even though it had a mass grave out the back, it still held memories of homestead and friendship.

James and Gwen slept together on the girl's bed. She refused to let him go and she still hadn't spoken. The youth removed his gun belt and Kevlar vest, and they slept on top of the bedclothes in each other's arms. Nina's bed was in the same room but she didn't want to intrude; neither did she want to be alone. She was eventually persuaded to lay down on the double bed that Auntie Marjorie and Pops had shared, and even smiled at the memory of the elderly lady informing everyone that the arrangement was 'purely plutonic'. Her nerves were eased when Kev took a mattress from a bed and lay it on the floor of the landing outside her door.

'You want anything, just call,' he said.

Reaper and Sandra stayed downstairs with the dogs that Nina told them were called Butch and Sundance.

Sandra took the settee and Reaper sprawled in an armchair.

They woke with the dawn, as was their practice. Ronnie went scavenging and returned with a dozen eggs that had been overlooked and left behind in the hen runs before the birds were taken to Haven. They found a stale loaf for toast and Kev cooked breakfast.

Time was no longer an issue. The girls packed what belongings they wanted and at mid-morning, Ronnie on his trail bike, and a Rover containing James and Kev and the rescued girls left for Haven. Reaper and Sandra planned to remain a while longer to wait for Pete Mack. If he hadn't arrived by noon, they would leave another note and return home themselves.

As they were about to, Pete returned. Following him were two black BMW 4x4s. Each had an aerial attached from which flew pendants bearing the Scottish Saltire – a white cross on a blue background. Pete seemed relaxed as he got off the motorcycle but Reaper and Sandra cradled their carbines across their bodies as they waited outside the farmhouse for explanations and introductions. The dogs ran around the yard, barking at the intrusion.

The vehicles carried two men in each. The passenger in the lead car got out. He wore military combat fatigues, a blue beret and a side arm. He was close to six feet tall, well built and looked to be in his late thirties, with a face that was handsome if you liked granite.

Pete sensed the awkwardness and stayed by his bike.

'This is Sandy Cameron,' he said. 'He and his men have been looking for a rogue gang. They could be the ones we're looking for. Sandy, this is Reaper and Sandra.'

Cameron stayed by his vehicle. He nodded and held his hands up, palms outwards in a sign of friendship. 'I understand the need for caution,' he said, in an unmistakable Scottish Highland accent. He held a hand out and took a couple of steps forward.

Reaper considered for a moment, then let his carbine swing behind him on its strap and walked the rest of the way. The two men shook hands and each took the measure of the other.

'Why don't your men step down?' Reaper said.

Cameron made a motion with his hand and his three companions – all dressed similarly – got out of the cars. If they had rifles, which Reaper guessed they undoubtedly did, they left them in the vehicles.

Pete said, 'I met them near Durham.'

'We're looking for a gang of four, possibly five,' said Cameron. 'They were three when they left Scotland. They're led by a man called Merrick. Tall, stringy sort of guy. Wears khaki.'

'What did he do?' Reaper said.

'Escaped. He was serving life with the other two. For murder and rape.'

'You have a prison?'

'We have a mine. An opencast coal mine. They were sentenced to a life of hard labour.'

'Until they escaped.' Reaper's words sounded close to admonishment.

'They were the first.'

'We found them,' Reaper said. 'They won't rape and murder again.'

'Ye killed them?'

'We did.'

Cameron nodded and looked round the farmyard. 'This was the place they raided?'

Reaper nodded. 'They killed five, took two women. We brought the women back.'

'I'm sorry.' He shook his head, his expression grim. 'We've been trying to bring justice back. Sentenced to the mines, instead of instant death. The people wanted a show of clemency. Violence begets violence? They wanted to break the cycle. Ye've no tried anything similar?'

'No. We kill them.'

'Mebbe we should have killed them. Merrick and his gang raided two other settlements that we know of on their way down here. Ten more deaths. We've been trailing them for three weeks.'

'Well, it's over now.'

Cameron looked past Reaper at Sandra, who still remained alert in the doorway of the farm, the carbine in her arms. Loud enough for the words to be directed at them both, he said, 'Reaper and the Angel. We've heard of ye.'

'Don't believe all you hear,' Sandra said.

'All we've heard couldnae possibly be true. We thought it was a legend. Like Camelot. King Arthur and Guinevere?'

'I prefer Angel,' she said.

'The Angel of Death,' Cameron said.

His three companions focussed their attention on her, probably wondering how such a slim teenage girl could have gained such a reputation.

'Take a good look,' she said. 'See if you can spot the horns.'

Sandra laughed as she caught one of the three fix his stare on her hairline. He blushed and looked away.

'We already have a King Arthur at Richmond,' Reaper said, and Cameron raised an enquiring eyebrow. 'There's a legend that Arthur and his knights are asleep beneath Richmond Castle. That they'll rise in time of need. The leader of the community there is a local historian who lives the legend. He claims to be Arthur and carries a broadsword. Nice guy. Settled community.'

Cameron said, 'We have a Robert the Bruce in Glasgow and I believe Rob Roy is alive and well on the banks of Loch Lomond.' He shrugged and smiled. 'It takes all kinds. Mebbe this new world needs heroes.' He glanced between them. 'Like Reaper and the Angel. Mebbe they need heroes tae believe this new world can grow.'

'Where are you from?' said Reaper.

'Outskirts of Edinburgh. Naebody wi' any sense lives in cities anymore.'

'Haven's not far away. Come and visit. Our people would enjoy talking to you. Exchange ideas.' A ghost of a smile flickered at his lips. 'You could tell them how hard labour works.'

'You have liberals, too?'

'They, more than anybody, have found the new realities hard to accept.'

*   *   *

Cameron and his men spent the night in Haven. Reaper could tell they were impressed. Duggan, one of the younger Scots, tried chatting to Sandra in the obvious hope of a brief liaison. What a story to take back to Edinburgh. The man who slept with not just an angel, but the Angel of Death. He had no chance. But Sandra, Reaper sensed, enjoyed the attention. At last, she might be getting over the death of Jamie, the husband she had had for such a brief time.

He had to admit, he was allowing his own feelings to grow towards their doctor, Greta Malone. He would never forget Kate, the woman who had reignited the passion he thought he had lost forever. Wonderful Kate with the lustrous red hair who had led him into a relationship he had been almost too scared to contemplate. They had not had long together, but the time they had, had been memorable.

Now he had a relationship with Greta that was developing slowly. There was a mutual attraction between them and he liked Greta very much. She was a beautiful woman and a beautiful person. But was he ready to love again?

After Cameron had met the members of the Haven council, Reaper took him to the Farmer's Boy and they sat outside in the evening sun to drink a glass of beer.

'Our place is not so much different,' the Scot said. 'Back tae the land. Hard work and simple pleasures.'

'Any territorial problems?'

'We've had our moments. We didnae have a plan, like you seem to have had when you brought people here. For us it happened by chance. People moved into the country to escape the cities. Our community grew around a village. Elphinstone. Close to the coast and good farmland and still close enough to Edinburgh. We've had no major threats but the vagabond gangs posed a problem. That's why we formed the Guards.' He flicked his uniform. 'We do our share of work but, when needed, we're expected to deal with trouble. From what I was told, ye've had war or the threat of war since ye started.'

'That's why we have the Blues. We're permanent. Plus we have a hundred part-time militia. We're responsible for a big area. And there are more people south of the border to be jealous of what we've got. That's why we fought two wars.'

'And won two wars.'

'At a cost.'

Cameron nodded. 'Always at a cost. I was in Afghanistan.'

'You should talk to Ashley, head of security.'

Cameron nodded. 'I met Ashley.'

'Except he doesn't like talking about it. He was a sergeant in the Paras. He had it rough.'

'Many did. Many dinnae talk about it. War is war and it's always hell.' He laughed disparagingly at himself. 'Cliché.' They paused to ruminate and Cameron continued the conversation. 'And now ye might have another war. Redemption? The Council mentioned it.'

'I was worried in case we had a threat from the north, as well,' Reaper said.

'Not from us. Not from Scotland, I dinnae think. Glasgow is a no-go area, mind. And, when the food finally runs out, the gangs there'll cause trouble when they come hunting in packs. By then, I might have persuaded our council to think again about hard labour in the mines. Sometimes the solution has to be permanent. We have contacts with other communities, like you do. Near neighbours we'll go and help and they'll reciprocate. When the Glasgow gangs move, that will be the time for us to take real action. Take them out before they think they can win.

'Every city or town has urbans, still clinging to familiar surroundings, even though grass has started growing in the streets. And all of them are in fear of the ferals, the ones who have chosen to run wild. The problem ye might have will be Newcastle. It has a reputation. The ferals there are organised. One major gang. Unified. As many as a hundred, hundred and fifty street soldiers, all armed. Plus their dependants, gofers and sex slaves. At the moment, they're content to live out of supermarket warehouses and they take a percentage from the farmers and fishermen who are operating on the fringes of their territory. They call it danegeld. Like the ancient tax to pay off the Vikings?

'But everyone will eventually leave the cities. There'll be too many rats to compete. Even the feral rats in Newcastle. When they do, Haven may tempt them. Of course that might not happen for a couple of years yet, as they work their way down the country. But eventually…'

'I appreciate the warning. So we have Newcastle and Redemption.'

'We've heard Redemption is near Windsor?'

'We think they moved to Banbury. Why, we don't know. We know little about them.'

'And they've got Prince Harry?'

'So they say.'

'Ye dinnae believe them?'

'I don't know. But it made a great rallying call. A lot of survivors from the military camps around here answered it. They all went south. We heard one morse code message back from an RAF group to others who were waiting to follow. It said "stay where you are". It said "don't go to Redemption".' Reaper sipped some beer. 'We don't know what regime is down there but if they have attracted military from around the country, they could have a proper army. We were told they were at battalion strength. That's a thousand men. If they decide to come north and wage war, it would be one we couldn't win.'

'What're ye going to do?'

'I think we have some time before they expand their boundaries. They'll have to consolidate their own area first. Then they'll move into neighbouring areas. The south of England is a big place. Then there's the West Country. When they eventually move north, they will have a lot of territory between them and us, a lot of communities we don't know about. It could be a couple of years or more before they reach us.'

Cameron said, 'On the other hand, ye're a viable community. A big community. A successful community. And they're... what, five or six hours away by military convoy?'

Reaper nodded. 'That's why we need to go and have a look at them,' he said.

'They could be friendly? They could be stabilising what's left o' the country?'

'We met some of them. They murdered a group in a village down the A1. Friends of ours. No reason for it. They killed and raped.'

Cameron stared at him for a moment, before saying, 'Did ye get them?'

Reaper nodded. 'Military. But poor discipline. We got them.' He paused and then continued. 'We haven't looked beyond the Pennines, either. Manchester, Liverpool, all those huge conurbations. We don't know what they hold. There could be gangs as organised as Newcastle. This is Year Two. There's a lot more trouble to happen before society re-invents itself. At least the Wild West had sheriffs. Some of these places just have outlaws. Sheriffs haven't been invented yet.'

'Of course they have, laddie. We're sheriffs. And from time to time, we have to ride out into the Badlands.'

Dr Greta Malone came down the steps of the manor house and walked towards them. She wore tan shorts and chukka boots and a short sleeved white shirt. The colours emphasised the blackness of her smooth skin and long legs. Both men watched her with appreciation and they stood as she joined them. Reaper kissed her on the cheek and introduced her to Sandy Cameron.

'This is our doctor. Greta Malone,' he said. 'Greta, this is Sandy Cameron.'

'I have never seen beauty and brains so well packaged together,' said Cameron, as they shook hands.

They sat down again, Greta alongside Reaper, and she responded with a tired smile.

Reaper said, 'Bad day?'

'I've been down the coast. A woman with appendicitis. She died.' She looked at Cameron, as if the news put his flattery into context. 'These days, appendicitis can be a killer.'

'I'm sorry,' the Scotsman said, for both the death and his flippancy.

Her smile strengthened. 'No, I'm sorry. You were being gracious and I was being a bitch. Besides,' she glanced from one to the other, 'you had your own problems.'

'They've been resolved,' said Reaper.

'Aye,' said Cameron. 'Reaper resolved them.'

'When do you go home?' Greta asked.

'In the morning. But it was worth the trip. New contacts, new friends.'

'Do you have a doctor?' she said.

'No. We have a paramedic. She's training two others, but we have no doctor.' Cameron looked at Reaper. 'Ye're lucky.'

Reaper accepted that the words meant that both he and Haven were fortunate to have Greta Malone. He reached for her hand on the table and said, 'That is very true.'

*   *   *

The Scots left the next morning. Sandra and Reaper waved them off from the steps of the manor house.

'Nice people,' Sandra said.

'Duggan seemed to think you were quite nice, too.'

'Shut it, Reaper.'

'Young man, young woman ...'

'Reaper ...'

'Of course, Duggan doesn't know you like I do. I reckon he had a lucky escape.'

They exchanged a look and he grinned, put his arm around her shoulders, and pulled her into his body. She didn't resist.

'One day,' she said, softly, 'maybe I'll meet someone. But not yet.'

He squeezed her with affection and so that she couldn't look up into his eyes and see that they had dampened. It was the first time since Jamie's death that she had acknowledged she might love again. Was it her reticence that was holding him back from a full relationship with Greta? At the moment, they were content to hold hands, share chaste kisses and enjoy being together. Like old-fashioned teenagers in love. Wasn't it time to take it further? The only reason they hadn't was his fear of commitment. But what was there to fear? Everyone lived with uncertainty and threat. There was no golden age of peace around the corner when everything might be better. Now was as good as it was likely to get.

'We've decisions to make,' Sandra said.

She meant Redemption and the possible threat from Newcastle in the north.

'We have,' said Reaper. 'What do you think about me and Greta? As a couple?'

'What?' She pulled away from him and, when she saw that he meant it, a smile broke across her face like a sunburst. 'I think that would be brilliant.'

'She might not want me on a permanent basis,' he said. He put a finger to his lips. 'I haven't asked her yet. So not a word.'

'Oh, Reaper.' She put her arms around his neck and pulled herself up to hug him so that her feet dangled. 'I'm happy for you. And of course she wants you. It's been obvious for months.'

'It has?' He held her by the waist and lowered her back to the floor.

'It has. But you're just a man, so what do you know.'

'Still. I can't just assume. And I haven't talked to her about it, yet.'

'Then it's about time you did, you stupid sod. You're made for each other.'

Sandra had been pleased before, when he and Kate had become a couple, and he hesitated yet again over commitment.

'You don't think it's too soon?'

'Kate liked Greta. They liked each other. Kate knew you had to grab life, which is why she grabbed you.' She gave a tight grin, that was part sadness, part determination. 'Kate's probably looking down right now, saying, get on with it, Reaper. Time is too short to waste.' She kissed him on the lips. A daughter's kiss. 'It's not too soon.'

The Rev Nick came out of the manor house behind them, almost running in his excitement.

'There's been a radio message from Bob Stainthorpe,' he said. 'The Royal Navy. They've landed at Brid.'

Chapter 6

THE HARBOUR AT BRIDLINGTON WAS LINED with more than a hundred people. They had come from Filey and Scarborough, too. Tied up at the far end of the harbour wall, was a dull metal-grey boat about seventy feet long. At its short mast at the stern flew the White Ensign of the Royal Navy. The number P273 was emblazoned on its bow.

Those watching did so from a distance. Reaper noted two machineguns on the vessel and a bigger weapon mounted on the upper deck. The four sailors on board, who wore navy blue blouson uniforms, were not actually manning the guns but were standing nearby.

Bob Stainthorpe of the Bridlington Yacht Club and fisherman Nagus Shipley were among a small group who stood alongside the boat. With them was the fiery preacher Charlie Miller from Filey and Richard Ferguson – the Prof – from Scarborough. They were talking to a naval officer. One step back from the officer on the dockside was a man in green camouflage uniform and combat vest, cradling an automatic rifle. He also had an automatic in a holster at his waist and wore the green beret of a Royal Marine Commando.

Assessing the firepower on the boat, Reaper was glad that he and Sandra had left their carbines in the Range Rover. They eased their way through the group of watchers and walked along the empty expanse of the harbour wall. The small group parted as they approached and Ferguson said, 'About time.'

Up close, the boat looked top heavy. A big square structure lined with windows at the bridge and an open command position on the superstructure. Even so, it also looked to be built for speed.

The officer was in his late thirties. Good looking, average height, dark hair and a beard that already showed touches of grey. He saluted, which rather took Reaper aback, and then held out his hand. Reaper and Sandra both shook as the introductions were made.

'I'm Commander Harvey.'

He smiled at them both, but looked longer at Sandra. Reaper was tempted to tell him that looks could be deceptive.

'It's good to see you,' Reaper said.

'Perhaps now we should go aboard? Gentlemen?'

Reaper was surprised when the others remained on the harbour wall rather than follow the Commander.

'It's all right, Reaper,' Stainthorpe said. 'It's been discussed. Limited space.' He said it as if he didn't believe it but had accepted the reality. He handed Reaper a folded largescale map of Great Britain. 'Here. This might be useful.'

Reaper nodded and followed Sandra. They stepped down onto the deck and Commander Harvey led the way, opening a door, and into a mess area with two fixed tables and benches. The marine remained outside. A sailor put his head round an inner door.

'Coffee, sir?'

'Splendid, Jones.'

He gave an inquiring glance at the two of them.

Reaper said, 'Black, no sugar.'

Sandra said, 'White, with two.'

Jones appraised her with a sailor's eye before ducking back from whence he came.

'We are a little cramped for space, but I'm sure we'll manage,' the Commander said.

'But that's not why the others have stayed ashore,' Reaper said.

'No. I've been through this process before and found it is easier to speak to the one or two people in command rather than a committee. Usually, those in command have a grasp of reality. I can make judgements about them, which becomes a judgement on the community they represent. That way, I decide how much to tell them.'

Sandra said, 'Do we have to pass a test?'

The Commander smiled. 'You've already passed the test. I've heard about you down the coast.'

She raised her eyebrows dismissively.

'Don't be modest,' the Commander said. 'I can

distinguish between fable and fact. Like it or not, you two are legends.'

'Don't tell me,' Sandra said. 'Haven is the new Camelot.'

He smiled and said, 'I haven't heard that one before.'

They sat at a bench, Reaper and Sandra one side, Commander Harvey on the other. The sailor called Jones returned with a tray on which were three mugs of coffee and a plate of biscuits. He transferred them to the table.

'Thank you, Davy.'

'Aye, aye, sir,' he said, and left.

Reaper looked at the Commander. Davy Jones? This time his eyebrow was raised.

The Commander smiled and said, 'Good man. His name is Roland but, of course, everyone calls him Davy.' He looked back at Reaper and Sandra. 'There will be lots you want to know. I, too, am compiling information.' He nodded towards the map that Reaper had placed on the table. 'We can help each other fill in the blanks. Where people are surviving. Trouble spots, safe havens.' He smiled at his choice of words. 'Let me tell you now, from what I've heard, your group is the most successful we know about. You must be doing something right.' He looked at Sandra. 'Even with your reputations.'

Reaper said, 'Are you from Redemption?'

'Straight to the point.' The Commander shook his head. 'No, we're from Portsmouth, but we've heard of Redemption. Not good things.'

Sandra said, 'Is there a government in Portsmouth?'

'No. But we are another safe haven. A hundred and five naval personnel and more than six hundred civilians. This patrol boat is exploring the east coast and we have another exploring the west coast.' He shrugged at her disappointment. 'I'm sorry. It's the same across the Channel.'

'You've been there?' Reaper said.

'Calais, Bordeaux, Ostend, Zeebrugge. The situation is the same as here. Same the world over.'

Reaper nodded. 'We assumed as much, but I suppose there was always a sliver of hope that somewhere might have escaped the worst.'

'We almost did.' Commander Harvey made the statement with a grim smile. They waited for him to continue. 'I was aboard HMS Vengeance, one of our nuclear submarines. We were on our way to the Falklands when the virus began to spread. We were silent running. When we made contact with Port Stanley, we were told the virus had become a pandemic. It was worldwide and getting worse. The last reports we had gave us a good indication that this was a global disaster. That populations were being shredded, society on the edge of collapse. No one was safe.' He paused. 'Except us. Beneath the ocean on the other side of the world. Then radio signals started dying.'

He pushed his coffee mug on the table with one finger, perhaps moving the submarine through uncontaminated waters.

'A nuclear submarine has a range of twenty years. Virtually unlimited. We distilled our own water, recycled our own air. We had plenty of supplies. We could surface and fish, if we wanted to. But the isolation was total. Aboard were fourteen officers and a hundred and twenty-one men. They had families, loved ones at home. I had a wife and two children.'

He pushed the coffee mug some more.

'We came home six months ago. Back to Faslane in Scotland.'

They nodded. Reaper knew Britain's nuclear submarine base had been on the west coast.

'We thought we might be safe. Our medical officer said the usual SARS virus was spread by close person-to-person contact. Droplets that are spread by sneezes and coughs. Touching contaminated surfaces. Persons with SARS were mainly contagious when they were suffering from the symptoms – fever, cough, sneezing. The contagion might last as long as ten days. We'd been away a lot longer. Long after the last person died. The Doc said the virus was a mutant. It might still be alive. Even so, we were determined to take the chance.' Commander Harvey stared across the mess room at another place, another time.

Sandra said, in a soft voice, 'What happened?'

'Only a handful of Navy had stayed at Faslane. A Royal Marine commando from the Fleet Protection Group, a chief petty officer and six ratings. They were providing protection for about forty civilians. They welcomed us as if we had come to save them. We remained disciplined, but we wanted to find out what had happened to our families. We wanted to go home. We agreed to stay together for another week before setting off in organised groups to check on who had survived. Some of the ratings had families who lived on the base. All had died apart from one child, a girl of eleven.

'It was winter and she had a cold. Within a few days, her father had it. The Doc put him in isolation and we all feared the worst, but he got better. Then others went down with it and we realised it wasn't flu – it was the virus. I got the symptoms but pulled through. The people there, the original survivors, said it didn't seem as strong as it had been during the pandemic. It still killed a hundred and twenty-four of us. Out of a hundred and thirty-five officers and men, eleven of us survived. Apparently that's good odds. They reckon the pandemic left one in a thousand. The Doc had warned us that the virus was a mutant. He said it had lain dormant in the girl. Probably other people, too. He said, hopefully, those of us who had survived this last outbreak, had built an immunity, but I'm not so sure. I still stay away from people with colds.' He took a deep breath, the end of the lesson. 'The Doc, he died, too.'

'You've had it rough,' said Reaper.

'So has everybody. Now we have to try to make it better, if we can.'

He finally drank the coffee, in one extended gulp, before he continued.

'We found Portsmouth was still operating. Contacted them by radio. Nine of us took this patrol boat, the HMS Pursuer and sailed there. Once we confirmed the base was good, we went back and brought the rest of the people from Faslane. We run Portsmouth on naval lines. There's order and discipline and a sort of democracy. That's why the civilians stay with us. That's why hostiles stay away. At Portsmouth we have a Commodore, a Captain, several junior officers, a Warrant Officer, a chief petty officer and assorted ratings. We have a doctor and a dentist.'

Sandra said, 'I don't understand ranks. You're a Commander? Is that like a Commodore?'

He grinned. 'No, I'm lower on the chain of command. I'm third senior officer, after the Commodore and the Captain.'

'What about your family?' Reaper said.

Harvey lost the grin. 'Dead. We all knew that would be the case, but some of us had to make sure. I found them. Said my goodbyes.'

They both knew sorry would be a facile thing to say, so they said nothing.

'Anyway, it was decided we should expand our horizons. We are the senior service, after all. We had a duty to discover how the rest of the country was faring and whether we could forge links and alliances. So another patrol boat went west, and we came east.'

'Dangerous?'

'Not really. At sea, we're fast. We're also well-armed. We can mount three general-purpose machineguns and have a 20 mm canon on the fo'c'sle. There's a crew of four ratings, a petty officer, and a Royal Marine Commando.' He smiled. 'And you mess with those guys at your peril. So far we haven't had to fight anybody, although one group was hostile to our presence. Usually, we have been well received, but people have been disappointed when they realise we don't represent a return to the old society.

'There's no government, no central power that is going to switch the lights back on, start paying pensions and make everything right again. That's down to us. To all of us. It's in our hands and no one else's.'

He stood up and went to the other table.

'Now. Let's compare notes.' He unrolled a large scale map of Southern England upon which he had marked out coastal areas, and written notations within the boundaries. He grinned at them. 'I'll show you mine, if you show me yours?'

The Commander used four large-scale maps upon which he had marked the different communities he had encountered on his journey up the East coast, and had included inland territories about which he had been told, but had not visited. Reaper copied them onto the road map

Bob Stainthorpe had given him and took extra notes on notepaper supplied by Harvey.

They exchanged information in as much detail as possible. Intelligence was essential if they wanted to make progress. Reaper told the Commander about the bunker beneath the Pennines they had found. That the city of Leeds had burnt itself out, that the city of Newcastle might be on the brink of warfare with an army of a hundred and fifty street soldiers looking for somewhere to invade when the supermarkets were finally empty.

The Commander confirmed that people were trying to reassert themselves, that life was trying to reassert itself, mostly in rural and fishing communities, but there remained unrest in cities and stories of roving gangs who travelled the land looking for easy pickings.

'What's happened in London?' asked Sandra.

'From what we can gather, pretty much the same as happened in other cities.' The Commander smiled. 'I suppose everyone hoped a government of sorts had survived in a bunker beneath Whitehall. Like your Pennine bunker. Didn't happen, I'm afraid. Same pattern as elsewhere but with embellishments. Some group occupied 10 Downing Street, another set themselves up in Buckingham Palace.

'For a brief time we had a King Wayne in residence. He was usurped by King Edward IX who was, in turn, usurped by King Ian. No more kings after that. It proved an unhealthy occupation. King Ian was hung from the gates of Buck House.

'Greater London was six hundred square miles in size and had a population of nearly eight million. Central London had maybe half a million people. We don't know survival rates but there could have been up to five thousand men, women and children in Central London, maybe more. Many would have gravitated to the Palace or Whitehall in the hope of finding a government. What they apparently found was chaos. Gang rule. London has great parks but nobody was interested in cultivating them, not while the shops and hotels were still stocked and available to make life bearable.

'The gangs are still there. The usual pattern. Violent ferals in control are ruling groups of serfs or slaves and living off easy pickings. Sensible urban dwellers got out early, escaped to the country when they saw the way things were going, although there are bound to be some still trapped in inner city areas. The further out, the better the conditions became, but only because numbers weren't as great. Gangs claimed shopping precincts, warehouses and wholesale depots as their fiefdoms. Other gangs fought wars of possession.

'Sensible folk moved further and further away from the conflict. Some came our way, which is why we know so much detail. A ham radio operator in Lambeth kept us informed until his batteries ran out. Others made the unfortunate choice of heading towards Redemption which, like the capital, we have designated a no-go area.'

'Redemption.' Reaper said. 'Is it a threat?'

'We heard about them at Portsmouth. We are staying contained close to the coast, until we can work out what is happening elsewhere, but a few refugees found us who had left the place. It's no longer headquartered at Windsor. They've moved north to Banbury. Apparently it's run on military lines. They have gathered several hundred officers and men from the RAF and Army. We were told the leadership in charge are protected by a cadre of elite soldiers called the Black Berets. The rest of the troops are on guard duty.'

'Guarding what?'

'The workers. They have people working farms, looking after animals, operating water mills, steam engines. They have a slave labour camp – at least, that's what it sounds like – where they put anyone who is too vocal against the regime, anyone who might stir up trouble. They have a coal mine. The prisoners dig the coal.'

'Why don't people leave?' said Sandra.

'Fear and security. Back in the middle ages, all serfs wanted was to survive. They worked the land for their lord and master and, with luck, were left alone in peace. It's pretty much like that. If anyone does try to leave, they're brought back and punished, sometimes killed. It's an incentive for the modern serfs to keep their heads down and work. The refugees I talked to said the leaders promised things would get better in a few years time. That this was a period of transition where everyone had to work together for the common good until the country got back on its feet.'

'And they have Prince Harry as a talisman,' said Reaper.

'Yes.' Commander Harvey sounded doubtful. 'Of course, we don't know whether it's actually Prince Harry or an imposter. But claiming to have Prince Harry at your head is a hell of a validation.' He looked first at Reaper and then Sandra. 'What do you know about Redemption?'

Reaper said, 'We met a three-man unit that had come from there.'

Sandra said, 'Our fame had gone before us. They had been sent to find out who we were.'

'We found them in a village called Cromwell on the M1 in Nottinghamshire,' Reaper said. 'They had killed friends of ours in the village. Rape and pillage, it appears, is a modus operandi for Redemption troops on a recon mission.'

The Commander glanced from one to the other. Their faces had become masks.

'What did you do?'

'Killed them,' said Sandra.

Reaper said, 'Unfortunately, the last one died before he could give us a full briefing.'

Sandra said, 'He died too quickly. He should have suffered longer.'

Commander Harvey this time kept his eyes on Sandra who had made the comment with a cold assertion.

'Before he died,' Reaper continued, 'he said they had battalion strength. A thousand trained troops. They called themselves the New Army. Their leader is a General George Purcell. Redemption, they said, is the seat of the New British Government.'

'Then they are dangerous,' the Commander said.

Chapter 7

THE RADIO MESSAGE WAS URGENT. A woman in labour in Whitby needed the help of Dr Greta Malone. A motorcyclist had ridden top speed along the coast road over the moors to Scarborough from where the request was sent. It was coincidence that Reaper was at the manor house when it arrived but it was a spur of the moment opportunity that he took.

'I'll drive you,' he said. 'You can't go alone.'

Greta didn't argue and Sandra didn't offer to come with them to fulfil the two by two rule: the Blues always went in pairs. But she did exchange an amused glance with Reaper before they left.

'What?' he said.

'Nothing,' she said. And smiled.

He snorted, Greta climbed aboard the Range Rover and he drove out of Haven and headed north in heavy rain that fell from a dark and troubled sky.

They didn't speak much on the way although Greta had occasion to brace herself at the speed of his driving and in apprehension at their approach to bends on the wet road. He noticed and said, 'Sorry. I'm just anxious to get there.'

'In one piece,' she said.

'Yes. Sorry.'

And cursed himself for his bad driving and his need to apologise. What sort of message was he sending out?

He eradicated the risk factor and eased into the journey. Greta stopped gripping the edge of her seat. It stopped raining but the cloud cover remained. The countryside was heavy duty green. The rain had washed dust away and left foliage and grass with a new depth of lustre. The landscape changed as they entered the moorland. It rolled like waves, eternal and empty beneath the clouds.

Greta instigated conversation about the visit of the Royal Navy. His mind was on other things but he responded and the talk led onto the possible threat posed by Redemption and he realised the relevance. He couldn't put off a visit south much longer. A trip into the unknown. There were other aspects of life he couldn't delay either. But this was not the time. He changed the subject.

'The baby,' he said. 'You think having a baby is normal but now, nothing is normal.'

'This probably is,' she said. 'A long labour makes people worried. That's all.'

'I know, but. Well, before you had babies in hospital with nurses and doctors. All the essential equipment if anything went wrong.'

'Generations ago, women just had babies. It's a natural

process. Some births are easier than others, that's all. And men tend to panic the longer it goes on.'

He remembered the birth of his own daughter. It had been relatively quick. Two hours, start to finish. Like shelling peas, he had said light-heartedly to a colleague. His wife had not agreed. The experience had not been a happy one and she had wanted no more. The two hours might have been swift but the months preceding the delivery had been uncomfortable and undignified and boring. Never again, she had said. One was enough. Emily. She had been enough. A daughter whose presence filled and completed his life without him realising. His Emily. His eyes began to prick with tears at the memories. He coughed. 'Not long now,' he said. 'Let's hope it's just men panicking.'

The motorcyclist met them by arrangement at Hawsker outside Whitby. He led them off the main road and onto a country lane, the back way through the farmland towards the Abbey on the East Cliff above the town. Before they arrived at the Abbey ruins, he turned into a working farm. Two anxious men were standing outside in the yard, smoking roll-up cigarettes. One was in his forties, the other twenty years younger. A black and white dog came from a barn, barking at their arrival. The older man shouted at it to be quiet; he called it Homer but it ignored him. It stopped when the motorcyclist dismounted and it recognised his smell. Friends, it decided. It wagged its tail as Greta and Reaper got out of the car.

'We didn't know what else to do,' the younger man said to Greta.

'Martha's with her,' the older man said. 'Upstairs.'

'Don't worry,' Greta said and went past them and inside.

The two men nodded to Reaper. He knew them vaguely by sight. The motorcyclist removed the helmet and he was surprised to see it was a girl with cropped hair. She was new; he hadn't seen her before.

'How is she?' she asked.

'God knows,' said the young man.

A baby cried from inside the house and they all looked up at a bedroom window.

'That was quick,' said the older man. He looked at Reaper. 'She doesn't mess around.'

Reaper smiled. 'It's a natural process,' he said, as if he knew what he was talking about. 'The doctor arrived just at the right moment.'

They waited a while longer in the farmyard, the day muggy beneath the clouds. Thunder rumbled somewhere out at sea.

'It'll come down later,' said the older man, glancing upwards.

'It's been a dry summer,' said Reaper. 'The crops need it.'

Making small talk. All waiting for the verdict from upstairs.

A middle-aged woman appeared at the door. She looked tired but was smiling.

'It's a boy,' she told them. And then directed her next remarks to the young man. 'Healthy and well.'

'Everything …' the young man said, stumbling over what he wanted to ask.

'Fingers and toes,' she said. 'Everything in the right place.'

He smiled, the older man slapped him on the back and the woman stepped aside and said, 'Wash your hands before you go up to see him.'

They heard water splashing from a jug and his footsteps on the stairs. Reaper found himself grinning at the miracle of life despite all that nature and disease had thrown against them. The older man looked at him and caught his sentiment.

'And so it goes on,' he said.

*   *   *

Reaper drove back at a more sedate speed. The baby had arrived before Greta had entered the bedroom but her presence had been reassuring both to the new mother and Martha, who had, whether she wanted to or not, become Whitby's new midwife.

'There's nothing better than first hand experience,' Greta said. 'Besides, she was a farmer's wife. She's helped at lambing.'

'The birth really was normal?' he asked.

She had reassured everyone at the farm that it had been, even though a protracted labour of twelve hours had caused concern. But he had wondered whether she might have withheld the whole truth in case it undermined Martha's newfound confidence as the first line of resource in maternity care.

'Perfectly normal,' Greta said. 'Painful, but perfectly normal.'

He cut across country to the Pickering road then turned off again to drive down into the village of Goathland. It was raining once more although the threatened storm had not arrived. The place was deserted, the village green and the gardens of the cottages that ringed it were overgrown. The only inhabitants were sheep that cropped where they liked. Reaper parked outside the pub.

'Were you a *Heartbeat* fan?' Greta said.

The long running television drama series had been centred on Goathland, which in fiction had been called Aidensfield. Country stories set in the nostalgic 1960s, following the lives and investigations of rural police officers, with a soundtrack of even more nostalgic music.

'Actually, I was,' Reaper said. The sound of the rain was heavy on the roof of the car now the engine had been switched off. 'But that's not why I came here.'

'Why have we come here?'

He paused, looked at the threatening sky, and said, 'Let's go in the pub.'

He got out without waiting for her reply, grabbed his carbine from the back seat, and dashed beneath the porch. The front door was already open and he pushed on into the pub itself. Inside, it was tidy and cared for. Kindling lay in the fireplace and stacked nearby were split logs for when a fire might be needed. The lighting was dim, even mid-afternoon in summer, because of the weather, but there was an oil lantern on the bar in case they needed better illumination. Reaper didn't think that would be necessary. He placed his carbine on a table and went behind the bar. Greta followed him in and stood in the doorway, unsure why they were here.

Reaper said, 'The sun should be shining and I should have brought a picnic.'

Greta said nothing but walked to the bar and sat on a high stool. He put two wine glasses on the bar and opened a bottle of red. The silence stretched between them while he poured.

'I thought it might be looted,' she said.

'It was famous on TV. The programme was nostalgia back then. The pub is even more nostalgic now. I think that's why people take care of it. There's one farm nearby that's occupied but, believe it or not, people still make a pilgrimage here. They still come as tourists. And they take care of it. They visit to remind themselves of a fictional past that never really happened.' He raised his glass and they toasted each other. 'Nostalgia,' he said.

'There's no future in it,' she said, with a smile and he laughed. 'Now. Why are we here?'

The bar was still between them. Reaper seemed to prefer it that way.

'I wanted to talk about us,' he said, almost in a rush, but the next part of what he had intended to say remained unsaid. The words had gone out of his mind.

'About us?' she repeated. Her eyes were big behind her big glasses. He felt as if their gaze was pinning his presumption to his soul. He stared back. She said, 'What about us, Reaper?'

'I ...' he shook his head and looked at his feet, his hands holding the bar as if for support. 'Probably a bad idea.' He looked up. 'We're good friends, aren't we?'

'The best.'

He nodded, somewhat reassured.

'Good. Good. That's what I thought. I ...'

His words were drying up again. Greta reached across the bar top and placed a hand on one of his.

'All men panic,' she said. 'Strong ones? They're the worst.'

She picked his hand up and led him from behind the bar so that they were face to face. She placed his hands on her waist and put her arms around his neck and kissed him. For a second he didn't react. Then he did. They kissed for a long time. When their mouths broke apart, they remained in each other's embrace.

'Us,' he said, still unsure. 'What do you think?'

'I think us is a great concept,' she said. 'What took you so long?'

They kissed again and, even though they were mature about their situation, their emotions began to develop along natural lines. Another break, and Greta said in a breathless tone, 'Do you think they do rooms?'

'I'm sure they do. I'll go and find out.'

Upstairs, the hotel was as well kept as the bar area. Perhaps for this very purpose, for when nostalgia gave way to something more demanding. They had a room with a double bed and a view, although they did not pay the view much attention. Reaper was surprised that, once the words had been said, although in such a clumsy fashion, his nerves had gone. They made love all afternoon, with both fierce passion and gentle understanding.

As they lay naked in the gloom afterwards, the storm finally broke. They lay side by side, only their hands touching, listening to the thunder and the deluge of rain.

'Why did you wait so long?' Greta said.

'I was afraid you might turn me down.' He shrugged and rolled onto his side. 'You are a beautiful young woman. You could have anybody. I suppose I didn't want to be disappointed. As long as I didn't ask, there was a chance you might say yes. But if you'd said no, that would have been it.'

They stared at each other.

'You look naked without your glasses,' he said.

She had put them on the bedside table when they had pulled each other's clothes off. She laughed.

'What about the rest?' she said.

His eyes caressed her body. They were content taking in every curve, every shallow shade, dark upon dark.

'The rest is very beautiful,' he said. 'I got the best of the deal.'

'You're not so bad.' She raised a hand to stroke his chest. Her fingers traced old wounds on his neck and shoulders. 'Rugged but serviceable. And you may have triggered a medical condition over which I have now no control.'

He frowned, half worried. 'What's that?' he said.

'I'm in danger of becoming addicted to you.' Her fingers touched his face. 'Can you do it again?'

He smiled. 'I can try,' he said.

Chapter 8

WHEN REAPER HAD KNOWN they needed to expand the Blues he hadn't expected Gwen and Nina to be the latest recruits. But, when he analysed the reasons, it made sense. They were both highly motivated after their experience and were determined never to be victims again. Besides, the community of which they had been a part, no longer existed. The Blues would be a new home for them.

Seventeen-year-old Gwen remained quiet and withdrawn and stayed close to James, although their infatuation with each other had not been consummated. A more unlikely relationship developed between Kev and Nina. This remained at a stage of mutual trust that Kev hoped might become something more.

The two women survivors of the Nab farm massacre had shared accommodation since their arrival at Haven. It had been their choice. They could relate to the trauma each had endured. It was better than having to face the sympathy of strangers who had not been there, and suffer their silent speculation about what had occurred.

When not with Nina, Gwen sought the company of James. The silence between them was comfortable; she needed no more, it seemed, than to be in his presence and hold his hand. The arrangement also suited him. It was the closeness he had wanted. They never referred to the circumstances that had brought it about.

It was natural that, because the two teenagers spent time together, Nina and Kev would come into contact. He remained bluff, compassionate and available. 'I'll sleep outside your bedroom, anytime,' he said, provoking a sad smile from her. Circumstances again. If the horror of Nab Farm hadn't happened, he wouldn't have needed to; and he wouldn't have got close to this attractive woman for whom he realised he had more than the usual thoughts of desire. Kev was surprised to discover his motives towards Nina were honourable rather than lustful.

Their recruitment happened naturally. The two women felt vulnerable and Nina asked Kev if he would teach her the rudiments of shooting. If there was ever a next time, she wanted to be able to defend herself. Sandra agreed it would be a good idea, and Kev and James introduced the two women to the intricacies of the Heckler and Koch carbine and the Glock handgun. Sandra and Reaper added lectures on discipline and survival and they became trainee Blues.

When James asked if he could travel to Cheshire to discover what had happened to his family, it was a mission in which all four could take part. Most people had experienced the deaths of their families and loved ones when the virus had devastated the world but James had been at school on the other side of the country. He knew there was little or no chance that his parents or sister had survived but he didn't know for sure. Reaper understood that it was important for the young man to resolve the doubts.

As the two girls were novice members, it would be normal for them to team up with a Blue with experience. It was obvious which way these four would team up, no matter what Reaper said. James would be with Gwen, leaving Nina paired with Kev.

'I'm not totally happy about this,' Reaper told James. 'You and Gwen are close. It might impair judgement if you get a tough call.'

'Sparta,' said James, nonchalantly.

Reaper nodded. He understood the reference.

'Spartan warriors in Ancient Greece took male lovers when at war and fought side by side. It made them fight all the fiercer.' James smiled. 'And to be honest, I never really fancied Kev in that way.'

Reaper laughed.

'Besides,' said James, 'we're all close, you know that. All the Blues. We'd all die for each other. Because I love Gwen doesn't mean I'm going to do something stupid. Rather the opposite.'

Reaper was impressed at how mature the young man was. 'You're right,' he said. 'Totally right. Just take care.'

Two teams usually travelled in two cars but on this occasion it seemed sensible for all four to use the one vehicle as the girls were still serving an apprenticeship. Next time out, they could split into pairs.

They completed loading the Rover for the trip on a hot sunny morning. The girls were already in the back of the vehicle.

'One thing,' Kev said in a quiet voice that would not carry. 'If shit does happen, there's no way we can let them fall into the hands of another gang.'

'I know that.'

'Do you? Do you understand what I'm saying?'

James raised his chin slightly, his eyes far too cold for a youth of his age. 'I understand,' he said.

Kev nodded, and suddenly felt the weight of the responsibility they were both shouldering because of the changed rules of survival under which they were living. They would shoot the girls to stop them becoming rape victims again. He snorted at having to consider such options when they were embarking on a trip on a summer morning that should have meant only excitement and having a laugh.

*   *   *

When the world was normal, the trip wouldn't have taken long. Motorway across the Pennines from Yorkshire into Lancashire and on into Cheshire. They might have stopped at a service station for coffee and an over-priced meal or looked for a pub in any of the conurbations through which the highway went.

Maybe a shopping detour into the giant Trafford Centre on the outskirts of Manchester, a retail mall of domes and doric columns, markets and food halls, the splendour of baroque and Ancient Egypt, and parking for 10,000 cars. Or a cultural diversion into the ancient streets of Chester with its Roman history, 17th century inns and tiered galleries of shops and tearooms.

Instead, they took their own food and drink, and drove carefully.

They had travelled to the peak of the Pennine range before, when Ronnie had discovered the secret bunker beneath the moors where government representatives had hoped to sit out the pandemic and restore order afterwards. It hadn't happened. The pandemic had found and destroyed them, like it had done everywhere.

Once they started down the long sweeping motorway into Lancashire, they were entering new territory, new dangers. The view ahead was vast. Urban areas lay on the plain before them on both sides of the snaking double carriageways. From a distance they looked normal, as if people still lived there and led lives of industry and going to the pub. As if mums were still picking up the kids from school or having coffee with their neighbours and talking about the holiday they planned in Florida. 'It's expensive but the children will love it.'

But there was no such thing as normal any more.

The skies seemed clearer, cleaner, without pollution. Smoke from one small fire rose straight upwards way over towards Oldham. Controlled smoke. Perhaps a cooking fire. A sign of habitation. No morning coffee for young mums but maybe roast rat or dog with a baked potato. Maybe roast human. There had been stories.

No barriers marred the highway ahead but they stayed alert. Kev drove at 50, James had his seat pushed back, carbine at the ready across his knees. They went beneath the walkway that linked the two sides of Birch Services, a few cars in each parking area but no people. Kev peeled off left to take the circular M60 around the southern edge of the city. It was a longer way, but avoided the Trafford Centre. They had discussed the route before they left and had surmised that the richness of the Centre, one of the largest retail parks in the country, might have attracted a gang with grandiose ideas to match the architecture. Buckingham Palace had had three kings, the Trafford Centre might have a pharaoh. At the least, the occupiers might have put up barriers on the motorway that ran past, to inspect, capture or barter with travellers.

They encountered no problems as they snaked along the swift road through the environs of suburban sprawl. There was the occasional crashed car, either driven by suicides in the aftermath of the plague, or by people going far too fast in thoroughbred vehicles whose power they had fatally underestimated. Two more small fires burnt on the far outskirts of Stockport, more signs of life in the desolated land. They encountered no travellers. In the early days, there had been plenty of fugitives on the roads in single vehicles or small convoys, looking for salvation. Now, it seemed, they had realised there was no salvation and many had decided there was no point in moving. Until the food ran out.

The motorway split again and they took the M56. Signs proclaimed this was the way to Manchester Airport.

'Where do you fancy?' said Kev. 'Three terminals. Destinations around the world. We flew to Cyprus from there. Smashing holiday. We had a villa at a place called Polis. Terrific time. Lovely bars and restaurants, great beach. Lovely people. Went snorkling every day.'

He ran out of things to say. The emotions of the holiday suddenly catching him out, memories of his wife and daughter, of the gentle, warm, family fun. No clouds of any kind on any horizon. He almost cried. He sniffed. 'Anyway, it was a lovely spot. Unspoilt.' He grunted. 'Unspoilt for ever now.'

Nina said, 'I've been to Cyprus. Nice place.'

'We flew to Majorca from Manchester,' said Gwen. It was the first comment she had made since the start of the journey. 'Family holiday.'

The silence threatened to emphasise her contribution out of proportion.

'How about you, James?' Kev said. 'Family hols?'

'We had a house in Ireland,' James said. 'On the coast in Wicklow. We flew from Manchester to Dublin a few times but mostly we drove and took the ferry.'

The signs showed the airport turn was approaching.

'Well, if there's nowhere exotic you want to fly, we might as well go to Cheshire.'

They surged past the turn and stared at the curve that had once taken passengers to the major international airport. Now weeds would be growing through the runways and the aircraft would be slowly rusting on the tarmac.

'No more holidays abroad for a while,' said Kev. 'Not until someone invents an airship.'

'That will be the way we'll go,' said James, meaning the future, and not them personally. 'Airships were the thing in the 1930s. Far superior to aeroplanes. The war and the Hindenburg disaster stopped their development. But they will be the best option for us. It's an easier way to fly.'

Kev glanced at him. 'You know some stuff, don't you?'

'It's called education, Kevin.' He said it with a smile to remove the sting.

'Me...' Kev said. 'I never went to a posh school. I'm a graduate of the University of Life. How about you Gwen?'

'My parents were teachers. It was all mapped out for me. Sixth form and university.'

Kev couldn't care less about her educational aspirations. He was pleased that she was talking. 'Were you going to be a teacher?'

'That's what they wanted.' Kev saw a hint of a smile in the rear view mirror. 'They meant well. But it wasn't for me. I didn't know what I wanted. I was in sixth form. I had a vague idea that I wanted to be a social worker.'

'By heck, me hearty,' Kev said. 'I never had you down for the open-toed sandal brigade.'

James said, a little defensively, 'Gwen just wanted to help people.'

They had obviously discussed this before.

'Fine thing too. Don't get me wrong. It's a vocation, like being a priest. All power to your sandals, Gwen.'

'I've never worn sandals,' she said. The smile stayed.

How about you, Nina?' Kev said. He realised he didn't even know if she'd been married. Come to that, she didn't know if he had. Many people chose not to talk about the past, keeping the memories precious and for themselves alone.

'Me?' she said. 'I was in local government.'

'Tea lady?' Kev said it mischievously.

'I was an architect in the Planning Department.'

The declaration of her past profession immediately dented Kev's hopes. Being an architect meant she was clever. What could she possibly see in a former matelot with a tattooed arse? Before he could brood too deeply, James directed him to turn off. His family home was the other side of the town of Knutsford, which was still some miles away. They were taking country roads to avoid urban areas.

'Nice countryside,' Kev commented.

'I hadn't noticed before,' James said.'Just taken it for granted.'

'It's gentle,' said Gwen.

They drove along a narrow road that was canopied with overhanging tree branches. The road dipped past a lake and rose again to emerge at the crossroad of a small village with an ancient parish church, a pub and a solitary shop that said VILLAGE STORE. Terraced cottages meandered away along two of the roads and more substantial houses were in secluded spots among trees and overgrown foliage. Parked on the road were two cars that might have been abandoned for a year, and a sit-up-and-beg bicycle that had been left propped against a hedge, and was now part of it as the undergrowth had gradually absorbed the frame.

Kev stopped the Rover and switched off the engine and they got out. Both he and James carried their carbines casually but ready to use. Gwen and Nina stood behind them, holding their weapons in the same manner but self-consciously. This was the first time they had been in an active situation. Except that it wasn't very active. They were in the peace of the countryside and listened to the birds and the hum of insects. From somewhere, they could hear the cooling sound of water in a stream.

They stretched and relaxed.

'Hello,' shouted Kev, but no one replied.

James, with Gwen a pace behind, walked towards the

Parish Church of St Stephen. He too, shouted, but still there was no response. He looked at Kev and said, 'We might as well eat. I'll check the pub.'

He went cautiously towards The Black Swan, even though all the signs suggested the village was deserted and hid no hordes of ferals. He motioned to Gwen and she levelled the carbine to the ready. James entered the pub, whose door was unlocked, and Gwen followed. Kev waited but there were no shots or shouts of alarm or discovery. He went to the Village Store; Nina was behind him, also with carbine ready.

The whole village looked as if it had gone to sleep eighteen months before and missed the turmoil that had followed in the wake of the virus. It was a neat and civilised village where the inhabitants had probably died neat and civilised in their beds, without causing a fuss.

Kev was not surprised that the front door of the store wasn't locked. He pushed it open and the shop bell rang, a sound of normality in a village that had died. It was an old building with a nicely preserved old frontage but, inside, it had undergone modernisation to better utilise the space. The counter was on the right as he went in. A door to the interior was at the end. A row of shelving in the middle of the store on the left created two aisles. Against the far left wall were two refrigerated units that had long ceased working. The shelves were reasonably well stocked with household items but there were spaces where foodstuffs had been. A rack of newspapers was inside the door. *State of Emergency* and

Martial Law were headlines on the nationals. *May Day Festival Cancelled* declared the local weekly.

He indicated for Nina to stay at the front door. He opened the interior door that led to a passage and a flight of stairs.

'Hello,' he shouted.

Nobody answered but three cats ran past his legs, giving him a start.

He inspected the shelves. They had brought their own food but anything that might augment it would be welcome, although he was inclined to leave the store intact. He had done his share of liberating supplies in other places but here it would seem like looting. That was until he discovered the SPAM. He first found a couple of cans on a middle shelf alongside a solitary tin of pilchards. He found himself smiling and reached for them. Two 12 ounce cans of the pork-based meat product were too good to pass up. He dropped one can and, when he crouched to recover it, he saw that extra supplies had been stored at ground level below the bottom shelf. There was a whole cardboard carton of SPAM. Twenty-four cans.

'Oh yes!' he said out loud. He put his carbine on the counter with the two spare cans.

'What is it?' said Nina.

'Food of the gods,' he said, and went back and picked up the carton.

SPAM was never top of the list when scavenging groups went out from Haven, but to Kev it was a delicacy he had missed over the last year. He was back at the counter when a voice behind him said, 'Stop right there!'

It was an old voice that trembled, but it spoke with an authority that suggested its owner might have more than justifiable outrage to back up his demand. Kev stopped. Nina had stiffened on the doorstep of the shop, her gun pointing past him, her eyes unsure. He motioned with the palm of his hand for her to calm down.

'Turn round.'

Kev turned and faced an elderly man in the shadows beyond the interior door. He held a shotgun that shook as much as his voice. He wore glasses, baggy trousers, a shirt buttoned to the neck and a cardigan. From her position, Nina would be unsighted.

'I'm sorry,' Kev said. 'I didn't know anyone was here. I did shout but you didn't answer.'

'Put it back where you found it.'

He waved the gun to encourage compliance and the shake got worse. Kev thought it would be a hell of a way to go – shot over a case of SPAM. No greater love hath man than to lay down his life for his SPAM. The chap was so old and the gun so unsteady that he couldn't take the situation seriously. Except that he should.

'I'm sorry. I'll put it back. No harm done. Okay?'

He moved carefully past the gun barrel and replaced the carton below the shelf.

'And them,' said the old man, and Kev returned for the

two cans, his hands going temptingly close to the carbine on the counter, but what would he do if he grabbed his own weapon? Shoot the old bloke?

'I really am sorry,' he said, after replacing them. 'I wasn't really stealing. I thought the whole village was empty.'

'Well it isn't.'

'I can see that.'

He backed towards the doorway with his hands held out to his side at shoulder height, fingers spread, palms showing.

Then Nina pushed past him, her gun pushed behind her back on its strap, and said, 'I'm glad you're open. Do you have any shampoo?'

The old man lowered the shotgun and pointed.

'On the back shelf. Near the ice cream.'

Nina went where he directed and returned a few moments later with a bottle of Vosene.

'Great,' she said. 'But what do you want for it? I mean, you don't still take money, do you?'

'Do I look daft?'

'Certainly not. You look like a businessman. One who means business with that.' She pointed to the shotgun and he grinned at her.

'Don't you be worried about that, lass. It's not loaded.' He propped the gun in the corner by the door, lifted a wooden flap and shuffled behind the counter, and put the flap back down. 'Now then. One bottle of shampoo. Do you have any liquorice allsorts?'

'I'm sorry, I don't. But we're going to my friend's home on the other side of Knutsford. I'll stop in the town and see if I can get some for you.'

'Funny folk in Knutsford.'

'You mean since the plague?' said Kev.

'No. There's allus been funny folk in Knutsford. I keep my distance. Anyways, the liquorice allsorts aren't for me. They're for me wife.'

'You live here with your wife?' Nina said.

'I look after her. She's older than me. Has a condition.'

Kev said, 'So that's why you stayed?'

'Why should I go?' the old man said belligerently.

Kev held his hands up again. 'No reason at all.'

Nina held her hand out and said, 'I'm Nina.'

The old man took her hand and held it. The tremble turned it into a shake. 'Godfrey Green.' He relinquished her hand almost reluctantly and moved his head in a circular gesture. He was so frail, Kev hoped it didn't fall off. 'Folk round here call me God.' He looked at Kev, still aggressive. 'It's a joke,' he said.

'I'm Kev,' he said, but didn't offer a hand. James and Gwen had come from the pub and were now behind him in the doorway. 'These are our friends. James and Gwen.'

James and Gwen waved.

'It's not every day you meet God,' James said, with a smile.

God nodded, not taking offence. He didn't appear to be intimidated by the fresh-faced youth. He looked from one to the other until he had re-assessed all four. 'You're together, then.'

'Yes,' said Kev.

'I mean, couples. You're together as couples.'

'That's right,' said Gwen.

'That's good. Everybody needs somebody. It's good you're together. It's how it should be.'

Kev glanced at Nina but she didn't look back. He wondered how she felt about being partnered with him, if only in the mind of God.

'You go well together,' God said, staring at James and Gwen. 'I can see it. I can feel it. You're a couple. Like me and Beth. Married sixty-two years, me and Beth. Hope you last as long.'

Gwen said, 'Can we do anything for your wife?'

'No, thank you, lass. I do all that needs doing. She's not up to visitors. But I'll tell her you called. You and your young man.'

'Erm.' Kev waited to be noticed. 'About the SPAM.'

'That you were stealing.'

'That was a mistake. The point is, I'm a SPAM aficionado.'

God's expression didn't change.

James said, 'He means he likes it.'

'I'm a member of the SPAM Appreciation Society,' said Kev. 'Well, I was.'

James said, 'That means he likes it a lot.'

God said, 'The SPAM Appreciation Society?' as if it was a belief in aliens.

'Yes. Honestly. And I haven't seen any for yonks. That's why I was tempted. But now that I know it belongs to you, perhaps we can come to some arrangement. Liquorice allsorts? We can do that. Or anything else you want. What do you say?'

'Well for a start, I'd say it's not my shop and the SPAM doesn't belong to me. I just don't like your not-so-much-as-a-by-your-leave thieving.'

'You don't live here?' Kev said.

'Oh I do now. After Mr Barlow died. It's better accommodation than our cottage.'

Nina said, 'So you're not a shopkeeper?'

'No lass. I'm the caretaker at the church. Caretaker and churchwarden.'

The pause lasted long enough for them all to re-assess the situation.

'So I can take the SPAM?' Kev said.

'Can't stand the stuff,' said God. 'Don't like pilchards much, either.'

Gwen said, 'If Kev takes it, we'll bring you something back. What else would you like, if we can't get liquorice allsorts?'

'Any liquorice. Any sort of sweets, I suppose. Always had a sweet tooth, my Beth. All that was here's gone.'

James said, 'Is there anyone else in the village?'

'No,' he said. 'All gone. Mostly dead. I hold a service for them in the church every Sunday. Churchwardens can do that.'

'How do you know when it's Sunday?' said Kev.

'When I hold a service, it's Sunday,' said God. He cocked an ear and looked at the ceiling. 'Anyway. I have to go and see to Beth.'

'We'll bring you some sweets,' said Nina.

'Anything else?' said Kev.

God lifted the counter flap and shuffled towards the door. 'Aye,' he said. 'Cartridges for the shotgun would be handy.'

He went through the door and they heard him climbing the stairs. One of the cats went with him.

Kev saw James grinning.

'You got taken by an old man with an empty gun?'

'All right,' he said, and held his hands up in surrender. 'But I still got the SPAM.'

He collected the carton and the tins and took them to the car.

The old man had said they were couples and Nina had given him a cheeky smile in passing that could have meant anything, but probably meant don't hold your breath. Kev had always had the ability to make women laugh – all the way into bed, he had liked to boast in his youth – but he was no longer young. He had never had film star looks, even then. His face was more lived in than Hollywood.

Romance? Maybe he would settle for platonic and keep his fantasies to himself.

'What's the pub like?' he asked.

'The shelves are a bit empty but the cellar is well stocked,' said James.

'Why don't we have a picnic on the bench by the church wall,' Gwen said. 'Then if God wants to join us, he can.'

'Do you believe his wife is alive?' James asked Kev.

'Can't be sure, but it's doubtful.'

'So he's living with her memory?' Nina said.

'Or her body,' said James. 'It would be hard to be parted after sixty-two years.'

Chapter 9

THE CLOSER THEY GOT TO HIS HOME, the more memories bombarded James: every signpost, cross road, village green; every pub or church spire evoked his childhood and his past. Public school had taught him to control his emotions before the pandemic. Since then, he had clamped them shut because he didn't know how he might cope if they spilled free. But now he knew he had to face them, confront them. He needed the release.

They had eaten in the village, but God had not joined them. From the pub, Kev had liberated a can of lager for himself and a bottle of red wine, from which James, Gwen and Nina had had a glass each. The encounter had done Gwen good. She had been comfortable talking to a stranger. She still remained mainly silent by choice, but she was returning to normality.

Kev drove and James sat in the passenger seat. Gwen sat behind him, her fingers touching his shoulder, occasionally stroking his neck and stroking his hair. Her touch was good, it was a steadying factor on his memories. If that touch was all their relationship delivered, it was enough because he loved her. He still had to tell her, but surely, she knew that already.

James directed and they avoided Knutsford.

'It's a nice town,' he said, as if sorry not to drive through its streets.

'We'll call on the way back,' said Kev. 'Get some liquorice allsorts. I looked up Knutsford in an AA guide before we left. Did you know this was the most expensive place to buy a house in the North of England?'

The town was surrounded by open countryside and they went through another village, with church and pub and a cricket field, all deserted, and along a narrow road, trees leaning over a high brick wall on their left and farmland beyond the hedgerow on their right.

'It's the next left,' said James, and Gwen's fingers held his shoulder more firmly.

Kev slowed and made the turn left. Tall open frame metal gates blocked their way and he stopped. A sign on the stone wall said this was Purlow House. James got out and lifted the catch, the touch of the metal sparking another memory. Him, jumping out to open the gates, the rest of the family waiting in the car. He pushed them open, one gate at a time, and waited until the car was through. He closed them again and got back in the car.

'Just round the bend,' he said.

The car came out of the trees and the road curved up a hill to a handsome three storey Georgian house.

'Nice place,' Kev said softly. He hadn't realised just how privileged his young protégée had been.

He parked at the front next to a Land Rover and switched off the engine. The summer afternoon silence enveloped them. James took a deep breath and got out of the car. The other three followed his example and waited for his lead.

The front entrance was flanked by Doric columns. James climbed the three steps and tried the door. It was unlocked and he pushed it wide open. His carbine was hanging casually; he was taking no precautions.

Kev said, 'What if there's someone in here?'

'There isn't,' James said.

He stepped forward into a long hall. His feet clicked on the wooden floor.

Gwen followed him and said, 'Shall we wait here?'

James smiled at her and took her hand.

'I don't know what to do,' he said. 'Now I'm here, I don't know what to do. I don't want to find them. I want them to be in Ireland. I want them to be anywhere.' His eyes misted. 'I don't want them to be dead.'

She took him in her arms and they held each other until a cat meowed at their feet.

'Good grief,' James said. 'It's Tabatha.' He crouched and held out his hand and a large tabby cat butted it with its head. It purred. A second cat, pure black, appeared at the end of the corridor. It watched them from a distance. 'Oscar!' James called, but it did not respond.

Gwen knelt with him and Tabatha allowed her to fuss her, as well.

'I'm amazed they haven't turned wild,' Gwen said.

'Oscar was always unsociable. Perhaps he has gone wild. Tabatha was always soft.'

'Two survivors,' Kev said. 'And it doesn't look like they've gone hungry.'

They split into two couples. Kev and Nina went into the first room on the right. A large and ancient oak desk, a swivel chair behind it, and a more modern table at a 90 degree angle that contained a computer stack, keyboard and screen. Book shelves filled the walls. Sunlight shone in through tall windows. The floor was wooden again but mostly covered by a large oriental rug.

Kev stepped past the desk to look out of the window to the rear of the building. A large parking area was to the left, in front of several out-buildings. Formal gardens were immediately outside and the grounds swept away to the right to encompass what seemed like half the county. His heart gave a lurch.

Nina stepped alongside him and said, 'What is it?'

'There.'

Beneath a large tree, maybe thirty yards away, was the unmistakable mound of a grave. It was a pleasant spot, sheltered, and with an unrivalled view of the grounds and house. They stood side by side for long moments and Nina put her hand in his. He turned away first and saw the envelope on the desk. Nina followed his gaze.

He went into the hall.

'James?' James and Gwen were still fussing the cat. 'There's a letter for you. In here.'

The young man put the cat down and stepped past Kev and paused in the doorway. His eyes spotted the envelope immediately. He walked round the desk and sat in his father's chair. Gwen hesitated and then went into the study after him. Silent support. Nina left the room and she and Kev walked outside. The air was warm and pleasant. After a moment, they walked towards the tree and the mound of earth to pay their respects.

*   *   *

James held the envelope in his hands. His name, written in his father's hand, on the front. Gwen stood behind him. Both hands on his shoulders.

'I'll wait outside,' she said.

He touched her hand. He wanted to say stay, but his throat was too dry for words. She left the room. He took several deep breaths and licked his lips. This was a moment of truth. Since donning the Blues he had almost convinced himself that he was grown up. He had killed, therefore he was a man. But right now, he felt his age. He felt fifteen and that he was trespassing in the sanctity of his father's study. He looked at the letter in his hands. This was his formal permission to be here. His father had left it in the hope that one day his son would sit in this chair and read it. Another deep breath and he was prepared.

He used the silver letter opener that was on the desk to slit open the envelope and removed the sheets of ivory velum; unfolded them and began to read.

My dear James,

I write this in the event that you have not fallen victim to this dreadful virus that appears to be devastating the world. Who knows when it will end or what it will leave behind? Perhaps those who die will be the lucky ones.

When we realised the seriousness of the pandemic, our first instinct was to travel to the East Coast and bring you home. Unfortunately, Pippa became ill and we couldn't travel. That was the last time your mother and I spoke to you on the telephone. I tried calling later, but the landline at the school had crashed or developed a fault because of the volume of traffic, and you never answered your mobile.

We isolated ourselves here at Purlow and I told Mrs Tipton to go home and care for her own family in the village. I closed the gates to deter visitors and we tried to sit it out. We failed.

I had taken the precaution of obtaining alleviating medicines as soon as I realised the possible extent of the problem in the early days of the pandemic, so we were able to make Pippa comfortable. She became ill on Monday, a week ago. She lasted 36 hours from start to finish but she was in her own bed with both your mother and me at her side. You should know that her passing was peaceful.

Mrs Tipton returned on Wednesday. She came the back way on her bicycle. By then, your mother was showing the early signs of the virus although we both pretended it was a summer cold. Mrs Tipton realised she was infected but accepted the pretence. The reason for her visit was to bring us bread and scones she had baked, and news. She was devastated to hear that Pippa had died.

Half the village, Mrs Tipton said, had gone down with the virus and people were staying in their homes. The vicar had organised food distribution to help them through the crisis. You remember the Rev Harland? A nice man. A godly man. He and his wife had undertaken to visit the sick and, when a household died, they took what food was left and gave it out to those still living. He had lost his wife the day before but, Mrs Tipton said, he was still carrying on his work. I suppose it gave him a purpose. I wonder if he has survived?

Mrs Tipton stayed an hour and we have had no visitors since. Your mother died on Thursday.

Again, I was able to alleviate undue suffering. I kept waiting to become ill but didn't. I felt remarkably fit and thought that perhaps I was one of those very few with immunity, that the scientists have talked about. It angered me. I didn't want immunity if it meant being without my family. According to what the scientists had said, if I had immunity, you didn't. I had no desire to continue living under those circumstances.

On Friday I buried your mother and sister together near the old oak. It's a nice spot. Remember the picnics? Saturday, I started to become ill. I am not immune, which means there is still a chance that you are. Which is why I am writing this letter, to explain what happened. If you live through this, I know you will one day come here.

It is now Sunday and you will be amused to hear that I have spent the last few hours tidying and cleaning – not exactly my forte, as you know – but I wanted to leave things in order. Besides, like the Rev Harland, it has given me a purpose. I have a sufficient supply of pills and a good bottle of Bushmills malt. I have decided to take Muldoon with me; he would never survive alone. If you come, you will find me in the garden room in the top field.

Do not be distressed by what has happened, James. Remember we had a good life. I hope yours will continue to be a good life, although under entirely different circumstances. Remember to always be true. True to yourself, to friendship, to loyalty, to doing what is right, unto death. I always thought we would have a lot more time to get to know each other, but that is not to be, and it never seemed appropriate for me to tell you how much I loved you, and how proud I was that you were my son.

If you did not survive, then I will see you and your mother and sister in a short while and you can tease me for being sentimental.

Your loving father.

Minutes passed. James stared at the wall in front of him. His mind was back re-living the final days of his family. Now he knew exactly what had happened and every forlorn hope that they had survived had gone. At least they had been together and thank God his father had survived until the last to be able to ease their passing. To be able to make things orderly. Love had been an unspoken emotion but he felt it now: love for his sister, his mother and his father. Love and respect and reciprocal pride. His father need not fear. James would be true.

He returned to the present and called Gwen. She bent over him and wiped tears from his cheeks that he did not know he had shed. She kissed his eyes and his mouth tenderly. She said nothing but the question was in her concerned gaze.

'I'm all right,' he said. He stood up and gave here the letter. 'I would like you to read it.'

She sat in the chair he had vacated and he went to the window and looked towards the old oak. Kev was standing by the mound, head bowed, immobile. Nina sat on the grass by his side. Perhaps Kev felt James's eyes because he looked up and returned the stare. The older man nodded his head once as if to confirm that the mound was a grave.

His father was right. It was a nice spot. James remembered the picnics. Memories flooded back, memories he hadn't allowed since the plague. Then Gwen's arms were round him, bringing him back to the present. He turned and they held each other for a long time and he was glad he was alive, he was glad he was his father's son, and he was glad he had found a woman he loved. The boy had gone and he felt a man again.

'Come on,' he said. 'We should go to my father.'

*   *   *

Others might have called the garden room a gazebo. It was a stone structure, similar to a folly in that it looked like an ancient survivor from a bygone age, perhaps a remnant of an old church. But this had been purpose-built as a hideaway on a shallow hill in the corner of the top field. It was protected by a copse of trees at its back, and was built of old grey stone with unglazed gabled windows and had a red-tiled sloping roof. The rear wall was solid and the front was semi-open with two stone balustrades either side of the entrance steps.

They had walked through a meadow and across an ornamental bridge over a meandering stream to get there.

Kev glanced at James as they approached.

'You want me to go first?' he said.

'I need to see him,' James said.

They had all seen plenty of bodies in the last eighteen months but James realised this would be different. These were special circumstances. Kev didn't argue.

As they got closer, James let the memories back in and he smiled. This was where he had kissed his cousin Tamsin when they were both thirteen. They had taken shelter from a threatened storm, a storm that hadn't happened. But the darkening skies had given them the excuse to linger in the privacy of the stone walls and kiss, mouths open, tongues darting, sharp as electricity. The first time he had experienced proper kisses. It had been, he remembered, delicious. That was the word he had used to Tamsin and she had laughed. He suspected it had not been the first time she had French kissed and he had been grateful for the lesson.

Tamsin. What had happened to Tamsin?

Their footsteps slowed as they neared the structure. It had been built to catch the afternoon sun. From here, you could sit and gaze down at the house and the old oak and the new grave. They could see his father's shape inside, sprawled comfortably in a wooden armchair padded with embroidered cushions. James stopped. The others flanked him. Gwen took his hand.

His father was wearing tan corduroy trousers, a check shirt and a tan sweater. A whisky tumbler was still in his right hand and the remnants of a bottle of Bushmills was on the table by his side. Muldoon, their Irish setter, was on the floor by his feet, an empty food bowl nearby. It was easy to imagine what had happened. A bowl full of food, heavily doctored with sleeping pills for the dog who had the reputation for eating anything, and the rest of the pills for his father as he defied the plague and eased himself into the next life with the aid of a good malt.

James saw only the configuration of death and did not dwell on the desiccation of the bodies. He felt the tears prick his eyes again and sniffed them away. His father's choice. A good choice after he had put everything else in order. He nodded to himself and became aware of Gwen's hand in his. He squeezed it.

Kev said, 'Shall I dig another grave by the tree?'

'No,' James said. 'I'll dig the grave. Could you …?'

'Of course.'

*　　　*　　　*

James dug the grave alone, not far from the mound that held his mother and sister. Kev placed the remains of master and dog into a sheet and then into a tarpaulin. Nature had meant there was not a lot of substance to the corpses and they weighed very little. He carried them down the hill and lay them in the shade of the oak tree.

They buried them as the sun sank lower and the shadows grew longer. Kev filled in the grave as James watched, dirty and sweating from his exertions. When the mound was complete, the four stood side by side.

'Any words?' asked Kev, gently.

'No. No words,' James said. 'They know.'

James and Kev stripped to the waist and washed at a horse trough in the yard at the back of the house. An old-fashioned pump brought water from an underground spring. Nina and Gwen waited for them at the back door that led into the kitchen. James smiled, when he and Kev joined them.

'Thanks for being here. All of you,' he said. 'Now let me show you around.'

They hadn't gone exploring on their own; it would have been presumptuous. The ground floor rooms were large and luxuriously furnished; the dining room was big enough for banquets. James did not enter the bedrooms of his parents and sister, but was happy to show them his own.

A boy's bedroom, not a man's. A framed Star Wars poster on one wall, half made models on a worktable, a computer on a desk. A comfortable double bed, neatly made. Guest bedrooms and bathrooms were along a corridor. The tour revived more memories for James, and impressed on his companions, the wealth with which he had grown up.

The kitchen was equipped with both a small electric cooker and a classic four oven Aga. The house had an emergency generator that still worked. They did not risk putting on the lights but they did use the electric cooker. They ate in the kitchen, opening tins they found in the well-stocked pantry, which was also stacked with cases of beers, ciders and wine. Spirits were in a bar in the drawing room.

Gwen and James drank wine while Kev opted for cider, in the absence of lager. Nina also opted for the cider.

'Careful,' James warned. 'It's strong.'

'I was drinking scrumpy down in Portsmouth before you were born, young James. I know it's strong. That's why I'm drinking it.'

They enjoyed a companionable meal and light-hearted conversation. At one point, Kev asked him, 'Are you okay?'

James nodded.

'I'm okay. I had to come. I'm glad I did.'

'Your father was a remarkable man,' Kev said. He had also read the letter.

'Yes he was.'

'I suspect,' said Kev, 'you are a lot like him.'

'I hope so.'

Gwen leaned close and kissed James on the cheek. 'I know you are,' she said.

As it got darker, the unspoken question began to pose a problem. To help solve it, Kev said, 'I'll take a turn around the grounds. Make sure no one's around. Then, if you don't mind, I'll kip down in the family room. Nice big sofa, and I prefer to be on the groundfloor. Just in case.'

'First line of defence,' James said, with a smile.

'Something like that.'

'I'll go with you,' said Nina.

'I'll get the sleeping bags,' James said. 'We'll use my room.' He said it without looking at Gwen. 'Choose any of the guest rooms,' he said to Nina.

Kev got up, checked his equipment and he and Nina left by the back door.

The grounds were quiet, the night warm. He wasn't drunk but the cider had given him a buzz. He needed a walk to clear his head.

'Nice night,' he said.

'A beautiful night,' said Nina.

They walked as far as the stone gazebo, where James's father had ended his life, and he had to admit that a garden room was an apt and much richer description. They sat there for a while, although not in the chair that Robert Marshall had occupied, easy in each other's company. Nina was smiling at him in the dark and he grinned back and settled into the silence. After a long while, they walked leisurely back, past the house, down through the trees, all the way to gates.

The gates were still closed, the road beyond was empty and the night was still. This was a peaceful place that had avoided any troubles. It would stay that way for at least tonight. Trouble didn't travel at night unless it knew where it was going and Purlow House had been undisturbed since the plague.

'Can you imagine,' he said, 'growing up in a place like this? Beats the council estate I lived on.'

'You turned out okay,' she said, and he began to smile with hope eternal. 'You're a nice man, Kevin Andrews.'

'We'd better get back,' he said.

Nina waited at the front door of the house but he nodded towards the graves beneath the tree.

'You go on,' he said. 'I'll say goodnight.'

She smiled and went inside and he walked to the two mounds, one more than a year old, the other freshly dug. He paused for long moments and wondered what the family would have made of him. Eventually he nodded.

'He's doing well,' he said. 'And I'll be watching out for him.'

At last, he entered the silent house and locked the door. In the dim light, he saw Nina sitting at the bottom of the wide circular staircase, holding a sleeping bag in her lap. Was she nervous about going upstairs alone?

'Are you all right?' he said, in a low voice, walking towards her.

'This is yours,' she said, holding the sleeping bag. 'I don't want to sleep alone tonight.'

Her smile was tight. Her sleeping bag was by her side.

'You don't have to,' he said. Her smile wavered. Nerves? Fear? He guessed her concerns. 'We'll share a room. That's what friends do.'

They went upstairs together and he led her to a room at the end of the corridor in the guest wing that he remembered had twin beds. Nina briefly went into his arms and kissed his cheek. 'You are a very nice man, Kevin Andrews,' she whispered.

*   *   *

Gwen was happy that James had said they would share his room. She certainly wouldn't have wanted to sleep alone in what was a strange house. She had been worried about this moment and it was best that it was to happen away from Haven and its inhabitants. She still didn't know what the outcome would be, but she sensed James's need as well as his concern for her emotional welfare.

What had happened was done and couldn't be changed and, after her initial despair, she had become determined it would not change her or her feelings for the young man she had met so infrequently, but with whom she had shared the sort of intimate glances that needed no explanation. They had had a mutual attraction that she had known would develop into something more solid at its own normal pace. But then the men came, and normality went out of the window.

Gwen had been a virgin. She had hoped to give her virginity to James. Two virgins together. Now the circumstances were utterly different and, while she still loved the young man, she could not be sure that he still loved her after what had happened. Oh, she knew he would always be protective of her, but could he still love her with the knowledge that her body had been violated? He was, of course, honourable but he was also a young man. She knew he needed the physical element of a relationship and, perhaps, because of that, he might believe he loved her. But afterwards, after he had had his physical release, would he feel the same?

It was a risk, but one she had to take and one she had to instigate, for he was a hesitant virgin as well as honourable.

James opened two of the windows to air the room. Gwen unrolled their sleeping bags on top of the bed, unzipped them and then re-zipped them to make a double. He watched silently. Gwen unfastened the gun belt and lay it on the work table. His carbine was propped in a corner by the door but he still wore his holster.

They stared at each other across the room and she felt the tension. Her move. He was immobile. Unsure. Waiting to be led. She lifted her t-shirt, taking her time, and pulled it over her head. She draped it over the back of an easy chair and then sat on the bed to pull off her boots. Her socks followed and she stood to unfasten the trousers and push them down her legs. They, too, went over the back of the chair.

He had seen her undressed before, of course, but not like this. Wearing only her bra and knickers, functional and white, she walked across the room and put her arms around his neck. His hands went hesitantly to her waist. She had kissed him before, but they had been friendship kisses, comfort kisses. This time she kissed him with passion, her mouth opening his to allow her tongue to explore. His hands moved around her, still unsure but with a scarcely controlled urgency. She felt his arousal against her stomach.

Their mouths broke apart and she whispered in his ear, 'It's time, James. If you want to.'

His body began to shake and he released her as she stepped away. His eyes devoured her body. Honour was fighting his desires.

'Do you want to?' she said, climbing onto the bed.

'Yes,' he whispered.

He undressed swiftly, putting his holster and clothes on the same chair, until he wore only boxer shorts. She could sense his embarrassment at being almost naked. A tall youth, still growing into his body. She held out a hand.

'Come to me, James,' she said, and he did.

They lay side by side on the bed and he whispered, 'Are you sure? I mean, you don't have to. After all that …'

She silenced his quavering voice with her lips.

'I'm sure,' she breathed into his mouth, suddenly on the brink of tears as she realised she was having to seduce him because of what had happened. She was now the experienced one; she could no longer give him her virginity. All she could give him were the techniques she had been forced to learn at the hands of her rapists. It wasn't fair but it was a fact and she couldn't stop the tears appearing in her eyes.

He saw them and his face was filled with concern again and she felt his urgency wilt against her thigh.

'Don't cry,' he said. 'We don't have to.'

'But we do have to. Don't you see? We have to. I need you to make love to me. No one has ever made love to me. You will be the first. So love me, James. Please love me.'

They kissed again and his urgency returned and they made love.

The help she gave was subtle and, in truth, he needed little guidance at discovering what was so natural and so pleasurable. They made love into the early hours: fiercely, gently, demandingly and, amazingly for Gwen, with fulfilment. She had feared she might have been repulsed at the act, that a fraction of herself might have been repelled at the intimacies in which lovers indulged, but she wasn't. The memories of what the men had done were fresh in her mind at the start but they faded as the night progressed.

Their lovemaking was complete and totally satisfying.

They lay together in the aftermath, the sleeping bag loosely across their naked bodies, and James whispered, 'I was frightened.'

'So was I.'

'I didn't want to hurt you.'

'You didn't. You made me complete again.'

'I'll never hurt you.'

'I know.'

A long pause.

'Is it always so good?' he asked, with wonder in his voice.

'I don't know. That was my first time, too.'

He rolled his head to kiss her forehead.

'I love you,' he said, and she believed him.

'I love you, too.'

He suddenly sat up on the bed and she half raised herself on one arm, wondering if he had heard a noise downstairs. He slipped from the bed onto the floor and knelt on one knee.

'Gwen,' he said, reaching to take a hand. 'Will you do me the very great honour of becoming my wife?'

'James,' she said, a smile spreading across her face at the absurdity of the formal proposal after all the informal things they had just done. 'I would be delighted,' she said.

He climbed back onto the bed and he held her in his arms until sleep claimed them.

Chapter 10

KEV WAS FIRST DOWNSTAIRS AND cooked breakfast. Toasted SPAM sandwiches.

'Food of the gods,' he told Nina, who followed him into the kitchen, her hair wet from the shower.

They shared a glance and a smile. Best mates, thought Kev. He'd settle for that. They had each taken a single bed the night before but, sometime in the early hours, Nina had climbed into his. He had used his unzipped sleeping bag as a quilt and she had slipped beneath it as he faked sleep, lying there in his boxers and a t-shirt. She was in a similar state of undress, t-shirt and pants, and had simply snuggled against his side and gone back to sleep, one arm across his chest, one naked leg across his naked thigh.

For a time, he wondered whether he would be able to control himself but he had, of course. There was no way he would have added to Nina's woe by taking advantage of her need for companionship. Eventually, he had even gone back to sleep. When he awoke with the dawn, she was still there. She had rewarded him with a sleepy kiss on the cheek.

'Thanks, Kev,' she had said, slipped out of bed and, grabbing her clothes, gone to the bathroom.

Nice bum, he had noted, and no, he hadn't chastised himself. Sneaking a quick look had been his reward for being a saint. Or what was it? *A nice man*. How the hell had he become a nice man?

James and Gwen joined them and announced their engagement. James seemed to be walking taller. Probably on air.

'We'll talk to the Rev Nick when we get back. Get married. Have it done properly.' He frowned. 'There won't be any objection because of my age, will there?'

'I'll make sure there are no objections,' said Kev, giving the young man a crushing embrace and Gwen a softer and hesitant squeeze and a kiss on the cheek. 'Made for each other, you two. God   told you that.'

Nina held Gwen and whispered to her, 'I'm so happy for you both. So happy.' And the girls shared a tear until Gwen lightened the moment.

'Liquorice allsorts,' she said. 'We promised God. We should try and get him some on the way back.'

'We will,' said Kev. 'And cartridges for his shotgun.'

'We can do better than that,' said James.

He left them to go into the hall and run upstairs. A short while later, he returned holding a small bunch of keys.

'Come on,' he said, leading the way into the pantry.

The room was long with one small high window and, even though the day was bright, it was still gloomy. James took the torch from his belt and led the way to the back of the room to a tall metal cabinet. He used the keys to unlock it and opened both doors. Kev used his torch too, to add further illumination.

'I thought the old man might like these,' James said.

'By heck!' said Kev. 'That's a collection.'

'A pair of Purdeys, a pair of Holland and Holland Royals and a Perazzi.'

He took one of the Royals from the rack and held it to show Gwen. The walnut stock shone and the silver engraving was intricate.

'It's beautiful,' she said. 'How can a gun be so beautiful?'

'They were my father's pride and joy. They *are* beautiful.'

'Expensive?' Kev said.

'Trust you,' said Nina.

'It's my mercenary nature,' Kev said. 'That and growing up on a council estate.'

'Quality costs money,' said James, a little defensively.

'How much?'

'The Purdeys were about thirty thousand each, the Holland and Holland Royals closer to seventy.'

'Seventy thousand pounds?' Kev said, in awe. 'Each?'

'As I said. Quality.'

'What about the other one. The Italian job.'

'The Perazzi was about £5,000.' He put the Royal back and picked up the Perazzi. 'This was my gun. My father bought it for my fourteenth birthday.'

'Well, if you take my advice, you'll give that one to the old man. What would he do with a £70,000 piece of kit?'

'There's plenty of cartridges, too,' said James. The bottom of the gun cabinet was stacked with boxes. 'That's a fair return for a case of SPAM.'

'Plus the sweets,' said Gwen.

They left mid-morning, packing all five shotguns in their cases and the cartridges in the back of the Rover. They also packed a good proportion of the tins of food from the pantry.

The country road was as deserted as the previous day. A mile down it, they forked left and within two hundred yards had arrived in the centre of a village. A small overgrown green, The Blacksmith's Arms pub, an ancient church and a village shop. England must be full of such green and pleasant places, Kev thought. He'd just never noticed them when the world was normal.

'You never know,' James said, pointing at the shop.

A metal Walls ice cream sign stood outside on the pavement and the windows were intact.

They got out of the Rover, carbines at the ready, and surveyed the cottages and overgrown gardens. Weeds and grass were growing through the cracks in the pavement. The village looked deserted.

'Hello?' Kev shouted. 'Anyone?'

No one replied.

James tried the door to the shop. It was open.

'We'll stay out here,' Kev said.

He and Nina stayed by the car, watching the empty village. James and Gwen went inside. The shelves held no food, no sweets. Mop heads and household items remained, but anything edible had gone. An inner door led to a flight of stairs and a back room.

'Anyone there?' shouted James.

Silence and a scurrying from upstairs. Rodents disturbed by their presence.

'There used to be a stock room out back,' James said.

'How on earth do you know that?'

'I was friends with some of the village boys. They told me. They would occasionally sneak into the back and, if Mr Priestley had left it unlocked, they would take a can or two of pop.'

They went through a back door into a yard and he stopped abruptly in front of her.

'What is it?'

'I think it's what's left of Mr Priestley.'

The remains were mainly held together by the clothes the man had been wearing. Some bones were scattered across a yard, the result of rats or other animals.

'He's lying against the store room door,' James said. 'In the early days, it might have deterred anyone from going in there.'

He went back into the shop and Gwen gazed at the sad remains of the shopkeeper. Another life gone, another corpse left. They had all seen so many the shock value had dissipated long ago.

James came back with a garden rake.

He handed her his carbine and used the rake to move the corpse away from the door. Keys were left behind where Mr Priestley's hand had once been. Gwen picked them up and unlocked the door and pulled it open. More scurrying from inside. There were no windows so the only light came through the door. James used his torch. Small piercing eyes stared back at him from the shadows. Mice or rats. The debris they had left behind was all over the place. Every packet had been eaten open, the unrecognisable contents spread over shelves and floor.

Gwen shuddered alongside him and took a step back. He felt guilty at forgetting, so soon, the ordeal she had gone through.

'You okay?'

'Yes,' she said. She didn't sound it.

'Look,' he said, to distract her from the memories and fear of rats and dark, enclosed spaces, and his torch lingered on one shelf that held a row of large glass bottles. Old-fashioned sweet jars, containing midget gems, aniseed balls, pear drops, sherbert lemons, liquorice torpedoes. 'We've found the liquorice.'

His torch moved again.

'And the cans of pop your village boys didn't take,' she said.

She had recovered her composure and they stared at tins of Coke, Seven Up and Fanta. The rodents had damaged the packaging but the cans were intact. They were near the door and he raked them out. Gwen went back into the shop and returned with two wire baskets. She filled them up. James was nervous about entering the windowless store room that was infested with vermin but there was no alternative. He banged the rake on shelves and the low ceiling, causing more scurrying as rats moved away, dropped it on the ground and walked swiftly into the darkness, his torch fixed on the bottles.

It was not far away from the door but, even so, the darkness inside seemed to enclose him and make him vulnerable and he could only wonder at the fear Gwen had been subjected to when the men had locked her in the caravan. He picked up two of the jars, trying not to rush and show his fear, but was aware of near silent activity close by as the rats crept back. The noise of the rake being bashed about almost made him drop the jars in shock.

'Get away, you bastards!' shouted Gwen, with such venom that he heard them retreat.

He took the jars outside, exchanged a tight grin with her and went straight back inside. She continued to bang the rake and shout and the rats stayed away and he liberated all six untouched jars of sweets.

His relief was palpable and she hugged him briefly in acknowledgement of what he had done. Not much, if truth be told, but to her, it would have seemed an ordeal. They carried the baskets of drinks through the shop and onto the street. Kev, standing guard by the front of the Range Rover, glanced at them.

'Hey-ho, me hearties!' he said. 'What have you got?'

'Jackpot,' James said.

They went back and returned with the six glass jars and packed the lot in the vehicle. James volunteered to drive, as he knew the roads, and went along narrow country lanes, past a handful of substantial houses and the track to a farm, round a bend and into another village. He slowed. This hamlet was smaller than the last, no church but a pub and a shop and a collection of houses at a crossroads.

Kev, in the passenger seat, said, 'There are people here. I saw someone in the pub.'

James stopped the car.

'Should we try to talk to them?'

'They might not be in the mood,' Kev said, caressing the carbine in his lap.

Gwen lowered the back window and shouted, 'Hello? Anybody? We're friendlies! Just passing through!'

A woman's greeting might attract a more positive response.

'Anybody?' Gwen shouted again. 'We're from York! Passing through! We mean no harm!'

'But will they believe us?' said James, in a low voice.

No one called back. No one showed themselves.

'Let's get on,' Kev said. 'No point scaring them to death and I don't want to start shooting at farmers. Likely they've had a bad experience in the past.'

James drove on and, in a few miles, joined a major road that would take them to Knutsford.

'It's sad,' he said, 'when people are too frightened to make contact.'

'Country folk,' Kev said. 'They could have kept to themselves before it happened. Think how much more they'll want to stay on their own now, with the world gone mad.'

They approached Knutsford and exchanged the open fields for the start of residential housing. A petrol station was ahead on the right. Poles had been set on oil drums across the entrance and exit to block admittance. The houses near the road were substantial and in their own grounds, many hidden by foliage. This had been a wealthy town. They reached traffic lights and a sign that pointed down the hill to a railway station.

James drove slowly and almost silently across the junction.

'The place is packed with history,' he said, his voice soft. 'This is the bypass. The town is to the right. Nice shops, old pubs, great restaurants. Well, there used to be.' He caught a breath. 'Parish church coming up on the right. The Crown Court on the left ... oh my God...'

The impressive Georgian courthouse was a long building with a cobblestone forecourt for parking and central entrance steps between sandstone columns. The car park was empty except for a bright yellow mobile crane. Hanging from it was the body of a man. The body looked as if it had been there for some time.

'Barrier,' James said.

The roads off to left and right had been barricaded with vehicles. Behind them were men. The bypass road was the only one clear and James continued along it. They were being encouraged to drive through.

'Shit,' said Kev. 'Lower your windows,' he said to the girls.

This was normal procedure if there was the possibility of attack. Lowered windows meant less flying glass. The girls in the back lowered their windows and held their carbines at the ready. As the curving highway straightened out, they could see another barricade ahead of them, near a roundabout, blocking their way.

James immediately began a U turn, quick with desperation, but by the time he was heading back the way they had come, a flat back lorry had been driven across part of the road and a delivery van was being moved from the other side to complete the blockade. They had driven into a trap.

'Give me an angle on the van!' Kev said, and James slewed across the road and stopped. Kev aimed at the driver of the van and fired. Targeted shots. Deadly shots. The driver was hit and slumped sideways out of the open front sliding door of the van, which came to a halt. Kev turned his attention on the cab of the low loader, causing the driver to duck out backwards. There was just enough space between the two vehicles to get through. James didn't wait to be told. He reversed briefly, put the Rover back into drive and aimed at the gap.

Gunshots came from both sides of the road and Kev returned fire, shouting 'Get down!' to Gwen and Nina, who ignored him to lean out of the rear windows and return fire. The combined fusillade encouraged their attackers to keep their heads down.

Bullets pinged into the metal of the car and starred a corner of the windscreen but by now they were travelling fast. They went through the gap and accelerated away, back past the parish churchyard with its ancient dead and the courthouse with its more recent corpse.

No one said anything. Kev checked and replaced the magazine in the carbine. James drove back along the main road, past the petrol station, and left the large houses behind. They were back in the country. He slowed and stopped and they listened to their breathing and the sounds of the countryside.

James exhaled noisily.

'Perhaps that's why the people in the village didn't want to talk,' he said.

Kev looked over his shoulder. 'Well done, ladies!'

'Back roads,' said James. 'We have liquorice to deliver.'

*　　　*　　　*

Godfrey was pleased to see them again, although a little surprised.

'I didn't think you'd come back.'

'We made a promise,' Kev said.

They unloaded tins of food, cans of pop and the jars of sweets. The old man's eyes widened as they stacked them inside the village store.

'I've no more SPAM,' he said, defensively.

'That's all right,' Kev said. 'We've got enough.'

Nina said, 'You could come with us, you know?'

'No thank you, lass. This is my village. Has been, all me life. And Beth and I can't be moving, not at our age. No, I'll stay here, thank you very much.'

'Well stay out of sight,' she said. 'You were right. There are very strange folk in Knutsford. Not nice people at all.'

'Was it them made a mess of your car?'

'It was.'

God looked at each of them in turn. 'You weren't hurt?'

'No. We're okay.'

'That's good, then.' He seemed lost for words as he stared at the mound of goods on the counter. 'Eeh, I don't rightly know what to say.'

Gwen gave him a kiss on the cheek. 'Don't say anything. Just take care.'

James carried the Holland and Holland Royals into the

shop and laid them on the counter. He went back to the car and returned with boxes of cartridges. God held one of the guns in his hands.

'Thought you might need a new one,' James said. 'In these times, it's as well to be prepared.'

'Nay, lad. You can't give me these? They're grandly.'

'That's the perfect word for them,' said Kev, with a smile.

'They were my father's,' James said. 'I think he would be pleased for you to have them. For protection, for you and Beth. And perhaps you can use them to bag a bird or rabbit?'

God said, 'You're a good lad, but I'm all right for food. I set my traps for rabbits. Catch quite a few rats, too.' He smiled when they winced. 'They don't taste so bad. And there's plenty of fruit and veg in the gardens. We'll be all right.' He looked at the variety of tins they had brought and the glass jars of sweet confection. 'But this will liven up the diet a fair bit.' He stroked the silver engraving on the stock of the Royal. 'Mind, there are deer on the estate and I was always partial to venison.'

They said their goodbyes, knowing they wouldn't see each other again.

'You two take care of each other,' God told James and Gwen.

'We will,' said Gwen.

He shook hands with Kev and Nina and looked from one to the other, as if not quite sure. 'And you two, take care of them two, and yourselves.'

Kev nodded. 'We will.'

'Love to Beth,' said Nina, through the open back window as they drove away.

'Aye,' said the old man, and waved them off.

They drove down the wooded lane for a while until Kev broke the silence.

'You've left him with £140,000 worth of shotguns.'

'Grandly shotguns,' Gwen corrected from the back.

'Well you can't be mean when you give God a present, can you?' said James.

*　　　*　　　*

James and Gwen were married four days after they returned to Haven. The ceremony was in the Parish Church of St Oswald in the nearby village of Westfield. Sandra, Reaper and the Blues attended, along with Cassandra Cairncross, the widow of a Squadron Leader and now deputy farm manager of Haven, Ashley, Pete Mack, Dr Greta and a handful of others. Shaggy, a former rock musician and reformed druggie who had joined them from Scarborough, played the organ. Kev was best man and Nina was matron of honour.

A simple service, an exchange of vows, a burst of music and the couple were joined together. The Rev Nick hoped it would be for a long, long time.

Chapter 11

THE TRIP SOUTH COULDN'T BE PUT OFF any longer. The visit of the Royal Navy the previous month had instilled the varying communities of the Haven federation with new hope. The existence of the country's senior service was a continuity with the past that suggested that enough of civilisation had survived to aid the development of the new future. But Redemption remained a worry that they had, until now, deferred doing anything about. Nothing could be decided until they knew more about the place and its so-called New British Government.

Tales got exaggerated and distorted in the telling. Perhaps the threat was not as they imagined. There were those in Haven who hoped that Redemption might emerge as a force for good rather than the opposite.

They could hope all they liked, but Reaper had a bad feeling about a community that based its strength on a battalion of trained military personnel. And which had been home for a three-man reconnaissance squad which had travelled north and, once beyond the control of its superiors, had indulged in wanton slaughter and rape. Maybe they had been a rogue element. Maybe they would have faced court martial and punishment if their misdeeds had been discovered. But Reaper doubted it. He thought it more likely reflected the attitude of those in command. They needed to investigate and discover the truth first hand. It was a job for Reaper and Sandra.

They did not intend to enter the boundaries of Redemption itself: they would observe; they would talk to the nearest communities; they would assess from close range. They left Yank in charge of the Blues. The four teams would continue their routine patrols. They left early morning, Reaper driving, and took the usual route to the A1/M1 where the emptiness of the motorway gave him time to reflect.

He had moved in with Greta to share her cottage in the grounds of Haven and, at her suggestion, they had arranged a date with the Rev Nick for a wedding service. When he got back, he would become a married man. The thought warmed him, made him mellow. He wondered whether it would affect his combat attitude. He hoped not, otherwise Greta might become a widow before she became a bride.

They stopped for coffee and information at Trowell Services on the M1 in Nottinghamshire where a trading post was operated by one of those odd couples that had been thrown together in the aftermath of the plague. Percy was a rotund chap in his sixties with a glorious moustache, who could have been a throwback to the music hall, while Martha was a tall and ungainly lady of a similar age. They supplied coffee but little new information that added any dimension to what they already knew. They were, however, thrilled to hear that the Royal Navy had survived.

'All the nice girls love a sailor,' said Martha, apropos of absolutely nothing at all.

'The Navy are exploring the coasts,' Reaper said.

'That's nice,' said Martha, as if discussing a yachting holiday in the Greek islands.

'And we're going to take a look at Redemption,' added Sandra.

'Ahh,' she said.

'Do you think that's wise?' asked Percy.

Somebody has to, eventually,' said Sandra.

'And, of course, it has to be you two,' said Percy, nodding sagely as if understanding the logic.

When fronting Goliath, send in Reaper and the Angel.

Another vehicle arrived while they were talking. A white Transit with a double row of seats. A young man in his twenties and a woman perhaps ten years older got out and approached. They were unarmed and Percy and Martha waved a greeting.

'Jimmy and Fay,' Martha said in an aside. 'Nice people. From a group about ten miles away.'

She raised her voice to welcome them as they got closer. 'Good to see you,' she said, and got to her feet.

Percy strode to meet them. He shook hands with Jimmy and kissed Fay on the cheek. Reaper and Sandra stood up to be introduced and Percy had a twinkle in his eye when he said, 'This is Reaper and the Angel.'

The couple had been viewing their armaments warily and Reaper could now see the shock in their faces. Being a legend could be a bind.

They shook hands and Sandra said, 'My name is Sandra.'

Martha prepared more coffee.

Percy looked at them enquiringly and said, 'Market day's tomorrow.'

Fay said, 'We were visiting friends. Thought we'd call in on the way. We'll be back tomorrow.'

'They're our egg producers,' Percy said.

Fay smiled dismissively. 'Keeping hens is so simple you'd think more people would do it.'

'Yes, but you do it on a large scale,' Percy said.

'How big is your group?' said Reaper.

'Twenty-two,' she said. 'But we have links with another three groups. We all farm, but different types of farming. We're out past Derby.'

'Do you get any trouble?' asked Sandra

'We haven't had trouble for about six months,' said Jimmy. 'We're off the beaten track, so we usually avoid the travelling gangs. And we avoid places we know are dangerous.'

'Such as?' Sandra asked.

'Derby. Stoke. Nottingham. We stay away from the Black Country,' said Jimmy.

'We stay away from all cities and most towns,' said Fay.

Reaper nodded. 'Seems like a good strategy. We're part of a federation of villages and communities.'

'Haven. We know,' said Fay. 'We've heard about you.'

'Have you heard about Redemption?' he said.

'Everybody's heard about Redemption.'

'What have you heard?'

'That Prince Harry's there. That it has an army,' she said. 'That it's not a very nice place to be.'

'Do you know why it moved from Windsor?'

She shook her head.

'Do you know anyone who has been there? Or escaped?'

Jimmy said, 'Why are you so interested?'

'Because we think it's a threat. As Fay said, we've heard it's not a very nice place.'

'So what are you going to do about it?' the young man asked.

'First, we need to find out all we can about it and the people who run it.'

'And second?'

'That depends on what we find out. We need intelligence to be able to defend ourselves.' Jimmy looked from Reaper to Sandra and back again. 'There are more of us, if necessary,' Reaper said. 'But we don't want a war. We want intelligence. After all, they have the only army in the country.'

'How do you know they're the only army?'

'We have contacts in the north and in Scotland. We talked to a Royal Navy officer. Portsmouth remains a naval base. He was commanding a patrol boat that was touring the East Coast. Another boat is touring the West. The cities are dangerous because of the ferals. We've faced those before. But the only army is the one at Redemption. It's a thousand strong.'

'How can you stop an army that big?' she said.

'I don't know. But we need to know about the place and its leaders.'

'I thought Prince Harry was the leader.'

'Maybe, maybe not.'

'What do you mean?'

'He might be a pretender. He might be Harry but he might be being forced to act under duress. We were told the leader is a General Purcell. We need to find out.'

Sandra said, 'We need as much information as we can get. Do you know anyone who has been to Redemption?'

The young man and older woman exchanged a look. Fay looked at Percy. 'Do you vouch for them?'

Percy nodded gravely. 'You can trust them, Fay. These are honourable people.'

'Honourable?' she raised an eyebrow. 'We've heard the stories. They're good at killing. But is that honourable?'

Sandra said, 'Believe it or not, Fay, we're the good guys. We've met soldiers from Redemption. They were definitely the bad guys.'

Fay thought a second or two longer and sighed. 'Lesser of two evils, I suppose,' she said. 'There's a family. They escaped. They're at Bracken Hall. It used to be a country hotel. It's run by a bloke called Edgar Wiseman. He's known as the Major. They can tell you about Redemption.'

*　　　*　　　*

Bracken Hall had been someone's ancestral home before an American hotel chain bought it and converted it into an upper class residential country retreat for well-heeled guests. Reaper noted that the signs on the front gate had been wisely removed to render the entrance as unremarkable as possible. One half of the iron double gate was closed, the other partly open, as if the last person who had used it thought it unimportant to fasten it. Tangled undergrowth at the foot of the partly-opened gate added to the impression of neglect and hinted at dereliction within.

The undergrowth proved to be an illusion. It was loose and moved easily when he pushed the gate wide enough open for Sandra to drive through. It had been placed there on purpose. He put the gate back in its half-open position, replaced the undergrowth and climbed back in the car, and Sandra drove them through a copse of trees, over a slight hill and down a long road towards the country house hotel.

It was bigger and on a grander scale than the manor house at Haven. A central block with a dozen stone steps leading up to an imposing entrance. The steps stretched the length of the main house and led to a colonnaded frontage and double doors big enough for a coronation.

The lawns in front were overgrown, with splashes of colour from buttercups, daisies and dandelions, and were more natural and attractive than how they would have looked previously, when manicured to perfection by gardeners. As they got closer, one of the front doors opened and a tall, thin man came out and walked to the top of the steps. He wore shapeless corduroy trousers, check country shirt and a pullover, all in differing shades of lovat. If he had crouched in a hedgerow, he would have been invisible. He carried no weapons.

Sandra stopped the car. Reaper got out but left the carbine in the front seat. Even then, he was overdressed with two handguns and a Bowie knife visible about his body. He stepped away from the Rover. Sandra stayed where she was, eyes scanning the house, checking the wing and rear view mirrors, ready to take any necessary action.

'Good morning,' the man said. Being at the top of the steps made him look even taller.

'Morning,' said Reaper. 'Are you the Major?'

The man smiled. 'That's what they call me.'

His voice had the ring of familiarity.

'My name is Reaper. I'm from the other side of York. A place called Haven.' The man's gaze went to the car, trying to see the driver. 'That's Sandra in the car. We were directed here by a couple we met at the Trowell Services. Fay and Jimmy. We are trying to find out about Redemption. We were told someone here knows all about it.'

The Major nodded. 'Fay called. We have radio contact. Limited range but it works.' He smiled. 'Why don't you both come inside?' His voice was measured and mellifluous, as if trained to carry over distances.

'That would be good,' Reaper said. He turned back to the Rover and took his carbine from the front seat. He held it up in his right hand. 'You don't mind?'

'Not at all,' said the Major.

Reaper nodded to Sandra and she joined him, locking the car with the electronic tag. Her carbine rested easily in her arms and she climbed the steps cautiously, still watching, still alert for any untoward movement by a third party.

The tension eased when they entered a large carpeted reception area. A sweeping staircase, redundant reception desk to the right, equally redundant lift next to it. The Major shook hands with them both and guided them with a sure and unworried step down a wide corridor and into a room through whose window they could see their Range Rover. Tables and easy chairs looked as if they were waiting for guests.

'Please?' The Major indicated the chairs. 'I'll organise some coffee. Perhaps a sandwich?'

They both nodded.

'Thank you,' Sandra said. She, too, recognised his voice.

As he turned away, a middle aged woman appeared in the doorway. 'Hello,' she said, with a smile directed at them. 'I'm Mary.' She looked at the Major. 'Let me guess? Tea and sandwiches?' She looked back at Reaper and Sandra. 'Or coffee, if you prefer?'

'Tea would be nice,' said Sandra.

'He'll want to talk to you first. Always does. Perhaps later, we could have a chat. Bit of gossip livens the week.'

'Of course,' Sandra said.

The woman disappeared and the Major came and sat with them at a table near the window. He looked at them both with undisguised curiosity, especially Sandra.

'Forgive me,' he said. 'But you are famous. Besides, we don't get many visitors. We try to discourage them.'

'What if they aren't put off by the moveable undergrowth?' Reaper said.

'If they seem a threat, we have places to hide within and below the house. It's old enough to have secret passages and the owners left them in situ when they redeveloped. They used to have Murder Mystery Weekends and the passages added to the air of mystery. Even our larder is hidden, so there is no incentive for any unwanted guests to stay. We cultivate fields that are out of sight of the house, and a casual invader is unlikely to go tramping across empty countryside looking for cabbages and carrots.'

'Is that what you grow?' Sandra said.

'We grew much more and we also keep animals. There

are two farms on the estate, which is where most of our people live. A casual visitor soon gets tired of a big house with no food, alcohol or prospects. They move on.'

'Has it happened often?' Reaper said.

'Three times. The last time four months ago. Four men, two women, two children. That last time, we observed them and decided they were no threat. They conducted themselves in a civilised manner and, after three days, when they were preparing to leave, we invited them to stay. They were shocked when we popped out of the woodwork, so to speak. But they stayed.'

Sandra smiled. 'A rather neat vetting procedure.'

'It only happened the once. The other two occasions, our visitors would not be on anyone's guest list. Vile behaviour. Just because society has collapsed is no reason to allow personal standards to slip.'

'Quite,' said Sandra, with a straight face. She hesitated and added, 'This may seem strange, but I have the feeling we've met. That I know you?'

The Major smiled and spread his hands in a sign of modesty. 'I, too, in a small way, can claim a modicum of fame. I was an actor. Royal Shakespeare Company and Stratford, but never got the leading roles. My height, you see. Who would believe a six foot six Hamlet thin as a hairpin? I moved into BBC radio and also made quite a decent living from voiceovers. If they wanted a cultured voice but couldn't afford Sir Patrick Stewart, they sent for me. One of my best known voiceovers was – '

'The Major,' Sandra said, with a smile.

'Exactly. In command of a company of cleaning products. I did their voices, too.' Sandra laughed and Reaper smiled. The Major was unabashed at finding fame as the leader of bathroom and kitchen cleaners. 'I also hosted the Murder Mystery Weekends here at the hotel.'

Reaper said, 'Major fits you perfectly. You look and sound like a major. Were you in the forces?'

'Sadly, no. My gravitas and military bearing were fine tuned at RADA not Sandhurst. I was a grave disappointment to my father. He was a colonel in the Irish Guards.'

'And now you're the Major of a country house community,' Sandra said.

'We are a democratic community, but yes, the residents do tend to look to my leadership, for some strange reason.' He smiled disarmingly. 'Must be the RADA training.'

Mary returned carrying a tray which she placed on another table, then unloaded the contents onto the table around which they sat. A silver tea pot, silver water and milk jugs, silver sugar bowl, china tea service and side plates, and two larger plates filled with sandwiches.

The Major smiled again. 'I hope you don't think us ostentatious,' he said. 'But tea tastes so much nicer drunk from china and there are stacks of the stuff in the kitchen.'

Mary left and they sipped tea and ate sandwiches and they told the Major about Haven and the visit of the

Royal Navy. The people of Bracken Hall hadn't ventured far, fearing what they might find if they went exploring and not having much in the way of weapons to fight any enemy. Their peaceful nature had made them insular and they relied on information about the outside world from Fay and Jimmy and contacts from other communities.

'I know it seems as if we're sticking our heads in the sand,' said the Major. 'Hoping that eventually someone will call round and tell us everything is all right and we can start socialising again, but once you get into a routine like this, it is difficult to persuade people to change their habits. Their attitude. It's like acting. You fit into a role. That's what the people here have done, and I don't blame them. I can't really, I'm their de facto leader. But I'm not sure that if it came to a fight, they would be able to. They would be more inclined to run away or surrender.'

He shrugged, before continuing. I'm not brave myself, but I can play the role of bravery. My Henry V was excellent. Radio, of course. But for the others, it's all down to attitude. Their attitude, unfortunately, is to pursue a peaceful life without conflict, which is why we hide. I just hope someone will eventually call round to tell us that Redemption has fallen.'

'What do you know about Redemption?' asked Reaper.

'Nothing good. First we heard rumours. Then, two months ago, the Stuart family arrived. Bob Stuart, Margo and Emily. Emily's four. Bob found her in the aftermath of the plague in a neighbour's house in Bexley. He and Margo got together and they became a family.' He shrugged. 'I suppose that's how most families are made these days. Anyway, they went to Windsor. What they found, they didn't like and it took them nine months to escape. But they're the best people to tell you about it. No point me telling it second hand. They're good people.'

'When can we see them?' said Reaper.

'How about dinner tonight? If you'll stay?'

'It would be ungracious to refuse,' said Reaper. 'Thank you for your hospitality.'

The Major grinned. 'Mary will be delighted.'

*   *   *

They were shown to rooms on the first floor. There were water tanks in the roof and a generator was switched on for an hour from six and they had the luxury of hot showers. It was as civilised as the Major's voice.

Twenty-four residents of Bracken Hall sat down to eat with Reaper and Sandra. Tables were arranged in a T formation so that everyone could be within close sight and sound of the two guests. The meal was wholesome, tasty and informal and red and white wine was served.

'We're working our way through the hotel stocks,' the Major said. 'Usually we drink our own homemade but as this is a special occasion…'

Visitors were a rarity and they were treated like show business on tour. Appearing soon at a venue near you: Reaper and the Angel. They talked about Haven and shared stories of survival, speculated about the future and answered questions.

Eventually, most of the residents headed back to the farms where they lived and worked. Bob and Margo stayed behind. Mary served coffee in the same room where they had taken afternoon tea and then joined them. Six of them sat around in comfortable chairs and sipped a good brew.

Bob was a sturdy, patient man. Margo bright, even flirty, in an innocent way. Sandra wouldn't have put them together as a couple before the virus, but the aftermath had created unlikely bedfellows and, in an odd way, they complemented each other. He mainly told the tale; she smiled, glanced at him, nodded agreement, interjected once or twice, but overall left it to him.

Redemption had started at Windsor but had moved north to Banbury after a fire had destroyed the castle. General Purcell said the move had been planned anyway because of the increasing number of its citizens and army.

'What do you know about Banbury?' Bob said.

'Ride a cock horse to Banbury Cross,' said Sandra.

Bob nodded. 'It's most famous for its nursery rhyme. Before the plague, it was a market town of 43,000. It's 64 miles from London, 50 miles from Windsor. The M40 runs past it, giving it good road access. The River Cherwell runs through it. So does the Oxford Canal. It has water and road connections. The canal is still navigable. The railway runs through the town. A direct link between London and Birmingham.'

He grinned and paused.

'All I knew about Banbury was the nursery rhyme so I looked it up in the library when I heard that was where we were moving. At that time, the atmosphere was tense but not unfriendly. Newcomers like us were being organised and chivvied along. After the chaos, it was comforting to be chivvied by British soldiers. We all went along with what we were told. We went north, in a convoy of buses and trucks, to Banbury.'

He paused again, to marshal his thoughts.

'The railway line cuts through the northeast part of the town. The Oxford Canal and the Cherwell River roughly parallel the line. It was into that portion of the town that we were taken. They used the railway line as a boundary on one side and the M40 on the other and guards restricted movement. They kept us in this sort of enclave of urban housing. Said it was for our own good, that the buildings in the main part of the town were still filled with the dead. But they didn't allow us across the railway.

'We realised we were in a work camp, but a civilised one. They took Emily into nursery every day, along with all the other kids. She's four. She'd been through a lot. What she needed was stability. She needed us, not a nursery.' Margo squeezed his hand. 'But me and Margo were sent out to work. I was bused out to a farm, Margo to do clerical work in Banbury itself. For the New Army. It was difficult to complain because everything was so well organised. The soldiers weren't cruel but they became indifferent. I mean, they heard the moans but their sympathy wore thin. They were in the same boat, to an extent.

'When I asked about leaving, moving out and trying somewhere else on our own, I was given a form to fill in. It came back with *Refused* stamped across it. Then we heard that things took a turn for the worst for people who persisted in trying to leave. After the third application, the blokes were taken away and put in a labour camp.' He shrugged. 'There were two, that I know of. One of them in a football ground, at least for a time. Two hundred men living in tents, barbed wire round the perimeter fence, appalling conditions.

'They used these men to clear the dead from the houses. They use them for hard or nasty work. Cleaning drains and sewers, digging latrines, moving refuse. Others were sent up the M40 to a coal mine near Coventry. So it seemed best to keep your head down and do as you were told and see what happened.

'We weren't paid wages but we were fed. Given groceries once a week. If there was stuff you didn't like, you had to try and swap it with a neighbour. The area was divided into regions and they had a raffle each week. A lottery. One winner from each region. They got a basket of luxury goods – whisky, chocolates, perfume, toilet paper. It might sound daft but people looked forward to it. Like they used to look forward to the Lottery. You know, before the plague.

'General Purcell made speeches to keep up morale. Hard work and discipline were necessary to secure the future. Two years and everything would be different. But for now, we had to buckle down and work. It was for the common good, he said. For the good of the nation and the future.'

He paused again, before continuing.

'Most of the work was rural. Men and women were taken out to work on farms. Couples were separated; they worked on different farms. It meant the only time couples and families got back together was at night time, in the enclave. Or on Sundays – day of rest. There was light industrial work. There are a few industrial units within the enclave. They had a steam mill and ran a steam train on the main line. They have an oil depot at Kingsbury in Warwickshire. It's on the motorway – M40, M42. They have soldiers based there. As I said, it was civilised. They had sanitation engineers and the sewage system still worked. Toilets flushed. There was running water, although you had to boil it before drinking.'

He glanced around, from one to the other.

'It was almost normal,' he said. 'Except for the working girls. And the quarantine section. It was the soldiers, you see. All the civilians there had had the chance to meet the opposite sex. The soldiers had been more restricted, particularly as they had gone to Windsor after the appeal had gone out to all military camps. There were women in the military, of course, but only a few compared to the number of men. So when it came to finding new partners, the soldiers had lost out. A few of the civilian partnerships broke up when women saw a soldier they fancied more, and relationships were formed between soldiers and single girls, but there was still a shortfall.

'They started the quarantine section first. This was where all new women went who were between fifteen and fifty and who arrived at Redemption without a partner. It was all very civilised. The quarantine section was protected by soldiers and they had the chance to meet and chat with the women without competition from single civilians.

'Of course, this system relied on mutual agreement and compatibility. While the soldiers might have been keen, not all the women were. The usual length of stay in quarantine was three months. If no relationship had happened by then, the women without an attachment were released into the enclave or taken out to live on farms. At least, some of them were. About the same time, the brothels opened. There are two of them. Civilians became worried, but the authorities said they were being operated by female volunteers. They were enjoying first class working conditions and being well looked after and could leave at any time. That's what we were told.'

Reaper said, 'Did all the soldiers use them?'

'The soldiers didn't talk about them, so it's hard to say. I think a few did. The soldiers accepted what they were told.' He shrugged. 'General Purcell dug up some old military regulation authorising hostels of rest and recuperation. One of the brothels was for the exclusive use of the Tans.'

'The Tans?'

'That's the nickname for the Black Berets. They wear normal combat uniform, like the rest of the military, but have black berets. The officers wear black tunics. Well, they're navy blue, actually, but they look black. Black jackets, tan trousers. They're known as the Black and Tans or the Tans. They're in charge of the labour camps and are a sort of personal guard for General Purcell.'

Sandra said, 'Did you see Prince Harry?'

'Yes. Mostly at the beginning. He made two speeches. The first time was at Christmas and then he made another speech about two months before we left. He used the same phrases General Purcell used – working for the common good, the sacrifice of now for a better tomorrow. Tomorrow would be better, he said. He knew what we were going through was not ideal but seemed to really believe in a better tomorrow.'

'Is he really Prince Harry?' Reaper said.

'There was a lot of speculation within the enclave but it looked like him, sounded like him, from what I remember of seeing him on television.'

'Did he mingle with the people?'

'No. He always had a close protection unit round him from the Tans. And he was always with General Purcell. He would drive through the enclave occasionally, on a Sunday, and wave to people. He doesn't live in Banbury. He stays with the General in a village about three miles south, where the Tans are based.'

He paused again and exchanged a look with Margo before saying, 'One thing... There are no black or Asian civilians or soldiers. There were, but they seem to have been silently removed. Almost without anyone noticing. I suppose you can do that with a growing population of strangers. You'd notice a black or brown face a couple of times, and then they'd be gone. If you asked where they had gone, you were told they had moved on. Decided to try elsewhere. Then you learned not to ask. Some of the soldiers seemed uncomfortable with the question. Then I heard black and brown faces had turned up in the labour camps. The women in the brothels.'

The Major said, 'This was accepted?'

Bob said, 'You accepted most things after a while. Routine. Military discipline. Obeying orders. And these were only rumours. No one wanted to push it so much that they would be able to confirm it by being sent to the camp themselves.' He gave them a thin self-deprecating smile. 'When you feel a permanent threat, not just to yourself, but to your wife and child as well, you find it's better for your conscience and your survival to believe the lie.'

Reaper said, 'But you didn't believe, did you? You escaped.'

'We were lucky. We used a boat on the river. We went up river instead of down. Rowed through the night. A soldier saw us at one stage. Young chap on guard on a bridge. He just watched us go and never raised the alarm.'

They sat in silence for a while and mulled over what they had heard.

Sandra said, 'How many people are at Redemption?'

'In the town and on the farms?' He mulled it over. 'Ten thousand. Maybe more. Plus more than a thousand military, mainly army, some air force. Plus a hundred of the Tans, the special guard. There's no love lost between the ordinary soldiers and the Tans. There was a tension about the place. Not just from the civilians, but from some of the squaddies, as well. I got the impression they were not totally happy with what they were being asked to do.'

Reaper said, 'Does Harry seem to be part of it?'

'You're wondering if he's being held captive?'

'Yes. If it really is Harry, he wouldn't condone the practices you've told us about. But they might be keeping all that from him.'

'It's possible,' said Bob. 'He never looked comfortable.'

Sandra looked at Reaper and said, 'There's only one way to find out.' When the others looked at her, she added, 'Go and ask him.'

Chapter 12

REAPER AND SANDRA LEFT BRACKEN HALL the next morning. Another friendship consolidated; another group to add to the growing list of communities. Perhaps, eventually, they would all be part of one giant federation. Perhaps, eventually, they would come back together as a nation. Reaper preferred the idea of a federation; nationhood would tempt someone to declare himself dictator or king or president. Like General George Purcell.

They drove south towards Redemption, staying on B roads and avoiding towns and urban centres.

'The Black Berets,' Sandra said. 'I didn't notice at the time, but those three in Cromwell. They had black berets.'

'That's right. So now we know how they operate.'

They kept stopping on high ground to check the land ahead through binoculars. It was on their third stop they saw the aeroplane. They heard the drone of its engine first. An alien sound in the empty skies, like a clockwork motor.

'It can't be,' Sandra said.

Reaper initially thought the shape was a bird until he realised it's movement lacked the elegance.

'It is,' he said.

'Is it a toy plane?'

It was the most obvious explanation. Someone flying a toy plane in the afternoon sun. Then it came closer and it was unmistakably a full size light aircraft with a man at the controls. They stepped back into the shade of trees on the hillside. Bob had said nothing about the New Army having aircraft but that didn't mean they hadn't acquired one since he left.

The engine stuttered and the aircraft turned away from them, dipped and headed southeast at a low altitude. Not the height he would have expected if it was travelling all the way back to Redemption, many miles away. It looked as if it was heading for a much nearer landing zone. He scanned ahead and saw, in the distance, a limp length of cloth hanging from a tall pole. Maybe three miles away.

'See it?' he said. 'The windsock.' He pointed. 'White farm. Then a couple of degrees to your left and further away. Do you see it?'

'Got it,' said Sandra.

They watched the aircraft get smaller in the sky, bank to the left, straighten up and then drop towards the ground, disappearing behind a line of trees.

'Come on,' he said.

He fixed the area in his mind and they drove in the same direction. They reached the white building easily enough but it wasn't a farm. It was a big handsome old house with a thatched roof, roses round the door, a converted barn turned into a three car garage, a Jaguar saloon sitting outside and what had been formal gardens. A rich man's hideaway. Reaper drove on but the lanes criss-crossed after that, and made it difficult to navigate in a straight line. They kept looking for the windsock without success. Eventually, he stopped the car and climbed on its roof to scan the field around them with binoculars. How had they missed the windsock? Then he saw the pole and realised they hadn't; someone had taken it down.

It was a grass airfield, long and smooth and no wider than fifty feet and it nestled behind hedgerows. Unlike similar fields, this had been freshly mowed. A long caravan in one corner faced down the runway and to one side was a grouping of innocuous farm buildings and barns. Beside the caravan was a wide and deep shed with a closed green roller door that stretched the length of its frontage. No sign of an aeroplane, a pilot or a vehicle. But perhaps a smell of fuel oil in the air.

They parked next to the caravan and got out of the Rover with carbines at the ready. They listened but could hear only nature. A soft wind, sounds of insects, the movement of leaves in the trees behind the shed.

Sandra looked at Reaper. A question in her gaze. Was this the right place?

He looked down the length of the field and she saw the soft wheel tracks in the grass.

She stayed by the car, alert for any eventuality. He walked round the side of the shed and disappeared briefly from view. When he returned he was smiling.

'There's a Cessna behind there,' he said.

They checked the caravan first. The door was unlocked and it was empty. Maps were pinned to boards that were fixed to the wall. At one end a radio set was on a desk by a window with a view of the field. Behind a leather swivel chair was a shelf that held a computer, TV and landline telephone. The middle area had cooking facilities, cupboards and seating that stretched to a bathroom and wc at the far end. This had been a functioning office. The hub of a very small airfield.

They left the caravan and went to the shed and Reaper banged on the door.

'Open up,' he said. 'We're friends.'

Someone moved inside, the scrape of a boot on a concrete floor, a lock was turned and the door began to open. It was being pushed sideways on its rollers by a dishevelled middle-aged chap in glasses, a boiler suit and wild red hair. He looked like a mad professor. He stopped pushing when there was enough space for him to step through. He eyed them warily.

'Are you alone?' said Reaper.

'I left my harem at home,' he said. His voice was educated Irish. 'Nice girls. Used to be artistes in Wigan. They were much in demand for their Dance of the Seven Clogs.'

'Are you alone?' Reaper said.

The man pushed the door some more and opened it wider. He waved a hand in a *be my guest* manner. Reaper glanced inside. It contained a Land Rover. Work benches were down both sides and boxes and presumably spare parts for aeroplanes were stacked at the back of the shed.

'I'm Declan de Courcy, and now you have me at a disadvantage.' His eyes moved between Reaper and Sandra. 'Who might you be?'

'I'm Reaper. This is Sandra. We're from Haven.'

None of the names had an affect on de Courcy. He maintained his composure but couldn't hide his worry.

'Haven? Where's that?'

'North. Near York. A big community. A big peaceful community.'

'So you're not with that lot down south, then?'

'Redemption? No.'

'Redemption.' He said it in a mocking way. 'A misnomer if ever there was one. Gulag would be nearer the mark.'

'You know it?'

'By reputation.'

'Do you live near here?'

'The White Cottage.'

'We drove past it. A handsome place.'

'It suits my needs.'

'You're the first pilot we've seen.'

'There's probably more. Thirty thousand held licenses BV.'

'BV?' said Sandra.

'Before Virus.'

'Thirty thousand?' said Reaper.

'In the UK.'

There had been continual speculation about how many people had died from the virus. At first, Haven's Brains Trust had thought one per cent had survived, but the more intelligence they had gathered, the figure had been revised. Their brightest minds had suggested it could be out by a decimal point: that there were less than seven million survivors on the planet; less than 60,000 in the UK. On those figures, maybe a dozen pilots might have been expected to survive.

'Do you know of any other pilots?' Reaper said.

'Redemption had one but he crashed.'

'How do you know that?'

De Courcy stared at Reaper for a long moment and then raised his voice slightly and said, 'Mandi. You might as well come out.'

A young Asian man in his twenties emerged from the far side of the shed. He was medium height, clean-shaven and muscular. He wore a t-shirt and jeans and stood hesitantly under their scrutiny. His eyes moved over the weapons they carried.

'Mandeep Singh,' de Courcy said. 'He was there.'

'You left?' Reaper said.

'Escaped,' said Mandi.

'We need to talk,' said Reaper, staring from one to the other.

*   *   *

De Courcy made coffee in the caravan and they sat around on the grass outside on canvas chairs. The Irishman lit a long cheroot. Reaper told them about Haven. The fact that they had come from an apparently peaceful community reassured them. Once the carbines had been laid aside, the original nervousness of the two men dissipated. They told their stories of survival after the virus – or AV, as de Courcy called it.

'I have kept to myself,' de Courcy said. 'A conscious decision.'

'No harem, then?' said Sandra. 'No clog dancers?'

'Only in my fevered imagination, dear lady.' He smiled. 'I lived alone until Mandi turned up a month ago. My choice. I saw what was happening in the cities. I wanted no part of that kind of survival. I'd rather prang out than be part of that kind of a new world.'

Sandra said, 'What did you do? BV?'

His smile returned. 'I was a poet and conceptual artist.'

'I beg your pardon?'

'I wrote poetry, and I once covered half a field in orange plastic sheeting.'

'That was art?' said Reaper.

'At the time it was a very pertinent comment on the rape of the countryside. At least, that's what I told people. Then the virus came and knocked conceptual art into a cocked hat.'

'Did you make a living doing this?' Sandra could not hide the incredulity in her voice.

'It was grand while it lasted. I was on the long short list for the Turner Prize, if that's not too Irish for you. I exhibited at the Tate Modern. It was all a bit of a game. I mean, I can actually draw and paint, but showing off was more profitable.'

'And people took you seriously?'

His smile widened. 'The first time, I did it as a dare to meself. I made a tree out of kitchen implements and someone took it seriously enough to buy it for £500. I already had a reputation as an artist, so it was not too difficult to take a step sideways and see if I could fool some of the people, some of the time. The very act of pretending a piece was art was, in its own way, an act of conceptuality. Their belief provided its validation.' He raised his eyebrows as if waiting for a nod of understanding. He didn't get one.

Mandi said, 'I've heard it umpteen times and I still don't get it.' His accent was pure Midlands.

'Emperor's new clothes,' Reaper said.

'I have to admit, I did take it to extremes in the latter part of my career. Real horse dung served in a Royal Dalton tureen? A comment on celebrity chefs? No? That one made the tabloids. They took the piss, of course, so I added a carafe of urine to the tableau. Double the publicity.'

'Is the White Cottage your home?' Sandra said.

'It belonged to an old school chum of mine. We met at Trinity in Dublin. Then I went to Oxford for my Masters and Tom went into business. He was very good at it and made lots of money. I visited from time to time. We kept each other's feet on the floor and he kept a good cellar.' His mood changed. 'I was always a loner but he had the perfect life. Beautiful wife, happy marriage, two kids, wonderful home, wealthy. A made man. And then everything was wiped away. I was here at the end. I'd come to get away from the contagion of the cities. Escape to the country and be safe.' He shook his head. 'I was safe. I had the immunity. They didn't.'

They sat in silence for a moment until he said, 'I buried Tom and Suzie and the kids, then I went back to the city. Drove there. I had this belief that civilisation would have survived, no matter what. But it hadn't. Birmingham was awful beyond words. I tried the dreaming spires of Oxford as a last resort. Oxford was bestial.'

He shrugged, as if shaking off the memories.

'So I came back here. It's off the beaten track. I stayed hidden. Hoped the madness would subside. Mad itself out. Then I met Mandi and he told me about Redemption and I thought about relocating. Moving back to Ireland to get away from them. They don't sound like very nice people and they are a mile too close for comfort.'

'How about you, Mandi?' said Reaper.

'I escaped Birmingham,' he said. 'And ended up in the madness of Redemption.'

'What did you do?' said Sandra. 'Before?'

'Motor mechanic in Handsworth. I went to college, got my diplomas and qualified. Worked in a main dealership before setting up with my cousin. When it happened, I stayed home. My family were poorly and I did my best to look after them. Mum, dad, grandma, sister, two brothers. They all died. All the neighbours died. The whole bloody street died. I went looking round the area. I shouted. You know? Anybody there? No one answered but somebody was alive because they'd been in the local shops. I went myself, for supplies. First time, I left money on the counter.' He shrugged. 'I'm no thief. Wasn't brought up that way. Then I saw there was no point.

'My family were upstairs in bed. I lived at home downstairs for the first few days until the smell got too bad. I left, found an office above a row of shops. Stayed there. When I heard someone in the shops I went down. There were two blokes, two Sikhs. They were from the temple. Twenty two people had collected there. I joined them for a while. A few more drifted in. Mainly Sikhs but white people as well. Then trouble started with other groups… fighting over supermarkets… with Muslims, with racists. It got nasty and I thought, bugger this for a game of soldiers, and me and three others left.

'We headed out of the city and fell in with a group of travellers. Gypsies, Romanies? There were a lot of travellers in Birmingham. Before. They seemed to know what they were doing and made us welcome. We settled down in Leicestershire near a village called Sheepy Parva. Worked the land, spent the winter there. I mended tractors. The travellers moved on in the spring. I went with them south. We heard London was not up to much and we heard stories about this new place, Redemption, that had a government.

'The travellers didn't fancy that and we went around London, staying in the country, outside the M25, until we were down on the south coast. Met some strange people on the way. The travellers were heading for Cornwall. They reckoned the West Country had been underpopulated BV so there was bound to be plenty of space AV. I thought a proper government sounded better. So I left them. Me and another bloke, we went to Redemption.'

He shook his head.

'We were separated almost as soon as we arrived. They made some excuse. My mate was white. I don't know where he went. I ended up in a labour camp. Most of the blokes in there were whites who had been listed as malcontents. Wouldn't tow the line. Apparently colour made you a malcontent, as well. Not that there were many of us. About a dozen out of a total of two hundred and fifty. We were kept in a football ground. Tents on the pitch. Then I was moved to the mine they have near Coventry. They have a small permanent workforce there. Twenty men. They kept us underground almost all the time. The conditions were pretty awful. People died while I was there but the guards didn't seem to care. I knew if I didn't escape, I'd die. So I got out. There was this chap there, ex RAF, who was sort of senior officer. He handled escapes. Bit like that film with Steve McQueen?

'He picked blokes who looked as if they wouldn't survive or who were likely to get picked on. They got first chance at getting away. Not that the odds were good. The guards would bring the bodies back. Harry said the chances were 70-30 against. But some of us had to try. He gave me the option and I grabbed it. Dark night, stormy weather, a diversion and I did a runner. Thank God I got away. I headed north and found Declan. That was two months ago.'

Reaper said, 'You say the guards were brutal?'

'At the coal mine, yes.'

'Were they regular soldiers, airmen?'

'They were Tans. The General's army within an army. I'm not sure that the regular service blokes down in Banbury knew how we were being treated.'

'How many guards? How many workers?'

'Ten guards and one officer. Five stayed on site, five came each day in the trucks. The officer usually came in his own car. They rotated after a week: seven days travelling, seven days permanent. None of the Tans liked working at the mine. A sergeant or corporal was in charge at night. There were twenty workers, give or take a death. The mine is both drift and shaft. There's a walk-in section, which is a half mile sloping walk to a coal face; and there's a 450 foot shaft, but they don't use that. Don't want to waste the power and the soldiers sure as hell don't want to risk the drop if anything goes wrong.

'The men at the face dig coal and load it on shallow flatbeds. Then they haul it out, two men to a load. They wear a harness to get a grip. Once a week, day men come and load it into trucks.'

Reaper stared at Mandi causing him to pause. 'The men *haul* it out themselves?'

'That's right.'

'They haven't operated a mine like that since the 19th century.'

'This is a punishment mine. I guess it's also an ego thing for the General. The fact that he has a mine in production, even though it doesn't produce a great deal of coal. But he has a steam train. I think he has plans for the train.'

Reaper nodded. 'A steam train could become a symbol of power. Of progress. Did you ever see Harry or the General?'

'No. Others in the camps had seen them. From a distance.' Mandi grinned. 'And no, I don't know if it really is Prince Harry. No one does.'

'What about Banbury?'

'I just passed through, saw very little. It's a work town but not a work camp, if you see what I mean. But the General doesn't live there. He and Harry live in a village called Baystoke.'

Reaper nodded and looked at a rough map of the mine that Mandi had drawn. 'What about hygiene? Water, lavatories?'

'There's a worksite loo. One of those blue plastic cabins with a chemical loo inside. It's changed every morning. We looked forward to loo duty. Two workers got to carry it out of the compound and dump the contents in an old pit. Twenty minutes of fresh air. Well, relatively fresh air.'

'Washing? Drinking?'

'A hosepipe. We never knew what it was attached to. Maybe a main's supply, maybe a river. We took our chances. Some got ill; a few died.'

'Food?'

'There's a chef. He's a day prisoner. He did a pot of stew. Two of them would carry it to the compound each night before they left at six. Actually it wasn't bad. The chef did his best. I suspect he put all the leftovers in it from the guards' meals. Apart from that, we'd get bread in the morning.'

They all fell silent for a while, trying to comprehend the hardships he had endured and that others were still enduring.

'You mention an RAF bloke called Harry,' Reaper said. 'Do you know his full name?'

'Harry Babbington. He was a Flight Sergeant. A great guy. Do you know him?'

'We know of him. Some of his people are with us at Haven. They'll be pleased to known he's surviving.'

Sandra said, 'He'll be a good man to use.'

'In what way?' said Mandi. 'How would you use him?'

'Liberation?' she said. 'Revolution?'

Chapter 13

THEY SPENT THE NIGHT AT THE WHITE COTTAGE and drank Irish whiskey.

'Black and Tans,' said Reaper. 'Extraordinary how potent cheap nicknames can be.'

'You're paraphrasing Noel Coward,' de Courcy said. 'But you're right. It makes you wonder whether Purcell chose the combination on purpose.'

'Probably not,' said Reaper. 'He calls them the Black Berets. Besides, would today's generation recognise the significance?'

'I don't,' said Sandra.

Mandi said, 'Harry told me.'

'It was nearly a hundred years ago,' said Reaper. 'The Irish War of Independence. The Black and Tans were recruited by the British Government after the Easter Rising.' He looked at de Courcy for confirmation.

'Actually, the Easter Rising was in 1916,' said the Irishman. 'The Black and Tans were recruited in 1920. They were First World War veterans and they were sent to Ireland to help suppress the revolution. They were military auxiliaries. There was a shortage of uniforms and they wore a mixture of their own khaki and Irish dark green. That's where they got their nickname. They were there two years before the war was won. By the Irish. Well, partly won. The Irish Free State came into being but the six counties of the north stayed British.'

Reaper said, 'The Black and Tans became renowned for their brutality, not just against the Irish Republican Army, but against the civilian population.'

'For many in Ireland, the war of independence was known as the Tan War,' said de Courcy. 'Now not many people know this…' he said, and grinned at his Michael Caine impression, 'but the medal awarded to veterans of the war had a ribbon with two vertical stripes in black and tan.'

'Memories run deep,' said Reaper.

'They do in Ireland. Well, they did in Ireland.'

'I didn't know any of this,' said Sandra. 'I thought Ireland was our best friend.'

'It was,' said the Irishman. 'We have a shared history and a love for all things Irish. Literature, music, the craic.' He held up the bottle, before pouring another measure into Reaper's glass. 'Good whiskey.'

Sandra and Mandi went to bed and left Reaper and de Courcy to finish the bottle of whiskey. It would have been far easier to save what was left for another time but the Irishman insisted, with a smile, that he had lost the top.

'When did you lose it?' said Reaper.

'When I threw it over me shoulder.' He shrugged. 'It's easier just to drink it. I'd hate it to go to waste.'

So they drank it and Reaper took the opportunity to persuade a reluctant de Courcy to take him on a reconnaissance flight the next day.

*   *   *

It dawned overcast and with little breeze.

'Perfect conditions,' de Courcy said, puffing on another cheroot, as he stared down the grass runway.

Reaper had drunk a gallon of water but his head still throbbed from a persistent hangover. De Courcy did not appear to be affected and looked disgustingly healthy. Sandra had no sympathy for Reaper's condition.

Mandi attached the two-seater Cessna to a quad-bike to haul it from its temporary hiding place behind the shed and line it up on the field. Normally, it would have been garaged in one of the farm buildings and barns, which also housed a four-seater Cessna, a ride-on mower as big as a small tractor, and drums of fuel.

Reaper left behind his carbine and had for once relinquished his Kevlar vest. He wore a maroon sweatshirt that de Courcy had loaned him after being told it could be chilly if they gained any height. The Irishman took the left hand seat and Reaper climbed into the right hand seat. He was disconcerted to discover that some of the flying controls in front of de Courcy were duplicated in front of him. He also had foot pedals and a two handled flying column.

'It's me that's doing the driving,' de Courcy said. 'Just don't touch anything.'

The cabin was cramped and felt flimsy, as if the aircraft had been built by children from a kit. De Courcy started the engine. It caught in a cloud of smoke and the propeller began to spin. The engine sounded clockwork and throaty. The flight controls were not as intimidating as he thought and wouldn't have looked out of place in an upmarket saloon car. He held a road map on his knee, open to their section of country. De Courcy had explained that without all the GPS signals the world used to take for granted, the navigation systems wouldn't work. They would be flying by compass and line of sight. Reaper had sudden qualms that this was a bad idea; the aircraft did not really feel safe.

'Don't worry. You're more likely to get knocked down by a bus,' said de Courcy, as if reading his thoughts.

'Not any more,' said Reaper.

De Courcy laughed.

He taxied to the end of the field and turned for take off. The small aircraft vibrated.

'Sure, we'll be all right,' he said, pulled throttles and pushed levers and checked flaps. He released the brakes and they were off down the field. Sandra was by the caravan. She waved. Mandi watched, hands on hips, and the Cessna lifted and they were airborne. The family car analogy did not change. It felt as if they were flying in a Vauxhall Astra.

'Now then,' said de Courcy, 'as long as we follow the road, we won't get lost.'

The sensation was not as smooth as an airline. The light wind buffeted them.

'Not what I expected,' Reaper said.

'You'll get used to it.'

De Courcy seemed to be having trouble keeping the craft in trim but Reaper didn't like to comment. He concentrated on finding the A515. They were heading for the mine from which Mandi had escaped.

'That must be the road,' he said, and they followed it south towards Lichfield. 'Everything looks different from up here.'

'It's just like following a Google satellite map,' said de Courcy.

'I wouldn't know. I rarely used a computer.'

Birmingham and the Midlands sprawl filled the horizon to the west but they avoided it by following the M6. The turbulence and disconcerting bumps eased out of the flight but Reaper decided he preferred the stability of four wheels on the ground rather than two wings in the air. Even so, it was exhilarating to look down and see the extent of England's green countryside. Man had made inroads with towns and cities but there was still a lot of fields and forests that were swiftly reverting to a virgin state and, on the occasional farmstead or hamlet, he saw people look up and wave. Not many, but a few, uncontrolled by urban gangs or the military influence of Redemption.

'How long have you been flying?' Reaper said. He was making conversation, not voicing a criticism about the vagaries of the ride.

'This is my second time.'

Reaper considered the information. 'No, how long have you been flying?'

'It's my second time. Yesterday was my first flight. I'm teaching myself. How else would I get back to Ireland?'

For want of anything else to say, Reaper said, 'A boat?'

'Good God, man. I hate boats. Hate the sea.'

'But you can't fly?' As he said it, he attempted to equate de Courcy's confession with the fact that they were several hundred feet above ground.

'I'm not doing too bad, so far.'

'But you haven't had lessons?'

'Never considered them necessary while Aer Lingus and Ryanair made Dublin so close. And old Tom, of course. He was happy to fly me whenever he had the chance. He was an enthusiastic aviator. Now, he did have a licence.'

'How reassuring.'

Reaper wondered why he was not yet panicking. Perhaps it was because the Irishman was not. He seemed content with the situation.

'Tom had a load of flight books and manuals and video simulations. Stuff he must have used when he was learning himself. He got the video simulation because he was trying to persuade his wife to learn but she wasn't interested. It's a full system – steering column, rudder pedals, trim wheel and throttle control panel. It's a grand device.'

'You learnt on a video simulation?'

'Well, I'd been up with Tom. I never would have taken the first step on my own if Mandi hadn't shown up. He's a very good mechanic. I didn't even know how to put petrol in the thing.'

'Yesterday was your first flight?'

'And a fine flight it was. Sure, the flying's easy. It's the landing that's difficult.'

Now it perhaps made sense why they were slewing around so much. Or maybe that was normal. Reaper looked at the dials and controls with a new respect. They had been mundane when he thought de Courcy knew what he was doing. Not much different from a Range Rover's. Now he realised they were far different.

'We need to go more east,' he said, wondering why he wasn't asking where the parachutes were kept. As they were up here, they might as well pursue their mission.

De Courcy adjusted their course and the Cessna responded. At least the aeroplane did not realise it was being flown by a novice. Reaper looked for landmarks.

'There's the reservoir.'

They identified a B road and followed it until they saw the grey scar of the colliery in the green countryside. An old slag heap, redundant machinery, grey and white concrete buildings. A man with a machinegun on top of a flat roof. People stared up at them. One or two waved. De Courcy went lower. Some of them were wearing uniforms. One of the soldiers raised his rifle and fired. De Courcy instinctively turned the Cessna away in a hurried movement that sent it dipping towards the ground before he regained a kind of control.

'Not very friendly,' said the Irishman.

The plane seemed reluctant to regain height. It coughed and spluttered. De Courcy glanced from one dial to another. He pointed it north but the engine was unhappy and they continued to slowly drop closer to the ground.

'Did he hit us?' Reaper said.

'I don't know.'

'So what's wrong?'

'Me, I think. I always was a clumsy idjit. The touch of a donkey when it comes to the fairer sex, it's been said.'

'Are we going down?'

'I think that's what she intends.'

Smoke began seeping from the cowling of the engine in front of them.

'Shit,' said Reaper.

De Courcy was looking ahead, presumably for a field flat enough for a landing. Unfortunately, they hadn't been mowed like the landing strip from which they had taken off.

'Are you a religious man, Reaper?'

'Not really.'

'Do you believe in God?'

'Only some of the time.'

'This might be a good time. You might say a prayer, and say one for me, too. I'm a lapsed Catholic but as an atheist I can't say one for meself. So if you'd mention me, I'd be grateful.'

'Anything else?'

'Brace yourself. And when we land, get out quick. We're carrying an awful lot of fuel.'

There was no time for anything else. Events happened quickly. They dropped and the ground rushed up and Declan de Courcy fought with the controls and guided the Cessna towards a straight stretch of B road that ran between hedgerows. The engine coughed and died and the last few feet was a silent descent and then they hit the tarmac. They bounced twice but settled a third time and Reaper thought they were going to be all right, but then the small plane veered and the port wing hit the hedgerow and they spun sideways and crashed and the world turned upside down.

He must have briefly blacked out although afterwards he could find no sign of a bang on the head. Perhaps it was simple shock that had shut off his senses. But when he returned to full cognisance he was hanging forward on the safety straps in the cockpit with the nose of the aircraft in the ground.

'Reaper.' De Courcy was shaking him. 'Are you all right?'

'I'm all right.'

'Then get out of here, man.'

The Irishman got out first which made it easier for Reaper to kick open the door, unclip the safety harness and struggle out of the cabin. He fell to the ground and was surprised his legs were steady when he stood up. He could smell leaking fuel and saw it dripping into the cockpit. He moved into the road to join de Courcy.

'Sorry about that,' said the Irishman.

'We're in one piece,' Reaper said. 'But I don't think we'll be alone for long. They'll come looking for us.'

'Then we'd better move.'

Reaper considered their options. 'You move. Get back to the others. I'll stay.' He stooped to unfasten the sheath on his right leg.

'You're staying?'

'Good chance to find out about Redemption.'

'They might just shoot you.'

'I don't think so. They wouldn't shoot a pilot, would they?'

'But you're not a pilot.'

'Neither are you.'

'Touche.'

He unfastened his gunbelt and handed it to de Courcy. 'With luck, they'll take me to headquarters. With luck, I'll meet General Purcell. Maybe even Prince Harry. It's too good an opportunity to miss.'

'If they find out who you are …'

'They don't know what I look like.'

Reaper unfastened the throwing knives from his left wrist and handed them over, too. De Courcy gazed at the armaments he now held and raised a quizzical eyebrow at him.

'You don't have a nuclear warhead in your vest, as well, do you?'

'That's it.' He gave him the map from the plane. 'I estimate we came down about here.' He pointed a finger. 'Get back home. You've got another Cessna and maybe next time you should just head off to Ireland. The fewer landings you attempt the better.'

'You have a point.'

'Tell Sandra I'll be back at the White Cottage in four days. If I'm not back in five, then they have me under lock and key or I'm dead and she's in charge. Hopefully I'll be able to escape. I'll pretend I've hurt my leg. If I limp around a bit, they might not watch me too carefully. If that doesn't work out, I'll tell them I have a spare plane back at the strip and return with an escort. Tell Sandra. She'll know what to do.'

'This is a dangerous escapade, Reaper.'

'I've been through worse.' They shook hands and Reaper said, 'Enjoy Ireland. If you've any sense, you'll go as soon as you can.'

'I'll do that.'

'One thing more. Do you have a spare cigar?'

'Of course.'

He took a box from his pocket and offered it. Reaper took one of the slim cheroots and de Courcy lit it for him.

'Time you were off.'

'Take care, Reaper.'

The Irishman bundled Reaper's weaponry in his arms and hurried off. He went through a gate into the field and stayed the far side of the hedgerow. He was immediately out of sight. Reaper went into the field, took a few drags on the cigar to ensure the tip was hot, threw it into the cockpit and stepped back swiftly. It caught fire almost immediately and he went back to the road and pushed through the hedgerow on the far side and lay down. When the Cessna exploded, the hedgerow took most of the blast. He got back to his feet and pushed his way back to the road. The smoke was rising high and proud. It wouldn't take the Tans long to find him.

*   *   *

The open-topped Land Rover in military markings arrived fifteen minutes later. Reaper was sitting in the shade at the side of the road. He raised his hand in acknowledgement. The Cessna was still burning fifty yards up the road behind him. The vehicle stopped twenty yards away. The driver remained behind the wheel. Two men in combat uniform jumped out, each carrying a sub-machinegun. They wore black berets. They glanced around, almost sniffing the air, as if they might smell an ambush, but the only aroma on the summer breeze was that of burning rubber and aircraft fuel.

'Where's the other one?' The soldier who asked had three stripes on his sleeve. He was stocky, late thirties and about five six in height. He wore a moustache as if he had been cast for a Second World War film. It looked incongruous.

'What other one?'

'There were two of you. In the plane.'

'No. Just me.'

'There were two of you. We saw two people.'

'There was only me.' Reaper pulled a face as if a suggestion had just occurred to him. 'My duffel bag was in the other seat. I had a coat over it. Maybe that was the other one.'

'So where's your bag?'

'It's burning along with everything else after you shot me down.'

The sergeant moved closer, still nervous in case someone was hiding. He motioned to the soldier with him, a younger skinnier man whose uniform was a little too large. The younger soldier pushed through the hedge and went into the field where the aircraft wreckage lay, flames still crackling, smoke still rising. 'We didn't shoot you down,' the sergeant said.

'Well someone did.'

'Where are you from?'

'Welsh borders. I'd heard there was a government in a place called Redemption. I was trying to find it.'

'You found it.'

'Redemption is a coal mine?'

'Redemption is further south at Banbury. The mine belongs to Redemption.'

'Impressive.'

The sergeant handled the gun as if he knew what he was doing. He looked as if he had been a regular soldier. He kicked the boot on Reaper's outstretched right leg. Reaper winced.

'Get up,' said the sergeant.

'I hurt my leg in the crash. Somebody will have to help me.'

'Taylor!' The sergeant had the requisite loud voice for his rank. The younger soldier reappeared through the hedge.

'No one there, sarge.'

'Help him up. He says he's hurt his leg.'

Taylor reached down his arm and Reaper took it and

allowed himself to be hauled to his feet. He hopped a little theatrically and then settled for taking the weight on his left foot while keeping one hand on Taylor's shoulder.

The sergeant waved at the Land Rover. 'Turn that thing round and reverse it up here!' he shouted. Then, to Taylor: 'Watch him.'

The sergeant went through the hedgerow to inspect the wreckage himself. While he was away, Taylor said, 'Where you from, then?'

'Wales,' said Reaper.

'All sheep-shaggers, there.'

The Land Rover reversed up the lane until it was alongside them. The sergeant came back. 'Get in,' he said, and Reaper made a show of favouring his right leg as he climbed into the back of the vehicle.

'Take me to your leader,' he said, a jocular quip that no one found amusing. Maybe they hadn't seen the same movies Reaper had. Maybe they didn't have a sense of humour.

'Go,' said the sergeant, and the Land Rover drove back the way it had come.

'Where are we going?' said Reaper.

'To the mine. And then Redemption.'

'Which is where I wanted to be in the first place.'

The sergeant looked at him. 'What's your name?'

'Tom Watson.'

'And you're a pilot?'

'Yes, I'm a pilot.'

'So far, you've been lucky, Watson. Now shut the fuck up.'

*   *   *

They arrived at the mine abruptly. One moment they were driving through countryside, then he saw the slag heap. One minute, greenery; the next the superstructure of an underground industry: dirty concrete and a perimeter fence topped with razor wire. A soldier opened tall metal gates. The Land Rover drove through and stopped outside a two storey building. On its roof was the guard Reaper had seen from the air. He peered down curiously but said nothing. They were in a fenced compound. Opposite was a single storey structure.

'Inside,' the sergeant said, jumping out.

Reaper took his time to follow and limped into the building. Private Taylor followed. There was a small counter with a raised flap. Beyond it was an open area that might once have contained desks and computers and office workers. It still had desks, pushed together at the back, upon which were portable stoves, a large metal tea pot and mugs, and half a dozen office chairs on wheels. There were also six camping beds in a row, presumably for the night guards, and a flight of stairs at the far end of the room. A partition on his right separated the ground floor into two. A door to his immediate right said MANAGER.

They went through the flap into the open office. Another door was in the partition. This now opened and an officer stared at him.

'Where's the other one?' he said.

His accent was only slightly refined North West – probably Manchester. Not exactly officer class. The sergeant didn't bother to come to attention or salute. He probably thought the same.

'He says there was just him.'

'Was there?'

'No sign of anybody else. The plane was still burning.'

The officer walked across the room to stand in front of Reaper. He stared at him. Reaper stared back. He was in his twenties and had two pips on his shoulder: a lieutenant. There was the smell of alcohol on his breath.

'Name?'

'Watson.'

'Where are you from?'

'Welsh borders. I was looking for Redemption.'

The lieutenant continued to stare. Perhaps his gaze was intended to make Reaper feel uncomfortable. The gaze of authority, of evaluation. Possibly the gaze of life or death. Except that Reaper knew it wasn't. Anyone arriving seeking sanctuary would be taken to Banbury to be interviewed and assigned. Anyone captured would be taken to HQ to be interrogated and assessed. Any pilot would be treated like gold dust.

'Where in the Welsh borders? What town?'

'Near Wrexham.'

'What's the size of your group?'

'No group. Just me.'

'Why just you?'

'I saw what was happening in towns, so I decided being antisocial might save my life. It has, so far.'

'Where are you living?'

'I have a farmhouse and a landing strip. It belonged to a friend. Now it's mine.'

The lieutenant paused and looked at Reaper's leg. 'You're hurt?'

'Yes.' Reaper looked down and patted his leg. 'It happened –'

The lieutenant hit him in the face with his right fist, a swinging blow that Reaper partly rode, even though he saw it late, but which sent him to the ground. He rolled and exaggerated his pain, holding onto his jaw. The officer had drawn a revolver and was now standing over him, the gun pointing at his head.

'It's better if you tell the truth now,' he said. 'It could get painful if you don't.'

'I have told the truth. I'd heard there was a government here. I heard there was Prince Harry. That's why I came.' He rubbed his jaw. 'I thought you'd be pleased to get a pilot. I didn't expect to be shot down and beaten up.' He looked the lieutenant in the face. 'What's your CO going to say when he hears you shot me down and beat me up?'

The officer put the gun away. 'Put him in detention,' he told the sergeant. 'We'll take him back tonight.'

Reaper looked past the officer. A girl with blonde hair and red lips was standing in the doorway of the room he had just left. She was watching him and what was happening. She was in her early twenties and wore a loose red silk dress and high heeled shoes that seemed more suited to a cocktail bar than a colliery. Her look was disinterested, as if she couldn't care less whether the officer hit him, kicked him or shot him.

The officer followed Reaper's gaze, turned and saw the girl. 'Get back in there,' he said. She shrugged her shoulders and did as she was told. 'Have him in the truck at six,' he said to the sergeant. He turned on his heel and followed her.

'Up!' said the sergeant, and when Reaper struggled he nodded to Taylor and the private reached down a hand to help him to his feet.

They left the offices and crossed the yard to the single storey building. The door wasn't locked and they pushed Reaper inside and left him. It was the canteen.

'You've missed lunch.' The man speaking was on the far side of a counter. He had red hair and wore civilian clothes. 'I could make you a sandwich.'

'Coffee would be better.'

'Coffee it is. Take a seat. How do you take it?'

'Black is fine.'

'Black it is.'

He sat at a Formica topped table on a chair with a plastic seat and metal legs. The floor was heavy-duty vinyl. There was a smell of food cooking, invasive, not unpleasant, but it didn't tempt his taste buds. The man brought a mug of coffee. He placed it on the table and stood hesitantly in front of Reaper before he held out his hand.

'Tim Jepson.'

Reaper shook, and said, 'Tom Watson.'

'You're the pilot.'

'I'm the pilot.'

'I'm the poof.' He grinned disarmingly. 'Which is why I'm the cook.' He shrugged. 'It was either that or hairdresser. Our New Army has very fixed ideas about gender roles.'

'You're the poof?' Reaper felt obliged to double-check what he had just been told.

'The hierarchy don't believe in euphemisms. I'm lucky to have such a cushy job but there's a manpower shortage. Not as many people are seeking Redemption anymore. Word must have got round. Mind you, there's a manpower shortage everywhere, these days. What about you? Are you from a big group?'

Jepson sat in the chair opposite.

'No. I was on my own. Didn't fancy company, until now. And now I'm not so sure I did the right thing in looking for it.'

'You'll be all right as a pilot. No fear. You'll be wearing the black beret in no time. If that's what you want.'

'What's a black beret?'

'The mark of the elite. The chosen few who live the life or Riley while everybody else does the work.'

'Do all the soldiers wear the black beret?'

'Good grief, no. They just follow orders. Even though I seem to recall that was a defence that lacked credibility at Nuremberg.'

'So what category do you fit into – to become a poof cook?'

'Sexual deviant. Although that isn't actually in any order of the day. The General operates a sort of Nazi code without actually putting it into writing. It's all very politically correct. Apparently, I lack the moral fibre for normal duties and I can't be let loose among the general population in case of cross-contamination.' He smiled. 'Chance would be a fine thing. They say my views are not conducive to the public good. But I'm safe enough here. They don't mind if I cross-contaminate the poor sods who work down the mine. They're the lost souls. Only way out for them is in a winding sheet.'

'Who's the General?'

'George Purcell. He runs things.'

'I thought Prince Harry was in charge.'

'Purcell uses his name like a banner, but the General is in charge.'

'But is Harry really here?'

'People like to think so.'

'What's Purcell like?'

'He's a believer. He believes in a better tomorrow. He believes it's necessary for ordinary people to suffer. He believes racial and sexual cleansing is necessary.'

Reaper sipped his coffee. 'So you wouldn't recommend Redemption?'

'If you are white, male and heterosexual and don't mind hard work and blinkers, you'll be okay. And you? A pilot? Officer class. You'll be a Squadron Leader in no time. Play your cards right, you could be Air Chief Marshall.'

'They shot down my plane.'

'They'll find you another.'

Reaper studied Jepson. Red hair above a chubby white face. He was a cook, after all. It wouldn't be difficult to stay chubby. Not bad looking, intelligent eyes and an expression of self mockery. Make that self defence. He had probably taken a lot of abuse. Behind the eyes, were pain and resignation.

'You're very open with your views. What if I were to report you for sedition?'

'I'm supposed to be seditious. That's why I'm here.'

'Wouldn't it make it worse for you? You could get sent to the mines?'

He shrugged. 'That might not be so bad. There are other forms of hell.'

Reaper could only guess the form of hell the man had

already been through. Ridicule, bullying, punishment, assault, torture. Indecent abuse?

'Are you really gay?'

'Yes.' Said with defiance.

'There must be others. What happened to them?'

'The few that were found – or suspected – were sent to a work camp.' He moved his head to indicate outside. 'Not quite as bad as this – this is a death camp – but bad enough. Any others learn to keep their heads down and pretend to be straight. I know of at least one marriage of convenience. There must be others.' He smiled again, as if the only way to talk about the subject was with a leavening of humour. 'At least white gays have a chance. If you are black and gay you have no chance at all. They all end up in a camp.'

'Who is the General? What's his background?'

'That is shrouded in the mists of chaos and plague. He emerged with Harry in tow along with a dozen soldiers, all wearing black berets. The lure of the Prince attracted nearby military elements and he put out a radio call nationwide. Word spread and people flocked, as they say. His command, though, was not established without overcoming voices of dissent.'

'What happened?'

'Divide and rule. The voices of dissent were quietly removed to other duties. After a few disappeared, the others learnt to be more cautious in their criticism.'

'Did no one complain? Offer resistance?'

'I suppose no one wanted to risk a civil war between the only troops left in the land. It was a delicate balancing act. And there were few real officers. No more than a handful plus a few NCOs. Besides, the General has the Beast.'

'The Beast?'

'Colonel Barstow. He was with Purcell from the start and arrived wearing a navy blue tunic and khaki trousers. He was the original Black and Tan. Officers promoted to the black berets adopt the same outfit. I think he chose it without irony or a sense of history. There are different stories about how he achieved his nickname. The Tans say he got it through bravery in action with the SAS. Then there are those who say he got it because of atrocities he committed. You can take your choice.'

'What do you think?'

'I think the Tans are as scared of him as everybody else. I saw him up close only the once. It was enough. He has this veneer of officer class. It's as if he got it from a kit and sprayed it on. But you sense it can crack at any moment. That the beast within is just waiting for an excuse to break out.'

'Hell of a way to run an army.'

'Madmen have run countries before,' said Jepson. 'And these are strange times. Anyway, I have food to prepare for the lost souls.' He got up and studied Reaper. 'They wouldn't send a spy in to listen to what I had to say. They know my views already. So you must be the real deal. I wonder which way you'll jump? Will you become a Squadron Leader for a dictator? Or will you end up as a lost soul, eating my stew?'

'Maybe there's another way,' said Reaper.

They exchanged a long stare in which Jepson's eyes seemed to dig deep into Reaper to try to understand what he meant or implied.

Finally, he said, 'One can only hope.'

Chapter 14

THE BUILDINGS WERE BLACK AND GRIMED *from old fires. The farmhouse had probably stood for 150 years and had been deserted since the plague but the soldiers had attempted to burn it to the ground anyway. They had failed, for the walls and half the roof still stood and provided shelter from the weather. The first floor had partly caved in but an old kitchen range remained defiantly in place, although he dared not use it.*

They had never found the cellar because, though the initial search had been cursory, subsequent visitors had assumed it had been thorough. Besides, there was too much debris and the floor and walls were not safe. The access to the cellar had been through a trapdoor. He had moved the debris and found it by accident. The debris included part of a charred body and a skull. Another reason soldiers had not investigated more thoroughly.

The cellar contained a stockpile for survival. Bags of feed for hens, tins and bottled water for humans, packets and jars, sleeping bags, torches, batteries, candles, matches. Tools and workbench. They had remained unused. The plague had fooled the farmer and his family, as it had fooled the world. Isolation had not been complete, the virus had reached them and they had died in their beds. Their bodies had fallen through the floor with the bedroom furniture in the fire.

Aiden Ford had removed bricks and dug through the earth to create a second access point and then replaced the detritus and body parts to cover the trapdoor to deter investigation. He had turned the hole below ground into a waiting room in Purgatory. It was located on the western fringes of Redemption's area of influence and had been his home for six months; just outside the boundary fields of the farms its citizens worked.

It was a good place, a safe place. The charred bodies protected him. He had told them his story and they had approved his intentions. Their home was his home. They would keep the enemy away by their presence.

It had been more than a year since the massacre of the innocents and the cleansing flames of the great fire. Almost time for him to act. Ellen had waited long enough. And Tony and Bertie and Nigel and Martha and the rest. Not that they complained. They were very patient. But the time was approaching when he must return to hell and kill his monsters. He had failed Ellen once, but wouldn't fail her again. Time, then, to join Ellen and the rest. Time, before he became too old.

During the good days, Ford lay in the fields and let the sun warm his bones and remembered the past. Remembered his two lives: the one before the plague and the one that came after.

His first life had been uneventful. He had been born into a middle-class family during the war in the 1940s, a time of austerity and shortages. He had attended local schools in Bournemouth and went on to a career with Barclays Bank, became a branch manager and took early retirement at fifty-eight; a decent pension boosted by property and investments he and his wife Pat had inherited from their parents. They had a house with a sea view, a villa in Spain and were comfortably off. No children, but you can't have everything.

The high points of his existence had been golf on Thursday, the acknowledgement and respect of his peers, and achieving retirement at an age when he was still young enough to enjoy it. His life had been dull but pleasant. His wife fitted into the same category, but again, you can't have everything.

He was a modest man and she was a modest woman and they had chosen each other from within their accepted boundaries of availability and prospects. They had always been fond of each other but love had never been mentioned. They had never shared a passionate relationship. Passion had not been their style. The only passion he had indulged was a small collection of adult magazines he kept locked in his desk at home. The fear they might be discovered, the only frisson of excitement in his life.

Pat had died six months after he gave up work. An aneurysm, swift and clean, sitting in her Rover in the multi-storey car park. The shopping was in the boot. By the time he got round to moving the car, the ice cream had melted. He was surprised at how easily he accepted her death. There was no trauma after thirty-two years of marriage. No sense of great loss. They had drifted into each other's lives, accepted the arrangement, and now she had drifted out of his life leaving hardly a ripple of sadness behind. The most difficult part of her dying was that he had to learn how to use the washing machine. But at least he didn't have to keep the drawer of his desk locked any more.

His life had continued without much change. Ford maintained the same routine for three years until one day, sitting on the patio of his villa outside Marbella, he wondered why he continued to visit Spain. He didn't particularly like air travel and sharing flights with hen-parties or extended families. Not that he had anything against other people's choices; he was no snob, but he could think of better ways to spend his time than sitting in airports, departure lounges and crowded aircraft waiting to go to a place whose only attraction was its climate. It was Pat who had liked the sun; he preferred good old British rain, whatever the season. He sold the villa and stayed at home with his sea view and bought a dog. Pat had never liked dogs.

His life meandered onwards in well-worn grooves. The Daily Telegraph with his breakfast, golf, Bournemouth Cricket Club in the summer, rugby on TV in the winter, a few pints in his local with the teatime crowd. He had never suffered serious ill health and never spent time in hospital and he took regular walks with Paddy, his dog. He was in his early seventies but felt younger and was fully active. He put his fitness down to never having had to worry about money. He had never really had a proper job, either, if it came to that. Digging ditches was a proper job, but he had been employed in an office in an occupation at which he had been proficient. He had found the challenges easy. No more difficult than the Telegraph crossword.

He suffered real sorrow when Paddy died. The dog had had a cancer removed the year before and had recovered well for his age but Ford had known he was on borrowed time: the walks they went on together became shorter, and there were times Paddy preferred to sit in the back garden rather than leave the grounds of the house. He called the vet when the animal's back legs went. He arrived with a nurse, an injection was made and Paddy closed his eyes and went to sleep forever.

Paddy was wrapped in a carrying blanket and taken away. Ford had been unable to speak once the injection had *been made and, as he watched the Range Rover depart, the tears came. He was surprised at the depth of his emotion. He didn't find it strange that he had shed no tears for his wife but was heartbroken about the loss of his dog. Days later, he collected Paddy's ashes from the vet's surgery. They came sealed in a package within a box. He kept the box on the dresser in the dining room, next to a framed picture of the dog. He touched the box each morning before he had his breakfast and again last thing at night.*

'Morning Paddy,' he would say.

'Sleep tight, old son,' at the end of the day.

Another routine.

He noticed the plague only when it began to affect his lifestyle. He read about it in the newspaper and watched the reports on television but this was Eastbourne, for goodness sake. You might have plagues in Camden Town or Birmingham, but this was Eastbourne. When his golf partners stopped turning up and the teatime crowd in the pub began to dwindle, he realised the situation might be serious. Then the pub no longer opened and the world, including Bournemouth, changed forever. And Aidan Ford's second life began.

His pantry and kitchen cupboards had always been well stocked. His wife had seen to that during their marriage and it was another routine that he had maintained. As society began to crumble, he realised it would be sensible to add to what he already had. He didn't know how long the virus would last, but he stockpiled bottled water and batteries and candles, just in case. He did this in a methodical fashion and without panic. He had never panicked in his life. Until he heard shots in the centre of the town.

He drove straight home, locked the door and sat upstairs in his bedroom. He stayed indoors for four days while he rationalised the situation. At the end of his deliberations, he still hadn't reached any conclusions. He didn't know what to do. That night, he left the house under cover of darkness to explore. Electricity was still working and street lights provided a hint of normality. But the silence was eerie. A few house lights were on but there were no signs of habitation. Perhaps the occupants had left the lights on for comfort when they had taken to their beds and died. The only sound was the echo of thumping music from a long distance away. Was a night club still open in town?

The next day the electric power died. The second night he went out was black and deep and primeval. He ventured in a different direction. He had been walking for half an hour when he heard screams and shouts. A domestic argument? There were lights in the front window of a semi-detached house. That's where the sounds were coming from. Then the window smashed and a girl screamed for help.

Ford reacted automatically. He ran to the window and saw, by the light of camping lamps, two men struggling with a young woman in the front room. They were all shouting, screaming, kicking, fighting, but the woman was not going to win. Already her blouse had been ripped open and her breasts exposed. Ford saw the fear and desperation in her face; saw the bestial gleam in the expressions of the men.

The front door was open. He walked into the hall, paused in the doorway to the room. The girl was sprawled backwards on a settee, the men above her like beasts of prey tearing at her clothes, unfastening her jeans. He picked up a baseball bat that was leaning against the wall. Perhaps one of the men had been carrying it as a weapon? He walked into the room and swung it against the head of the closest of the attackers. The man went down without a sound, a collapsed heap on the floor. The second man half turned, his face losing the lust and sensing the danger, and Ford swung again. A blow straight to the side of the head, powered by adrenaline and anger and fear. Blood spurted, the man toppled. He lay groaning on the floor. Ford looked at the girl. She stared back at him, unsure, still waiting for rape. She looked at the baseball bat in his hands; he dropped it.

'I think we'd better leave,' he said.

She nodded and allowed him to help her to her feet and lead her from the house. They walked quickly, but did not run. When they were two streets away, they paused and listened for sounds of pursuit. The girl held her torn clothes about her.

'I'm Aidan Ford,' he said, and held out his hand to shake.

She stared back a long moment before saying, 'Ellen Staithes,' and placing her hand in his. They shook.

'I think we are temporarily safe,' he said. 'Do you live round here?'

'That was my house,' she said.

'Oh dear. If you don't think it presumptuous, perhaps you would like to come to mine?'

That was how he met Ellen, a nineteen-year-old student nurse, father dead in bed upstairs and about to be ravished by a former neighbour and a complete stranger.

Much later, at Ford's house, she said, 'You saved me.'

'Anyone would have done the same.'

'No, they wouldn't.' She saw the puzzled look in his face. 'Haven't you seen what's happening?'

'I don't suppose I have. I've stayed here. Till things blow over. I've plenty of food and – '

'Things won't blow over. It's the end. The apocalypse. The only people out there are like the two you just met.' She paused, her eyes wide. 'You saved me.'

He shrugged, embarrassed at being a saviour and a little disturbed by talk of apocalypse. This was Eastbourne, for goodness sake.

'You called my name,' he said.

'I... I don't know what I called.'

'You shouted help. That's what my name means. Aidan means help.' He smiled and blushed, in case she thought that knowing such trivia might categorise him as a trivial man.

She smiled in return. 'I don't know what Ellen means,' she said. 'But I'm grateful.' She touched his hand. 'It was a brave thing to do. Thank you.'

Ford had never been brave in his life and he didn't consider his actions had been brave until now. In retrospect, he realised what the consequences might have been if he had lost the fight. A sound beating, perhaps death. He had reacted to a situation; a young woman being attacked. Any decent chap would have done the same. He was also trying to come to terms with the feeling of power he had experienced when he had hit the two men with the bat. Had he badly hurt them? Killed them? He could claim self defence. Except, according to Ellen, no one would be interested in what he had done or what had happened. Was this really the apocalypse?

He and Ellen adopted and looked after each other, as they eventually embarked on an odyssey out of the suburbs that led them to meet a handful of others seeking salvation or peace or an alternative. A group that moved haphazardly from farm to village hoping to find a reason, a resolution, a place to stay. He carried a knife in a sheath at his waist and a shotgun he found behind the bar in a country pub. The rescue had empowered him, made him a new man.

Eventually, they came together with like-minded others at Stonehenge on Salisbury Plain.

The prehistoric site had existed for thousands of years and had seen plague and apocalypse before. Echoes of the past lurked in the shadows of the ancient stones and sunrise on a clear day seen from within the circle seemed to put humanity into perspective. The aura of the place held them for longer than anywhere else.

They were an oddball group from all walks of life and different ages. Ford was the eldest but was not looked upon as an elder. The mantle of leadership had been taken by Tony, a charismatic young man with lean limbs, handsome profile and biblical beard. Tony had been attracted to Stonehenge, with his own small group, through a sense of history rather than New Age philosophy. He believed in peaceful coexistence but also carried a shotgun in the back of his camper van.

Relationships were inevitably being formed and Tony and Ellen were attracted to each other but did not rush into a partnership. Ellen became his girlfriend but continued to share a caravan with Ford. The two young people were serious about each other but, even in the new circumstances, Ellen was not the kind of girl to indulge in instant sexual gratification. It was plain to see her future lay with the young man; they were both smitten; and Tony was happy to play the suitor and woo her affections. Ford was delighted that, at least in their small part of England, chivalry and romance had not died along with most everything else.

Three travellers in a Bentley told them Prince Harry was rallying survivors at Windsor. They stopped for a meal before they headed off to join the royal encampment. The news caused long discussions within their own company. A faction had been suggesting heading into the West Country but the dominant feeling tilted towards Prince Harry and a newly established authority.

Ford kept his own counsel but Tony spoke eloquently about new beginnings. Harry could be exactly what they needed. Not a new monarchy, but a popular figurehead to attract the best among the survivors. Thugs would be deterred. The promise of order would send them elsewhere; they would not expect royal patronage. Perhaps Harry was the answer to their search.

That night, Ellen asked for Ford's approval. She wanted to move in with the young man. He was touched. In only a few short weeks, she had become a daughter to him and he had become part of a family. It was more, much more, than he had expected to achieve in his later years, but it had happened and he was grateful. Grateful, even, for the virus that had made it happen, although he kept that to himself.

He gave his permission and the two young people exchanged vows as the sun rose. It was a clear day in late June, close to midsummer's day, and the golden rays touched the Heel Stone before blazing through the standing stones like God's blessing.

And later that day, they went to Windsor.

Chapter 15

GENERAL GEORGE PURCELL WAS ENJOYING the sunshine. He was sitting in the shade on the terrace of Brownley House, a Georgian mansion named after a local man of industry, that was his general headquarters, located in a village to the south of Banbury. He gazed across a manicured lawn at the Oxford Canal that, at this point, flowed almost in tandem with the River Cherwell. A large gin and tonic, served by Adams his batman, was on the table next to him. He wore combat fatigues with his tabs of rank and a black beret was on the table alongside the latest pages of his memoir that were held down by a swagger stick.

He knew his writings were prompted not by ego but a sense of destiny. His intention was to leave behind a new England: an Albion of strong and willing workers; an embryo nation that would, in time, expand to absorb within its boundaries all the lands of this island, before once again embarking upon a mission of empire. This was not foolish fantasy but a natural progression of reality.

The first part was in place. He had the only army in Great Britain. With that at his back and a captive workforce, the future was inevitable. Sacrifices would have to be made initially, but the long-term benefits were indisputable. Safety was in strength and first he would consolidate mainland Britain. Then he would look to continental Europe and, gradually, life would become easier for the people here in Redemption who had been with him from the start, because his conquering army would ensure that the vanquished of other lands would become the workforce, just as in days of empire. His people would then enjoy the better future that he had promised.

The naval base at Portsmouth was still operating. It would be necessary to coerce the Royal Navy into his scheme of things. So far, they had not responded to his calls for unity under Prince Harry but he was unperturbed. He would seek meetings, parleys and, if those failed, he would infiltrate and change the order of the naval command. He didn't believe force of arms would be necessary. As he had done here, the removal of the occasional recalcitrant officer could work wonders. Other officers would see the sense of combining resources and it was only right that the potent force and threat of the vessels at Portsmouth should be held in responsible hands for the good of the nation he was building.

The federation of settlements based around Haven was another target. He intended that they benefit from his rule sooner rather than later. Reports suggested they had become an agrarian success in a very short time. He could use such expertise; he could use its stockpiles of food and its people. With proper encouragement, Haven would help supply the needs of Redemption's citizens. Let his people see the benefits that were to come.

One or two minor problems needed removing first, such as the pair known as Reaper and the Angel of Death. Strange how people so quickly reverted to legend and fireside tales once they lost the panacea of television. A gun-happy duo survive a couple of skirmishes against rank amateurs and their names are whispered in the same terms as Robin Hood. Let them have their temporary glory. People tended to forget that, in history, the winners were the Sheriff of Nottingham and Prince John. And so it would be again.

He would also eventually take London. He had a steam train ready to take military units to Marylebone Station as the first part of a triumphal journey to the capital. Buckingham Palace and Downing Street were symbolic and would be better off in his hands.

In the meantime, there were his daily duties to perform to ensure the smooth running of Redemption. And his memoir to maintain for the benefit of posterity.

He sipped the gin and tonic and savoured the cool freshness. Down at the far end of the lawn, three camp workers swung scythes to ensure the grass was neat. They had petrol for mechanised mowing machines but he preferred the old-fashioned way. Wielding a scythe was skilful; the work kept the men in their place. They were stripped to the waist and their torsos gleamed with sweat. The sight was aesthetically pleasing and made the coldness of the gin taste all the sweeter. A guard stood beneath the shade of a tree, a sub-machinegun hanging from a strap. He held it at waist height. All was peaceful. All was as it should be. The birds sang in the trees and there was order in his world.

'Have you heard?'

Colonel Barstow came through the French windows like a force of nature. He flopped into a chair. Behind him, the faithful Adams waited, a look of apology on his face that he had been unable to warn the General or divert his deputy.

'The airman?' said Purcell.

'Damn right, the airman.' Barstow raised a hand, the index finger upright. 'Gin and tonic, Adams. You shouldn't need telling.'

He was an unkempt officer, the very antithesis of his general, with a libertine's taste for women and an alcoholic's thirst. Purcell could smell the stale drink on the summer air. His clothes were rumpled as if he had slept in them, and he probably had. He wore combat fatigues and a handgun in a holster strapped to his thigh. He had a navy blue jacket draped across his shoulders that was unadorned except for an enamel lapel badge that showed the distinctive winged dagger of the SAS. He shrugged the jacket off so that it lay trapped between his back and the chair. His black beret, which he didn't remove, also carried a cap badge of the SAS.

Barstow claimed he had been a member of the 22 Special Air Service Regiment based at Hereford. It had been the elite special service unit of the British Army to which many applied but few were chosen. Purcell suspected his deputy had not actually been a member but he allowed him to wear the emblem. It gave him a degree of kudos that might be needed if they were ever confronted by a real threat of military might.

'A pilot would be useful,' Barstow said. 'Shoot a few rockets at anyone giving us a hard time and they'll soon surrender. London. Haven. That place in Cornwall.'

'He was flying a Cessna,' Purcell said.

'A plane is a plane. He can fly one, he can fly another.'

'I don't think it works like that.'

'The principles must be the same.'

'There is a great deal of difference between a Cessna and a Typhoon jet fighter.'

The batman appeared from inside the house and placed a large gin and tonic on the table next to Barstow.

'Bring another,' Barstow said. Then, to Purcell, 'All right then, if you're going to be so bloody pessimistic, I'll go up with him in his Cessna and drop bombs from the bloody thing.' He took a long drink. 'The point is, it gives us another string to our bow.'

'Precisely. Perfect for reconnaissance and impressing the natives of the north. Big metal bird in the sky. A potent symbol of power and technology. And, if necessary, you can drop a few bombs to make the point.'

'When does he get here?'

'Tonight. Solitary confinement. Let him sweat on his future for twenty-four hours. Then we'll talk to him. Discover the extent of his abilities – who knows, he might be able to fly jets? Invite him to join us.'

'I'll talk to him,' said Barstow.

'You may be a legend as a soldier,' Purcell said carefully, 'but you are not known for your subtlety, Brian.' He rarely used Barstow's first name and did so now to diffuse any argument before it started. 'If my approach doesn't work then, by all means, I will leave it to you to make him see sense.'

Barstow finished the first gin and tonic, ruminated a moment, and nodded his head.

He looked round to shout for Adams, but the batman was already at his shoulder with the second glass.

'You do a very fine gin and tonic, Adams. Have I told you that before?'

'Yes, sir. You have.'

'Good. Well get me another.'

The man departed silently and Barstow looked around. The drink had mellowed him.

'Where's Harry?'

'In his rooms. Miss Finlay is with him.'

'No more problems?'

'No more problems.'

'Carrot and stick,' said Barstow. 'I can be subtle.'

'Quite,' said Purcell and stared across the lawn at the men sweating in the sunshine.

When Harry had continued to complain – about the confinement of the people, conditions in the work camps and his own role in the scheme of things – Barstow had brought him swiftly back to heel by suggesting that Miss Finlay might be better employed in the Pussy Shack, the brothel reserved for the Tans, who were not know for their gentility. Harry's complaints had stopped.

'Maybe I should go and visit her,' Barstow said. 'Reinforce the point.'

Judith Finlay was a good looking girl.

'I don't think that's necessary. He got the message. Besides, I thought you had an inspection.'

'The Tramways Work Camp. Two newcomers. They're mouthing off, can't take the hint. Either I make an example or send them to the mine.'

'It's your decision, of course, but we should be careful of manpower. People have stopped coming. Before long, we will have to go and find more, conquer fresh fields.'

'About time.'

He finished the second gin and tonic as Adams arrived with the third. Barstow stood up, put his jacket on his shoulders without putting his arms in the sleeves, picked up the third glass and drained it.

'Bloody good gin and tonic,' he said, nodded to Purcell, and marched back through the French windows and through the house, followed by Adams.

Purcell breathed more easily and picked up his own glass and sipped.

Barstow might eventually become a problem that would have to be dealt with. But Purcell was not stupid. He realised his deputy might come to the same conclusion about himself. At some point, one of them would have to go. When that time came, it would be done with finesse, and he would need another officer ready to step into Barstow's rank and be grateful for the promotion.

The chap in charge of the regular military would not do. He had already promoted Colonel Maidstone above his ability. He had been a captain in recruitment and was less than inspiring. But he had the right accent and he was safe and malleable. A duffer who would do until someone better came along. His thoughts touched on Reaper once more. There was a man with obvious ability, even though it may have been overstated. He had half a mind to attempt to recruit him to the cause. He seemed to combine ruthlessness with leadership abilities. If only he could make him the right offer, the road to Haven might open up without a shot being fired.

Command weighed heavily. Particularly as so few officers had survived the virus. This had been both a boon and a problem. He had been a major in the Adjutant General's Corp, more specifically in Staff and Personnel Support. His was a career that had not gone according to plan after he had sneaked into Sandhurst with high hopes.

His own sense of destiny had not been shared by his superior officers. Instead of glory he had been consistently shunted sideways into administrative work. Glory had been handed to other chaps. He suspected that in the final months before the virus took hold, he had been marked for the list of redundancies in an army that was being skimmed to the bones.

When the grip of the virus tightened, he was at the army base in Colchester. No one else had been available and he had been sent to help smooth over a potentially embarrassing scandal involving buggery among soldiers being detained at the Military Corrective Training Centre. A detention centre, not a prison, where inmates served up to two years or were kept on remand before being sent to a civilian prison. But these were the last days of normality and everything went very wrong, very quickly. His presence was hardly noted as officers and personnel started dying around him.

He was proud to say he wasn't scared. He just didn't believe he would succumb. He visited officers and men in makeshift wards that became morgues, without the facemask that many were wearing. He felt invincible. He felt destiny calling. This was what he had been born for: to survive and to lead.

But as a major from Staff and Personnel Support?

There were plenty of uniforms. He chose one without regimental distinction and attached the crown of a lieutenant general. He added campaign ribbons that denoted an active career in Iraq and Afghanistan, a Conspicuous Gallantry Cross and a Military Cross. He took a black beret that had belonged to an American soldier who, for some unknown reason, had been at the camp. The beret was a distinctive touch. Black was only worn by the Royal Tank Regiment although it was standard issue in the US Army. Black would be the colour.

Look the part and others will follow. He had seen it happen throughout his career. And, after all, he was invincible. His first recruits were from the detention blocks. He carried no weapon apart from a swagger stick. He released all surviving inmates. Some were ill and destined for death but two had the arrogance of the immune. One of them was the Beast.

He never knew precisely what Brian Barstow had done but he suspected he was capable of just about anything. Each acknowledged the worth of the other. They would be a lesser force on their own but together they could do great things and they entered into an unspoken collaboration. They recruited the other detainee and three regular soldiers. They piled weapons in a truck but, before they left, Barstow disappeared for thirty minutes. When he returned, he was wearing a navy blue military jacket over his combats, with the flying dagger of the SAS on the lapel. There had been a brief argument.

'This unit will have no regimental badges or flashes. This unit will be the Black Berets,' insisted Purcell. 'Besides, you were never a member of the SAS.'

'Listen,' Barstow said and held up a combat knife with blood on its blade. 'I've killed for this badge. I'm the biggest fucking hooligan that ever came out of Hereford. Remember that... *General*.'

Purcell had remembered. And perhaps Barstow had served with the Regiment. He smiled to himself. At least his claim was as valid as Purcell's assumed rank and decorations.

They had stopped in the town of Colchester for *bonding*, as Barstow had put it. The men had got drunk, found women, and sated their appetites. They recruited two more to their ranks and also found an Army and Navy store. They kitted their new recruits in combat fatigues and found a box of black berets. It was the start of his army.

By the time they reached Chelsea, Purcell and the Beast had twelve men, all of proven violent disposition and adept with weapons. It was in Chelsea they found Prince Harry. London was too wild with gang warfare to be the birthplace of his new nation. They were left alone because they had a discipline imposed by Barstow. They were merciless bastards and they wore uniforms. Look the part and others believed. But London was the wrong place at the wrong time. They recruited half a dozen more men to the Black Berets but Purcell knew it was best to leave the capital for the present. He resolved to return when the idiots had stopped killing each other. He picked Windsor for the next stage of his grand design.

Windsor had been a good idea. The home of the monarch, the cradle of British history. The plan had lasted only a short time before they had to leave because of the consequences of the madness of the Beast. Leaving had been the easiest way, the only way. Leave the secret behind before it became knowledge among the people.

At that time, keeping his plans on track had been a fine balancing act. Encouraging civilians to believe they had found organisation and safety after the chaos that reigned across the land, while attracting groups of military personnel to build his army. Gradually, the roles had eased themselves into place. The soldiers had first been protectors against the threats that lurked in the wilds of the outer reaches. Then they became the guards that kept the population under control and within the boundaries of his grandiose strategy.

Along the way, some had fallen. Those officers and soldiers who had been outspoken against his regime had, without fuss or threat, been moved to other duties, usually in the work camps. As inmates. The rest had been compliant, as soldiers were under strong leadership. They understood discipline and they wanted to believe. They had himself as general, an officer without blemish, they had an SAS hero they nicknamed the Beast and, to sweeten the cake, they had Prince Harry as Commander in Chief.

The Black Berets had become his elite. They had become known as the Tans, not a name of which Purcell approved but one that had made Barstow smile when he had explained its implications. It suited his rag tag stormtroopers perfectly, he said, for the men he recruited were not the finest soldiers. He preferred the ruthless, the arrogant, those easily led and swift to obey orders, no matter what those orders were. Many had never served in the military but had been chosen from the ranks of the gangs they had encountered as they had made their way to Windsor.

Now Barstow had eighty Tans of varying quality, plus a captain, four lieutenants, four sergeants and eight corporals. Purcell's regular army of combined services numbered 1,150. Officers and NCOs had been in short supply, particularly after those removed to other duties, but the right promotions, he believed, had consolidated its loyalty.

The future was bright. And next on his agenda were Haven, the naval base of Portsmouth and then a glorious return to the capital in triumph.

Chapter 16

DECLAN DE COURCY GOT BACK TO THE White Cottage four hours after the crash. Three miles into his homeward hike, he had managed to find a motorbike in a barn. Much to his surprise, it had started. He guessed someone must have been using it AV. Perhaps they had abandoned it in favour of a car.

The White Cottage was empty and he rode the bike to the airfield where Sandra and Mandi were waiting.

'Where's Reaper?' Sandra said.

He dismounted and held out his hands in an apology. 'We crashed.'

Sandra took a step forward and hit him with a right hook that carried all her power. The blow caught him by surprise and he stumbled backwards and fell onto the grass. Mandi moved to her side and put his arms around her hoping to both calm and restrain her.

'Where's Reaper?' she said.

'He's fine. He stayed behind.' He shrugged from a sitting position. 'He wanted to go to Redemption and this seemed the best way.'

'What seemed the best way?'

'We flew over the mine, they shot at us and we went down. We landed okay, about a mile away. We could have both walked away safely but he stayed. He set fire to the plane and waited for the soldiers to find him.'

'He wanted to be captured?'

De Courcy shrugged again. 'He's pretending to be the pilot. He hopes that will make him a protected species. The soldiers will take him to Redemption and he'll meet the General and Harry. That's his plan.'

'What if somebody recognises him?'

The first flush of anger was leaving her andMandi released his restraining grip. He held out a hand to de Courcy and pulled him to his feet.

De Courcy watched her warily in case of any more blows. 'He won't join the hoi polloi. He'll be treated differently, kept apart. If they think he's a pilot, then he can't be Reaper.'

'You're not even a fucking pilot,' she said, and tensed as if about to release another punch.

De Courcy held up his hands defensively. 'I'm sorry. Really, Sandra. I'm sorry. But he's fine. I'm rather good, as it happens. I made a perfect landing. It wasn't my fault that the bastards shot us down. Reaper told me to leave, to get back here and tell you what was happening.'

Her anxiety had made her lash out. Now it seeped away. She took a deep breath and nodded. 'I'm sorry,' she said. 'That I hit you.'

'Think nothing of it.' He tentatively stroked his chin where the blow had landed. 'It's obviously been a trying time.'

'But if he doesn't come back, I'll kick your Irish arse all the way to Ireland.'

'He'll come back. You know he'll come back. He told me to tell you he'll be here in four days. His instructions were specific. He'll try and escape. If he can't, he'll tell them he has another plane here and they'll bring him back under guard. He said you'd know what to do...' He hesitated.

'Go on,' she said.

'He said he would be back in four days... but if he wasn't back in five, he wouldn't be coming. He said he'd be either a prisoner or dead. He said you were to take charge.'

The anger began to return but she controlled it. It wasn't de Courcy's fault. It was Reaper being bloody Reaper.

They returned to the White Cottage and Sandra debriefed Mandi again about his time at the mine and what he knew or had heard about Redemption. She took notes and had him draw better and more detailed diagrams of the mine and the location of workers and guards. She used an Ordnance Survey map to mark out the lines of occupation of the town and the location of the village of Baystoke, where Purcell was based.

Rain next morning reflected their mood.

'The odds are Reaper will come back,' she said, as much to convince herself as them. 'The odds are he will be under guard. General Purcell will want a pilot and if Reaper says there are things here that he needs, like a spare plane, they'll bring him back.'

'What will you do?' said de Courcy.

'We'll set him free.'

'We?'

'I'm going back to Haven for help. We'll set him free.'

'And then?'

'Reaper will have a plan. And I'll have a plan. In the meantime, you might want to make plans of your own. You have the other Cessna. You and Mandi could try for Ireland.'

'We could,' said de Courcy. He glanced at Mandi. 'But I think we might stay around for a while longer. See how things work out.'

*　　　*　　　*

Sandra left within the hour. The distance was not great but the detours she made to avoid the dangers of urban areas extended the trip. She needed to stay clear of trouble to ensure she was able to bring back help. Except that when she arrived at Haven, she sensed immediately that trouble had preceded her.

Ashley was in the command office at the manor house. He was, unusually, wearing combat uniform and sidearm and had an automatic rifle on the desk.

'Good to have you back,' he said, his eyes going past her. 'Where's Reaper?'

'Long story. What's going on?'

'We got a call for help from Richmond yesterday. The ferals have broken out from Newcastle and are looking for easy pickings. Last heard, they were in Darlington. Yank took the Blues. All four teams. I've put the militia on standby and have a platoon already under arms.'

'Shit,' she said. 'Perfect fucking timing.'

Ash raised an eyebrow. 'If Reaper were here, he'd tell you to mind your language.'

She gave him a tight smile.

'Where is he?'

'In Redemption. He's gone undercover and I think he's plotting revolution.'

'As you said,' Ash replied. 'Perfect fucking timing.'

Chapter 17

THE FERALS HAD MOVED OUT OF Darlington and settled into the complex of hotels and restaurants at Scotch Corner, the famous junction of the A1 and A66 that had been the accepted gateway to the North for generations.

The sensible Mavis Wilburn, one of the committee members of the thriving and growing community based around the market town of Northallerton, gave Yank and the Blues this latest intelligence. Northallerton wasn't a part of the federation but a close ally. Richmond was the next major town north, just below Scotch Corner. Mavis said its inhabitants were worried.

'Even with King Arthur to lead them,' she said, with a straight face.

Yank smiled.

Richmond was at Haven's frontier. The town and surroundings were run by a group headed by Arthur Dobson, local historian who claimed to be the reincarnation of King Arthur. Legend said the King and his knights slept in a secret chamber beneath Richmond's 11th century castle, awaiting the call to awake at a time of greatest need. Dobson's forename and ownership of a big sword inspired him to interpret the legend to his own elevation. Not many believed him, but he was an excellent and benign administrator.

In the aftermath of the plague, many strange leaders making equally strange claims had arisen. York had produced the charismatic Brother Abraham, now part of Haven along with his flock. The New Army in Redemption claimed Prince Harry. As Reaper had said, each to his own. Haven tolerated King Arthur and had friendly, if distant, relations with his 'subjects'.

Mavis said, 'They stayed ten days in Durham City and a week in Darlington. They simply ran wild, my dear. No sense of responsibility. You would have thought they would learn, after all that the world has been through. They pillaged, took slaves and women. They set fire to Durham Cathedral, if you can believe that. A most beautiful building, and now much of it destroyed.' She shook her head. 'Vandals, dear. Simply vandals.'

'And Arthur's worried?' said Yank.

'They're next in line and so very close. Then they will probably come here. After that, they'll march into Haven.'

'Maybe they haven't heard that we fight back?' Yank said.

'Perhaps they don't care.'

Yank studied a map again, although she new the lay of the land. The A1 was a blue ribbon that cut straight through Yorkshire, south to north. Northallerton was to the east of it; to the west, a mere five miles from Scotch Corner, was Richmond.

'We've had a look at them from a distance,' said Mavis. 'Charlie and Brian are still out there, keeping an eye. They reckon there are about a hundred and twenty of them armed – mainly men, but some women. Plus slaves and camp followers. A total of about two hundred and fifty.'

Not bad odds, Yank thought: eight against a hundred and twenty. Maybe if she offered them terms, they might surrender.

The four Range Rovers containing the Blues crossed the A1 and drove to Richmond. They crossed the river into the town, the castle dominating on their right, and drove into the cobbled and sloping Market Place, the large central area that was the main car park. A few abandoned vehicles remained and vegetation had started growing in places. The buildings that fringed the square – shops, pubs, restaurants, banks – were a reminder this had been a thriving tourist town. In the middle of the Market Place was a medieval church that had been converted into a regimental museum for the Green Howards, a pub and restaurant. Beyond it was a distinctive obelisk market cross.

An elderly man came from the museum and waved. They stopped and Yank got out to talk. She had only previously visited Richmond twice and didn't know him.

'I'm Anna. We're Special Forces from Haven.'

He shook her hand, holding on as if grateful at her arrival. 'I know who you are,' he said. 'Thank God you've come. I'm Gordon Beavis. They left me here just in case.'

He didn't say in case of what. 'The women and children are in hiding. Arthur and some of the men are on the Darlington Road.' He glanced from vehicle to vehicle. 'Where's Reaper?' he said, with a hint of disappointment. 'Shouldn't he be here?'

'He's on a scouting trip,' said Yank. She didn't tell him the scouting trip was two hundred miles in the opposite direction. 'What does Arthur plan to do?'

'He's built a barricade across the road. He plans to resist.'

*   *   *

The town was compact. Before the plague it had had a population of 8,000, boosted at weekends by soldiers from nearby Catterick Garrison who used its pubs. At the last count, it had about a hundred and twenty people, most of them living to the north of its centre, where they cultivated the golf course and nearby fields. King Arthur headed a committee that met at a round table, as in days of yore. But today he was manning a barricade across the main road that led into town from the north.

The area was residential, the road running past schools and through an estate of semi-detached and detached homes and gardens. This had been a very nice place to live. The barricade was about sixty yards from open country.

Arthur carried a broadsword in a scabbard that hung down his back. The hilt was behind his left shoulder. It looked incongruous when worn with corduroy trousers and a checked shirt. The eight Blues got out of their vehicles and the two groups assessed each other. No contest, thought Yank. The uniforms alone gave the Blues the edge, plus their youth. And that was before you got to the deadly weapons they were carrying. In contrast, Arthur's hodgepodge of twenty homespun heroes held shotguns, pitchforks and spears that looked as if they had come from a museum. Two carried longbows, one a crossbow and two had handguns. Several also had knives in sheaths at their belts. All were men and ranged from a boy who looked about fourteen, to a tall and thin but gnarled looking chap who had to be seventy-plus. Arthur Dobson was overweight and wore glasses and was in his fifties. He had mutton chop sideburns and a pleasantly rounded face, although it now held an expression of anxiety.

'I'm Anna,' Yank said, and they shook hands.

They had met before but only briefly.

Arthur nodded and gripped her hand firmly. 'Reaper?' he said.

A girl could get a complex, she thought. 'He's on other business.'

Arthur glanced at the other Blues and nodded. Their apparent confidence reassured him. Yank made a visual inspection of the barricade. It was substantial, mainly made from vehicles, some half stacked upon others. A tow truck and farm tractor were nearby and had obviously been used in the construction. Other vehicles lined the road facing back towards town. Escape vehicles. She guessed resistance would be token.

A man came from the far side of the barricade and joined them. He was small, middle aged and wore jeans and a t-shirt and a battered waxed hat like Indiana Jones. He saw Yank had noticed the hat and raised it to reveal a totally bald head.

'When you're follicly challenged it's essential to protect against the sun. You'll never believe it, but I once got sun stroke sitting outside a pub in Whitby.' He held out his hand. 'I'm Brian Jones from Northallerton. Mavis has told me all about you.' His grip was firm and his smile wry. He was good-looking in an eccentric sort of way. Yank liked him. He was calm and quiet and looked fit from working the land.

'Brian's been scouting them since Darlington,' Arthur said.

'Me and Charlie,' Brian explained. 'Charlie's in woods above Scotch Corner keeping watch.'

'One of our chaps is with him,' said Arthur.

'We need to talk,' Yank said to Brian.

'Please,' Arthur said. 'Come into my office.'

He held an arm out indicating a set of patio furniture in the nearest garden. The three of them sat round a white plastic table. Arthur sat down only when he had removed the broadsword from its scabbard and laid it on the table in front of him.

'Impressive,' said Yank.

'It's really only ceremonial,' he said, slightly abashed.

'Tell me about Scotch Corner,' she said to Brian.

'There are service areas on both sides of the road,' he explained. 'They've picked this side for their camp. The Holiday Inn is this side, plus lots of facilities and a caravan park. They're in a convoy so they need space. Twenty white vans – some of them pulling caravans. A dozen mobile homes, two enclosed trucks, one open truck, eight 4x4s, and a Bentley.'

She was impressed that he was so specific.

'What sort of weapons?'

'Shotguns, rifles, handguns, crossbows. We reckon up to ninety men and perhaps thirty women are armed with something. They also have sub-machineguns. Like Uzis? Not that I've ever seen an Uzi, except in the movies.'

'Uzis make a lot of noise but aren't very accurate. It's a close quarter weapon. How many do they have?'

'Maybe a dozen.'

'Have you identified the leader?'

'Not one hundred per cent.'

'The Bentley?'

'That's what we thought. It's used by a bloke in a designer suit. Hardly looks like a gang leader, but he obviously has authority. He's in his forties. He also has two very attractive women with him. They carry Uzis. I don't know if they can use them but they look the part.

He has a driver, a small bloke, who's never far away. Then there's a big bloke. Jeans, biker boots, black leather jacket. About thirty, a lot of hair and a black beard. As I said, he's big, but he carries no excess weight. Looks dangerous. He drives a Nissan 4x4 with huge wheels and has a sawn-off in a holster on his hip. We've seen him with a girl but, if it's a relationship, she doesn't appear to be too happy about it. She's young, blonde, quite probably a recent captive. When he speaks, people jump.'

Yank smiled, sat back and ran a hand through her short spiky hair. 'You and your friend have been thorough,' she said. 'How long have they been there?'

'Three days. It seems as if they were waiting for others to catch up. Looks like they had foraging parties out going through outlying villages on the way.'

'But they are all there now?'

'Looks like it. And probably ready to move on.'

'But which way?'

'If I was a betting man, I'd say this way.'

'How long have you been watching them?'

'Since Durham. I saw them arrive. They caused havoc. Some people tried to talk to them, come to an arrangement, but they weren't interested. They killed the men that resisted, took what women they wanted. Some took refuge in the Cathedral. They set it on fire. They have slaves. It's that sort of group. But they should be careful. Too many slaves can spark a revolt. The balance gets out of kilter. Quite a few made a run for it from Durham. I helped where I could. Sent a few families to Northallerton, some here. Some opted to head for the Dales where there are fewer people and fewer stockpiles to pillage.'

Yank said, 'If there's a lot of them – a big caravan of vehicles – they must be slow on the road.'

'I watched them enter Durham, I watched them go into Darlington. Same method. The 4x4s and the open truck go first. Mostly fighting men, a few women. Fighting women. The sort you wouldn't want to meet on a dark night. They go in and establish a base. Impose themselves. Then the rest of the vehicles follow. The rest of the armed ferals are spaced throughout the convoy and two of the white vans bring up the rear. They carry half a dozen each.'

Brian and Arthur had accepted Yank was the professional without demur but she couldn't very well command the men of Richmond. Not that she wanted to. She had a military background with her time in action in Afghanistan and knew more than the basics about how to pick a battle and when it was best to avoid one. But this situation was dictating a conflict, whether she wanted one or not. What would Reaper do? What would Sandra do? She ran her fingers through her short spiky hair and smiled to herself.

They weren't here so it was academic. It was what she was going to do that was important, and at least she had more army experience then either of them. But Afghanistan had been a war and this was survival and a different kind of fight where, sometimes you could not wait to consider morality and peripheral casualties.

'Have they sent anybody to scout Richmond?' she asked.

Arthur said, 'Not that we know.'

She looked at Brian: 'How about your way?'

'One car went as far as Catterick, saw the damage, and went back.' The soldiers who had survived the plague and who had remained on base, had blown up any equipment they couldn't take when they had headed south to join Harry.

'So we still don't known which way they'll jump.'

'It has to be this way,' said Brian.

'I agree,' said Arthur.

She stared at Arthur. 'If it is, what will you do? Fight?'

He frowned and dipped his head. 'My heart says we should but I know it would be suicide and there's no glory in that.' He stroked the blade of the sword. 'I had thought that if we gave them a show of force they might go somewhere else and leave us alone. They're bullies, after all, and bullies prefer to avoid a fight where they might get hurt. But the more I hear,' he glanced at Brian, 'the more I realise we would be better hiding until they've been and gone and try to pick up the pieces later.'

'I hope you've got a good place to hide,' she said. 'They only need one prisoner to tell them where you are and then you could all be slaves. Or dead.'

He shrugged. 'We'll make a show at the barricade. Maybe it will deter them. If it doesn't, we'll get away. We have the cars ready and it will take them time to move that lot.'

Yank thought he was talking sense, although she didn't put their chances too high of remaining undiscovered in their hiding places. The forces at Haven would put up a better fight, but it would be costly. And as Reaper often said, the one commodity this world couldn't afford to waste was mankind. The fewer good guys who died, the better. The ferals? That was a different matter.

'I'd like to take a look at them myself,' she said to Brian. 'Can you take me?'

'Of course. We can drive most of the way and walk the last mile.'

'Then let's do it.'

They got to their feet and Arthur re-slotted his sword into its scabbard with a deftness born of practice. As they walked towards the barricade, the young boy shouted: 'Rider!'

The Richmond home guard milled around anxiously, Arthur trying to calm them. The Blues unslung their carbines and stepped to the barricade. Yank peered through the shattered glass of a broken car window. A man on a motorcyle approached.

'It's Dick Mason!' the boy shouted, and the home guard relaxed. He was their own scout.

Mason rode the machine through a garden and round the wrecks that blocked the road.

'They're moving,' he said, before even dismounting. 'Charlie's still up there but they were getting ready to move when I left.'

'Which way?' said Arthur.

'This way.'

'How long before they get here?' Yank asked Brian.

'It will take them time to get organised. They'll want all the vehicles packed before any fighting men leave. Maybe an hour?' He took the motorcycle from Mason and stepped astride it. 'I'll find out.'

'Here,' said Yank. 'Take this.'

She handed him her Clansman handheld radio. He slotted it on his belt, nodded, and rode off without another word.

Yank turned to Dobson, who looked less than majestic, despite the sword.

'Arthur, I'm going to need your help. Make me a gap to get my cars through. We're going to the tree-line to check the lie of the land.'

A gap at one side of the road was soon ready. Yank climbed back into her vehicle and led the Blues up the road. They stopped sixty yards away at the tree line on the left that marked the end of the housing complex. To the right there were four more houses before the flat countryside began. It wasn't perfect for an ambush but it would have to do.

'What are you thinking?' Jenny said.

'We either fight or run. And I sure as hell don't like running.'

'There's a lot of them.'

'They're little more than soccer hooligans.'

'I've seen soccer hooligans,' said Kat. 'Not nice.'

'Arthur called them bullies and he's right,' said Yank. 'Give them a bloody nose and they might go somewhere else.'

'A short, sharp, shock,' said Kev.

'Exactly. Hit them hard, make them think twice. Consider the alternatives.'

'So what do we do?' said Jenny.

Yank looked around again and pointed to the last two houses on the right. 'The upstairs windows of those houses need breaking,' she said. 'Kev and Nina, the end house. James and Gwen, the one next to it. Smash all the windows so it looks like they've been wrecked, then pick your positions. They'll be your firing stations. Check the back doors are open for escape. Through the back yards to the nearest road. We'll place a Rover there for a speedy getaway. I'll brief you in fifteen.'

A metal gate led into the field opposite and she crossed the road, pushed it open and stared at the tree line from this side. It was dense and afforded cover but no height advantage, unless they climbed the trees, which was never a good idea unless someone had a death wish. The field was also edged with a low stone wall that would provide shelter for the enemy. They needed height. They needed the tractor.

'Jenny, get the tractor from the other side of the barricade. I want it in this field.' She stared down the empty road that curved away across flat countryside. Green fields beneath blue skies across which floated a few scattered fluffy white clouds. A beautiful day. For a battle.

Chapter 18

THEY WERE AS READY AS THEY WOULD ever be when Brian radioed in. A few minutes later, he came into sight riding fast along the narrow two lane road and skidded to a halt, surprise showing on his face.

'How long?' Yank asked.

She and Dee were sitting on the white plastic chairs that had only recently been part of the furniture of King Arthur's office garden. The plastic table was in front of them and two empty chairs were on the other side. On the table were four sets of cups and saucers and a teapot. A plate of biscuits, found in one of the nearby houses and well past their sell by date, added to the incongruity of the scene. They wore only side arms.

'Five minutes,' he said.

'Same system and numbers?'

'Same. About fifty fighters.'

'You'd better get behind the barricade. Arthur has his instructions but he might need a steadying hand. When they arrive, I want a show from behind there. Wave the spears, shout threats, let the bastards know war is waiting.'

'And then what?'

'When it starts, get ready to run.'

He shook his head and rode past the girls. They had set up their welcome opposite the gate into the field, behind which now sat an old yellow tractor with giant wheels that looked as if it had been abandoned years ago. Their position was exposed. Brian continued to shake his head. It was obvious he thought they were crazy.

Dee said, 'Shall I be mother?' She poured black coffee into two of the cups, trying not to let her nerves show. In a lower voice, she said, 'Is this going to work?'

'We'll find out anytime soon,' said Yank, sitting back and crossing her legs, as the first of the vehicles from the feral convoy came into view down the road.

Behind the girls, parked in the middle of the road, was a dump truck that had been requisitioned from Arthur's barrier. A big red tipper bucket and a white cab. The Richmond home guard had replaced it in the barricade with two other vehicles from nearby houses. Yank had briefed Arthur and his men. She had briefed her own teams separately. Each knew their roles, knew what was expected and had planned escape routes in case everything went wrong. But what could go wrong? Everything was as she had planned it. All she could do now was hope it worked.

The point car stopped fifty yards away. A man got out and studied them through binoculars. A 4x4 with big wheels – the Nissan Brian had talked about – pulled alongside it and a giant of a man, dressed in black, climbed out and also took a long look through binoculars. Yank couldn't be sure, but she thought he laughed. A smaller man approached from behind: the man in the designer suit. They exchanged words, nodded in agreement, and the big man got back into his vehicle and drove forward slowly. Designer Suit returned to his Bentley, which nosed past the point car and followed in its wake.

Come on, urged Yank silently. The rest of the convoy continued after them, side by side, filling the two lanes. 'Yes,' she said.

The Nissan and Bentley stopped twenty yards off. The biker in black and Designer Suit got out and stared at Yank and Dee. The vehicles behind them emptied and armed men spread out for a better view of the Mad Hatter's Tea Party.

'I should have been called fucking Alice,' Yank said, and Dee laughed. Dee was nervous but the laugh wasn't. It was loud and it carried.

Some of the men at the back of the convoy climbed onto the roofs of the 4x4s, some levelled guns to keep the girls covered. Yank's throat was dry and she hoped the tic at the side of her face wasn't noticeable. She sipped some coffee and put the cup back in its saucer. Two women climbed out of the rear of the Bentley. They wore shorts and boots and tight t-shirts over large breasts. They had really nailed the Lara Croft look. They hung Uzis on straps from their shoulders as if they were Gucci handbags. They were both taller than Designer Suit.

Yank got to her feet. Dee didn't. Dee stretched her legs out in front of her as if enjoying the day. She held the cup in both hands and sipped. Yank put her hands on her hips. A statement of authority. Behind her she could hear the home guard shouting and making noise. It didn't sound particularly threatening.

'I think you took the wrong road,' she said, her voice loud and clear.

The big man with the black hair and beard laughed. Designer Suit said something to him in an aside, and the big man nodded. They walked forward, the two Lara Crofts a pace behind. A small man, also in a suit, got out of the Bentley and hurried after them. The big man appeared to be armed only with the sawn-off shotgun that was in a holster on his right thigh. It was a big thigh; it could cope.

Yank wondered whether she had made a mistake. Too late now. She had dealt the cards; now she had to play them.

The party stopped at the other side of the table.

'We like this road,' the big man said.

'It's a toll road,' said Yank. 'I don't think you'd like to pay the price.'

'What price is that?'

'You'd lose a lot of people.'

Designer Suit looked past her at the barricade and laughed. 'From that?' he said.

'We're from Haven,' Yank said. 'Maybe you've heard of

us. Richmond is under our protection. Cross that barricade and Haven will mobilise. We'll destroy you.'

'But you'll be dead,' the big man said, staring into her eyes.

'We're from Haven!' Yank shouted, past him, towards his followers. 'This is a no go area! You mess with Haven, you'll have Reaper and the Angel on your ass!'

'What's a Yank doing in the middle of Yorkshire?'

'I'm a UN peacekeeper. Keep the peace and I won't kick your butt.'

'This is bullshit,' Designer Suit said. He was on edge, a bundle of nerves. Maybe the result of too many drugs. He abruptly grabbed the edge of the plastic table and threw it to one side. 'I'll have this one,' he said, and grabbed for Dee who was attempting to stand up. And, inevitably, it kicked off.

He grabbed Dee and the cup she was holding fell and broke on the road surface. He held her in a clumsy embrace as if they were dancing to silent music and he began to giggle. He had his left arm tight round her, so that her right arm was pinioned and she couldn't make a move for the Glock on her hip. His other hand mauled her between the legs.

'I'm going to enjoy you,' he hissed. His mouth close to her neck, his tongue licking her flesh, one thigh now between her legs. His hand had moved to her buttocks. The Lara Crofts were laughing behind him. 'And then they can have you.'

The big man in the black leather reached Yank before she could draw her weapon. He spun her, so that his body pressed against her back. His huge left arm pinned both her arms to her side.

'I admire your balls, Yank. Although I sincerely hope you don't have any.' He laughed and stuck his tongue in her ear.

'Only my friends call me Yank,' she said, and stomped down hard with her heel on his instep. Her arms were held but she could still use her hands. She grabbed his genitals and tried to pull them off. He yelled and let go, attempting to push her to the floor, but she pivoted on her left foot and reverted to her Taekwondo training to deliver a roundhouse kick hard with her right boot as he lowered his head in pain. And then the shooting started.

Dee let Designer Suit maul her bottom and reached behind her with her left hand for the Ladysmith .38 in the back of her belt. She didn't have much room to manoeuvre but she had enough. She shot him in the foot and he screamed and released her and she fell to the ground. She fired two more bullets into him, both body shots. Fuck, she thought. Should be head and chest. Then the man's driver, the small man in the suit, ran into her view and she shot him twice with the two remaining bullets in the gun. It didn't seem to matter that the man was unarmed.

Yank pulled the Glock from its holster, high on adrenalin. The big man, blood coming from his nose, had staggered behind the two Lara Crofts, who were open mouthed in surprise but fumbling with the Uzis. She shot them: chest shots in their large bosoms, totally fatal at such close range, and, as they fell, she saw the big man's fist rising fast clutching the sawn off. Then the single shot from behind her, from the bedroom window where James had been positioned with strict orders. Take out the leaders. And the big man's head exploded in a red mist and he went down for good.

Only now was she aware of the chaos around them. The gunfire and explosions. She grabbed Dee and hauled her to her feet and they ran to the dump truck behind them and launched themselves over the metal sides into the rear bucket where their back-up weapons were waiting.

Yank had attempted to choreograph the carnage in advance. Jenny and Kat were on the tractor, which provided elevation and protection behind its giant wheels. They opened up first on the convoy, Jenny using a light machinegun, propped on its tripod on top of the engine casing, to drive the enemy into cover on the far side of the vehicles. This then gave the four Blues in the bedrooms of the last two houses a clear field of fire into their ranks. Kat used a grenade launcher for added power and, although her first shot didn't go exactly where she intended, it wreaked havoc when it overshot the front of the convoy and landed in the open truck that contained ten ferals. Other grenades landed indiscriminately in and amongst the vehicles.

Kev also had a light machinegun that he wielded in his arms. Nina, in the next room, fired three-shot bursts from an automatic rifle. In the next house, James, the acknowledged sharpshooter of the Blues, used his preferred single shot carbine to pick and take down his targets. Gwen was alone in a box room. She stood at the window, automatic rifle levelled, in plain view of those outside, but had frozen at the noise, chaos and bloodshed outside. People were dying, blood was spurting, limbs being blown from bodies. She shook, mouth open and gasped as if she had sprinted a hundred metres, hyperventilating and unable to react, a feeling of numbness tingling in her fingers, fearful that the dizziness would make her collapse.

Gunfire from below hit the brickwork and windowsill and sent splinters of concrete into her face and it was if a spell was broken. She fired, not accurately. She simply fired the pre-set three bullet bursts, without aiming at targets. When the bullets ran out, she changed the magazine and fired again. An automaton without thought. She didn't want to kill but it was her duty to support her friends. So she kept firing and her breathing settled and, as she calmed, she fired with more purpose and deliberation.

In the dump truck, Dee grabbed an Uzi and knelt up and fired a full magazine of forty rounds in a ten-second burst. She dropped it, picked up a second Uzi and did the same. It was all about firepower, Yank had said. Get their guard down and hit them hard. Yank was throwing hand grenades. She hurled two as far down the convoy as she could before picking up another light machinegun which she rested on the rim of the bucket and added another blitz of bullets. Dee now reached for an automatic rifle; three-shot bursts, straight down the road.

On the tractor, a shotgun blast hit Jenny and knocked her backwards onto the grass below.

'Fuck!' she shouted, a word she would never have used when she had been a schoolteacher.

Kat dropped to her side, a worried and wild look in her eyes.

'Get back up there!' Jenny yelled. 'Take this. Keep killing the bastards!'

The young woman took the offered light machinegun. She had always been fit and athletic and her body felt more powerful than ever with the pulsing excitement of the action. In a second she was back on the side of the tractor, the weapon in its place, and firing again into an enemy that was reeling and hugging cover. Jenny, her left shoulder numb and blood trickling down her face, climbed to rejoin her and used the Glock.

'They're running,' she said, almost in disbelief.

Those that were able were indeed running. The convoy was trapped by the blown-up truck at the rear. Other vehicles blazed and it was impossible to turn any round in the narrow road. In ones and twos, the invaders were running. Back down the road or across the fields on either side. Yank stood up in the bucket and climbed onto the cab of the dump truck and watched them go. There were maybe a dozen in total. Their guns fell silent. All except the single shots from the carbine of James. He was leaning out of the upstairs window and continued to drop the fleeing figures with unerring accuracy. Yank suppressed the doubt that it was cold-blooded murder; it was, as Reaper so often told them, survival. Let them go and they would rape and kill again. They had stepped outside the rules of society and, in this world, there was no way back in.

The Blues gathered in the road. All were sober in the aftermath of the killing, except James. He climbed onto the roof of the Nissan 4x4 to look for targets, found one and shot. Paused and fired again. Then, finally, he lowered his carbine and stepped down to join them.

King Arthur Dobson came from the barricade. He had unsheathed the sword and carried it over one shoulder.

'Is it over?' he said.

'For now,' said Yank.

'You mean they'll be back?'

Yank stopped herself from snapping at the middle-aged man. He was obviously suffering from the stress of the action. Not many civilians had seen a full-blooded gun battle. It would have shaken him and his men. It had probably shaken the new members in the Blues as well. She looked them over as she replied to the leader of the Richmond forces. Everybody was shaken, which was only natural, but of the new recruits only Gwen looked as if she might not cope.

'Nothing is certain, Arthur,' she said. 'We gave them what we intended. A very painful lesson. We've removed their leaders and many of their front line troops. But there are probably another eighty or so more back with the main group. I think we may have persuaded them to go somewhere else. They have the numbers but they can't match our firepower.'

He nodded, relief sloping his shoulders. 'Do you think we should keep the barricade?'

'For the moment, yes. Best to be safe.'

'I'll er, I'll tell the men.' He turned and walked back to the untested barrier in the road behind him.

Yank had noticed the blood on Jenny's face and that her arm hung limply.

'Are you all right?'

'I'll live,' Jenny said, and handed the Glock to Kat. 'I can't reload. My arm …'

Kat took the handgun, released the empty magazine and replaced it with a fresh one. She pulled the slide to put a bullet in the chamber and handed it back. Jenny exchanged a look with Yank and then glanced at the smoking wreckage of the vehicles and the littered bodies. Cries could be heard: of pain, despair, asking for help.

'Somebody has to do it,' Jenny said.

Reaper's rules. Yank nodded, placed her rifle on the ground and took out the Glock. 'You take that side, I'll take this.' She glanced at Kat and Dee. 'Cover,' she said. 'James, top of the dump truck. I doubt they'll come back, but you never know. Kev, collect the weapons. Take them to the side of the road. Gwen, Nina. You bring them back here. Any questions?'

Gwen said, 'What are you going to do?'

She really was on the edge.

'Only what's necessary.'

'It's murder.'

'They made their choices. They're all guilty of capital crimes.'

'But ...'

James said, 'There's no other way, Gwen. We shoot the wounded for good reasons. We haven't the resources to look after them. They'll die anyway without treatment. This is mercy killing.'

She looked shocked at his choice of words.

Jenny said, 'If they live, they'll do it again. There are enough rapists in this world without them.'

Maybe it was the use of the term that stiffened Gwen. Maybe she reflected it was not just her that had been a victim. So had Jenny. So had many women in this brave new world.

'Right,' Yank said, and the Blues went to their allotted tasks.

Gwen, white faced but in control, followed Nina.

Chapter 19

THERE WERE FEW ENOUGH TO SHOOT. Badly injured ones they left to save ammunition. Those who were incapacitated got a bullet in the head. So did those who had just dived for cover when the battle commenced and had remained in hiding ever since. Yank and Jenny allowed no emotion into a task that might have been repellent but which they accepted as a duty. They closed their ears to pleas for mercy. How much mercy had these men shown during their days of pillage on the road? How many women had begged? How many people did they burn in the cathedral at Durham?

One wounded man, half beneath a vehicle, realising what the girls were doing and that there was no way out, raised a handgun and waited for Yank to appear between two cars. Kat, on the other side of the road, saw him first and put a three-bullet burst into his upper body. Yank stopped in mid-stride, assessed the situation, and nodded her thanks.

When they were almost at the end of the convoy, a young blonde woman rose from the last car before the still burning truck, her hands above her head. She wore a dress and carried no weapon. Her make-up had run with crying and she could hardly speak from fear.

'Please. Please…' she said. Other words were lost amidst terror and tears.

Jenny raised her gun, but Yank motioned for her to wait. The girl looked out of place. She was no warrior. She half guessed who she might be.

'I'm not one of them,' she whispered. 'I'm not. Please, I'm not.'

'Where are you from?'

'Neville's Cross. They took me.'

'Where's Neville's Cross?'

'Near Durham. Brewster took me.'

'Who's Brewster?'

'The Big Man. The Leader. They call him Rambo Brewster. He took me.'

'You were his woman?'

The girl's tears started afresh. 'I had no choice. He took me. He said he owned me.' Her arms collapsed and she held her face in her hands and her shoulders shook as she cried.

Jenny said, 'What's your name?' Her voice was soft and understanding. She'd been there.

'Kirsty,' she said.

'Well nobody owns you now, Kirsty,' Jenny said. 'Rambo is dead.'

They counted thirty-six bodies but James said they should add another four to the tally for those he took down at distance as they ran off. They also collected a varied arsenal that showed that, while the invading army might be big, it was not well armed. Shotguns were the main weapons, followed by single shot rifles and eight Uzis or copycat sub-machineguns. There were also about two dozen handguns of various types. Ammunition was limited.

'No wonder we were able to hit them hard,' said Kev.

'No wonder they ran,' said Yank. 'We had surprise and firepower. They were a disorganised mob who had nothing more than numbers.'

'They have more numbers back in the main group,' said Kev.

Yank smiled. 'These were their best. The vanguard. These were the best armed. What have the others got? Slingshots?'

'Of course, we didn't know that,' said Jenny, in a low voice, and Kat chuckled.

James said, 'Fortune smiles on the brave and frowns upon the coward.' The others looked at him and he added, 'It's a Latin proverb – from Ancient Rome.'

'Well, she sure smiled on us today,' said Yank.

At which point they heard gunfire in the distance.

'Oh shit,' said Dee.

'Back to positions,' said Yank, turning to return to the dump truck.

The Blues dispersed. They waited, nerves again strung taught, guns ready and, minutes later, Yank saw, through her binoculars, two black BMW 4x4s coming along the road towards them.

'I don't believe it,' she said. 'I don't fucking believe it. Hold your fire!' She had seen the Saltire pennants. 'It's the Scots!'

Yank climbed on top of the cab of the dump truck and waved. The two approaching cars stopped and Sandy Cameron got out of the lead vehicle, levelled field glasses to identify her and waved in response. He got back in the BMW and the both vehicles turned off the road and into a field to avoid the wrecks and impassible debris. They parked alongside the end house and Cameron and his three men climbed out. They seemed amazed at the smoking clutter and bodies.

'Good God,' Cameron said. He stood for a moment, hands on hips, taking in a scene from hell. Yank approached and they shook hands. 'Any casualties?' he said.

Jenny appeared, still bloodstained.

'We got off lightly,' Yank said. 'What was the shooting?'

'The ones who got away. We drove into them.'

'Were they organised?'

'No. Just running.'

She grinned and took a deep breath of relief. 'And what the hell are you doing here?' she said.

'We heard about Newcastle and came to keep a watching brief. They could have turned north. We knew ye widnae hear about them.' He smiled. 'We thought ye might appreciate an intelligence report on numbers and potential. But ye seem to have had it covered.'

'Not completely. There are still more of them.'

'True, but they were disorganised to begin with and after this...' His gaze swept the battlefield '... they'll no be back.' He continued looking at the bodies. 'No prisoners?' he said.

'No prisoners.'

'Did ye get the leaders?'

'We think so. A big guy in black leather and a smaller guy in a designer suit with two well endowed girlfriends.'

'That's them. So they'll be completely lost. Power vacuum. One or two may fight for dominance. Mair likely they'll break up intae gangs, go different ways.'

'It would be nice to finish it,' Yank said. 'But I don't fancy driving into open country to take the rest on.'

'They'd run,' Cameron said.

'They might not. I can't take that risk. Reaper might, but I can't.'

'Where is he?'

'He went to Redemption. Scouting operation. He and Sandra went before we heard about this lot.'

'I see your problem.'

'My priority is to protect Haven.'

He nodded in agreement and turned to the young Scot standing closest. 'Bad luck, Duggan,' he said with a smile. 'Sandra's away south.' Duggan blushed but said nothing.

Yank said, 'Come and meet King Arthur and have something to eat. He's behind the barricade. We're staying here until our own scout gets back and tells us what's happening.'

*   *   *

Kev and Nina remained on lookout in one of the houses and the others retreated behind the barricade.

'Are you okay?' Kev asked.

'I'm better than I thought I'd be. I'm still alive and I'm worried.'

'Worried?'

'Because I don't feel guilt.'

'There's no guilt. They made their choices. We had no choice. We had to stop them. We had to kill them. It's been said before… if we don't, they'll do it again. The time to feel guilty would be if we let them go and they raped again. Or killed again. Ask the next victim which would they prefer? I know which they'd pick.'

'I didn't think I could be so cold blooded about it.'

'You're not because you're still worried.' He put an arm out, wrapped it around her shoulders and gave her a squeeze. 'It's not your fault, Nina. It's their fault.'

She allowed the intimacy for a moment then moved gently away. She nodded. 'I know.'

She remembered. She knew.

*   *   *

Arthur sent for Richmond's medic, a young man who had been in the St John's Ambulance Brigade. He cleaned the wound on Jenny's face and dressed it with a temporary pad and bandage that covered her left eye. He was embarrassed when she removed her Kevlar vest and cut off her t-shirt to reveal the wound on her left shoulder. He cleaned it, applied another dressing and put her arm in a sling.

'You need a doctor,' he said. 'There are probably pellets in there and I'm not sure I can take them out.'

Jenny was positive he couldn't take them out. The sight of her white bra had made his hands tremble and she didn't think he would have enough composure to wield a pair of tweezers in an open wound with any success.

Yank took the medic's report and joined Jenny.

'You should get back and let Greta treat that wound,' she said.

'I'll wait awhile. See what's happening.'

'We've got Cameron and his boys. We can spare you, Jenny. You need attention.'

'Don't we all?' She grinned. 'Thanks, but I'll wait till the scout gets back.'

'Car!' shouted the boy on the barricade, and he pointed back towards Richmond.

Yank stood up and stared. 'It's one of ours,' she said. She raised the binoculars. 'It's Sandra!'

Sandra was riding shotgun and Pete Mack was driving. When she jumped out of the car, she immediately saw Jenny and said, 'What happened?'

'We faced off the ferals,' said Yank.

Cameron shook his head. 'It was a wee bit more than that.'

'Okay, we beat the shit out of them.'

Sandra shook hands with Cameron, touched fists with Yank and raised a hand in greeting to Arthur at the barricade. She went to Jenny and said, 'You need to get back to Haven.'

'I've already told her, but she thinks she's indispensable,' said Yank.

'She is. We need you treated and ready to go again,' Sandra said softly to Jenny. 'We've got a bigger war coming with Redemption.' She looked up and shouted: 'Kat! Get your vehicle! You're taking Jenny back now.'

Jenny's shoulders slumped a little but she didn't argue. If there was a new battle looming, she needed treatment. The two girls left immediately and Sandra turned to Yank and said, 'Tell me again. What happened.'

'Come and take a look,' she said.

They walked around the barricade and Sandra and Pete stopped at the sight before them. Sandra was both shocked and impressed.

'Jesus, Anna,' she said. 'And our only casualty was Jenny?'

'We were lucky,' Yank said softly. 'We staged an ambush and they were too cocky to see it.' She paused as they surveyed the desolation. In a soft voice, she added, 'Everybody was great, Sandra. They stood and they fought.'

Sandra nodded. They didn't know it yet, but they would have to stand and fight again, very soon.

After Yank had described the encounter, Brian reported on the make-up of the invasion force and how they had behaved in Durham and Darlington. Cameron added what he could and described how they ran into the remnants of the defeated.

'They were broken,' he said. 'They had nae fight left in them.'

Yank said, 'I had half a mind to follow up and hit them again before they could organize. But that was, maybe, a risk too far.'

Sandra nodded. 'You did the right thing. They'll try somewhere else now.'

'But that's the problem, isn't it?' said Yank. 'Somewhere else might not be able to fight back.'

Cameron added, 'Somewhere else might be us.'

If Redemption wasn't demanding attention, Sandra would have had no hesitation. She would have followed up the victory with an attack of their own. But?

The boy on the barricade shouted: 'Rider!' And, a moment later, 'It's Charlie!'

The second scout from Northallerton drove his motorcycle onto the field and approached slowly. When he got off the machine, he stared in amazement at the bodies and wrecks of vehicles. He stared at the men from Richmond who were peering over the barricade, at the Blues and the Scots standing to one side, and at Sandra and Yank who were forward of everyone else with Cameron and Brian. He walked towards them, almost in shock, a man in late middle age, wearing jeans, walking boots and a green military camouflage jacket. He was six feet tall, lean and, like Brian, looked capable. Around his neck was a pair of binoculars.

'Bloody hell!' he said to the two girls. 'You don't mess about, do you?'

'It made them run,' Brian said.

'Oh, I saw them running,' Charlie said. 'They ran straight into the convoy. Caused chaos. Panic, people arguing, some turning their cars round, others forming a barricade. Some have already headed back to Scotch Corner.' He looked from one to the other: Sandra, Yank and Cameron. 'One more push and the balance will go.'

'The balance?' Sandra said.

'You've taken out the worst of them and they were top heavy to start with. Now there are only seventy or eighty of the bastards, and they're not exactly the crème de la crème, and a hundred and thirty or more slaves and gofers. All it needs is another push and you'll have a Spartacus reaction.'

'Spartacus reaction?' Yank said.

Brian said, 'Charlie was a history teacher.'

'One push,' he said, 'and you'll have a slave revolt and that lot will be finished.'

Sandra and Yank glanced at each other. Sandra looked at Cameron. He grinned and said, 'Count us in.'

*   *   *

The two scouts went first on motorbikes, carrying Clansman radios to provide intelligence: Brian to check on the strength of the barricade across the road; Charlie back into the woods above Scotch Corner.

Sandra and Pete Mack were in the lead Range Rover. They went at speed, through the deserted village of Skeeby, around an S bend and paused. Brian radioed in. There was four hundred yards of empty straight road ahead of them, then another slight bend and, according to Brian, another four hundred yards before the barricade. Beyond that was another bend and a short distance to Scotch Corner. The wood from where Charlie was watching, was on the hill to the left.

Brian reported there was still chaos at the barricade, which was a lot less substantial than the one built on the outskirts of Richmond, and the rest of the convoy was strung out all the way to the hotel and service area on the A1.

Cameron and the two vehicles flying the Saltire turned off the road and into the field to the right. Yank and Dee took the left flank across the fields, teamed with the Rover of Kev and Nina. Sandra and Pete stayed on the road, Gwen and James alongside them, the two vehicles filling both lanes. Sandra gave final instructions over the Clansman radios and added, 'No heroics. Let's just get it done.'

The two Rovers on the road went quickly, took the slight bend side by side, and saw the barrier ahead: two cars echelon parked forming a V. They stopped a hundred yards short and ignored the feeble barrage from two or three shotguns.

On the radio came the voice of Brian: 'They're already running. Over.'

James climbed out of his Rover and onto the roof. He aimed the grenade launcher and fired. The car on the left blew up, orange flame and a cloud of acrid smoke. The burning vehicle was pushed backwards into the hedge, creating a gap.

He jumped down and got back in. Pete started forward in the other car, Sandra leaning out of the rear passenger window firing an Uzi. It was inaccurate but had the right angry sound and she was using the rear window so she could hold it in her right hand rather than her left, to keep it pointing in the right direction. As one magazine emptied, she dropped the gun in the rear foot well and picked up another, but by then they were through the broken roadblock.

The other cars of their attack force were paralleling the road, the occupants shooting at targets with discrimination.

They didn't want to take down innocents in their onslaught, only the guilty, and at first it was only the guilty who were at this end of the road. They scythed them like grass. The two cars on the road soon had to stop because of abandoned and bullet damaged vehicles in front of them.

Charlie in the wood radioed: 'They're shooting civilians at Scotch Corner. The revolt has started. Over.'

Cameron had also heard and now his voice came on the line: 'On our way. Over and out.'

'Shit,' said Sandra.

'We've still got work here,' said Pete, and she realised he was right, as shots were being fired in their direction and hitting the Rover. The rear window starred from a shotgun blast. 'Everybody out!' he shouted.

They bailed out as their second Rover stopped behind them and James and Gwen also took to the road. Sandra had an Uzi, Pete a light machinegun, James a carbine and Gwen an automatic rifle set for three shot bursts. They moved cautiously but swiftly among the abandoned vehicles but their firepower was too daunting for the opposition. Some were taken down by accurate, dispassionate shooting, some indiscriminately by bursts from the Uzi and machinegun. Those who had stayed to fight now ran or attempted to surrender.

'No quarter!' Sandra shouted, although the noise of the guns had already half deafened them, but no words were needed. They all knew Reaper's rules and it soon dawned on their enemy that the only course of action was to run. Not many made it.

As they went further up the road, the vehicles became transports, caravans, mobile homes, and they saw the frightened faces of men and women, and some children, peering at them from inside.

'It's okay!' Sandra shouted. 'You're okay! You will be safe. We only want the ferals. If they're hiding among you, throw them out! You will be safe. We're Haven! Reaper and the Angel. You will be safe!'

A shot was fired in one van and then a man was thrown out of the back door. He fell on the ground and looked round in fear and half got to his feet to run before Sandra shot him. A short burst from the Uzi that spit chips along the road surface before it stitched into his body. There were the sounds of scuffles in vans, another shot and this time the body that came out was already dead.

This part of the battle seemed to be in its dying embers.

*　　　*　　　*

It hadn't taken much. Just the spark that Charlie had suggested and the revolt had happened. They estimated afterwards that maybe a dozen of the ferals escaped. Yank's two-car squadron on the left flank had taken out most as they tried to break. Cameron and the Scots had simply tidied up at Scotch Corner itself, where the captives had seen the balance of power tilt and had taken advantage. The slaves had lost people in the fight but, where they had captured ferals, they had taken a terrible revenge. After all, Charlie said afterwards, they were entitled. Their suffering had been terrible.

Sandra itched to get back to Haven to start planning the move south and the rescue of Reaper, but once the fighting was done, there were still the survivors to look after. As Charlie said, they had suffered and were still in a daze from their experience and sudden freedom. They needed advice about where to go. Richmond, Northallerton and Haven would all offer sanctuary, or they could go home.

King Arthur came with a small delegation and their medic to give aid and advice, and Charlie and Brian also helped this disparate group that numbered more than a hundred. Sandra knew the young women who had been used as sex slaves would certainly need understanding and compassion. They did what they could. Most of the girls in the Blues knew what these victims had gone through. They moved among them, touching, talking, holding, helping. Some of the girls were very young and Gwen had tears in her eyes.

Yank put an arm round her shoulder and said, 'Now you see why we do what we do? It's the only way.' She squeezed her. 'Why don't you go to them. Just being there helps.' And Gwen went to two girls who looked no more than twelve and simply held them. For a few moments, they remained wide-eyed and in shock. And then the realisation

275

sank in, the comfort was felt, the humanity of an embrace, and they cried.

'This needed doing,' Yank said to Sandra, and she nodded her agreement.

This was a deliverance and it had needed doing. Another war won and another to fight.

Chapter 20

REAPER WAS TRANSPORTED to Banbury in the back of a military truck. It stopped at a civic building and he was transferred into the back of a Transit van for a twenty minute drive made in total blackness. When the rear doors opened again, the van was in an enclosed yard alongside a large house.

He was led down outside stone steps and put in a cellar that had one small horizontal window at ceiling level. The cellar contained a camp bed and an old-fashioned kitchen sink. There was no other furniture. He guessed that the yellow plastic bucket was his toilet. At least it had been washed out. The sink's single tap worked so he had water, although it was probably unfit for drinking. A bottle of water was by the bed.

The room was about four metres square with whitewashed plaster walls and a stone flagged floor. He lay on a camp bed, put his hands behind his head and wondered how long they would make him wait.

He woke early when first light provided poor illumination through the high window. He got up, had a piss in the sink and turned on the tap to rinse it clean, and lay down again. An hour later, wide awake, he exercised. Push ups, sit ups, physical jerks. He worked up a sweat and lay down again and waited some more.

The day dragged on. Nobody came. He became hungrier, but that was their intention. Make him uncomfortable, make him worry about what was to happen, make him nervous. He napped. He had another drink. He did more exercises. He napped again. The hours dragged. He tried not to make plans. It would be better if he just reacted. He thought of Greta and a future together. He thought of Sandra and wondered when she would find another chap. He thought how the dying of the old world had given him a new life. But that was the same for everyone. For some, the new life would never compare to what had been lost. For him, it had been a chance at redemption. But not this Redemption.

He thought of his daughter, a suicide at fourteen. The hurt was as deep as ever. He thought of the crime that had caused her to take her own life. Back then, when the world was supposed to have been civilised, men raped. Now that society's safeguards had gone, men raped more than ever. A vile crime that was often worse than murder. Had men always been prone to such evil?

Throughout history, it had always been a by-product of war. Part of the victor's spoils. Defeat the enemy, sack the city and take the women. Give men the veneer of a social life, jobs, wages and respectability, and most would never contemplate abusing women: they were the fairer sex, to be protected. But how soon respectability was shed when there was nobody to enforce the law, the rules, the moral code.

Was it any different here, under the New Army of General Purcell?

He fell asleep when the darkness deepened and was startled from a dream that was instantly forgotten when they came in the dead of night. A bright torch shone in his face, a boot kicked the camp bed. 'Up, up!' said the voice. Harsh, brutal, portending pain.

Reaper got to his feet and was pushed towards the door. He couldn't see clearly but guessed there were two of them. He took a step before he remembered to limp. He turned it into a stagger, his hands out like a blind man. Someone knocked his arm away.

He stumbled up the outside stone steps into a cool night. The air was fresh and pleasant, a scent of some kind of blossom he couldn't identify. He was pushed and guided by the beam of a torch, along a path at the back of the house. Light spilled from an open doorway. He was shoved inside and stumbled again, held his leg and winced.

The room was a scullery. A washing machine, drier, freezer and refrigerator lined one wall. It was lit by electric light. They had a generator. Two doors led from it. One of the guards moved past him and opened one of them and pushed him again. It was a room without windows and a stone flagged floor. The walls were plaster and had at one time been white. Now they were dirty and patchy. A kitchen table was in the middle of the room, two hardback chairs either side of it. The only light in the room came from a high-powered desk lamp on an adjustable arm, that was pointed at the one vacant chair on his side of the table. A man sat in the other chair. The shadows made it difficult to see him but he was bulky and silent. A brown cardboard file was on the table next to the lamp.

A second table was against a wall. Upon it were pincers, pliers and DIY tools that could also be used as weapons of torture. Two large hooks had been embedded in another wall; chains hung from them. They hung nicely over stains on the plaster that could very easily be blood.

A guard pushed him to the vacant chair and he sat down.

'Good morning,' Reaper said.

The hulk in the shadows said nothing. The two guards remained behind him, standing either side of the door, which they had closed.

They waited.

At last, the hulk said, 'Name?'

Reaper said, 'Tom Watson. And you are?'

'Where are you from?'

'The Welsh borders.'

'Whereabouts?'

'That's close enough.'

'No it isn't.'

'Perhaps I'm missing something here, but I came looking for organisation, leadership, a new beginning. Prince Harry, for God's sake. I came to offer my services as a pilot. And what do I get? Shot down, locked up, kept in a cellar and now given a third degree straight out of a B movie and instruments of torture from Hammer horror. Now we both know my value as a pilot. You start damaging me and I may never fly again. As it is, you've hurt my leg and it's going to be at least ten days before I can get up in a kite again. So cut the bullshit and take me to your leader. Or at least back to that camp bed. I was having a very nice dream when your goons woke me up. Jane Fonda in her heyday. Remember Barbarella?'

Silence again. The hulk twitched. This was not going the way he had intended. He opened the file, took out a map and unfolded it on the table. He thumped it. 'Show me where you came from,' he said forcefully.

'No.'

A long pause. Reaper suspected the man did not have too many brain cells and his attitude was challenging the three that were active. 'No?' Pause. 'Why not?' He sounded genuinely puzzled.

'Because I have another aircraft there and I don't want you sending a lorry load of idiots to tie it to a tow truck and haul it back here.'

The hulk scratched his head. Maybe he was trying to find another brain cell. 'We can hurt you.'

'No you can't,' Reaper said patiently. 'I've already explained why.'

'We can starve you.'

'Now that is plain stupid. Why would you want to?'

'So you'll tell us what we want to know.'

'What is it that you want to know?'

'Where you come from.'

'No problem. I'll take you there when my leg's better. But I'm not telling you. Now, unless you can provide me with a cup of tea and a bacon sandwich, perhaps you can get your chums to take me back to my room. You are beginning to piss me off.'

The man got up suddenly and kicked his chair back across the room with a clatter. He took two strides around the table and pulled back his right fist as if to swing a punch. A bulky man, overweight, with broad shoulders, a beard and small eyes. He had a sergeant's stripes on his uniform and was wearing black leather gloves. Probably had delicate knuckles that needed protection when beating up prisoners. Reaper didn't move. He was almost sure a blow would exceed the chap's authority. He didn't throw one. Instead, he turned around and returned to the shadows.

'Take him back,' he said, and the guards escorted him back to the cellar and the camp bed.

*   *   *

He completed his limited ablutions in the dawn light and waited for Round Two. Two guards came again. He didn't know if they were the same two. They wore combat uniform and black berets and side arms. The day was cloudy but warm. He was taken into the scullery and along a shadowed corridor, into the wide hall of a handsome house. He was guided upstairs and into a bathroom.

A guard said, 'There's hot water,' and they left him.

A stack of white towels, fresh underwear and socks and a blue Polo shirt.

Reaper stripped and showered. It was a wallow in luxury. They were extravagant with their display of oil-fired affluence. He washed his hair and shaved, dressed in the clean items and threw his old ones in a bin. He felt better already and suspected the bacon sandwich might not be beyond the realms of possibility. He exited the bathroom and rejoined the waiting guards who took him downstairs. One knocked at a door, opened it and he was ushered inside.

The room was wood panelled and had a dining table with a dozen chairs round it and an array of dishes on a long sideboard. He could smell the bacon. A man who could only be General Purcell was already at the table, eating breakfast. A neat man who sat erect and used his knife and fork precisely. He looked up and nodded a greeting.

'Help yourself,' he said.

The guards departed and Reaper limped to the sideboard and heaped bacon, sausage, eggs and fried tomato onto a plate and cut himself a wedge of bread. Tea and coffee were both on offer and he poured himself a mug of black coffee. He took the food and the drink to the table and sat opposite the general.

The general smiled and said, 'Eat. Plenty of time to talk.'

He ate. Purcell finished, refreshed his cup with tea and walked to the window to stare out at the garden. He sipped the tea, comfortable in a silence broken only by Reaper devouring the food. It did not take Reaper long. He was starving. When he had finished, Purcell returned to the table and held out his hand. Reaper stood up and shook it.

'I'm General Purcell.'

'Tom Watson.'

'I hope you didn't mind last night's little pantomime?'

Reaper shrugged and said, 'I much prefer this approach. My compliments to your cook.'

They resumed their seats.

'Ah, Adams. He's indispensable. Not much of a soldier but he looks after me well. The *other* approach was standard military procedure.' He smiled again and Reaper couldn't tell whether the man was being patronising or sincere. He also didn't think being threatened in a cellar in the middle of the night was standard military procedure, but who was he to dispute the point? 'I never did think it would work with you. As you made quite clear, you know your worth.'

'I've had time to consider it. I estimate we are getting down to the bare bones of civilisation. A few more gone and we may never recover. That's why I came here. It seems you have started the recovery. Stopped the rot. It seemed to be the best place for me and somewhere I could be useful.' Reaper fixed Purcell with a look. 'And be rewarded for my usefulness.'

Purcell nodded. 'I admire both your honesty and your grasp of the new reality. We live in a meritocracy. Skills and leadership will always be rewarded. And you have a very special skill.'

'There were 30,000 pilots in the UK before the virus,' he said, re-quoting de Courcy. 'I reckon maybe a dozen survived. Take out the suicides and the victims and the ones who went insane, and there are not a lot left.' Purcell nodded. 'Which makes me, as you say, special. What makes me more special is that I can teach others to fly.'

He saw the gleam in the general's eyes. This was a development Purcell had not considered.

'You can teach?'

'Back at my modest HQ, I have everything you need to teach others – including a simulator.'

'A simulator?'

'Nearest thing you'll get to flying without leaving your living room. The latest technology, before technology collapsed, that can help those with the right aptitude become a pilot.'

'It's that good?'

'It is.'

'And you can do this?'

'I can. This is for light aircraft but, with your backing, we can find other simulators, more advanced, so that pilots with the basic knowledge can learn to fly helicopters and jets.'

'These simulators exist?'

'They have them at Heathrow, Gatwick and Manchester airports. They must be at other places, too. And I've landed at RAF airfields in the north. There are jet fighters just waiting for a team of mechanics to give them a service and they would be ready to go.'

Purcell was obviously interested but controlled his emotions well. 'You believe that all this is a possibility?'

'I know it is, general. You could have a real air force.'

The general nodded as if it made perfect sense so Reaper fed him some more.

'When the military units moved south to join you, they destroyed all weapons and explosives they couldn't carry.' He shrugged. 'It made sense to be cautious. But there is one RAF station I know that has a bunker full of missiles. It's sealed and safe and ready when we are. I'm not just talking about an air force, general. I'm talking about air power.'

'Which station?'

'It's in Yorkshire. But it's safe. No one else can access it. The missiles will wait until we have the pilots. It was up there that I found a mechanic. He's waiting for me back at base.'

'A mechanic as well? You seem to have been very fortunate.'

'He was a motor mechanic. I introduced him to aircraft engines. He is now first class and a trained man on the ground is indispensable. There are plenty of light aircraft sitting on airfields and in hangars, but it takes time to make sure they're safe. It's a long way down if something goes wrong. That's another reason to go back. For my mechanic and an aircraft I know I can trust.' Reaper gave the general a smile of optimism and caution across the table. 'Of course, at the moment there's just me and a mechanic. But I've had time to think things through. This mission you have undertaken will take years. Building an air force will be a slow process, but I guarantee you'll have your first pilots flying light aircraft within three months. Once they're proficient, some can move on to helicopters. Easier than road transport, excellent for fast troop movement. The best pilots can move on to jet simulators. That will take a lot longer. But in, say, eighteen months time, you could have a jet fighter at your command.' Reaper worried momentarily that he was laying it on a bit thick, but it seemed exactly what Purcell wanted to hear.

'Mr Watson, if you deliver only a fraction of what you promise, you will be an undoubted asset and will be very welcome here in Redemption. The rewards will be considerable. We shall endeavour to make up for the rudeness of your arrival and the loss of your aircraft.'

'No problem. I was probably flying too low and invited trouble.' He patted his leg and said, 'There's no lasting damage.'

'As regards your leg, I shall have our medical people do what they can. As regards an airfield, there is one that might be suitable not far from here at Hinton – the other side of the M40. Or you could scout around the village to see if there is anything suitable?'

'Is Hinton in good repair?'

'I shall ensure that it is.'

'Then that will be fine.'

'As regards Redemption itself, you may have questions?'

'Not really. I know the mine is a work camp and that you operate other camps for troublemakers.'

The general raised an eyebrow.

'They put me in the canteen at the mine and the cook was talkative. I was impressed with what I heard. Redemption has discipline, control, an army, a civilian population and a plan for the future. What you have created isn't just a chance for survival. It's the start of a new nation. I'd like to be part of it.'

Reaper had taken his attempt at 'sincerity' as close to patronising as he dared and hoped Purcell would accept it. Megalomaniacs usually did. Purcell did.

'I think we will get along, Mr Watson. We share a vision

that others are often too small-minded to see. But there is one thing you haven't asked me about, and I am intrigued to know why?'

'You mean Prince Harry?'

'I do, indeed, mean Prince Harry.'

'A popular figurehead always appeals to the masses and you can't get much more popular than Harry. But he's a fake. Everything I've heard about Redemption has centred around you, General, not Harry.'

He could see Purcell was again flattered.

'You seem very sure, Mr Watson.'

'The real Harry has a pilot's license. In fact, he has more than that. He can fly both fixed wing and helicopters and he's a qualified instructor. By now, you would have had Harry – or the men he's trained – flying reconnaissance all over the country. I haven't seen any. I wonder why?'

Purcell smiled. 'The real Prince Harry would be too valuable to risk in an aircraft.'

'Maybe, but I'm still betting the one you've got is a fake. He's a figurehead. But he's a fake. Am I right?'

Purcell said, 'You'll find out at dinner, Mr Watson. I do hope you will join us?'

Chapter 21

REAPER SPENT THE DAY IN BROWNLEY HOUSE. He had the run of the place and explored as much as good manners allowed. Guards were few; they were not deemed necessary during the absence of the General, but two were outside patrolling front and back, and two were inside, trying not to appear to be keeping an eye on him. Also inside was Adams, the General's batman, who was always available to provide coffee, sandwiches for lunch, and fresh clothes.

'I would guess you are a 42 chest, 33 waist and medium leg, sir,' he said.

'Close enough.'

'Sixteen and a half collar?'

'Seventeen.'

'Nine shoe?'

'Eight and a half.'

'Sir will need a change of clothes. I shall see what I can find.'

'That's good of you.'

'It's what I do, sir.'

'What you do?'

'I facilitate the smooth running of the household, sir. For the good of the General. He likes things to run smoothly. That's what I do.'

Adams wore the regular combat uniform that other soldiers wore but did not look much like a fighting man. He was in his middle thirties and there was a softness about him. He carried a little too much weight and his uniform fit particularly well, as if he had tailored it himself. He was medium height with dark hair that was short and neat with a side parting, and a regular but expressionless face like a blank canvas.

A paramedic, dressed in the familiar green trousers and shirt of the civilian ambulance service, still with an NHS badge on the right breast, turned up with an army corporal wearing a Red Cross armband, to look at his leg.

'The MO is busy,' said the corporal. 'If your leg is serious, we'll take you to the medical centre.'

'It's not serious,' Reaper said. 'Just a sprain. It's inconvenient more than anything but it's getting better. I shouldn't be wasting your time.' The paramedic gave his leg a cursory examination and they shared a stare which suggested he knew there was nothing wrong with it. 'I'll be fine in a couple of days.'

The MO, he discovered, was an army doctor who was conducting a minor operation at military headquarters in Banbury. The corporal was training with the paramedic.

'You're not a member of the Tans, then?' Reaper said.

The corporal rolled his eyes but said nothing.

'Perhaps when you're fully trained? Then you'll join the elite?'

'The elite?' The corporal was on the verge of saying something more but the paramedic said, 'Andy…' a warning that caused him to be less forthright than perhaps he might have been.

'I'm in the army, sir,' he said. 'A professional soldier. That'll do for me.'

After they had gone, Adams served Reaper coffee. Reaper suggested the batman stay and join him. He wouldn't sit or take coffee but he did stay. Reaper noticed the generator had been switched off in Purcell's absence.

'How long have you been with the General?'

'Since London, sir. I joined the New Army in London.'

'That was before Windsor?'

'Yes, sir. We were a small group then, but the General had a vision and he made it happen. He was the sort of officer to follow.'

'Were you in the regulars?'

'I had been, sir. Twelve years in the Catering Corps.'

'Do they still call it the Catering Corps?'

'Actually, they called it Logistics. I don't know why they changed it. Perhaps they thought it didn't sound warlike. But the Catering Corpse has served everywhere and with everyone, including the SAS and the Paras. I didn't.'

Adams was happy to talk. Reaper was a civilian – until

he became a Wing Commander – and perhaps the batman felt more at ease. His world seemed to revolve around the General.

'Why did you pick the Catering Corps?'

'To learn a trade.' He smiled. 'Simple as that. I went to the Army School of Catering, got my City and Guilds, and had the finest training possible.'

'But you weren't in the army when you met the General?'

'No. When I left the service, I went into the kitchens at a four star London hotel. When you can cater for squaddies in a field kitchen, a hotel is a piece of piss. Sir.'

Reaper smiled and said, 'I'm sure it is.'

'Then I moved to the Savoy after its refurbishment. Trained at the Savoy Academy and became a butler. It was one of the happiest periods of my life. I was working in the finest hotel in London. Arguably the most glamorous hotel in the world. I felt I had come home.'

It made sense to Reaper. Adams seemed to glide about Brownley, appearing when needed as if summoned by telepathy. He was calm and unflappable. A perfect butler and a perfect batman.

'Were you married?'

'Divorced. A service marriage. There were no children.'

Reaper nodded. 'In a sense, you were lucky.'

'I agree, sir. Luckier than most. I was at the Savoy when the end happened.'

'What was it like? London? The Savoy? When it happened?'

Adams did not speak immediately. Instead, he topped up Reaper's coffee cup from the silver pot. When he had resumed his position, legs slightly apart, hands cupped gracefully at his front, he replied.

'People didn't believe it could happen. Not at first. Trains stopped running, the Tube closed, there were no buses. Soon very little traffic. Guests had stopped coming and many of those who remained tried to get home. The ones who lived in Britain had a chance but our clients came from all over the world. They were stranded. Then there were a few who decided to stay and sit it out regardless. The spirit of the Titanic, Sir Geoffrey called it. He died in the Beaufort Bar. I moved him back to his suite.'

'You stayed at the hotel?'

'A few of us did. You were not just staff, you were part of tradition. You were the Savoy. At the very end, three of us were left. Myself, an American gentleman called Winslow and a Peruvian lady, a Mrs Vargas. The gentleman was in his middle years and had been on holiday with his daughter. She had become ill with influenza and he assumed she was infected with the virus. He kept her in isolation in her room and they missed their chance to return to the United States while flights were still available. Her illness was actually unrelated to the virus. But, once she recovered from the flu, she became a victim.

'Mr Winslow had no other close family. He was a widower. He was a gallant gentleman. Mrs Vargas was an elderly lady. Her husband died at the hotel leaving her alone. She was confused and bereft. Mr Winslow shot her before he shot himself. He also gave me the option of a bullet but I declined.'

Reaper said, 'I've heard many stories about what happened. I'm amazed they can still have an effect.' He shook his head sadly. 'You tend to think of what happened in world terms. The end of civilisation as we know it. But what it came down to was the end of individual life stories, personal tragedies.'

They shared a silence, a token remembrance to the departed.

'What happened to you?' Reaper asked. 'Did you stay at the hotel?'

'There was nowhere else to go. I had a cellar of the finest wines and a kitchen of the finest foods and my choice of suites. But London soon became a dangerous place. I locked the doors against scavengers and that worked, at first. The location helped. People went looting in the West End. There were plenty of hotels on Piccadilly and Park Lane. Buckingham Palace was an attraction, I learned later. There was a minor incursion when someone tried to enter. A group of four. They smashed a window. I fired a shot to deter them. I had Mr Winslow's revolver. But one of them fired both barrels of a shotgun at me. Smashed a chandelier. So I shot him. They soon left then. Easier pickings elsewhere. I left his body there to deter others. And then the General arrived.'

'He came to the Savoy?'

'Four days later. He had six soldiers with him. You don't know how reassuring it was to see those uniforms. I heard them outside, saw the way he handled himself. A born officer. I actually thought martial law had been declared. Here, at last, was law and order. I unlocked the front doors and let him in. I served him gin and tonic in the American Bar and told him of my military career. And do you know what he said? He said, "Right, Adams. You'll come with me. You'll be my batman and you will be at the side of history. You will watch the birth of a new nation." And I am, sir. And I shall.'

'Lucky he went to the Savoy.'

'Not really. He said it was a pilgrimage. He had always celebrated important events at the Savoy. His commission, his engagement, his wedding, his divorce. His return from active duty, his awards for gallantry.'

'The birth of a new nation.'

'Exactly, sir.'

Reaper paused, sitting in an easy chair, a cup of coffee in his hand. Adams standing before him, at his ease and ready to perform his duties. Anxious to be of service.

'You like the General?'

'I like order, sir. The General provides it.'

'You know about the work camps?'

'It is always necessary to break a few eggs, sir.'

'For the greater good?'

'Exactly.'

Reaper nodded as if he agreed. 'Tell me about Prince Harry.'

'I'd rather not, sir. It's not my place to speak of His Royal Highness. You'll meet him this evening, in any case. Dinner will be at seven.'

*   *   *

When Reaper retired to the bedroom to which he had been assigned, he found a grey lounge suit on a hanger behind the door. On the bed were two shirts, still in cellophane wrappers, a choice of ties, a pair of navy blue slacks and a short-sleeved shirt in a lighter blue with patch pockets and epaulettes. Draped over a chair was a leather jacket with fur lining. He guessed these latter items comprised the start of his flying uniform. More items of underwear and socks were on the chair, and a pair of black shoes beneath it.

Adams had trained in the Army, which had been a kind of home environment, trained again at the Savoy, which had become his declared home, and, when the world ended, had found his final reason for life as valet, batman and butler for the man who was building a new Albion.

Reaper didn't know whether to pity or admire Adams. His needs were simple: he had found his role and would follow wherever it led. Like the Nazis who were tried at Nuremberg.

As evening approached, the generator was switched on and Reaper luxuriated under the shower and shaved and added a touch of cologne that was among the items in the well-stocked bathroom. He dressed in the suit with a white shirt and blue tie. He hadn't dressed like this in years and stared at a stranger in the full-length mirror in the corner of the room. What on earth would Sandra have said?

Two days and, if everything went according to plan, he would guide a team of soldiers to the White Cottage and Sandra and the Blues would be waiting to set him free. He wondered if he would get really lucky? Could he persuade the General to go with them?

It was 6.30 and Reaper wondered whether he should go downstairs. A discreet knock on the door relieved him of the decision. He opened it to reveal Adams holding a tray upon which was a sparkling drink.

'G and T, sir?'

'That's absolutely perfect, Adams.' Reaper took the drink. 'How do you do it?'

'Savoy trained, sir.' He ran a practised eye down Reaper. 'And may I say, sir, that you wear the suit superbly. You have the physique for fine clothes.'

'Steady on, Adams. This is only our second date.' They

shared a grin and Reaper added: 'What's the form?'

'The drawing room in five minutes and dinner prompt at seven. Your fellow guests are Prince Harry, the Honourable Judith Finlay, Colonels Barstow and Maidstone and, of course, the General.'

'Who are Barstow and Maidstone?'

'Colonel Bardstow leads the Tans. Ex-SAS.' He tipped his head slightly. 'A bit of a rough diamond. Colonel Maidstone commands the regular forces based in Banbury.'

'And the Honourable ...'

'Judith Finlay. She is Prince Harry's companion.'

'Delicately phrased.' Reaper finished the drink, put the glass back on the tray and licked his lips. 'You make a bloody good gin and tonic, Adams.'

'It has been said before, sir.'

Reaper looked towards the stairs and said, 'Now?'

'Now would be good, sir.'

The General was absent but the other guests were already in the drawing room. Prince Harry and the Honourable Judith Finlay were near the window. Harry wore a light grey lounge suit and white shirt with the top button unfastened and no tie. Reaper felt overdressed. The girl wore a knee length white cocktail dress with a flared skirt in some kind of taffeta material. It was strapless and showed tanned shoulders. She had brown hair cut in a bob and a pert and attractive face that carried a worried expression. Across a less than crowded room, Harry looked the real deal. The right shade of hair, the light freckled complexion, the even features and slightly upturned nose. He seemed to be reassuring his companion. She held a wine glass in both hands; he held a whisky tumbler in his left hand while his right stroked her shoulder. They both glanced in Reaper's direction as he entered, and then returned to their conversation.

Two military men were standing by a drinks trolley. Reaper identified the portly officer in dress uniform as Colonel Maidstone. The wild looking man in navy blue tunic and khaki trousers had to be Barstow. He half turned at Reaper's entry and the winged dagger of the SAS could be seen on his collar. Barstow fixed him with a stare like a stag at bay. No. Reaper immediately changed that assessment. This was no stag at bay, this was a bear stating its territory. The uniform appeared to be struggling to contain the man's energy. By comparison, Maidstone was portly, had a receding chin and wore glasses. He blinked in Reaper's direction. An owl being patronised by a bear.

Reaper limped across the room and joined the two men.

Barstow said, 'So you're the flier.' A statement, not a question. His accent was nondescript. He didn't seem impressed.

'And you are Colonel Barstow.'

Barstow didn't change his stance. He remained only half facing Reaper, as if half was all he warranted. He also accepted that he would be known by sight.

'Roger Maidstone,' the owl said, holding out his hand.

Reaper took it and they shook. 'Tom Watson.' He smiled, deprecatingly. 'Flier.'

'Welcome to Redemption. A pilot is exactly what we need. I'm sure you will be a great asset in our endeavour.' His voice had touches of upper class drawl, as if he had acquired them with promotion and was still unsure how they worked. It was obvious he wanted to be liked; accepted. Reaper accepted him.

Reaper looked at the SAS emblem on Barstow's collar. 'I'm impressed,' he said.

'So you should be,' Barstow said. The words sounded like a challenge. Tension palpitated within the small triangle they made.

'Sir?' Adams materialised at his side, tray proffered, gin and tonic upon it.

'Thank you, Adams,' Reaper said, and took the glass.

'Ah. You are all here.' The General had arrived. He was wearing a red cut-away mess jacket with epaulettes, braid on the sleeves and a row of medals on his left breast, over a white shirt and black bow tie. Now Reaper felt underdressed. He approached the three men. 'Introduced yourselves?'

'Yes, indeed,' said Maidstone.

Adams was back, tray proffered, and Purcell took the glass.

'You wanted to meet Harry,' he said to Reaper. 'Now you shall.'

He escorted him across the room and the young couple stopped talking at their approach. The girl tried to hide her concerns behind a smile. Harry adopted a languid posture and raised an eyebrow in Reaper's direction.

The General made introductions and the three of them shook hands. The girl's hand was damp, her touch light. Harry's grip was firm, as if he had practised it, his gaze steady.

'Welcome aboard, old chap,' he said.

Reaper smiled. 'There's nothing like a royal welcome,' he said.

And this was nothing like a royal welcome.

He glanced at the General. 'Where did you find him?' he said.

'In London.' The General was also smiling. 'He was dressed in the uniform of the Blues and Royals.' He chuckled. 'Don't tell Maidstone. He thinks this is the real Harry.'

Harry followed the conversation without amusement. 'I am here, you know. I am a person.' His cheeks had flushed and he was angry.

'He's right,' said Purcell, the humour dropping from his voice. 'He *is* Harry. There is no room for ridicule, or even speculation. Harry is playing an important part in the reconstruction. We treat him with the respect due to the heir who would be king. Except that Harry is an egalitarian. He has declined the throne to work for the good of all. Which, of course, is exactly what you would expect of him. Which is why he insists most of his titles are outmoded. He will always be Prince Harry to the masses but, to fellow officers, he is Harry.'

'My apologies, sir, if my remarks caused offence,' said Reaper, and dipped his head.

Harry stiffened his backbone a little, nodded and said, 'My apologies for a lack of humour. These are trying times.' His glance moved to the two officers across the room. 'Particularly where Colonel Barstow is concerned. General, we must have words.'

'We will. Later, Harry. Later. Now it must be almost time for dinner.' He guided Reaper away and when they were out of hearing he said, 'He can be sensitive. He was an actor and a professional look-alike. Apparently, there used to be a demand for such people.'

'And the Honourable Judith?'

'She really is an Honourable. We found them together and she was rather pleased to see us. London was no place for a young woman alone. She has reason to be grateful to us and she and Harry make a handsome couple.'

'And she helps him polish the image?'

'Exactly.'

*   *   *

Dinner was a desultory affair. Conversation was stilted, with Purcell speaking in platitudes and Colonel Maidstone agreeing with everything he said. Judith Finlay contributed little and Harry joined in when required and asked, again, for a private meeting with the General and was, again, fobbed off. When he made the request, Reaper noticed that Judith's head dipped even lower as if pretending she wasn't even present.

Barstow was a lurking presence who had poor table manners and drank too much. His grin became lascivious every time he looked towards the girl. There was obvious tension between the couple and the leader of the Tans and Reaper could easily imagine what it was. The girl was attractive and Barstow had all the social attributes of Attila the Hun. Harry might not be a real prince but he was protective of the girl and his role was important in Purcell's scheme of things. The General was obviously aware of the situation but Maidstone hadn't a clue. He also believed Harry was Harry and his demeanour towards the couple was deferential.

'The General tells me you're going to build us an air force,' Barstow said with a sneer.

'That's long term,' Reaper said, without irony. Like Harry, he had to fit his own role. 'Of course, Harry could have started the process before now, but the General is quite right. It would have been foolish to have risked the Prince in actual flights.' He glanced towards the young man. 'I have suggested to the General the use of simulators to train new pilots. Your help in that area, sir, would be invaluable.'

'Here, here!' said Maidstone. 'An air force?' He obviously hadn't been party to the possibility.

'That seems a sensible idea,' the General said. 'What do you think, Harry? Agreeable?'

It was part of the charade being played for the benefit of Maidstone, who would pass on the information to his fellow officers and reinforce Harry's credentials.

'Of course, General,' Harry said. 'Anything to help the cause.'

Reaper caught the hint of sarcasm in the response. The General and Maidstone didn't, but smiled and nodded approval. Barstow nodded to himself and grinned as if amused by the whole joke. When he raised his eyes, it was to look at the young woman. The stare undressed her where she sat.

'Tomorrow is Sunday,' said the General to Reaper, 'And you shall get the tour.' He looked across the table. 'Harry, you will be with us, of course. It will do the troops and the people good to see you out and about.'

'Of course, General.'

'Right. Two o'clock start, I think. Unless your leg is good enough to go and retrieve your other aeroplane?'

'Maybe the day after,' Reaper said. 'It's getting better all the time.'

'Good, good.' he placed both hands on the table and got to his feet. Maidstone, Harry and the girl followed his example, so Reaper did the same. Only Barstow took his time about rising, and even then he made it appear as though it had nothing to with respect for the General, but that he wanted another drink. 'Then I shall leave you. Good night.'

They all dutifully replied, apart from Barstow, who grunted.

As the General departed, Harry looked nervously in the direction of Barstow and took Judith's arm.

'I think we'll retire, too. Goodnight, gentlemen.'

He guided the girl from the room. Maidstone bowed stiffly from the waist and said, 'Goodnight, sir. Ma'am.' Reaper nodded to them, and Barstow muttered, 'Shame', as if he had parlour games in mind that could not now be played.

Maidstone looked unsure what to do now that the important people had left. He was obviously intimidated by the Colonel of the Black and Tans and did not relish an evening that might develop into a drinking bout with the man they called the Beast. He made his excuses about duty in Banbury and left.

'Drink?' said Barstow to Reaper, holding a half empty bottle of Merlot and looking at it with disdain. 'I mean a proper drink,' and he nodded towards the drawing room where there was a selection of spirits.

'A nightcap,' said Reaper, and followed him.

'What that girl needs,' the Colonel said, 'is a bloody good fucking.'

He poured two whiskies, his own neat and left Reaper to take the other. Reaper added water.

'And you're the chap to do it?'

'I'm the chap.'

'I don't think Harry would agree.'

'That jumped up prat.'

'Or the young lady.'

'She'd see it my way eventually. Or ...' He stopped and took a drink.

'Or what, Colonel?'

'She'd learn.'

'I would have thought a man with your reputation wouldn't have difficulty finding a woman.'

'I don't.'

'So why this particular one?'

Barstow was about to answer then changed his mind. He didn't know Reaper well enough. Had yet to place him in the order of things. Reaper saw it in his face. The man would have liked to be boastful and loud, but he wasn't yet sure whether he would be able to dominate Reaper like he dominated almost everyone else. And if he couldn't, Reaper suspected, Barstow might think the only alternative would be to kill him and bugger the chance of an air force. Until he made that decision, it would not be in his own interests to provide any information at all to this new man.

'Forbidden fruit?' Reaper suggested.

Barstow snorted dismissively, drained the glass of whisky and said, 'I'll see you again,' as a threat rather than a parting farewell.

Chapter 22

SANDRA BRIEFED A COUNCIL meeting at the Manor House in Haven. She told them about the new people they had met on the journey south and of the rise of General Purcell and his New Army and the sort of order they imposed. She told them of the work camps, slave labour, the Black and Tans, the brothels and Purcell's racial policies. And how Reaper had let himself be captured.

'What about Prince Harry?' asked Cassandra Cairncross.

'Prince Harry appears to be under the control of the General and his Black and Tans. He doesn't go anywhere without them.' She paused. 'I should add that we don't know if he really is Prince Harry. But the people in Redemption seem to think he is.'

A pause.

'Something else, Cass...'

The older woman looked at Sandra.

'Another Harry. Flight Sergeant Harry Babbington is alive. He's in the mine work camp. But he's alive.'

Cassandra gasped and a voice from the back said, 'Of course he is.' Leading Aircraftman Clifford 'Smiffy' Smith, who had joined them from RAF Lemington, along with Cassandra, added: 'He's a flight sergeant.'

Cass smiled and nodded at what Smiffy had said.

'Clifford is right. Flight sergeants are difficult to subdue.'

'He's head of the escape committee at the mine,' Sandra said.

Smiffy and Cass both nodded, as if they expected nothing less.

Sandra glanced round the group. 'That's about as much as I can tell you. We have a plan to get Reaper back. Ash and Yank and me just have to work out the details.'

The committee left and Sandra asked Sandy Cameron to stay behind with Ash and Yank. Pete Mack and Smiffy talked in the doorway before stepping back into the room. Pete Mack said, 'Whatever you decide, Smiffy and I are going with you.'

'We're only going to get Reaper back,' said Sandra.

'Bollocks. If he doesn't turn up, you'll be going in. I know you. You should know me. Me and Smiffy are going with you.'

Sandra smiled. 'Thanks.' She nodded to both of them. 'You're in. Now bugger off while we work out what we're going to do.'

*   *   *

The first part was easy. They would go to the airfield near the White Cottage and wait. If Reaper turned up with an escort, they would remove the escort and release him. They were confident of their manpower and skills to mount such an operation. The problem came if Reaper didn't make the rendezvous.

'If he turns up, he'll have a plan,' said Sandra. 'If he doesn't, he'll be either dead or locked up. Then *we'll* need a plan.'

'And we'll need it pretty damn quick,' said Ash. 'We'll need to strike while they're being cocky about catching the legendary Reaper. The obvious first target is the mine. Get Harry Babbington onside. The guy has to be an asset. He'll know people. Targets. If we take the mine, we increase our forces straight away from among the prisoners.'

'They might not be in a good state,' Cameron said. 'This is slave labour.'

'Who'll be itching for the chance to fight back,' said Yank. 'They're there cos they're troublemakers. I guess they'd jump at the chance to cause more trouble.'

The Scot said, 'There's still the wee problem of doing this without word getting back to headquarters.'

'True,' said Sandra. 'Silence is essential. If they know we're coming, we've no chance. Surprise is our best weapon.'

'It can be done,' said Ash. 'Two teams. One to release the prisoners. The other to drive up to the gate and ask to be let in.' They stared at him. 'Bluff it. Dress in military uniforms, take a military vehicle and bluff your way in. Then first priority is the radio. We need to know its location.'

'Mandi will be able to tell us,' said Sandra.

'Sounds like a plan,' said Yank. 'But then what?'

There was silence round the table until Sandra said, 'We bluff again.' She smiled. 'I think we may have a secret weapon.' She looked at Cameron. 'Can you come with us or should you go back?'

'Purcell is a threat to everybody. After Haven, we could be next. We'll come.'

'Good.' Sandra looked round at her companions and felt the strength of their commitment. 'I've an idea that might work. Let's start planning. And when the plan falls apart, we'll just have to fight.'

Chapter 23

REAPER WORE THE BLUE slacks and the blue shirt with epaulettes and carried the flying jacket. Might as well get into the role for the General's sake. They met at breakfast and Purcell, who was already at the dining table and had almost finished, nodded his approval.

'Fourteen hundred hours,' he said.

As he left, Harry and Judith Finlay entered. They exchanged good mornings with Reaper and served themselves with bacon and eggs. Adams brought a fresh pot of coffee for Reaper and a pot of tea for the couple.

The resemblance with Prince Harry was striking although Reaper noticed small differences in attitude and expression. He wore jeans and an open necked white shirt. The young woman was more relaxed than she had been the previous evening. She wore jeans and a Union Jack t-shirt. Adams made a discreet withdrawal and they ate in silence until most of the food was gone.

Harry glanced across the table and said, 'You must have questions.'

Reaper smiled. 'You don't mind?'

'Not at all.'

'You know, the pair of you really do look the part.'

'Good casting,' the young man said. Then he glanced at the young woman and briefly covered her hand with his and said, 'Sorry.'

They shared an intimate look of friendship and mutual reliance.

'We are alone in here?' Reaper asked.

'No one bothers to eavesdrop anymore,' he said. 'If they ever did, I've got over my paranoia.' He gave a tight smile. 'I'm not the man I thought I was.'

'So who are you?'

'Harry Kaplan. That's with a K.'

'An actor?'

'And celebrity look-alike. I was quite a good actor. I went to LAMDA – the London Academy of Music and Dramatic Art. I did good stage work, a few parts on TV. *Casualty*, *EastEnders*. But my looks got in the way. Someone noticed a resemblance and I dressed up for a party. A woman from an agency saw me and, before I knew it, I'd signed up. Acting parts were few and far between and it paid the bills. I only intended doing it for a short while until something else came along, but nothing did. The look-alike stuff killed other work.'

'Were you good as Harry?'

'I was an actor. I perfected it. The work rolled in. It was not particularly satisfying but, let's face it, it could have been a role for life.'

'Family?'

'I'm an only child and my parents died years ago. No wife, no serious girlfriend. I was too busy having a good time. I thought, fuck it. If I can't win an Oscar, I'll take all the royal perks I can get.'

'The General said he found you in Chelsea. Is that where you were living?'

'Found me? He makes it sound like he discovered Elvis. No, I'd gone to Chelsea for an end of the world party. That's what they called it. End Of The World in big letters. By then, you didn't need a crystal ball to know this was as bad as it was ever going to get.

'The party lasted a week. People kept coming and going. Then mainly going. People died, but there were so many drugs you couldn't be sure what of. I know at the end I slept for two days. When I came round, three of us were still alive and there were four bodies in the bedrooms. The apartment was in Sloane Square and pretty swish. It belonged to Lola Wright, the daughter of a millionaire. She was one of the bodies. She overdosed rather than get flu and have a runny nose. Well, that's what she said, but we were all saying pretty stupid things at the time.

'Anyway, the bodies were an inconvenience. And one of the others started sneezing and the third chap wandered off into the night, so I went flat hunting in the same building. Got a nice one, first floor. It was for sale. There was a brochure in the kitchen. Seven million quid they wanted for it and I just walked in. Lola had a spare key. I took all the remaining booze and drugs with me.

'I'd gone to the party as Harry, of course, wearing the Dress uniform of the Blues and Royals. You know: the one he went to the wedding in. Those were the only clothes I had. I nipped out, at one stage, looking for a hardware store to get a camping stove. Fat chance in Sloane Square. Anyway, somebody saw me and shouted. They thought I really was Harry. I legged it back to the flat.

'I was an actor, so I knew how to look after myself. When the power went, I lived on walnut oaties, plum pickle, truffles, strawberry shortbread, and a dozen boxes of cheese and onion crisps. Lola had a thing for Fortnum and Mason's hampers and cheese and onion. I tell you, Beluga caviar and Krug champagne can get a bit boring after a while.'

Reaper said, 'And then the General arrived?'

'Somebody told him Prince Harry was living near Sloane Square. The General was in uniform. Had soldiers – what looked like an armoured convoy. I thought, at last, someone in charge. He had a megaphone. Announced himself. Invited people to come forward. Especially any officers from the armed forces, which was about as close as he got to asking for Harry by name. I thought what he offered had to be better than the chaos that was going to happen. I'd heard windows being smashed, screams in the night, that sort of thing. So I decided to go out. That's when we met.' He nodded to the young woman. 'I hadn't known it, but Judy was living in the same apartment block. We met in the foyer.'

Judith said, 'I was peeping through a window. I still wasn't sure what to do. I was a bit paranoid myself after being on my own. I hadn't a clue Harry was in the building. He gave me quite a shock when he came down the stairs. For a minute, I thought it really was him. The other Harry, I mean. I'd met him a few times. Nightclubs, events. Our social circles overlapped. Harry, this Harry, introduced himself. Very much the gentleman. "Hello, I'm Harry." And we shook hands. And I said, "But you're not, are you?" And he said something like, "If we pretend I am, it might help." He gave a cheeky grin and held out his hand and I took it. I thought, this is bizarre. The world is ending and I'm holding hands with Prince Harry. So I told him my name and we went outside.'

Harry said, 'The General believed us. It was Barstow who didn't. Later, when he realised the truth, the General was a bit cross.'

'A bit cross?' Judith said. 'I thought he was going to shoot us.'

'Then he realised it didn't matter. The rumour had started and all that mattered was that others believed it. We thought it was a bit of fun, at first.' He paused and looked sideways at Judith. 'Actually, that's not true. At first, we just wanted safety. Then we thought it was an easy way to be looked after. Then we realised what he was doing. He was using the name of Harry to give him legitimacy. He was ruling in Harry's name. By then, we were trapped. Nothing we could do. We had to play along.'

'Had to?' Reaper said.

Judith took Harry's hand on the table in a show of solidarity.

'Had to, Mr Watson,' she said. 'The General pretends to be civilised, even though he's a madman. Barstow has no pretences. It was made clear what would happen if Harry was unwilling to go along with the role. I would be the first victim. Barstow didn't use euphemisms. I was to be raped. First by the Beast himself, and then his men. He was blunt. He looked as if he rather hoped Harry would be awkward.'

The threat had been so stark that Reaper did not know what to say.

Harry said, 'Do you know about the work camps, Mr Watson? About the General's unspoken policy of racial purity? About the brothels? Of how people can disappear? Of course, it's all wrapped up in platitudes about the public good. About building for the future. The new Albion.'

'We have no way out,' said Judith. 'But do you want to be a part of all this? You still have a chance to escape.'

Reaper smiled. 'Sadly, I don't think I have. I do believe I have made myself as indispensable as you. The General is unlikely to let me walk away. We appear to be prisoners together.'

＊　　　＊　　　＊

Reaper was served with a lunch of sandwiches and coffee and, at two o'clock, he made his way to the hall to join the tour. Harry looked every inch a prince in the khaki service dress uniform of the Blues and Royals. A Sam Browne belt and a blue lanyard on his left shoulder, the distinguishing hat with the broad red stripe and a swagger stick under one arm.

'I have uniforms for all occasions,' he said in a stage whisper, when he saw Reaper's nod of appreciation, when they met in the hall.

'I'm sure they suit you,' Reaper said. He himself was dressed as Flying Officer Watson. 'This one does.'

'Much better than civvies, I agree.' The voice seemed more authentic than earlier. He was back in the role. 'Most people never look past the costume. You dress like the Demon King and people believe you are the Demon King. Dress as a prince, and they believe that, too.'

'You've played pantomime?'

Harry gave him a hard stare. 'This is pantomime.'

The General came down the stairs and joined them and they went outside where a Hummer was waiting. It was a vehicle with an open top. Two sets of seats, and a truck bed at the back in which two guards, sub-machineguns hanging around their necks, already stood holding a roll bar. Reaper was directed to sit alongside the driver and the

General and Harry climbed into the rear seats. The clouds had broken and were now a patchwork across the blue sky.

'Don't forget, Harry,' the General said. 'Be gracious.'

There were no checkpoints on the road into Banbury, but when they passed military personnel Harry raised a regal hand. The soldiers saluted in return. The suburbs were deserted. They entered The People's Park, where the gate was manned by soldiers who came swiftly to attention. The car followed narrow tarmac pathways through the trees and they stopped at the head of an open space that was packed with people, sitting around in groups on the grass, having a picnic. Harry was on his feet again and waving before the car stopped and people stood up and cheered. Not full-blooded cheers, but a throaty welcome augmented by a round of applause.

A dozen Black and Tans were lined up and, as the Hummer stopped, a sergeant called them to attention. They climbed out of the car and the General led the way to a flatbed truck where a Captain with regular army insignia waited. Salutes were exchanged.

Purcell said, 'How's it gone?'

'Fine, sir. Even the weather brightened up.'

The General and Harry climbed steps to get on the back of the truck. Reaper hesitated but was ushered upwards by the Captain who followed on his heels. The General went forward to a microphone on a stand.

The muttering of the people died. Purcell raised his hands as if for silence, but silence had already fallen. The people knew their place. Reaper guessed there were perhaps 2,000 men, women and children present. He also noticed two large white vans with side doors open, a catering truck and tables on which were tea urns. It appeared the picnic had been provided.

'Well, even the weather brightened up!' the General started his address with an attempt to be jocular, and Reaper stole a glance at the Captain who had provided the line, as the crowd attempted a polite response of amusement.

'In fact, other things are looking up as well. The road we have chosen is hard but it is fair. We have security in our numbers, unlike the poor souls beyond our boundaries who are still prey to the vultures of banditry and rape.' He said the last word almost as a whisper as if he did not want to offend children present. Now his voice became strident again: 'We are getting stronger! We have cemented our ties with the Royal Navy at Portsmouth and we will soon expand our frontiers to the north and take within our protection peaceful groups who want nothing more than the chance to prosper. And prosper we will!'

He paused and looked out at his subjects. When he continued, it was reflectively, sharing his thoughts with friends.

'Do you remember before the terrible scourge happened? We had family life then. We had a caring society. We looked after one another. In adversity, neighbour stood shoulder to shoulder with neighbour. It had always been so. Our ancestors did so when they faced the Blitz, for Britons were slow to anger but resolute when roused to action. But even back then, we had the disaffected. Those who wanted something for nothing. The underclass of society that believed the rest of us owed them a living. The urban filth that polluted our streets, caused mayhem and violence and made ordinary citizens prisoners in their own home. They ran riot in our streets and our courts were soft and our police had their hands tied.'

Murmurs in the crowd suggested that people agreed.

'Today, those vermin still pollute our land. But we do not have our hands tied. We do not have judges passing soft sentences on violent criminals. We lock them up and keep them away from honest folk. We make them work for the public good. Because no one in this society is owed a living. We all have to work to survive. Shoulder to shoulder for a better tomorrow – and we *will* have a better tomorrow. I promise that we will all reap the benefits, sooner rather than later, because we are moving forward.'

He looked round and nodded to Reaper, then waved for him to approach.

'One way forward is through our latest recruit. Tom Watson heard about us from the other side of the country and sought us out because he wanted to be part of Redemption. Like many have done. Like you did, yourselves. So what makes Tom so special?'

321

Purcell squeezed him round the shoulders, a manly expression of welcome or pride in a new specimen.

'Tom is a pilot. Yes, that's right, a pilot. He is also a qualified instructor. Of course, we have had a pilot with us all along.' He released Reaper and indicated Harry with his other hand. 'But it was not reasonable to risk Prince Harry at the controls of an aircraft that might not be fully serviceable. But now Harry has volunteered to help Tom train pilots. He will be, you might say, Ground Control to Major Tom!'

Purcell risked a chuckle at his joke and, after a pause at the implausibility of the General knowing anything about the music of David Bowie, the laughter started and once it got going it was difficult to stop. Was this the first time his audience had seen the human side of General Purcell? The General let it roll across the park before he held up his hands for silence.

'That's enough from me. Enough for you to know we are going in the right direction. With our New Army, Prince Harry and Major Tom.'

This time his raised arms invited applause, which he duly received. As he backed away, the Captain approached him with congratulations and a muttered request.

'Yes, yes, of course.' He looked at Harry. 'Time to be gracious again, Harry. Draw the numbers.'

Harry looked at Reaper, gave a minute shrug of the shoulders and mouthed the word *pantomime* before walking forward to where the Captain had now placed a large box on a folding table.

'And this,' said Harry into the microphone, 'is what you really came for' which brought another appreciative and warmer round of laughter from the crowd. People sat and took notice. Harry plunged his hand into the box and pulled out a slip. 'Blue region...' he said. 'One Six Seven.' He drew five numbers in all.

Duty done and back in the Hummer, Reaper said, 'What was that?'

'The draw,' Purcell said. 'It happens once a week. A winner from each of the five residential regions gets a hamper. A touch of luxury and whimsy. It's well received.'

Reaper remembered he and Sandra had been told about it. What next? Gladiators? Bread and circuses? He must remember not to suggest it. Especially to Barstow.

They drove through town, past occasional groups of off-duty military, some of whom may have been inebriated. Harry waved, and they waved back. The Hummer stopped outside a handsome old building that sat at the junction of two streets. Opposite was a Debenhams store and the entrance to what had been a shopping mall. Two Land Rovers and a military half-track were parked outside.

'Military HQ,' Purcell said.

'For the Tans, as well?' Reaper asked.

'The Black Berets,' the General corrected, 'are based at Baystoke.'

Colonel Maidstone hurried from an office to greet them. He saluted smartly to both the General and Harry, and shook Reaper's hand.

'Welcome to the hub,' he said. 'Tea?'

'How lovely,' the General said, without enthusiasm.

It was a routine call, designed to show off Harry. Soon they were back in the Hummer and crossing a bridge over the railway. At the far end was a checkpoint where soldiers pulled aside a barrier, stood to attention and saluted.

'Civilian areas,' the General said.

Scattered groups lined the route, that went through an estate of semi-detached houses, as if they had been chivvied from their homes.

Harry smiled and gave his royal wave. Some waved back, others stared, a few cheered half-heartedly and, towards the end of the brief trip, as they neared a Holiday Inn, there was a single female cry of: 'Harry!' that was almost a plea. They exited the residential area through another checkpoint at a bridge that crossed the M40 motorway. The road back to Baystoke was through countryside.

*　　　*　　　*

As the Hummer stopped outside the front door of the hall, they could hear a disturbance within. Raised voices, cursing and something crashed. The General's face was grim and he marched briskly towards the front door, but Harry got there before him.

Adams was on the landing of the grand staircase. A silver tray lay at the foot of the stairs, smashed china on the steps. Adams was frightened but trying to retain his decorum as he backed down the stairs. Above him on the landing was Barstow. No tunic and shirt unfastened. He was shouting: mainly threats about what he was going to do to the General's batman.

Harry ran up the stairs, past Adams, onto the landing and past Barstow, bouncing off his shoulder as the military man deliberately barged him into the wall. Harry didn't stop but hurried on towards the suite of rooms used by himself and Judith Finlay.

The General stopped in the middle of the hall, feet apart, hands behind his back holding his swagger stick. His neck was stiff with fury.

'Adams? What's going on?'

The servant regained his composure and courage and stood to attention at the foot of the stairs.

Barstow screamed from the landing, 'That twat burnt me. I'll flay his fucking hide.'

The General hardly raised his voice but it seemed to fill the hall.

'I asked Adams, Colonel Barstow. I would be obliged if you dressed yourself as befits an officer and a gentleman, and remain silent. Adams?'

'Sir. I took afternoon tea to Miss Finlay. The Colonel was in her rooms. Miss Finlay asked me to stay and serve tea. The Colonel asked me to leave. In fact, he took my arm to guide me towards the door and the tray inadvertently tilted and he was unfortunately splashed with hot water. I immediately offered to bring cold water to bathe the affected area but he insisted on helping me leave and, in so doing, sir, the tray became dislodged and fell down the stairs.'

'The twat splashed me on purpose. He's on a charge.'

'Colonel?' Again Purcell's voice carried without being raised. 'Perhaps you will join me in my office? When you are properly attired. Adams? Perhaps you could bring me a gin and tonic?' He turned and walked away along a corridor as Harry burst back onto the landing. He threw a jacket at Barstow and shouted: 'You bastard!' as he ran into him, pushing with both hands. It caught Barstow off balance and he staggered back to the head of the stairs. The man they called the Beast grabbed a handrail. His whole body seemed to bristle with rage. Harry was still shouting. 'You come near her again and I'll...'

'You'll what?' The words were spat like venom. And then Barstow had his hands round Harry's throat. 'You'll what? You sad little prick.'

Reaper ran up the stairs and got between them. He tried to prise Barstow's fingers apart but they were like steel.

'Now is not the time,' he muttered urgently at the

Colonel. 'There's too much to lose. Don't waste it. Leave it till later.'

The fingers slackened and Harry began to breath again. Down below, Adams was still watching and Reaper nodded to him that everything was okay, even though it wasn't. Adams went off to prepare a gin and tonic and Barstow turned away and appeared to be re-bottling his anger. Just for a moment he had let it out and it had been a fearsome sight. He snatched up the jacket from the floor and walked to the stairs. He paused and looked back.

'You are fucking lucky,' he said, enunciating each word. Then he looked at Reaper and added, 'Later,' as if he blamed him for stopping his strangulation of the pretend prince. At last, he stomped downstairs, kicking the tray across the hall with a clang.

'Are you okay?' Reaper asked and Harry nodded, although he held his neck.

'He tried …'

It was Reaper's turn to nod. 'Is Judith all right?'

'Adams stopped it. Hot water in his groin.'

'Brave bloke.'

'He has the General's protection.'

'I don't think that would be much help if Barstow really loses it. And he will do, one day.'

Harry practised breathing for a few seconds and looked up at Reaper and said, 'He's marked you down, too, you know? You can see it. He'll kill you.'

Reaper smiled and said, 'Not if I kill him first.'

*　　　*　　　*

Adams served Reaper with dinner in his room.

'I believe your conduct today was above and beyond,' Reaper said.

'It was an accident, sir.'

'A perfectly-timed accident. Harry told me. Judith didn't ask for tea.'

They exchanged a non-committal look.

'Miss Judith is a nice lady,' Adams said.

'She is. And she's grateful.' Reaper paused. 'It was a brave act.' He raised a hand as Adams was about to object. 'A brave accident. Will there be any repercussions?'

'No immediate repercussions, sir. The Colonel accepted it was an accident.'

'There could be danger in the future?'

'There will undoubtedly be danger in the future, sir.'

Reaper couldn't fully understand Adams. He seemed devoted to the General because he offered order in a devastated world. He accepted work camps. He accepted the need for Barstow and his Black and Tan gangsters. Yet he had stood up to the Beast when a young woman was threatened.

'Will you give a message to the general for me?'

'Of course, sir.'

'Tell him my leg is much improved. Tomorrow, if it is convenient to him, we could take a trip and collect my other aircraft.' He smiled. 'It might cheer him up.'

'I'm sure it will, sir.'

*   *   *

The General was in buoyant mood at breakfast.

'I've sent Colonel Barstow to inspect the mine at Coventry and then to our oil depot at Kingsbury in Warwickshire. The travel will do him good. Captain Beaumont and Sergeant Logan of the Black Berets will accompany you with a platoon. Captain Beaumont will fly back with you. The airfield at Hinton is in good order. It's a concrete strip and I've had it checked and weeds and undergrowth removed.' He passed over a map. 'I hope that is all in order?'

'You've covered everything, General.'

'Good.' The General had dined early and now stood up from the table. 'Then I'll see you off in ten minutes.'

'I'll be there.'

As Purcell left, Harry and Judith came in, followed by Adams with a pot of tea. He put it on the table and Judith touched his arm and they exchanged a glance. She nodded her gratitude. He smiled and left the room.

The young couple were subdued and not hungry. Reaper was. He carried on eating.

'So you're off,' Harry said.

'That's the plan.'

'You could just fly away in the other direction.'

'That's not their plan. Captain Beaumont is flying with me.'

He was aware of the time and didn't want to keep the General waiting. He finished quickly and drank coffee.

'You two okay?' he asked.

Harry nodded.

Judith said, in a voice of resignation, 'It will happen again.'

Harry took her hand on the table but he didn't dispute the possibility.

'Hey,' Reaper said, getting to his feet. 'Look on the bright side. You never know what tomorrow might bring.'

He put on the flying jacket and took a step towards the door, which opened before he got there. Sergeant Logan, his bearded interrogator, entered together with a soldier wearing the black beret of the Tans. Logan looked at the soldier and back at Reaper.

'You sure?'

'I'm sure, sergeant.'

Logan swung a beefy fist that Reaper was too surprised to avoid. The blow knocked him onto the polished floor. 'You don't seem so tough,' Logan said.

'What the hell is going on?' said Harry, pushing his chair back as he got to his feet.

'Didn't you know?' Logan said. 'You've been having breakfast with the famous Reaper.'

'Reaper?' said Harry.

'Oh my God,' said Judith.

Reaper was aware of the General striding towards him.

'I had high hopes of you,' he said.

And then he kicked him in the side with one of the black shoes to which Adams undoubtedly gave a high polish every morning. No more Mr Niceguy, then.

'Still, not everything is lost. We have one of our major enemies and we will be able to demonstrate to the people that the Grim Reaper is no folk hero. He is just a man who is susceptible to pain and, eventually, death. When we hang you in the People's Park next Sunday.'

Chapter 24

THE FORCES OF HAVEN WERE at the White Cottage two days in advance. Their group was formidable. Four teams of Blues, two teams of Scots, Ash, Pete Mack, Smiffy and Sandra, plus an impressive array of armaments. Dr Greta Malone had insisted on coming with them. Her logic was simple: there would be action, there would be casualties, there would be need for emergency treatment. Besides, she needed to be as near as possible to Reaper.

They stood to the day before deadline. By evening, they realised no one was coming and relaxed. The next day, they were in position with the dawn and waited again. Still no one came.

Doubts deepened with the dusk.

'One more day.' Yank said. 'There's still one more day.'

Reaper had said he would be back in four days but to allow five in case of unexpected contingencies. Five meant the unexpected had happened. Sandra didn't like the implications.

They spent an uncomfortable night. Some camped at the airfield, some stayed in the White Cottage. Sandra remained at the field to be that much closer; she sat in the caravan that had served as control for the strip, drank coffee and watched the night. At two in the morning, she heard a sound outside and reached for her carbine.

'It's only me.' Greta pushed open the door and came inside. She helped herself to coffee and sat on the couch.

'He'll be all right,' Sandra said.

'I know,' Greta said. But she did not sound convinced.

They sat for a long time in silence, staring through the wide window at a clear sky.

Greta said, 'You've known him from the beginning, haven't you?'

'Dad and daughter.'

'You could be. You're very alike.'

Sandra was pleased Greta thought so. It hadn't occurred to her before. Others might not have appreciated such a comparison but, yes, she was pleased.

'I never knew my dad. He went absent without leave. I've never thought about it before, but if I could have chosen one, it would have been Reaper. You know about his daughter? His real daughter?'

'Yes.'

'We're the same age. And the same thing happened to me. You know?'

'I know.'

'We were the first. Me and Reaper. He found me, rescued me, trained me.' She gave a sort of laugh that was tinged with sadness for a lost life and, maybe, a lost father.

'He put a gun in my hand when I was still in shock and that probably helped. I was desolate. I mean, that sounds like a wrong word but it's not. Desolate land. A desolate girl. I was a wasteland. No feelings. Nothing but self-pity and fear. I had nothing. He gave me anger. He gave me belief. He gave me a gun. Two days after he rescued me, I killed my first man. That night I slept in his arms. He was a shield. He made it all right.'

They lapsed into another silence. Greta didn't break it. Eventually, Sandra did.

'I have no regrets about the people I've killed. That sounds cold but it's true. They deserved to die. The Reverend Nick and some of the others, they talk about how wrong it is to be judge and jury and deliver death, but you know what? They're secretly grateful. They can't do it but they know somebody has to.' She sniffed, took her time. 'I was an assistant in Top Shop.' She laughed. 'Can you believe that? I sold silly dresses to silly girls. Bought them myself with staff discount.' Silence again. 'But you know what I really wanted? I wanted to better myself. Sounds daft now, I suppose, but I wanted to go to university. We had plans, me and my mum. She was helping me.' She turned for the first time and stared at Greta sitting in the shadows. 'I'd have done it, too.'

Greta said softly, 'I have no doubt you would.'

Sandra went back to staring at the night. 'Reaper could have had me, you know? Sex. I wouldn't have minded. But he never once … never once …' She began to cry and Greta went to her and knelt on the floor in front of her chair so she could hold her. Sandra welcomed the comfort. 'I don't know what I'd do,' Sandra said. 'I don't know what I'd do. He's my dad and I can't lose him. I lost my mum but not him, too. I can't lose Reaper.'

'You won't lose him,' she said. 'He's indestructible.'

* * *

Reaper wasn't feeling indestructible. He was hanging from chains against a wall in the interrogation room, his hands manacled above him. They had stripped him to the waist and, in the process, had found the throwing knife he carried on a cord around his neck and which had hung down his back. Logan had given him a beating, not with his fists, but with a piece of wood to the body. The General had ordered that his face was not damaged.

Then he had been left to ponder his fate, as Purcell had said, until the arrival of Barstow the Beast, back from his tour of outlying facilities. The fate he was supposed to ponder, he guessed, included more beatings and the application of the Hammer House of Horror implements that were on a table on the other side of the room. They had thoughtfully left a lamp on so he could see them.

Barstow was in a good mood when he arrived.

'I knew you were wrong,' he said. 'I knew it.'

Then he aimed a kick at Reaper's genitals. Reaper

twisted and turned, grateful that at least his legs were not chained apart.

'The great bloody Reaper. The Grim fucking Reaper.' He kicked him again. 'Well, the world's now really grim for you, you bastard. And it's going to get a lot worse.' Another kick. 'Now, first things first. You were in an aeroplane and you sure as hell didn't fly it. So, where's the pilot? The General is hoping you'll cooperate. I don't give a toss. We don't need an air force. We'll be flying in balloons before we're flying jets again. But you managed to paint him a pretty picture that he swallowed hook, line and sinker. So I said I'd ask. And as I know you're not going to give me an answer, that means I can carry on kicking you.'

He kicked Reaper again.

'Want to tell me? I thought not. Ah well, happy days.'

He picked up the same length of wood that Logan had used and swung it. The piece of wood broke in half, which only made Barstow laugh. He chose instead a length of rubber hose and beat him some more. When he had worked up a sweat he dropped the hose on the floor, snorted with derision at his captive and left the room.

It's only pain, Reaper told himself. Only pain. Others have been through far worse. His daughter went through far worse. Most of the world had gone through far worse. It was only pain; he could deal with it. He could endure. That's why he had been spared; to endure so that others could have a chance. He'd made a mess of the past life, he would not make a mess of this one.

But by Christ, his body hurt, and he wondered how many ribs must be cracked or broken. Or maybe he was being soft. Sandra … he remembered when he first saw her and he almost cried. Almost cried at what she had been through and what she had become.

'Come on you bastards!' he shouted. 'You've got the Angel to deal with yet!'

But no one heard. No one was listening. And he was glad. He knew Sandra would come and it would be best if he didn't tell anyone else. But the thought helped him through the pain.

He wouldn't have believed it possible, but he fell asleep hanging from the chains. A kick brought him awake and he tried to stand upright and discovered his legs ached as much as his body. When he focussed, the General was standing in front of him, arms behind his back. The guard left the room and closed the door.

'We could have done great things together,' the General said, his voice tinged with sadness. 'I'm not talking about flying. I'm talking about a partnership. You could have joined me, been part of the New Army. You could have brought Haven into what we are building. Together, no one could have stopped us.' He stared at Reaper for a while and shook his head. 'What did you hope to achieve? Assassination?'

'It occurred to me.' Reaper's throat was dry and his voice cracked.

'If you had tried, you would never have escaped. Why take the risk of coming here?'

'To see the opposition. We know nothing about you,' he lied. 'We needed intelligence.'

The General shook his head again. 'You were recognised by one of the guards at the People's Park. He joined us from Whitby. Once seen, never forgotten.'

'The curse of celebrity.'

The General smiled. 'Being a celebrity means there will be no bullet in the back of the head. We have to show the people that we are untouchable. That we have captured the great Reaper. Your death will be a showpiece.'

'As long as it's not boring.'

'Next Sunday, the People's Park in Banbury will hold its first games and you will be the star attraction in a gladiatorial contest to the death.' Another smile. 'Sadly, you do not get choice of weapons.'

'Who's going to fight me?' he said, and knew as soon as he had asked the question. 'Barstow.'

'That's right. He will face you in the arena. You will fight with swords. So there you have it. I should warn you that the Beast is quite a fearsome warrior. He will take his time killing you and make it as unpleasant as possible. And if you think you might have half a chance against him, think again. Your face will be unmarked but your body will be damaged.' He brought his hands from behind his back. He was holding his swagger stick in his right hand and he used it to prod Reaper in the body. Reaper winced. 'Cracked ribs will make it rather painful to wave a sword about. But I'm sure you'll try. It's a shame, Reaper. It really is.'

He left and the lights went out. At least Reaper now knew they would not damage him too much until the day of combat. No broken legs or arms. And he would retain his rugged good looks.

*   *   *

The next day, he was moved to the basement where he had first been kept and where he collapsed gratefully onto the camp bed. He was left a bottle of water but no food. Another way to ensure he would be weakened when Sunday came. At least he could nurse his pain in peace for a while.

Barstow came midday.

'Snug?' he said. 'You really do have a soft number here, don't you Reaper? Comfortable bed, plenty to drink.' He grinned. 'Never fear, there'll be more pain tomorrow. Just enough. On Saturday we'll lay it on a bit. By Sunday you won't be up to much at all. You'll be hungry and hurting and just wanting it to end.'

Reaper said nothing. There was nothing to say.

Barstow laughed and looked across to the guard by the door and nodded.

The guard opened the door and Harry and Judith were pushed inside. The girl gasped and tried to cross the room to him, but Barstow grabbed her arm and pulled her against him. Harry began to step forward to help her and the Colonel back-handed him across the face and knocked him to the floor.

'Make sure he stays there,' he said to the guard. He held the girl closer than he needed to, pushing against her from behind. One arm holding her, one hand teasing her breasts. 'This is how it ends for the great man,' he said. 'Take a good look. Both of you. This could be you.'

Harry said, 'You wouldn't dare.'

'You're not indispensable, Harry. We could arrange for you to be shot by terrorists. You'd die a hero. We would all mourn. And I'd step into the breach and take care of the Honourable Judith.' His hand tightened over a breast and she screamed. Harry was kicked by the guard when he tried to get up. 'I might even marry her. Something you haven't done. Make a proper woman of her. Give her kids, start a dynasty. How does Prince Brian sound?' He laughed and threw Judith towards the door. 'Go on. Get out. You, too,' he said to Harry.

The pair paused and looked back. Anguish in their eyes. Harry trying to let Reaper know there was nothing they could do. Reaper trying to let them know it was okay. But they had seen the bruises on his body and had heard what was in store, so how could they believe anything was okay?

The guard ushered them out and Barstow exchanged a last look with Reaper. 'I shall enjoy killing you,' he said, conversationally. 'I'm glad you came.'

Then he turned and left and Reaper was alone.

*   *   *

The daylight from the high window was dimming when the door next opened. He was surprised when Judith Finlay came in. The guard said, 'Ten minutes.'

She carried a bowl and cloths and a small wicker basket.

His puzzlement showed and she said, 'I went to the General. I told him the cuts needed treating. They could lead to infection. They need you to at least look normal on Sunday.' She crouched by the bed and began sponging away blood on his body. He hadn't really noticed that he had blood on his body.

The guard eyed the girl with open lust. She gave him a dismissive look in return and he shuffled his feet and went outside.

'The General allowed this?' Reaper said.

'Not really. But is the guard going to take the risk that he didn't?'

'If Barstow finds out – '

She stopped him with a look. 'Barstow plans on taking over. And when that happens, nothing can save us. Harry will be killed and I'll belong to the Beast.'

'And I'll be dead.'

'You'll have a chance on Sunday.'

Reaper smiled sadly at her optimism.

'I know,' she said, 'but it's a chance.' She passed a cloth to him. He lifted a corner and saw cooked steak. 'Adams gave it to me. He knows what Barstow is up to as well.'

Reaper pushed the bundle beneath his pillow.

'Has Harry ever thought of appealing directly to the people? Maidstone believes he's real. Wouldn't he help?'

'Maidstone bends whichever way the wind is blowing. Harry thought of making a stand but he was told there would be reprisals if he gets out of line. Civilians would be sent to the camps. There could be random executions. He has to obey.' Her eyes were desperate. Her only hope? Pieces of steak wrapped in muslin.

He nodded. 'There's always a chance, Judith. Remember that. There's always a chance.'

'We'll try and get more food to you,' she said. 'We'll try.'

The door opened and the guard said, 'Time's up.'

The girl gathered her things and left. Reaper watched the soldier eyeing her from behind as she climbed the steps and then the door closed. He was her only hope. A forlorn hope.

Chapter 25

HE FOUND ANOTHER SHOTGUN IN A FARMHOUSE near Henley-on-Thames. Double-barrelled, plus two boxes of cartridges. The gun was difficult to hide, so a week later, he broke into a workshop and filed through the barrels and created a sawn-off shotgun. He tried it out with two cartridges, half expecting it to blow up in his hands, but it didn't. From ten feet away, it blew a door off its hinges. Against a human being, its force would be sufficient.

Ford made a strap for it so that he could hang it from his shoulder beneath his coat. To anyone he met, he would look like a shambling old man on the road to nowhere. Not worth bothering. Nothing worth stealing. He preferred it that way.

He joined people only to obtain information. He stopped one night with a group that had a horse-drawn caravan. They were heading for the West Country and said they were prepared for when the petrol ran out. It would have been impolite to say so, but he thought that might take quite some time and that they could have travelled west a lot quicker in a truck, but the changed world had changed people. Some had become violent, some religious, some slightly unhinged. Not enough to be committed but just that percentage off centre that might lead them to strange decisions.

They told him Redemption had moved. They said it was now based in Banbury. Prince Harry was at Banbury.

He went towards Banbury and scouted the fringe areas of Redemption. He tested its perimeters. He had plenty of time. He continued to make occasional contact with people, some of whom worked the land, but only when the soldiers weren't there. They told him the General lived in a village to the south of the town. They said the work was hard but they were protected. They were part of the new beginning. They said life would improve in the future. They were working to a five-year plan and it all made sense. The General made sense and the plan had the royal approval of Prince Harry.

Ford listened and said it was good someone had a plan. But surely, such a plan needed a lot of protection, and they said the General had an army and, with a little prompting, told him about the stormtroopers who lived with him in the village south of Banbury. The Black and Tans. He nodded and said he had heard about them; that they were commanded by an officer from the SAS. That's right, they said. Colonel Barstow. And so he found the Beast and the people of the Beast.

He slept in barns and hedgerows until the autumn began to bite and he realised he would need something more permanent. He had to survive the winter. He had to survive to give peace to Ellen and his friends. He told God this, and that night stumbled into the ruins of the farm looking for shelter, and made a fire, and found the skull. He kicked it by mistake in the dark and immediately apologised.

He treated it with reverence and held it in his hands as he sat by the fire and wondered to whom it had once belonged, whether man or woman. He decided it was a man and, sometime during the night, he began to talk to it and it became his friend and confidante and he smiled at the thought that he, too, had become slightly unhinged, but in a nice way. Not enough to be committed but enough to make a friend.

In the morning, he returned the skull to where he had found it and discovered that his stumbling about the night before had revealed the outline of the trapdoor. God had heard him and sent him the skull to guide his way.

This was where he spent the winter, isolated for weeks on end, talking to no one but the skull. Among the stockpiled goods he found a delivery note with the name William Hodge and the address Royd Beck Farm. He was pleased he had found a name for the skull and he and William talked every day. It made his isolation bearable because he was still grieving at his failure to protect Ellen and he often cried when the memories took him unawares. William helped.

Ford was surprised one day – late January, he figured – at how weak his body had become and he realized that he needed exercise to bolster his strength and keep him mobile. He went for walks and tried to make occasional contacts, although the workers at outlying farms were wary of him. He didn't know why until he entered an abandoned house and saw his reflection in a mirror. He hadn't shaved or washed for six months. William hadn't mentioned it. His hygiene hadn't bothered William, but it bothered people who were trying to lead normal lives.

He didn't shave or cut his hair or bathe. He didn't want to fit in. He was only here for a short while longer. Some people still talked to him and even gave him food, if he stayed downwind and pretended to be an eccentric old man whose brain had been damaged by events. And who was to say that wasn't true?

With the spring, he ventured closer. He slipped through woods and overgrown fields and hid in ditches. He watched the village of Baystoke from hides he constructed in hedges, wearing foliage so that he blended with nature. He chuckled when he told William. He could blend in so easy because he had the smell of nature; like a cowpat. Once he lay in the same place, in a ditch opposite the village *crossroads, for two days without moving. He was in no hurry; had nowhere else to go. This was the purpose of his life. He lay unmoving beneath his camouflage, he pissed there, he slept there, he made friends with the creatures that crawled and slithered over and around him. And he saw the men he wanted. He saw Barstow the Beast and, at his heel, was Logan, wearing a uniform and a sergeant's stripes: Logan, the creature of the Beast.*

He had placed his targets. Now he had to plan his killing ground. He would only get one chance and he could not fail. Ellen and the rest were relying on him. Windsor had to be avenged.

*   *   *

Windsor. They arrived with high hopes. The place was busy with troops and civilians on the streets in larger numbers than they had seen since the plague. Their small convoy was guided into a parking area outside St George's Chapel, below the Castle. They were told they needed to register and were directed to the Castle itself, past the ancient Round Tower on its raised motte and into a huge quadrangle. He remembered the overwhelming sense of history as he looked around at the buildings. They were directed into the state apartments and walked past two cannon on display and up a red carpeted staircase. Vaulted stone rising to lofty windows and a wood-panelled ceiling. Two full-sized knights mounted on horses, displays of medieval weaponry on the walls, suits of armour. History.

If anything gave credence to the claims of Prince Harry leading a new beginning, this was it. Perhaps this was why it had been chosen as the location to register new recruits, new citizens to the cause. This was a powerful first impression.

A soldier sat at a table at the top of the stairs, documents in front of him, a black beret alongside them, a line of red plush chairs for waiting applicants.

Perhaps things would have been different if they had arrived an hour earlier or later. If Barstow had not stumbled drunkenly from a chamber as they reached the head of the stairs. If they had not had among their company Ellen and Martha, two young and attractive girls. Barstow had immediately taken notice.

'You ladies' he said, without preamble. 'Follow me.'

'Why?' said Tony, unhappy to relinquish his grip on Ellen's hand.

'Why?' For a moment Barstow bristled, then he smiled. 'We are short of nurses. These ladies will be interviewed to see if they are suitable for training.'

'It's alright,' Ellen said.

'They will be just along the corridor,' Barstow said. 'When you've registered, you'll all be interviewed for job prospects. It doesn't take long.'

Ellen and Martha did as they were told. He was an officer. They were in Windsor Castle. What could be wrong? The rest of them sat in the chairs and waited. The soldier took their names, ages, occupations and special skills, if any, and wrote the information on cards. And they waited.

Ford, Tony, Bertie, Nigel, Jim, Barry, Susan and Marie. It hadn't occurred to them to question why the other two women had not been considered for nursing duties; Susan was middle-aged and Marie was elderly. They assumed age excluded them. They sat. And at the end of the row was Roy Logan.

Logan had already been at the Stonehenge camp when Ford and Ellen had arrived. He lived alone in a camper van, a large bluff man whom Ford had attempted to befriend simply because he was alone and because his large size seemed to deter others from making the effort. He was perhaps forty and had a reserved nature, as if experience had taught him to keep his own counsel.

The rest of what happened was not clear in detail to Ford. It was as if his mind had attempted to delete events that were too painful. His recollections were fuzzy and incomplete.

He remembered a scream and Tony was off his chair and moving quickly along the corridor. Ford followed. Had there been an accident? He only became aware later of confusion behind him as the guard tried to stop everyone else from following, but by then he was in a room of expansive size. Couches and chairs in sets and still enough space to hold a ball.

Ellen was being held by a soldier from behind. Barstow stood in front of her and had ripped open her shirt. He was cutting her brassiere in two with a knife between the cups. An impression of bottles, glasses and a sense of lust. Martha was face down over a settee, trousers round her ankles, a soldier behind her. Another soldier stood grinning inanely, a bottle in his hand.

Tony ran at Barstow who batted him to the floor with one blow. Ford also attempted to get to grips with the Beast, who simply smiled, avoided his flailing arm and bodily threw him across the room. He hit his head and lay stunned.

He heard Barstow's voice, echoing in the back of his mind.

'Might as well bring the others in,' he said.

He was kicked and returned to consciousness on a wave of nausea. He stopped himself from vomiting and sprawled against the side of a gilded chair. How could this be happening? In a royal palace? His head was still not clear but he was aware of the others. Susan was kneeling on the floor by his side. She was holding his body upright, one arm around him. He could feel her shaking with fear. Someone was sobbing rhythmically. Someone pleading. Voices were shouting. Blows were struck and a body fell to the floor.

'We could have done this nice and easy.' Barstow was speaking as if disappointed with the way things had turned out. 'Now you've made it complicated. It's your own fault.'

The shot was unexpected and unbelievably loud. It shocked Ford wide awake. Marie, the elderly former schoolteacher, lay sprawled backwards on the floor. Blood bubbled from her chest.

Someone shouted, 'No!' as if they couldn't believe what had happened.

'It's your own fault,' Barstow repeated, almost sadly. He levelled the gun at Ford and fired again.

But not at Ford. The bullet hit Susan. A neat hole in her forehead, blood and matter sprayed from the back of her head. She was flung backwards and Ford went with her. He lay over her and gazed into dead eyes. His hands were covered in her blood. The overwhelming urge was to fight back but how? At his age, he found it difficult getting up swiftly when he was on the floor. The memory of how he *had saved Ellen the first time they met taunted him. This time, he could save nobody.*

'You see the problem?' said Barstow. 'You can't live and tell the tale. It's just not on.' It was Martha who was sobbing rhythmically as she was raped. Ellen was naked to the waist, eyes wide in horror. 'There is one way out.' He glanced along the line of men who had been forced to their knees. 'Join us and you live. Otherwise …?' He raised the handgun.

'You're mad,' Bertie said, a large overweight man whose shirts never seemed to fit.

'No. I'm totally rational.' He raised the gun and fired again and Barry, a mild mannered elderly chap in glasses, slumped sideways, a bullet to the head. 'Too old to be useful.' Barstow explained.

His gaze began to wander towards Ford when Roy Logan said in a low but steady voice, 'I'll join you.'

Tony said, 'Bastard,' but whether that was to the soldier or the turncoat, it was difficult to say.

Barstow smiled and said, 'Death is a wonderful motivator. But there is a test. To prove yourself you have to be complicit.' He could see that Logan didn't understand what 'complicit' meant. 'You have to take your turn with the girls.'

'What?' Logan said.

'You're nothing but an animal,' Nigel said.

Jim just shook his head in horror. Tony, nursing what looked like a broken arm, struggled to his feet and took a step towards the Beast, who laughed, and clubbed him back to the ground.

Into the silence that followed, Logan said, 'I'll do that.' The words clear and strong. When Ford looked at him, he no longer saw fear. He saw lust.

Barstow saw the same emotions in his face and laughed. 'There's always one. There's always at least one. Get up.'

Logan got to his feet. He seemed to stand straighter, making the most of his full height. The sobbing had stopped. The first man had finished. Barstow nodded in the direction of Martha.

'Go ahead,' he said.

Their erstwhile companion ignored the others and moved to the settee, unfastening his trousers with slow deliberation.

'Bastard,' said Bertie, heaving his large frame to his feet, followed by Nigel. Jim was also trying to get up from the floor and Ford rolled onto his hands and knees to join them in last ditch resistance, when someone opened fire with a sub-machinegun. The bodies spun and fell and

blood splattered and they dropped in a row, one upon the other in an untidy barricade. Ford was not hit by bullets but banged his head again, and lay beneath the gentle giant that had been Bertie, covered in his blood.

'What about this one?'

The words faded in and out.

'Let him watch.'

An incoherent shout of rage and despair. Ellen saying, 'I love you. I love you' and the sound of clothes ripping, a scream and he lost consciousness.

He awoke after it was all over. He felt dead, or at least in hell, but was strangely comforted by the bodies of his friends around him. He opened his eyes. The two girls lay naked on richly cushioned settees. Tony, who had only married that morning, was tied to a chair. His body had slumped forward against the cord that held him. Blood ran down his front and Barstow held a blood-stained knife in his hand. Tony had been the last to die. Perhaps it had been his scream that had awakened him? Perhaps Ford had preferred unconsciousness to listening to the horror that had occurred?

Logan was grinning. Another soldier slapped him on the back and made a comment and they both laughed. Another man in uniform looked worried.

'What do we do with this lot?' he said.

Barstow wiped the blade of the knife on the shirt he had ripped from Ellen. He looked unconcerned. He gazed round at the paintings on the walls, the rich furnishings, the curtains and the bodies.

'We have a fire,' he said. 'A cleansing.'

'The General?' the same doubting soldier said.

'Is away with Harry. We'll burn this room. Burn the evidence.' He glanced at the settees holding the two bodies. 'Bloody women.' As if it had been their fault for making such a fuss about rape. He looked around at the living. 'This goes no further. This stays with us. Right?'

'Right,' they all answered.

'Get some petrol and we'll do the job properly. And you,' he said, turning to Logan. 'We'll have to get you a uniform. You're a natural.'

Eventually, they fired the room and closed the doors on the flames. Ford didn't move, at first. He was among friends. Then he felt the desire for revenge building. They deserved justice. All of them. These had been innocent women and brave men. This had been his family. He crawled from beneath the beefy arm of Bertie and shuffled backwards away from the smoke and the bonfire of furniture that had been built. Petrol had been splashed over the bodies and four canisters had been left nearby. He took two of the cans and stumbled to the double inner doors. He pushed through into the next room, opened the canisters and tipped them over and let the petrol run across carpet and floorboards. Let it all burn. Let the conflagration build. Beth and his friends deserved the biggest funeral pyre he could arrange. On a thousand years of history.

He went back for the other cans and spread the petrol to other rooms and then he left.

And now he was ready to go back. For Barstow if he could, but especially for Logan.

Chapter 26

THEY HAD WAITED ANOTHER day with fading hope. On the morning of the sixth, they moved. A mile from the mine they split into two columns. Mandi and Greta Malone went with the Blues and they parked in the cover of a wood and left their vehicles to make the rest of their journey on foot.

The second column was led by an open army Land Rover driven by a uniformed Ash with sergeant's stripes on his sleeve. Sitting next to him was the Major from Bracken Hall, in full uniform and with an impressive row of medal ribbons on his chest. Pete Mack, also in uniform, followed in another military Land Rover, with Smiffy standing in the back behind a machinegun mounted on the roll bar. Both these vehicles were flying the cross of St George on their pennants. Behind them came the two black BMWs flying the Scottish Saltire.

'Well, we look the part,' Pete said to Smiffy.

'Just don't try to salute,' Smiffy said. 'Your salute is rubbish.'

They took a detour so that they could approach the mine gates from the south and the direction of Banbury. They timed their arrival precisely for noon. Lunchtime for the guards. The convoy came quickly and showed no hesitation. It stopped and waited for the guard at the gate to approach, which he did with a puzzled expression on his face, his eyes moving from the tall officer in the front seat to his black driver. A soldier on the roof of the two-storey administration building manning a machinegun, stared down openmouthed.

The Major gave the guard an imperious look that was tinged with distaste.

Ash shouted in his best NCO voice: 'Salute, man. You will come to attention and salute a superior officer. Now!'

The guard straightened his shoulders and gave an approximation of a salute. He was beginning to look nervous.

The Major flicked a return salute and pointed at the gate. 'Open,' he said.

'What are you waiting for, you horrible little man?' Ash was in good form. 'Open fucking sesame? At the double!'

The guard ran back and opened the gates and the convoy drove in. Ash and the two Scottish vehicles echelon parked in front of the administration office. Pete Mack parked behind them so that Smiffy could cover the building opposite with the machinegun. Everyone but Pete and Smiffy got out of the cars. Sandy Cameron had a captain's three pips on the front of his combat tunic. He carried only his holstered handgun. Duggan, behind him, had the stripes of a sergeant on his arm. He carried an Uzi. The two other Scots carried automatic rifles.

'Attention!' shouted Ash at the soldier who came out of the building. The man obeyed, eyes darting and frightened.

The Major went inside and Ash and Cameron followed. They walked past a raised hatch at a counter and into an open-plan office that had been turned into a dormitory. There was a flight of stairs at the far end. A sergeant was standing by an open interior door in a partition. He came to attention at the approach of the Major and gave a smart salute. The Major returned it and nodded in approval. 'At last. A real soldier,' he murmured, and the sergeant straightened his shoulders a fraction, at the praise. He was below medium height and had a moustache and looked capable. 'Communication room?' the Major said.

'Sir.' The sergeant pointed to the second door in the partition. 'Just there, sir.'

The Major nodded and looked at Cameron. The Scot opened the door and went inside. He came out a moment later.

'Empty, sir.'

The Major glanced at the sergeant.

'It's not manned full time, sir.'

'Good.' He nodded. 'And your officer?'

'Off duty, sir.' The sergeant's eyes glanced towards the other door in the partition. 'He'll be here directly, sir.'

The Major nodded. 'Other ranks?'

'Two at the mine, the rest in the canteen, sir.'

'Lunchtime?'

'Yes sir.'

'Good. I'm a bit peckish, myself. Ash, check the roof, will you?'

'Sir.' Ash came to attention and looked at the sergeant until the man realised he needed directions.

'This way, sergeant.'

He led him across the room to the staircase. As they ascended, the lieutenant finally made an appearance, still fastening his tunic.

'Sir,' he said, coming to attention and saluting. 'I must apologise. We weren't expecting …'

The Major flicked a return salute and then drew the Glock from the holster on his hip.

'Don't worry about it, old chap. Regime change.'

'What?'

'You are now under arrest.' He smiled and added, 'For you, the war is over.'

'What?' The lieutenant wasn't wearing a weapon.

'Who is in the room?' the Major asked.

'What?'

'Good God, man!' He pointed the gun at his face. 'Get a grip!'

'A girl. A … young lady.'

'Introduce us.'

'What?'

'Call her out.'

'Vicki? Come out here.'

A girl with short blonde hair and smudged red lips, wearing high heels and a silk dressing gown appeared in the doorway.

'What?' she said.

'I do despair,' said the Major, in exasperation glancing at Cameron, but at least she wasn't carrying the lieutenant's gun.

Shots were heard from outside. At a distance, probably the mine. Several shots. A pause, followed by two more bursts. A moment later, more shots from the roof. Two quick, followed by two that were more deliberately spaced.

Cameron said to the lieutenant, 'Sit on the floor.'

'What?'

'Oh my God,' said the Major.

The lieutenant sat on the floor.

'You, too,' Cameron said to the girl.

Shooting from directly outside was loud enough to make them start. Single shots then a burst from Smiffy's machinegun. More single shots, then silence. The girl stared from the Major to Cameron, realisation dawning that something important was happening, and that it might be time to change sides. She sat on the floor with the lieutenant.

Ash returned from the roof, clattering down the stairs, a Glock in his right hand. There was no elation at killing two men. His face was stony at completing a job that had been necessary. He went straight to the main door and shouted from it without going outside.

'Status?'

'Five hostiles down.' The voice that of Smiffy. 'Duggan and Pete checking the canteen.'

Ash went outside cautiously. Five down and the ones they had already accounted for meant the only possible survivors were at the mine where the shooting had started. Duggan came out of the canteen and shouted: 'Clear.' Pete followed him with a chubby civilian with red hair.

The razor fencing and barricades at the mine itself were to the right. A gate squeaked in the silence that seemed intensified in the aftermath of the gunfire. A group of men staggered forward, some being helped by others. Kev carried one in his arms; James walking alongside, shouldering both his and his comrade's weapons. Mandi half carrying another who was limping heavily. Sandra emerged from the group, alongside her a tall, battered but unbowed man in the ragged remnants of an RAF uniform.

'Problems?' she said to Ash.

'None. Everything is secured. No casualties. No message was sent.'

The Major appeared in the doorway. The ragged Harry Babbington attempted to come to attention.

'Certainly not, old chap,' said the Major. 'Lunch, I believe, is served.'

*　　　*　　　*

Greta set up a first aid station in the admin building and five of the mineworkers were laid in cots. The others ate in the canteen, served by a grinning Tim Jepson, the red headed chef. He sliced up large steak pies he had made for the guards. They had them with potatoes and vegetables. There wasn't enough for the troops from Haven, so he added soup, bacon and eggs, chips and fresh bread.

Babbington and the walking mine survivors ate like the starving men they were. Half remained dull eyed, as if they couldn't believe their change in fortune, the rest were excited; with the food, freedom, possibilities of finding lost friends and loved ones, possibilities of revenge.

Sandra, the Major, Yank and Sandy Cameron sat apart and ate sparingly. Jepson served them coffee. Afterwards, Babbington joined them. He was led over by a grinning Smiffy.

'I told you,' he said.

Babbington looked puzzled about what Smiffy might have told them. He took a seat and accepted coffee from Jepson.

The chef said, 'Reaper was here. I knew something was up then. He called himself Tom Watson.'

'Do you know where he is?' Sandra said.

'They took him to Baystoke. It's a village south of Banbury. He's at Brownley House. That's the General's headquarters. They know who he is. The Tans were full of it this morning. Somebody recognised him and they've got him locked up.'

'He's still alive?' Sandra said.

'He's alive. But they say he's taken a beating. They plan to kill him in Banbury on Sunday. A public execution.'

Greta Malone joined them and realised, from their looks, they knew something she didn't.

'What?' she said.

'Reaper's alive. He's a prisoner. He's been beaten but he's alive.'

Her face tightened but she simply nodded.

'How are the walking wounded?' said the Major.

'Suffering from bad diet, abuse, overwork, exhaustion,' she said. 'One has a serious leg injury. He'll need an operation. But they will recover, given time.'

'We need to move quickly, before anyone realises we're here,' Sandra said. She looked at Babbington. 'If we take the General and the Tans, what will the real military do?'

'Probably be grateful. But you'll have to be careful. Purcell removed officers and NCOs who didn't agree with him and promoted those who would follow orders.'

'How many Tans are we up against?'

'I don't know. I've been in here a while.'

'Time to ask the lieutenant,' said Yank. She pronounced it loo-tenant.

'Turner's alive?' Babbington said and Sandra nodded. 'Then I'll get you exact numbers and disposition.' He rose from the table. 'Give me ten minutes. Where is the little bastard?'

For a moment, Sandra thought the Major or Cameron might object to what Babbington obviously intended. They didn't.

'It would be helpful if we knew routines. Where Purcell and Barstow will be in particular. Where they are holding Reaper.'

Babbington nodded and Yank said, 'I'll take you.'

'Jimmy! Tank!' Babbington called, and two of the group of mine survivors looked round. Babbington nodded towards the door and they got to their feet and joined him.

'I take it that Lieutenant Turner is not a popular officer,' the Major said.

'He's a bastard of the first order who deserves everything that's coming to him,' Jepson said, in a low voice. 'He hung Tank's friend Boris on the razor wire. Left him to die. Wanted to see if he could last a week without water. Boris didn't give him the satisfaction. He slit his throat on the wire that night. More coffee, Major?'

*   *   *

Sandra, the Major and Cameron gave the flight sergeant thirty minutes before they crossed to the admin building. Yank was sitting outside drinking a bottle of beer.

'Bud,' she said, holding up the bottle. 'The loo-tenant's private stock. He doesn't need it any more.'

She got up and led the way inside. The five men in the

cots were being cared for by Smiffy, Kev and Nina. They had taken food and drink and three of them were sleeping, one was lying on his back staring at the ceiling while Smiffy sat by his side, and the fifth was holding Nina's hand and talking to her softly but with a glaze in his eyes that was abnormal.

'He thinks she's his wife,' Yank said, softly. 'Harry's upstairs. But what are we going to do with Barbie?'

She nodded at one of the offices whose door was open. Inside sat the blonde girl in the silk dressing gown. She was tied to a swivel chair and the gown had slipped from her legs and showed a stocking top and white suspender strap. Her eyes were wide and frightened.

'I've done nothing wrong,' she said. 'It wasn't me. I never did anything.'

Sandra stared at her and said, 'You know, you give blondes a bad name.'

'I couldn't help it.' Desperate tears burst from her eyes and ran down her cheeks. Her smudged make-up ran even more. 'I had no choice. You don't know what it was like.'

'Yes I do,' said Sandra.

'I had no choice.' The girl's head dipped and the tears didn't stop. 'He said he'd give me to the men if I didn't. I'm sorry. I'm sorry.'

Sandra's anger dissipated like the plug had been pulled.

'Shit,' she said, and glanced at the two men and Yank in the doorway before looking away.

Victims came in all categories. The girl might have dolled herself up to order, she might have done everything she was told, she might have taken advantage of her privileged position. But what choice had she had and how precarious had that position been?

Sandra pulled the Bowie knife from the sheath on her leg and stepped forward. The girl screamed and said, 'No!' and Sandra cut the ropes that tied her to the chair.

'Have you got anything else to put on? Anything … more suitable.'

She had a vision of how she must have looked herself when Reaper had found her when it had all begun in those first horrendous weeks of the plague.

'I can find something.'

'Then do it. And wash that stuff off your face. You don't need it now.'

The girl staggered when she got to her feet and walked unsteadily into the inner room. Yank went past Sandra.

'I'll keep an eye on her,' she said.

They went back into the main hall and footsteps crossed the floor above them and Babbington, Jimmy and Tank came down the stairs at the far end. The flight sergeant was holding a map. Tank, who was a big man, was holding his knuckles.

'Dispositions and manpower.'

Sandra, the Major and Cameron didn't ask the whereabouts of Lieutenant Turner. Flight Sergeant Harry Babbington didn't say.

*　　　*　　　*

The Tans had potentially forty-eight men in the village of Baystoke, along with one captain, two lieutenants, two sergeants and two corporals, General George Purcell and Major Barstow. Four patrols would be out. These would each consist of two vehicles containing six men led by a corporal: twenty-eight men in total. They would return at six sharp. Returning early was frowned upon.

The work camp, which was located between the canal and the river on an industrial estate, contained about a hundred men. They did light industrial work when they were not needed to clear sewage, dig drains or remove and dispose of corpses. They were guarded by a lieutenant, a sergeant, a corporal and five Tans, aided by five trainees, who were not necessarily from the military. Thugs, according to Babbington, were better recruitment material to the Tans than British soldiers and airmen.

One road ran through the village. Two-man checkpoints would be in place on the outskirts, both north and south.

The thousand genuine military personnel were based in Banbury. They would have patrols on the outer reaches of Redemption's territory, ostensibly to keep intruders away, but effectively to encourage the civilian population to remain. Not that it was feasible that many would try to move on. People in relationships were split apart during the working day. It had proved unlikely that men or women made a run for it on their own. Besides, their lives might be dull and the work hard, but they were not in danger as long as they kept their heads down and caused no trouble.

'That's how it works,' Babbington said. 'That's how they maintain the status quo.'

'Which is why it needs to change,' said Sandra.

Maps were before the group on a table in the admin building: Banbury and the army HQ based in the Town Hall buildings was highlighted, along with the work camp on the Tramways Industrial Estate. The outline of the village of Baystoke had been hand drawn and buildings identified courtesy of the late Lieutenant Turner. Even the interior of Brownley House was mapped out with information supplied by a more than willing Vicki, the blonde girl who had been the lieutenant's paramour. She was keen to rehabilitate herself, had dressed in a track suit, washed her face clean of make up and was helping tend the mine workers in the cots. She had not asked about Lieutenant Turner, but she had volunteered she had once been a guest at Brownley House.

They had learned that Purcell was always in his quarters at Brownley House by four o'clock at the latest. He was a man of habit who spent at least an hour working before preparing for dinner at seven. Barstow was far less assiduous in his duties, which he usually completed by lunchtime when he started drinking, although, Turner had said, he held it well. The pub in the village was used by the men, but didn't open until six, and the village hall had been converted into the officer's mess. There were five officers, including Barstow: a captain and three lieutenants. The captain had taken a girl for himself, as Turner had, but the mess also had two ladies who were expected to serve more than drinks and food.

Barstow ignored even the basic rules of etiquette, drank when he liked and took whatever woman aroused him at the time, no matter to whom she might be nominally attached. Vicki confirmed this assessment of his behaviour. He was usually at Brownley house at five for a staff meeting with the general. This did not take long. By five thirty, he would be in the mess to carry on drinking.

The Tans brothel – the Pussy Shack – was open to NCOs only in the afternoon and became available to the rank and file after six.

Standing around the table were the Major, Cameron, Yank, Ash and Pete Mack.

A clatter on the stairs and Smiffy and Mandi appeared, behind them two of the healthier survivors of the mine. They all carried boxes.

'Sorted,' said Mandi. 'I'd better get off.'

They carried the boxes outside to a waiting vehicle.

'Time we were all going,' Sandra said, looking at her

watch. They were running to a timetable. She looked round at the expectant faces, at the doubt, determination and excitement. 'Good luck.'

Like Reaper had done, a few short days before, they were now flying by the seat of their pants.

Chapter 27

THE MAJOR WAS IN THE LEAD vehicle in the convoy. Ash drove and Flight Sergeant Harry Babbington, wearing a new combat uniform, sat behind them. Pete drove the second vehicle with Smiffy manning the machinegun, and the Scottish vehicles followed. Finally, came a military truck carrying ten of the survivors from the mine, all in fresh uniforms and armed.

Combat uniforms had been packed in the hope the first part of the plan would be successful and they would have volunteers from among the liberated men. All those capable of standing had volunteered. The men had all showered and shaved; long hair had been hacked short, those with less lustrous locks had shaved their heads. Their bodies might be thin but their eyes burnt with desire. They no longer looked like slave workers.

The five recovering survivors remained at the mine being cared for by the five least fit, plus the girl, Vicki and chef Tim Jepson.

They needed to be at their destination by five, an hour before the return of troops to their barracks, which were mainly in hotels in the town. A vehicle with military markings approached them.

The Major said, 'Make him stop,' which Ash did by driving in front of it.

A captain jumped out of the passenger seat, unsure how to react to a strange officer leading a military convoy sitting alongside a black sergeant.

The Major stood up where he was, holding onto the windscreen. The elevation plus his natural height gave him a distinct advantage, even before the captain noticed his rank. The man came to attention and saluted. A sergeant, who had disembarked from the vehicle, did the same. The Major touched his cap with his swagger stick.

'Major Wiseman of the British Army of the North,' he said, in a compelling voice. 'You are?'

'Captain Selby, sir. Er, sir? We didn't know there was an army of the north.'

'Quite. Doesn't surprise me. Purcell's a bounder. I'd be obliged if you could escort me to army command.'

'Army command in Banbury, sir?'

'Of course, Banbury. That, I believe, is the only army command there is. Purcell's rabble are not worthy to wear the uniform. Now, if you would be so kind?'

He waved his swagger stick and the officer saluted and went back to the vehicle, which made a three point turn and set off into town. The convoy followed.

'You really are very good,' Ash said.

'It's the role I've been waiting for all my life,' the Major said, with a smile.

It didn't take long to reach the Town Hall buildings, which were at the junction of High Street and Market Place. Ash pulled up alongside the front door. Pete Mack turned his vehicle so that it faced down Bridge Street, which Smiffy now covered with the mounted machinegun. The two Scottish BMWs drove past and parked and three of the occupants took up position behind their vehicles to cover Market Place and the Castle Quay shopping centre. The truck stopped short on the other side of the building, manoeuvred on the roundabout and reversed so that its rear faced the High Street. The tailgate was dropped to reveal a manned heavy machinegun in a nest of sandbags. Other men climbed out and spread among the vehicles, at ease but in a defensive formation. Jimmy and Tank took positions by the Major's lead vehicle.

The Major was out and staring around like he owned the place. Cameron, wearing only his side arm, joined him. Ash and Babbington, each carrying an Uzi, took up position behind them. Their guide, Captain Selby hurried up to the group, his sergeant following hesitantly as he eyed the weaponry on display.

'Lead on, captain,' the Major said, and the officer did so, still followed by his sergeant.

Their arrival had already been noted and two privates and a corporal were standing in the entrance hall. Colonel Maidstone appeared at the open door to an office.

The Captain said, 'Colonel, this is Major Wiseman of the British Army of the North.' He turned to the Major. 'Major, Colonel Maidstone, Officer Commanding the New Army.'

'Thank you, captain.' The Major and the Colonel exchanged salutes. Ash had gone to talk to the corporal. The Major walked straight past Maidstone into his office, where a sergeant came to attention. 'This won't do, it's not big enough. Colonel!'

His voice filled the room and, probably, the entire building. The Colonel was confused. He followed him into the office, along with Captain Selby and Sandy Cameron. Babbington stood in the doorway, his back to the room, the Uzi held across his chest. No one else entered.

'Major, I do believe I am senior officer,' Maidstone said, with a bleat.

'Of course you are. Apologies. But the exigencies that now apply call for an unorthodox approach in the way we work together. By the way, when did you become colonel?'

'General Purcell appointed me seven months ago.'

'Ah. Purcell, a rogue who is not a general and who has no right to suborn members of the British forces into a so-called new army. What was your rank before, Colonel? In *Her Majesty's* army.'

'Captain.'

'Quite. However, that is by the by, and I am sure your new rank will be confirmed when this little mess is sorted out.'

'Little mess? Sorted out? Major, what is going on? Why are you here?'

'I am here to restore order, colonel. We have been in secret communication with Prince Harry. We are here to restore order.'

'But the Prince is with the General. He is commander in chief.'

'The Prince is a captive of the General. I take it you have seen him?'

'Of course.'

'And doesn't it strike you odd that he is always surrounded by these damn Black and Tans? This rabble of non-soldiers. He is being coerced, man. He is being threatened. Not him, personally. That wouldn't bother, Harry. I know him. He has so far stayed silent because the threat is to the people. Purcell, and this damnable fellow Barstow have said they will kill innocents if he doesn't obey. They have possibly done so already.'

'Windsor,' Maidstone whispered.

'Speak up, man!'

'Windsor.' Maidstone looked up, his eyes clearing as if they had been covered in wool. 'There was talk of people killed in Windsor. They said they fired the castle to hide it. That's why we moved here.'

Maidstone glanced past the Major at the sergeant, still at attention, and Captain Selby, searching for confirmation.

'There was a rumour,' said the captain. 'But surely …'

'We are here to remove Purcell and Barstow,' the Major said. 'No blame is attached to any military personnel. Damn difficult times, I know. No blame at all. But now the reckoning is due. Now is the time to make a difference. As we speak, units are moving on Purcell and his Black and Tans.' He spat the name with utter contempt. 'Those units will extradite the Prince safely and will deal with Purcell and his rabble with extreme prejudice.'

The words, delivered with Churchillian depth, reverberated through the building. It sounded as if two of the privates outside actually gave a cheer before they were glared to silence by an NCO.

'To ensure a smooth operation with the least confusion and unnecessary shedding of blood, we will call all officers and senior NCOs to a briefing here. My sergeant is already taking care of that. So, is there a room big enough.'

He turned and stared at the sergeant.

'Yes, sir. Just about, sir.'

'Good man.' He tapped him on the shoulder with the swagger stick. 'Could you organise that? Get rid of any chairs or clutter?'

'Yes, sir. Right away, sir.'

He saluted and the Major saluted in return. The sergeant left without looking towards Maidstone for confirmation of the order.

'And while we wait for the chaps to arrive, perhaps you can supply a list of officers, colonel. Flight Sergeant Harry

Babbington here, will help you go through it.' Babbington now stepped into the room. 'And you and Captain Selby can point out which officers may be supportive of Purcell. We don't want misguided loyalty getting in the way of the Prince's safety. When did you last see him, by the way? I trust he is well?'

'I saw him on Sunday. Had dinner with him on Saturday. He is in fine health. Although ...'

'Yes?'

'He did seem subdued. There was tension, between him and Colonel Barstow.'

'No surprise, there. He cannot stand the man.' The Major looked round at the others present. 'But then who can?'

Chapter 28

THE VILLAGE HAD A SQUARE patch of grass and a pond, although no ducks. They'd been eaten the previous year. The main road paralleled the canal. Brownley House stood back from the road, solid, detached and smug in its own grounds, facing the green. A low wall ran along the frontage, gates were wide open and a gravel drive led to the front door. The substantial gardens at the back meandered down to the water.

Cottages, a shop, a terrace of three storey houses, and the pub – The Woodman – were to the right of the green. This housing was used as accommodation for the Tans. Three large detached houses were to the left. The middle house was the Pussy Shack, the Tans' brothel, the two flanking dwellings housed the NCOs, sergeants in one, corporals in the other. Lance Corporals bedded down with the men, ostensibly to instil a modicum of order.

An 18th century church dominated the fourth and upper side of the green. The stern, weathered stonework and sainted windows did not seem to approve of the changes to its village. The large detached vicarage on the left was being used as officers' quarters; the village hall on the right was the mess hall for the Tans.

The first casualties were the guards at the checkpoints. They were lax and lazy. Sandra led Pete Mack, James and Gwen to take out those to the north. Yank was tasked with removing the ones to the south. Sandra stared at the 4x4 parked at the side of the road through the scope of her weapon. She shook her head at their stupidity.

'Do you want me to take the one on the bonnet?' James asked.

'In ten.'

Sandra slipped behind a hedgerow and moved towards the vehicle along the side of an overgrown field. She was soon close to the 4x4. One guard sat on the bonnet of the car leaning back against the windshield with his eyes closed as he enjoyed the afternoon sun. The other had lowered the passenger seat and was sprawled full length, the door open to catch the breeze. She could hear his snores. Sandra lay down her automatic rifle and took the Bowie knife from its sheath and chose a gap in the hedge. She did not have to wait long.

The noise from the sound suppressor on the sniper's rifle James was using from a hundred yards away was slight. The body of the guard who was sunbathing jerked briefly, as if he had had a bad dream, and blood bubbled from his chest. The bullet went through him, through the windscreen and through the rear window of the car. The second guard stirred and waved a hand at the sound of a bee and began to sit up. He was mid-thirties and a slovenly soldier. He had unfastened his belt and the top of his trousers for comfort.

Sandra rose from the side of the road, slipped the blade through his throat and ripped it forward. The knife was very sharp and she had experience. It went in easily at a point of little resistance. He gurgled, blood spurted and sprayed the interior of the car. She remained to one side to avoid the splatter.

Two down and, hopefully, two more down to the south. Time to move on.

Dr Greta Malone was staying with the vehicles they had hidden in a copse of trees along a dirt track. She was their radio link with Banbury. Sandra, Pete Mack, James and Gwen nodded goodbyes to her and went across country towards the canal bank. Their target was Brownley House. If all went according to plan, they could take Purcell and Barstow and free Reaper at the same time. They would then remove the NCOs, who would be in their quarters or the Pussy Shack. Then they would take out the remaining officers in the vicarage. The Tans would be a rabble without leaders.

They were going in at five fifteen. Their deadlines were tight. They needed to have won the war before the patrols returned at six. By the time those twenty-eight men arrived, it should all be over.

*   *   *

The lawns at the rear of the mansion house were neat and well-trimmed. Yank and the others joined them. They waited by the water and plotted a way through the bushes, rockeries, shrubs and trees. A covered terrace ran along half of the rear of the mansion house, equipped with tables and chairs. French windows onto the terrace were closed. Sandra's Clansman radio bleeped.

She thumbed the respond switch and said: 'Blues one.'

'Phase one is go,' said Greta.

'Roger, out.' To the others she said, 'The Major has taken Army HQ. Now it's our turn.'

They moved forward into cover, pausing once, when a guard sauntered into view smoking a cigarette, a carbine over his shoulder. The man stared down the gardens and took his time over the smoke. Eventually, he stubbed it out between his fingers and put the remains in a pocket. Perhaps the General was particular about litter. He turned and went back from where he had come.

Sandra had co-opted Nina to go with her round the house to the right, Yank and Dee went to the left. Jenny and Kat were to attempt an entry from the rear. Kev and Pete were being used as mules to carry equipment; James, who also had a bag of extras on his back, and Gwen were providing their cover. Just for a second, Sandra wondered at their chances of success. They were a motley group of young women, a mechanic, a middle aged ex-sailor and a public schoolboy, led by a shop assistant from Top Shop.

They were hardly the Magnificent Seven. But this was their only chance and they had to take it.

She was moving fast, a Glock fitted with a sound suppressor in her left hand, the Bowie knife in her right. As they rounded a rhododendron, the guard who had been smoking appeared. He was startled enough to stop and wonder where this blonde girl had come from before he realised she was a danger. By that time it was too late and the knife had gone into his stomach, driven by her momentum, and the long blade ripped into vital organs. He sagged and coughed and she removed the knife and, as he dropped to his knees, slashed it across his throat. This time she could not avoid the blood that splashed onto her legs.

Nina was a pace behind her, Uzi on a strap hanging down her back, a silenced Glock in her right hand.

Sandra wiped the knife against the dead man's uniform and moved on quickly. Keep the surprise. There was a side door into the house and steps down to a cellar. Nina went down the steps. The door was unlocked, the room empty. She investigated the cot and came out.

'Fresh blood on a camp bed,' she said.

Sandra led the way into the house. The first door she opened led into a room without windows. She tried the light switch and, amazingly, it worked. They saw the tools on the table, the chains, more fresh blood on the wall.

They moved on. Sandra first. Wanting to answer blood with blood. The rooms to the rear were empty. Handsome rooms. Dining room, drawing room, access to the French windows. A handsome house for handsome living by the wealthy of the past. They encountered Jenny in a corridor behind the stairs. She put a finger to her lips and pointed. Jenny and Kat had found the communications room which was manned at all times. Sandra nodded and she and Nina moved back the way they had come. Jenny would take care of the radio operator.

They moved towards the front of the house and she used a hand mirror to look around the corner. Two guards were in the hall by the front door. Sub-machineguns hung around their necks. One was sitting in an upright chair with carved arms and a back tall enough to be a throne. His legs were stretched out and crossed at the ankles and his hands were in his pockets. The other was leaning against the wall, arms folded, one eye on the stairs.

Sandra whispered in Nina's ear. 'You take the one standing.' She walked round the corner, taking care to stay out of Nina's line of fire.

'Hi boys,' she said, in a faux sexy schoolgirl voice.

The two men stared in surprise at the small figure of a blonde girl. Then they noticed the knife she held in her right hand.

'Who ...?' said the leaning soldier, straightening and reaching for his gun.

By then it was too late. Nina, unnoticed because of the distraction of the vision approaching them, aimed the silenced Glock and put two bullets into him. The second Tan was struggling to free his hands and stand up at the same time. Sandra reached him at the run and plunged the knife into his throat. The blade cut the carotid artery and the blood gushed. More on her, most on the floor.

'Oh my God.'

They turned at the voice. Gwen was standing at the other side of the hall, her eyes wide with horror. She had seen the blood spurt. Now she stared at Sandra, whose face, hair, Kevlar vest and t-shirt were covered with it. Yank appeared behind her.

'One hostile outside,' she said, in a low voice. 'Dealt with. We came through the kitchens. The kettle is still hot. Someone is here.'

Jenny and Kat joined them at the bottom of the stairs.

Sandra said, 'We'll go left, you go right.'

They ascended silently on thick carpet and went their separate ways. She found Purcell in the second room she tried, a large bedroom with two interior doors. The General was sitting at a desk before full-length windows that led onto a small balcony. He was writing on sheets of loose paper with a fountain pen. The window provided a view onto the village green.

He half turned as she came in and said, 'Adams?' as if surprised someone had entered without knocking. When he saw Sandra, he fully turned in the swivel chair. Nina stepped past her into the room and covered him with the silenced Glock. Sandra checked the other doors – a bathroom and a walk-in wardrobe – before returning to face the seated man.

The knife she held was bloody and so was she: in the past, her appearance had frightened enemies.

'General Purcell,' she said.

Purcell carefully screwed the top onto his fountain pen. 'I presume you are the Angel of Death.'

'Where's Reaper?'

'Ah. A rescue. I had heard you two were close. Such sentimental actions will be the death of you.'

'Where is he?'

'Colonel Barstow moved him.' He indicated the window behind him with a movement of his head. 'He currently resides in the parish church of St John. You can't miss it. Straight across the green, between the barracks of my troops, and alongside the officer's mess. I'm sure if you ask nicely, Colonel Barstow will let you see him.'

'Where's Barstow?' she said, with a sinking feeling.

'He's attending to Reaper.'

Things had been going too well. Their luck had suddenly changed.

Sandra stepped close to Purcell and put the knife to the side of his neck. He flinched but held her gaze. She carefully wiped the blood off the blade on his tunic and then replaced it in its sheath. His nose wrinkled at the close proximity of gore.

'The only way you will leave here alive is to go now, the way you came,' he said. 'This is a suicide mission. You can salve your conscience. You made the attempt. Now get out before you join him in the church. You wouldn't like what Barstow would do to you.'

'Barstow won't like what I do to him,' she hissed. 'Or maybe Reaper will do it first.'

He stared into the intensity of her eyes and a percentage of his bluff drained away. This was not a girl who had dressed as a Halloween vampire. She had the instincts of a wolf. He saw death in her gaze and he realised why people called her the Angel.

The door opened. Yank stepped in first and stood back to allow a young woman, a man who, despite wearing a uniform, looked nothing like a soldier, and Prince Harry to enter. They stood in a confused group and all three flinched at the sight of Sandra. Dee brought up the rear.

'Nobody else here,' she said. She indicated Adams with her gun. 'He was serving them tea.'

Harry was wearing jeans and an open neck shirt.

'Prince Harry?' Sandra said, hesitantly, and wondered if there was some protocol she should follow.

He smiled ruefully. 'The name is Harry but I'm not the prince.' He nodded at the General. 'That was his idea.'

'Who's he?' she said, meaning the soldier who was not a soldier.

'Adams. He's the General's batman.' Sandra began to raise the Glock. 'He's a good guy,' Harry said, hurriedly. 'He helped us, and he helped Reaper.'

She lowered the gun. 'You met Reaper?'

'He was a guest here, when they thought he was a pilot. Then they discovered who he really was.'

The girl said, 'Barstow has taken him to the church.'

'Why?' asked Sandra.

'The General didn't like the thought of prolonged violence in his own house. The Beast moved him to the church. Out of sight, out of mind.'

'What a delicate little soul you are,' Sandra said to Purcell. Then she looked back at the girl. 'Who are you?'

'Judith Finlay. I'm supposed to be the Prince's consort.' She smiled without humour at the General. 'You couldn't even get that right. I'm gay.'

'Good God,' he said, seemingly more shocked by the confession of her sexuality than being taken prisoner. 'But you …'

'No we didn't.' Judith looked at Sandra. 'If they had found out, the Beast would have taken me. I would probably have ended in the Pussy Shack.'

'You'll never get away with this,' the general said.

Sandra looked at him.

'Did you really say that?' she said. Then: 'Get Pete and Kev. We need to set up.'

Sandra pushed past the General to stare out of the window.

'You're mad,' Purcell said, turning in the swivel chair to follow her progress. 'You're all going to die.'

Sandra swung her arm back viciously: a stiff armed blow across his face that burst his nose and knocked him from the chair. Adams went to his aid. She didn't turn around, but said, 'From now on, you remain silent. Annoy me and I'll gut you.' She glanced back. 'Harry? Can you tie him up?'

'You don't know …' the General began to bluster, until she turned and kicked him in the face.

'No. You don't know. I've just come from the mine. I've seen what you do. Now shut up and watch what we do.'

Harry got to work tying up the man whose ego was deflating fast. Pete carried in a light machinegun and extra ammunition. He also carried an Uzi across his back.

'Kev's putting the other in a bedroom across the hall,' he said.

'James, you and Gwen join him. You too, Nina.' She was thinking fast. Could they still make the plan work?

Pete opened the double windows that gave access to the balcony and set up the gun on the desk, knocking onto the floor the stack of handwritten papers. They fluttered haphazardly to the carpet. The General, back in the chair to which he was now being tied, shuddered as if the act of discarding his memoirs was the first stage of the destruction of his vision.

Adams brought a wet cloth from the bathroom to dab at the General's face. Harry and Judith stood awkwardly, unsure what to do or how to behave or whether they, too, were under guard.

'Yank, you're in charge. Pete, you're with me.'

'Where are you going?' Yank said.

'We'll do what we planned, only quicker. It's five thirty, we've still got time. Pussy Shack and then Reaper. Hopefully Barstow on the way.'

Pete left the machinegun and Dee took over. He still had the Uzi on his back and was loaded with spare magazines.

Harry said, 'What's happening?'

'We're going to get Reaper back,' Sandra said, picking up a spare Uzi and slipping the strap around her neck. 'And we're going to destroy the General's private army.'

'What about Banbury? What about the army in Banbury?'

'Taken care of. This is a private war. Us and the Tans.'

'But who is us? Is this it?'

Sandra fixed him with a glare. She couldn't blame him for being sceptical. Seven girls and three men. Not much of an army.

'We've done this before,' she said. 'Make a decision. Which side are you on?'

He did not look away from her. His gaze was firm and intelligent, his chin set. He knew the odds and he was, she thought, rather handsome.

'Yours, of course. Give me a gun and I'll help.'

For some reason his reply cheered her. As if he didn't think the odds were hopeless.

'Do you know how to use one?' she said.

'The General insisted I learn.'

'What about me?' Judith said.

Sandra thought they were a pair of unlikely allies. But welcome, nonetheless.

'There are dead guards downstairs,' she said. They don't need guns any more. It would be good to collect all the spare weapons and ammunition. Yank will tell you where the bodies are.'

'Right.'

Sandra moved to have a private word with the American.

'If this goes tits up, radio the Major and tell him what's happening. He might have to talk his way out of Banbury. Then get the others out of here and back to Haven.'

Their eyes locked. Sandra didn't think Yank would be inclined to obey the last order.

'It won't go tits up, girl. Besides,' she smiled, 'there's more balls in this team than all the Tans put together.'

'You'll do what you have to do?'

'Bank on it.'

*　　　*　　　*

They were running out of time. They should have gone two hundred yards down the road before crossing to stay out of sight but they didn't. No one was on the village green; it was still too early for anyone to be waiting outside the pub for it to open. They crossed and entered the back gardens of the large houses on the left. They really should be taking more care but speed was more essential than caution.

Her intention was for them to be silent assassins in the Pussy Shack to at least reduce the number of NCOs, then head straight for Reaper and double back to take care of the officers. Even she knew it was ill conceived, but it would have to do. They entered the rear of the brothel and scared a young girl in the kitchen who was pouring a large measure of vodka into a mug of coffee. She wore a silk dressing gown.

'Who the fuck?'

Sandra held up a finger for quiet and said, 'How many girls? How many men?'

'What?'

Pete handed her the vodka bottle and said, 'Take a swig.' The girl did and coughed. 'Now, how many girls? How many men?'

'Eight girls, three men.'

'Eight girls including you?' Sandra said.

She nodded. She was totally bewildered and not a little distracted from the blood on Sandra's face.

'What are you?'

'We're going to kill the men,' Sandra said, and smiled. 'And then we're going to kill the rest of the Tans.'

'You're going to kill them? Really?'

'Yes. Now, take us to the girls.'

The house was a large Victorian dwelling that, in a city, might have been split into flats but in the village had survived as a single home for a wealthy professional. They were led into a large living room where four girls sat around with listless patience. The youngest wore a school uniform, an Asian girl was dressed as a nun, the other two were in silk dresses and high heels. They stared at the intruders in amazement.

Their guide informed them of their intention in a low voice. The pleasure was obvious on the faces of three of them; the fourth looked worried. 'What about afterwards? The Tans will take it out on us.'

Sandra said, 'We're going to kill them. All of them.'

The doubting girl didn't look reassured.

'Now, where are these men?'

The schoolgirl volunteered to show them the rooms where the three men were having sex. As they climbed the stairs, Sandra touched the girl on the arm.

'How old are you?' she whispered.

'Fourteen.'

Sandra looked at Pete and said, 'Okay?'

If Pete's resolve had needed stiffening, the girl's age had done the job. 'Okay.'

They went into a room on the first floor. It smelled of sex and sweat and fear. Pete held a Glock in both hands, Sandra held the Bowie knife in her right hand. The man was naked and the girl kneeling on the bed before him. His trousers were folded on a chair, the tunic hung on its back. They bore a sergeant's stripes. Sandra stuck the knife in the man's throat. The girl didn't know at first what was happening and mistook his convulsions. Sandra ripped the knife and blood sprayed and the girl screamed and the schoolgirl went to calm her and tell her what was happening.

'Come on,' Sandra said, her voice hoarse. 'The next one.'

A scream was not unusual in this house and no one came to investigate. The girl pointed to the door of the next room that was occupied and they went in quickly. A black girl was lying on the bed, half naked. A soldier was dressing, his trousers halfway up his legs. His mouth dropped open and Sandra pushed the knife into his stomach below his ribs. She aimed upwards, pushing and twisting. He gasped and fell backwards off the blade onto the floor. The girl screamed. What was wrong with these women?

Then Sandra saw her reflection in a large mirror. She looked like a character from a slasher movie.

One scream they could get away with, but two?

The schoolgirl went to the woman on the bed and the two held each other. Pete backed onto the landing. A door opened on the floor above and a man, half dressed, came to the top of the stairs. Before he could speak, Pete shot him: double tap, head and chest.

The man Sandra had stabbed was still gurgling, still alive. The schoolgirl pulled a pillow from the bed, dropped it over his face and knelt on it.

They were running out of time.

'The church,' she said to Pete. 'We must get to the church.'

As they reached the ground floor, the front door was pushed open. They turned and hesitated in case it was one of the girls. But it was a Lance Corporal who already had an automatic handgun pointing at them. He fired first, with fear but without great accuracy, the shots loud in the confines of the corridor. Pete returned fire, hitting him with three shots that sent him staggering backwards down the path of the front garden.

'Shit.' Sandra moved to slam and lock the door. All surprise was now gone. But she was determined to try for the church. She turned and watched Pete slide sideways against the wall and slump to the floor. 'Pete?'

'The bastard got me.' Blood was pumping from a wound in his thigh.

'Christ.'

A machinegun opened fire from Brownley House. The Tans had been alerted and must have been trying to cross the green. The battle had started and the odds had suddenly lengthened.

'Go get Reaper,' Pete said.

The schoolgirl came downstairs, took one look and ran into the room where the other women had been waiting. She returned, pulling behind her the Asian girl in the nun's outfit.

'Bernie's a nurse.'

Bernie was frightened but one look at the wound and her training took over. She issued instructions and the schoolgirl obeyed. Another woman came to help.

'Go!' Pete said.

And she did.

*   *   *

Sandra went through the back gardens and paused to look across the green to see what was happening. The Tans were being organised by officers. Did that mean the church would be empty apart from Reaper?

She crossed a lane and was through a side gate and into the vicarage garden. She ran round the back of the house, using cover, but moving too quickly to be safe. Hopefully the officers had rushed to take charge of their men after the opening shots. All but one of them had. A florid-faced captain came out of the rear door of the vicarage and collided with her as she ran past. Sandra was tumbled to the ground while the captain was knocked backwards into the stonework of the house.

For a split second, they stared at each other. Then the captain slung forward the Uzi he was carrying on a strap over his shoulder. He fumbled as he reached for the trigger and Sandra rolled to her feet and hurled herself behind a tree at the same time as the bullets began to fly. Thank God she was slim. She felt the tree shudder against her back; bark and splinters ripped past her.

Had that been the full magazine? Then she heard him trying to change it for a fresh one and she stepped out of cover, the Glock in both hands, pointing at her adversary.

'Bugger,' he said, which she thought restrained in the circumstances, and she shot him twice, head and chest.

Sandra holstered the handgun and took the Uzi from the dead man, completed loading it and took two extra magazines from his body. Two sub-machineguns were better than one. For some reason, she glanced upwards and saw the face of a woman at a window. The captain's woman? Their eyes locked for a second, then Sandra was off again, wondering if the gunshots might attract unwanted attention from the Tans.

The front of the church was hidden from the rest of the village by trees. She paused in the porch, held an Uzi upright and at the ready, and opened the door. It squealed on its hinges. Shadows gave the interior an aura of peacefulness and she slipped inside and let her eyes and ears adjust. Silence and shadows. Tall candles were lit near the altar throwing out more shadows. No creaks, no footsteps, no heavy breathing. Except? And what was that smell? Decay? Death?

She moved to the central aisle of the church, the gun at the ready, and gasped. Reaper was tied to the pulpit, arms stretched apart, stripped to the waist. It was his breathing she could hear. What had they done to him?

Her eyes searched the corners of the church but there were too many places to hide. She began walking forward towards the altar, the pulpit was on her left. As she got closer, she saw Reaper was gagged and that his body was bruised from repeated beatings. Perhaps her concern made her careless but she was taken by surprise by the voice that came from her right and slightly behind her.

'Drop the gun.'

The words had a slight echo in the high arched body of the church but they were said with a cold clarity that brooked no argument. She lowered the gun to the floor and stood up, her hands in a gesture of surrender. She turned from the waist to see the hulking figure of a soldier with sergeant's stripes who held a revolver in his very large right hand. He was smiling.

'And the other one.'

'It's over,' Sandra said, slipping the strap of the second Uzi over her head and putting the weapon on the floor. 'We've taken Banbury. We've taken the General. The army has a new leader. Only the Tans are left.' They could hear gunfire. 'And they're dying. If you have any sense, this is the time to change sides.'

The soldier moved carefully towards the aisle, the gun

never wavering. Sandra turned fully round to keep him in sight.

'It's only the officers we want,' she said. 'The rest of you can join the real army. No repercussions. Just put the gun down.'

He grinned. 'The Colonel will enjoy you,' he said. 'I will, too.'

So much for persuading him to change sides. She wrinkled her nose. Didn't he ever wash?

He stepped closer to her and she backed away towards the altar. She called to Reaper over her shoulder.

'I'll have you down in a jiffy,' she said.

He gurgled a reply against the gag.

Sandra tripped as she stepped backwards. A pretend trip that didn't take her to the floor but allowed her to put her hands down for balance to break her fall and make a grab for the Glock on her thigh. It fooled the sergeant for a moment, long enough for her to grip the butt of the gun, and then he realised what she was doing, cursed and fired. The shot flung her backwards onto the altar step and she stared down the church, waiting for the coup de grace, when a strange figure rose from the pews and howled.

The noise shocked both her and the sergeant, who turned and took a step backwards in horror at the sight of a creature in tattered clothing and long unkempt hair and beard that appeared to have arisen from a gothic horror story or perhaps a grave outside.

'Time, time!' shouted the undead man. He put his head back and howled again, shouting words only he could understand. Were they names? He lowered his gaze once more onto the sergeant, paused in his litany, and said, 'It's time, Logan. Hell is waiting.'

He raised his right hand. In it was clutched a brass cross. Sandra and the sergeant stared at it as if it was a potent symbol and the man threw it without warning and turned it into a potent weapon. The sergeant raised his arms to fend off the cross and its impact knocked the revolver from his hand.

The sergeant stooped to grab the gun from the floor as the man raised a sawn off shotgun from beneath his coat and fired both barrels. Sandra was not in the direct line of fire but even so, threw up an arm in protection and rolled sideways. The blast skinned the back of the sergeant's head and plucked at his shoulders and threw him forcefully onto the altar itself so that he banged into the table upon which was a tall cross and two brass candlesticks. The candles were lit and both fell to the floor. Without their light, the evening sun shone through the stained glass windows behind the altar more forcefully and cast a shadow from the tall cross onto the sergeant. He didn't notice the omen as he was intent on raising the handgun, which he fired repeatedly into the body of the tattered figure that staggered towards him.

'Hell! Hell!' the tattered man shouted, the bullets pausing the forward motion of his body like punctuation.

The six shot revolver clicked on empty but the sergeant was too badly injured to move. The ragged man fell to his knees on the altar step, tilted his head back and said, 'Ellen?'

His head lolled forward and, almost by chance, he looked at Sandra with eyes that were somewhere else, in some other time.

'Sorry,' he said. 'I didn't save you.'

'You did,' Sandra said. 'You saved me.'

His eyes changed, for an instant, and glowed a little more brightly, and the sergeant began to move. The old man's head swivelled on a body that should have collapsed already and he staggered to his feet and lurched forwards. The altar table stopped him and he paused, gathering his remaining strength. He grasped the tall brass cross that had been the focus of worship for generations of churchgoers, raised it above his head and brought it down like an axe, embedding an arm into the sergeant's neck. Once the blow was struck, it was as if the energy left him and he staggered sideways like a drunk and fell to the floor.

Sandra sat up and eased her arms in a stretch. The bullet had hit her in the chest and the Kevlar vest had once more saved her, although she would have been at the sergeant's mercy if her strange saviour had not appeared without explanation or warning.

She went to him now but he was dead, as was the soldier impaled on a cross. At last, she reached Reaper. She untied the gag and it fell from his mouth. He licked his lips and tried to spit and she wished she had water to give him. He finally found enough saliva to speak.

'You took your time,' he said.

She grinned and used the Bowie knife to cut him down and, once his hands were released, he fell to the floor, unable to stand.

* * *

They had opened fire from the manor house when the first Tans had tried to cross the green to investigate the shooting at the brothel. A couple of bursts from the machinegun had put three men down and sent the rest scurrying back to their own side of the village. Two of the prone men were wounded and shouted for help but no one ventured out.

For a while there was confusion in the houses and cottages along that side of the village, then order was imposed and fire was returned. It was obvious to Yank that officers had survived and taken charge. But how enthusiastic would the ordinary Tan be in an open gunfight? A group tried to cross the green beyond the pond where foliage and the lip of the land around the water provided cover. But gunfire from the Pussy Shack deterred them. Were Sandra and Pete still there? Had they got no further in their rescue attempt?

'Reinforcements,' Dee said, from behind the machinegun.

The patrols had returned and two vehicles had stopped on the road to their right. The men inside had taken cover behind them and began to fire at the house. Yank glanced in the other direction and saw the patrols from the south were also returning and taking up similar positions. They would soon infiltrate their flanks and enter the house.

'Jenny, you and Kat take the right side of the house. Try to keep the bastards out. Judy?' The girl nodded. She had a handgun in its holster slung bandoleer style across her body and carried a carbine. 'Go to the others. Tell Kev and Nina to take the left of the house. Okay?'

'Yes.'

'Then go.'

The girl went. Harry followed. Yank didn't ask why.

Time for trying something different.

'Time for your big moment, General,' she said. 'Time for a balcony speech.'

Bullets hit woodwork and splintered stone around the balcony.

'You must be mad.'

'Not mad. Just angry.'

She slung the automatic rifle across her back and took the knife from its sheath on her leg and cut the ropes that tied him to the chair.

Adams, the batman, said, 'You can't send him out there. It's murder.'

'It's his only chance.' She looked round the room. 'White flag.'

Adams went to the bed and returned with a pillowcase.

The machinegun was already silent as Dee, bleeding from a gash in her forehead caused by a stone splinter, waited for targets. Single shots and short bursts from automatic rifles continued to be fired by the opposition. Yank could hear the occasional shot from the other side of the house. 'Ceasefire!' she shouted. She put the pillowcase on the end of her rifle and waved it out of the window. Someone shot at it but then the firing stopped.

'You're on!' she said to Purcell.

'To do what?'

'To tell them we've taken Banbury and their war is over. To lay down their guns.'

'They won't.'

'There's a chance they will, if they see we've got you.'

'There's a chance they'll shoot me.'

'It's war, General. Somebody always gets shot.'

Purcell was pale but he squared his shoulders. 'If it works, what about me?'

'How about a role in administration?' Yank smiled. 'You can even keep your rank.' Not that she meant it. This was war. Somebody always told lies. But at this moment if Purcell could arrange a surrender it could only be to their advantage. He seemed to sense it might be the only way for him to survive.

He composed his face and exchanged a look with Adams. He held out his hand and the surprised batman shook it.

'When this is over, will you still be with me, Adams?'

'I will, sir.'

'Good man.' He smiled. 'Best gin and tonic ever.'

The General released his hand and walked past Yank and onto the balcony. He raised his arms as if offering himself to his people. And one of them shot him.

Purcell fell backwards, shock on his face, blood on his chest and Adams pushed past Yank to get to his side. He dragged the General back into the room and knelt alongside him. Purcell said no words. Blood bubbled from his mouth and his gaze fixed on his batman's face for an intense second before the light died within them.

'Shit,' said Yank, as the firing from outside intensified.

Showing surprising strength, Adams picked up the body of Purcell in his arms and carried it to the bed where he laid the General on his back in respectable repose. He walked back to Yank and said, 'Give me a gun and I'll fight.'

'What?'

'I'll fight.'

'Because of him?'

'He was hope. He had a vision. Barstow just killed it.'

Yank nodded to spare weapons and said, 'Help yourself.'

*   *   *

In one of the cottages held by the Tans, Brian 'The Beast' Barstow lowered his rifle and smiled. He couldn't have planned it better himself. The General was out of the way and, once this stupid incursion was dealt with, he would be in sole command. Harry would do as he was told and, he smiled again, so would the Honourable Judith Finlay. But first, they needed to take Brownley House.

He had a dozen men led by two corporals on each side of the house and about forty in the cottages. He had counted the gun positions at the house and the Pussy Shack and guessed he was facing no more than a dozen and probably less. The odds were massively in the Tans' favour.

He had no illusions about the quality of his men. They would be reluctant to fight in open combat and, at the first sign of the battle going against them, a proportion would break and run. They were mainly scum without the spirit or discipline of the regular army; dangerous in back streets, brutal when dominating a situation, but nothing like as good as they pretended to be when it came to war.

So best to get it over with quickly. He radioed the returned patrols and gave them orders to prepare to attack. He would feed more men to his left flank and send others round the top of the village, to deal with whoever was in residence at the Pussy Shack, and then join the right flank. A frontal assault wasn't possible. But he had enough faith in his men to trust they could gain entry into the house either at the sides or the back and then kill everyone inside. No mercy.

Except for Harry, who would remain their figurehead, and the Honourable Judith, who would become his plaything.

*　　　*　　　*

The arrival of Dr Greta Malone was a surprise. When the door burst open, Yank almost shot her.

'You should be on your way to Haven.'

'Shouldn't we all?'

'What about the Major?'

'I told him what was happening.'

'And?'

'I don't know. Where's Reaper?'

'In the church. Sandra's gone.'

'Any wounded?'

'Nothing desperate.'

Greta looked at Dee.

'It's just a scratch,' Dee said.

'Where are the others?'

'Follow the sounds of shooting,' said Yank. 'But announce your arrival. Accidents can happen.'

*　　　*　　　*

Lieutenant Simon Mason led eight men through the back gardens towards the church. He was to pick up Sergeant Logan along the way, and find out what had happened to Captain Blunt – 'probably drunk again', Colonel Barstow had said – before arcing round the village behind the houses to retake the Pussy Shack, then reinforce the dozen men on the right flank who should be attacking any time soon.

Barstow planned to use them as the diversionary attack while leading the bulk of the force against the left flank and the rear of the house. The odds were overwhelming; the outcome assured. That's what Barstow had told him and he believed it. But he was still unsettled at the way the Beast had shot the General.

Mason was pleased with his mission. It would keep him out of the firing line. There only seemed to be one gunman in the brothel and those odds suited him, as well. He would send two or three men inside to sort out that problem. Of course, they might want to linger to punish the women or to simply fuck them. Nothing like the whiff of battle to give a man an erection, especially when he was safely in the rear. He might partake himself, if they were quick about it. Then they could continue on to the battle proper, by which time it would hopefully be won.

*   *   *

Kev and Nina were at adjoining windows of a room at the

side of the house on the first floor, waiting for the inevitable attack. He carried the light machinegun, the ammunition box beneath it holding a hundred rounds of 5.56 mm shells. The odds, he knew, were not good. Nina glanced at him and gave him a tight smile. She knew, too.

'When this is over.' Her smile flickered. 'Maybe you and me?'

'You and me sounds lovely.' He grinned back. 'Gives me something to look forward to.'

'Kevin, you are a prize prat. But you're my prize prat.'

He took it as a compliment. More than that, he took it to mean that he was on a promise. Bugger the odds outside. They had just got infinitely better inside.

*   *   *

Gwen said, 'This is not good, is it?'

'No,' said James. 'It's not good at all.'

He understood the lull in the shooting was because troops were getting into position for an assault. He put the rifle down and took her in his arms. The weapon she carried rather spoilt the embrace and they laughed before she moved it on its strap into the small of her back. They held each other and gazed into each other's eyes.

'I love you,' he said.

'I love you.'

'Whatever happens, we are together and we are one. You made me very happy, Gwen.' He smiled softly. 'You made me a man.'

'You were always a man. You scared me, you know?'

'I scared you?'

'Being posh. I'm not.'

He crushed her to him and spoke into her hair. 'I loved you the first time I saw you. I would have loved you anytime, anywhere. It was written in the stars, Gwen. We were meant for each other.'

'Yes, we were.' They kissed, gently. 'I'm glad we found each other. I'm glad we've had what we've had. And now …'

'Now we're together. Always will be. No matter what.'

'No matter what.'

They held each other close and she tried not to cry that it might soon be over.

*   *   *

Jenny's eye was hurting from the previous wound. Smoke and irritation had caused her to rub it and the stitches were bleeding but she waved Greta away when the doctor offered repairs.

'Well use this,' Greta said, and gave her a black eye patch.

The former teacher laughed and put it on. 'What do you think, Kat? Do I look like a pirate?'

'More Captain Pugwash than Johnny Depp. More's the pity.'

'Did you fancy Johnny Depp?'

'Who didn't? Handsome, witty, intelligent, wealthy. What's not to like?'

'But I'm Pugwash.'

'Sorry.'

The machinegun from the front of the house rattled out a long burst and Kat risked a look from the window.

'Reinforcements crossing the road. Dee got a couple.'

'It'll be soon,' said Jenny.

They had shared the guns and ammunition and Jenny had a sub-machinegun on a strap on her back, two handguns, and an automatic rifle cradled in her arms and a determined expression on her smudged and bloody face.

'Forget Johnny Depp,' Kat said. 'You look more like Bruce Willis about to save the world.' Jenny gave her a reproving look. 'A sexy female version,' Kat added.

'That's better.' She glanced at Greta. 'Doc, when it starts, stay low. When it's over, whoever is left will need a doctor.'

Greta picked up a spare Glock handgun and pulled the slide back to arm it.

'Right,' she said.

Kat and Jenny exchanged a surprised glance. 'Right,' said Jenny.

*   *   *

Harry and Judy joined Yank and Dee in the room with the balcony at the front of the house.

'Good God,' said Yank.

Harry was wearing the dark blue and heavily gold brocaded dress jacket of the Blues and Royals, although it was only partially fastened. He carried a cavalry sword and a Glock handgun.

'I thought I might as well look the part. You never know, it might make the opposition stop and think. God for Harry, England and St George?'

Yank said, 'I'm American.'

'Colonies included.'

Dee said, 'The likeness is amazing.'

Yank said, 'They'll get inside. We can't stop them. We'll try to hold this floor. I doubt they'll take prisoners.'

Judith said, 'There is only so long one can be a prisoner.'

'Brave words, but...'

'Believe me, I'm scared witless about what might happen. But I'm even more scared of what I know will happen if I go and hide and wait for the Beast. Better this way.'

'Definitely better this way,' Harry said. 'Enough of faking it. Time to be a prince.'

*   *   *

The attack on the house coincided with Lieutenant Simon Mason walking straight into an angry Reaper and his guardian Angel.

Sandra had found a bottle of water and a bottle of whisky in the sacristy, plus a blue t-shirt. As he drank the water and took a nip of whisky, Reaper explained the Beast's plan to soften him up and then present him, with his bruises covered, for a ceremonial hand-to-hand combat for the entertainment and edification of watching civilians.

The dead sergeant had left his automatic rifle in the room and an ammunition belt. Reaper strung the belt over his head so that it hung to the left, and put the strap of the rifle over his head so that the weapon hung to the right. He staggered as he walked but was methodical as he went about his preparations and Sandra explained what had happened. He retrieved the sawn-off shotgun and reloaded it with cartridges he found on the tattered man; he took the gunbelt from the sergeant and put it on. The gun was an old .38 Webley service revolver with no safety. He reloaded it and put it in the holster that fitted uncomfortably at the hip.

He swayed slightly as he stood upright and Sandra said, 'Are you all right?'

'One hundred per cent better than I was ten minutes ago.'

'Do we have a plan?'

'Kill the bastards.'

She nodded as if it made perfect sense. 'Then let's do it,' she said.

They left the church by the front door as Lieutenant Mason and four of his men walked up the path from the lych gate.

'Where's Sergeant Logan?' Mason said, unsure of who they were in the shadow of the porch.

'In hell,' Reaper said, levelled the sawn-off and fired both barrels.

Mason and two of the men were blown backwards, and the way they fell, with limbs flapping, heads banging rag-doll-like on the ground, it looked as if they would be of no further threat. Another fell to the ground in shock, the fourth turned to run. Sandra dropped both with short bursts from an Uzi. Reaper calmly broke the shotgun, flipped out the used cartridges and replaced them with fresh ones.

The six other men, who had been waiting near the gate, took cover behind gravestones as Sandra walked towards them using the Uzi in sparing three shot bursts that put down two more before she crouched behind a tall and ancient stone herself. Shots were being fired at them. Long bursts, short bursts, wild firing from guns held over or around the cover behind which their owners cowered.

She looked back at the church to see Reaper had slung the shotgun on his back, alongside the rifle, and had taken two sub-machineguns from the dead. He now walked forward, the guns held in a steady grip, no hint of weakness in his stride. She stood and joined him and swung the spare Uzi forward so she, too, held a gun in each hand. They walked forward together, guns firing, and the men ahead of them broke and ran. Two went down. The two survivors, one limping heavily, disappeared beyond the wall and scuttled back the way they had come.

From the house came the sound of fierce fighting. They reloaded as they walked.

*   *   *

Kev and Nina faced the first attack. He stood at the broken window, not attempting to take cover, firing the machinegun at the men below as they ran from the trees to reach the side and rear of the house. Nina also stood square on at her window, using three-shot bursts. The Tans were widely spaced and only three went down as bullets from those still in cover returned fire. Nina leant out of the shattered window to gain a better perspective and fired a last burst before she was flung backwards into the room.

Kev dropped the machinegun and ran to her. Bullets had hit her Kevlar vest, forming a line of stitches upwards, the last bullet taking off the top of her head. He held her, unmindful of the blood and brains on his hands, and rocked her against his body. More pain than he thought he was capable of feeling spread up through his torso and arms at the death of such a good person who had suffered so much; a person he had loved, even though he had never spoken of it, never even acknowledging it to himself; a woman who might, in time, have loved him.

He howled in anger and rage and desolation.

He lay her down softly and kissed her chastely on the lips. Their first and last kiss. He got to his feet with deadly purpose, wiped her blood from his hands to his face like war paint and retrieved the machinegun. He changed the magazine and embraced it, felt it become a part of him. He left the room and headed for the stairs.

The assault on the other side of the house began but he ignored it. He went down. Behind him, he heard James shout but his brain was conditioned for only one purpose. He headed towards the rear of the house where the invaders had gone and where he could hear glass and doors breaking as they entered. He kicked open double doors and stared down a long dining room. Men in uniform were grouped by French windows. They fired, with automatic rifles and sub-machineguns, and he returned their onslaught with the machinegun jumping in his hands, unaware of the bullets that hit him, rocking with the ones that hit the armoured vest, not feeling the ones that took off an ear and ripped flesh from his arms.

The silence afterwards was louder than the gun battle. He was deaf and the empty gun was suddenly heavy in his hands. He dropped it and pulled the Glock from its holster, although now, he could feel the hurt in his arm and the strain it took to level it as he looked for targets. But there were none. He took a step forward and staggered. He swayed and saw the bodies on the floor at the other end of the room. Six, seven?

Now he should go and kill more.

He never felt the bullet that went into his brain, fired from behind by a Tan who had entered through the kitchen side door. A single bullet from a revolver that ended the pain and desolation and dropped Kev to the floor in front of his vanquished foes.

*   *   *

Two antique cabinets were against the wall at the top of the stairs. They were surprisingly heavy but James and Gwen pushed them across the top of the stairs as a makeshift barricade. They had seen Kev stride away and, moments later, had discovered why, when they found Nina's body. The single shot after the gun battle had sounded final. An execution. They did not shout his name. They waited, but he did not reappear.

Instead, a Tan peered cautiously around a door. James shot him. Another single shot. A decisive execution.

'Come on,' he muttered to himself.

Gwen crouched at his side, frightened but determined. They had friends to avenge before it was their time.

*　　*　　*

The main attack on the other side of the house began. Yank and Dee would soon be redundant in the room at the front.

'Barricade at the top of the stairs,' Yank said.

'What about the back staircase?' Judith said.

'Shit.' Yank had forgotten there was a smaller staircase that led up from the kitchen to the first floor. 'Block it. Wardrobes. Whatever. But we'll make our stand at the top of the main staircase.' Harry and Judith left to obey orders. 'We'll need that,' Yank said to Dee.

Dee stood up and leaned forward to pull the machinegun back when she shuddered, raised herself as if in surprise, then fell forward again. More bullets smashed into the room, knocking the machinegun sideways and bringing plaster down from the ceiling. Yank grabbed Dee's waist and pulled her backwards, easing her gently from the table to the floor, but she was past gentleness. A bullet had slipped in above the Kevlar protection as she leaned forward. Her expression was surprise at being dead.

Yank felt the loss deeply. Not long before she had lost the effervescent Irish girl Keira, who had died saving her life in a gun battle. She closed Dee's eyes with grubby fingers and her tears fell onto Dee's face.

'Take care of her,' she told Keira softly.

*　　*　　*

The Tans crossed the road behind the reconnaissance vehicles and swarmed in a huge wave through the shrubbery, trees and ornamental grottoes to reach the rear of the house. Jenny and Kat kept up a steady fire but the targets were unclear, the cover too dense. The enemy didn't even bother to pause and give covering fire.

'What now?' Kat said.

'Stairs,' said Jenny.

The two girls moved onto the landing to see their comrades already there. They noticed who was missing, received shakes of the head from the others, felt the grief and let it turn the fear into anger. They lined the landing with furniture to provide cover, picking heavy pieces that would stop bullets.

The salvo that had killed Dee had also damaged the machinegun. They collected all the weapons and ammunition they had and waited for the last onslaught. Their position at the head of the stairs meant they were looking down into the hall, towards the front door and the doors to the rooms on either side. They were at the crossbar of an H made by two legs of the landing that went to the front of the house with rooms off them, and two corridors that went back into the house and more bedrooms and bathrooms. From one of these corridors, stairs led up to a top storey that had once housed servants quarters, and down to the kitchen area. This back staircase had been packed tight with furniture. Adams, the batman, had booby-trapped it with two hand grenades. They had four more grenades but they were a dangerous option in the confined space in which the battle would be fought.

Greta tended to a wound on James's arm. They all had facial wounds from splinters, stone and glass but they hardly seemed worth bothering with, considering what was to come. Harry had a gash on his forehead, which she bandaged.

They could hear them in the building, moving through the rooms downstairs, not yet ready to make an assault. Heads took quick glances at their defensive position before ducking back behind corners and doorways and Yank saw the flash of a mirror as someone else assessed what they faced. The Tans might have numbers on their side but they still didn't like the odds.

'No speeches,' Yank said. 'Take as many of the bastards as you can. If they lose enough, the rest will run away.'

*　　　*　　　*

The wounded Tan dragged himself into the undergrowth at the bottom of a cottage garden and hid from Reaper and Sandra. The other ran back the way he had come, crashing through overgrown hedges and knocking down fences in his rush.

He found a squad of eight men under the command of a corporal in one of the last houses before the main road.

'Where's the Colonel?'

The Corporal pointed to the floor above from where came the sound of gunfire.

'What's your rush?' he said. 'You look like you've seen a ghost.'

'Worse,' said the breathless Tan. 'I've seen Reaper and the Angel.'

The men nearby caught the fear in his voice and repeated the news among themselves, as if talking of a mythical beast of retribution.

'What's going on?' Barstow appeared, looking pleased with himself.

'Reaper's coming,' the Tan said. 'Reaper and the Angel.'

Immediately Barstow's mood changed and he grabbed the soldier by his tunic and dragged him into another room. 'Tell me,' he said.

'We went to the church. They were there. Reaper and the Angel. Guns, knives. Everything. They said we were going to hell and then they opened up. We fired back but nobody could hit them. They killed everybody. I was the only one who got away.'

'Reaper and the Angel?'

'That's right. A girl with blonde hair. Eyes like lasers. Bullets didn't stop them. And they're coming this way.'

Barstow raised a finger of his left hand to calm the man down. He gave him a grim soldierly smile and placed the hand on his shoulder. A conspiratorial gesture. He leaned in close to say: 'We need to keep this to ourselves.'

The Tan's eyes opened wide, not in understanding, but because of the knife Barstow had pushed forcefully into his stomach and twisted upwards. Barstow held the man upright until he was sure he was dead, then moved him backwards and laid him down behind a sofa.

He rejoined the squad, who now stared at him with fear in their eyes. Barstow assumed a bluff, fatherly persona.

'There's always one,' he said. 'Always one who runs at the first shot. Smudger can't help it,' he nodded towards the room where the corpse lay. 'He'll be all right when the panic has gone. Best thing now is that he rests. He's no good to fighting men in that state.'

He grinned to let them know they were fighting men.

'It seems Reaper's escaped. Some cock up. But he's hardly a threat after the hiding I've given him these last few days. Lieutenant Mason's on his way round to the other side, to push the attack from the other flank. Smudger was supposed to be guarding Reaper. Not the best choice in the circumstances. So, now we'll get Reaper. And this time, shoot the bastard on sight. All right?'

*　　*　　*

Yank wondered how many they faced. Forty? Fifty? She looked along the landing at her companions: Jenny, the English rose schoolteacher turned pirate; Kat, the pale skinned athlete from the BBC who'd buried her husband and baby in the back garden; James and Gwen, star crossed lovers who deserved a future but who had at least shared what time they'd had; Harry, a pretend prince determined to die like a real one, and Judith, daughter of aristocracy, who preferred death to a fate that she considered worse. Greta, the doc, who could have, should have, driven away to Haven but who had walked into the Alamo of her own free will, partly from comradeship but mostly for love. And Adams, an unlikely soldier, overweight but determined.

What the hell had happened to Reaper and Sandra and Pete?

And what about herself? A Yank from Oregon who had washed up in Manchester – of all the godforsaken places. Still, she had packed a lot into the life she'd had so far. War in Afghanistan followed by a love affair that had brought her across the Pond, and an uncompromising battle for survival after the virus. She had taken no shit and shot first. And so to Haven and a new life and new friends; friendships deeper than she had ever known: Keira and the slightly built, but oh so brave, Dee. Kev and Gwen and all the rest.

Shit. If the shooting didn't start soon, she'd be going around kissing everybody.

And then the shooting started.

*　　　*　　　*

The Tans didn't make a frontal assault. They pushed out furniture from the rooms and crouched behind it to fire up at the defenders. Others smashed in the glass of the windows and front door and fired from there. For a time, there was a greater danger of being wounded by splinters than from bullets. The explosion from the back staircase gave everyone cause to pause and the attackers pulled back momentarily.

Jenny glanced in the direction of the backstairs and said, 'I'll go.'

She picked up two grenades and went down the far corridor, Kat at her heels.

They waited impatiently for the battle to recommence, sweating, nervous, trying to keep the fear at bay. Shots from the corridor. Incoherent shouts and a scream and then another explosion. Yank hoped the grenade had been thrown by Jenny and not the enemy. Then a sudden charge from below that took them by surprise. The staccato sound of sub-machineguns, the bray of automatic assault rifles, pistols going off like fire crackers. Bodies fell but some had climbed the stairs and there were pauses in the firing as magazines ran out.

Gwen was knocked backwards and slumped to the ground and James stood astride her, dropping one weapon and picking up another, standing upright to fire into the throng. Judith let an empty Uzi swing onto her back on its strap, and used the Glock at point blank range before crumpling against a Chippendale dresser, Greta fired a

424

handgun blindly down the stairs. Yank emptied one sub-machinegun and picked up another; she held it one-handed, not bothered that its rake of fire was haphazard, and used a Glock in her other hand. Harry surged above the barricade alongside her and swung the curved cavalry sword into the head of an attacker, Adams swung an empty carbine above his head and used it as a club before slumping to the floor.

The smell, the noise, the bloodlust, the anger and the fear were overpowering until an explosion from the body of the hall abruptly ended the chaos. Yank crouched behind cover and automatically changed the magazines of both the weapons she held. There was no point asking questions; no one could hear, but she saw that Judith was lying on her back, hands clamped over her side where blood seeped between her fingers. Greta ripped open her blouse and prepared to tend the wound. Gwen was sitting up and saw Yank looking; she pointed to the Kevlar vest that sported three shells. She also had blood running from a neck wound that she chose to ignore. Adams was clutching his shoulder, his eyes were wide with pain.

Yank realised that Harry was still standing upright, staring over the barricade. She tugged at his arm to pull him down and he sank beside her. His eyes were mad; he had lost his senses in the battle.

'Reload,' Yank said and, even though he couldn't hear her, he understood from her mime and put a fresh magazine in the Glock.

Now she saw that Jenny was sitting at the end of the corridor that led to the kitchen stairs, her back against the wall. Lying by her feet was the body of Kat but Yank couldn't tell if she was alive or dead. It looked as if Jenny had pulled her there.

Jenny felt her gaze and turned her head. She nodded. She held up an empty magazine and asked, with the raising of an eyebrow, if there were more. Yank reached for two from the few that were left, and threw them to her across the landing.

'Grenade?' Jenny mouthed, and Yank realised sound was coming back.

They had two left and she now realised Jenny must have used one in the stairwell and lobbed the other into the hallway when she saw the state of battle. She picked up one and sat up straight to lob it to her. Jenny caught it deftly, nodded and pointed down the corridor. That would be where it would go when the Tans attacked again. Kat stirred and Jenny shouted, 'Doc?'

Greta looked, nodded and finished taping a bandage around Judith who remained conscious. Harry moved to sit alongside her and put an arm around her shoulders. She handed him her gun and said, 'Load it.' Greta, staying low behind the furniture barricade, checked on Adams who whispered, 'See to the girl.' She picked up her medical bag and moved to Kat.

Yank wondered when they would try again. She knelt and looked over the barricade and was shocked at the devastation in the hall and on the stairs. A dozen bodies lay like extras in a movie; they lay at odd angles, some with staring eyes, some with missing body parts, others with half a face. A few moved and groaned, lifted an arm, pleaded for help. One screamed loudly. A scream that was repeated time and again. No one went to help. No one dared. A gunshot from a room and the screaming stopped.

God, she thought. Would they come again? Or would they call for armour and blow them out? Bomb them out? Burn them out? She sank back behind the solid wood and knew they would not try another frontal assault. But what would they try?

*   *   *

Reaper and Sandra moved quickly as they heard the gun battle raging at the house. It was time to end it, one way or the other. They followed the back garden trail left by the soldier who had escaped through hedgerows, flower beds and broken fences. The row of cottages on their right ended. A lane ran between the last cottage garden, whose owner had at one time cultivated vegetables, and the far more substantial garden of a detached house. Beyond that was the main road and the battle for the manor house.

A gate was open in a high fence. It led to an old fenced compost heap, a tall green plastic bin, and a garden shed. This was all hidden from view of the house and the rest of the garden by shrubbery that had become overgrown. Reaper hesitated. If the Tans knew they were coming they could be stepping into an ambush. An explosion from Brownley House put doubts from his mind and he went through the gateway quickly, moved to the right and dropped prone. Sandra was close behind and she moved to the left and also went flat on the other side of the compost.

He ignored the aches in his body and squirmed forward beneath the shrubbery. The movement was seen and bullets cut through the foliage above his head. He was behind a rockery, which provided limited protection, but he was in no mood for a protracted stand-off. He had friends in danger and he needed to be there. An overgrown lawn was beyond the rockery, and then a large circular paved area in front of French windows at the rear of the house. A pond with a low stone wall to the left, a separate brick garage to the right. There was a lot of open space.

Sandra began firing from her unseen position, long bursts from an Uzi, into the trees and bushes opposite. He heard cries and a body fell. He levelled the automatic rifle at the bedroom windows and fired when he saw a pale face behind the barrel of a gun. Another scream and the gun disappeared. Sandra fired again, same pattern, this time spraying the house. She did not attract return fire. The opposition were not the bravest of opponents and were keeping their heads down. Any return fire was coming in his direction. He slung the rifle on his back and took a sub-machinegun in each hand. He had had enough of lying in the dirt.

Reaper stood up abruptly and crashed through the bushes and over the rockery, both guns firing. He sensed Sandra was doing the same to his left. Perhaps it was the sight of them together – Reaper and the Angel – perhaps it was the concentrated firepower that caused more cries, more bodies falling, that turned the tide in their favour.

He stepped behind the edge of the garage and changed magazines. Sandra, he saw, was curled behind the low stone wall that surrounded the pond. A soldier showed himself as he attempted a shot at Sandra and Reaper put him down with a burst from his Uzi. The body spun out of cover and pirouetted before falling to the ground where it lay inelegantly, face down with its posterior in the air. So much for the dignity of death.

How many did they face? How many were left? When could they move on to help their comrades in Brownley House? More explosions came from across the road.

'Reaper!'

The call was unexpected. He recognised the voice.

'What do you want, Barstow?'

'You and me. What we planned. Why don't we do it now?'

He couldn't be serious? Reaper didn't trust the man but perhaps he was desperate. Perhaps his own men were ready to run and this was his only way to save the situation.

Perhaps his ego was bigger than he thought.

'You and me?' he shouted back. 'You and me fight?'

'Hand to hand. See if you're as hard as you think you are.'

'What are the stakes?'

'Well, if you win, you get to kill me. And you and your friends get to walk away.'

'What guarantee?'

'My word. You hear that, lads? If he wins, they go free.'

The situation was bizarre. A hand-to-hand fight would solve nothing. There could still be men hidden in the house or garden who could shoot him dead if he did win. He peered across the garden at Sandra. She stared back at him. She shook her head. He gestured with his hand for what he wanted her to do. She nodded and he stepped around the side of the garage and opened fire with both sub-machineguns. Sandra got up and ran across the paved garden area and into the cover of the garage with him.

Nobody had returned fire. As he thought, whoever was left, they were not very brave.

'Barstow?'

'What?'

'You still want it?'

'Yes, I want it. You and me.'

'All right. What's your choice of weapon?'

Barstow laughed. 'Knives.'

Reaper threw out the two sub-machineguns where

they would be seen. They clattered on the paving. The rifle he had left at the compost heap.

'If your men shoot, the Angel will cut their balls off and make them eat them.'

'I believe it.' Barstow laughed again. 'Just you and me?'

'Just you and me. My word.'

'Right.'

Reaper peered around the side of the garage. Barstow had stepped out from the shattered French windows, a large knife in his right hand and an insane grin on his face.

'Lend me your knife,' Reaper said, and she put it in his left hand.

He stepped out from cover. Sandra stepped out behind him, a step away, covering the back of the house with an Uzi. No one shot him.

'What's the matter?' Barstow said. 'Don't your trust me?'

'Not in the slightest,' Reaper said.

He began to walk forward and, as Barstow adopted a knife fighter's stance, moved his right shoulder to swing the unseen sawn-off from behind his body and up into his right hand. He fired both barrels. Barstow was almost cut in half and was blown backwards through the battered French windows.

'Anybody else in there should run now!' Reaper shouted.

Furniture tipped, something broke, footsteps left quickly. Nobody fired.

Sandra came to his side, still alert. He bent down and put the knife back in its sheath on her leg, retrieved the two discarded guns and put in fresh magazines.

'Let's hope we're in time,' he said.

They went through the house, picking up spare magazines as they found them, and stopped at the front door at the familiar sound of a light aircraft.

'I don't believe it,' he said.

'Mandi and de Courcy have been dropping leaflets over Banbury,' Sandra said. 'I don't know why they are here.'

The Cessna swooped low over the village and a few Tans fired at it. Then explosions had them running for cover.

'They'd dropping grenades!' Reaper said. 'The crazy, wonderful bastards are dropping grenades.'

Tans began to run from the side of Brownley House back towards what they thought of as the safety of their home cottages. They met unremitting gunfire from Reaper and Sandra. Some ran down the road towards Banbury. One tried to start a reconnaissance truck. He got it going as the Cessna came back and Mandi dropped a grenade on it. A few ran across the green, anywhere to flee the blitz and the bullets. As they neared the middle of the open space, an Uzi opened up from the front bedroom of the Pussy Shack. Bodies fell, Tans ran aimlessly in all directions.

'Pete,' said Sandra, with delight.

From Brownley house came single, spaced shots. They recognised James on the balcony: taking his time, target shooting, as if in competition. Not many escaped.

They had won. It was over. The energy suddenly seeped from Reaper and he sagged. Sandra stepped under his arm and supported his weight. They walked together through the front gate to the main road. The Cessna came back again, swooping low.

Reaper laughed.

'The mad Irish bastard just waggled his wings.'

Army vehicles approached from Banbury. Real army vehicles. The occupants fired shots at the Tans who were still attempting to run across fields or hide in hedgerows. An open Land Rover pulled up and the Major, Colonel Maidstone and Ash stepped out.

'You chaps all right?' said the Major.

'Absolutely,' said Reaper.

Smiffy pulled up behind, along with Cameron, Duggan and the Scots, then the truck containing the former prisoners of the mine, and regular army units.

The shots from Brownley House stopped and a small group came out of the front door and walked down the drive. James, a rifle held casually over his shoulder, his arm around Gwen who had a bandage around her neck. Yank, a pair of Uzis hanging from her hands as if she had forgotten she still held them. Her face was stained with war and fatigue. A young man with ginger hair and an eager expression in a brocaded blue dress jacket that was open over a white bloodstained shirt. He had a bandage around his head and carried a cavalry sword that was stained with close quarter use.

'He looks the part,' Sandra said. 'He's not bad looking, is he?'

Reaper squeezed her shoulders and then saw another figure come from the house, and run down the drive, past the group. Greta had seen Reaper. She ran across the road, as Colonel Maidstone and the Major saluted the Prince, and into his arms.

Sandra eased herself away and allowed her to take the load. Greta didn't seem to mind.

The Angel thought they deserved time alone and went to meet the others, determine the body count and say hello again to Harry. He was, she decided as she got closer, quite a dish.

Epilogue

They took their dead home and held a memorial service at Haven. Colonel Maidstone and officers from Banbury attended, along with Sandy Cameron and his Scots, and the Major. The butcher's bill had been heavy: Dee, the young Asian girl; Nina, a victim who had become a warrior; and Kev, her protector and surrogate guardian to young James.

Yank had come through it all with barely a scratch and Jenny, still in a black eye patch, had her arm in a sling and would walk with a limp for some time. James was unscathed although Gwen would carry a permanent scar on her neck, not that either of them cared. Kat had survived, although her wounds would take a long time to mend. Pete was on crutches; the nurse at the Pussy Shack had saved his leg and his life, and the schoolgirl had propped him up and changed magazines while he continued to fight from the brothel. The Honourable Judith Finlay was in hospital but would recover and Prince Harry sported a bandage around his forehead but was otherwise unharmed.

Adams the batman, who had ultimately fought with distinction, was also in hospital and would mend. He had applied to return to the Catering Corps, a request to which Colonel Maidstone had happily agreed.

The Reverend Nick held a moving service and, as they lay their comrades to rest alongside the previous fallen, Sandra said softly, 'We did it again. But how?'

Reaper said, 'Maybe we had God on our side. And God can be a right bitch when She gets angry.'